THE GIRL WHO WROTE LONELINESS

THE GIRL WHO WROTE LONELINESS

KYUNG-SOOK SHIN

TRANSLATED FROM THE KOREAN BY HA-YUN JUNG

PEGASUS BOOKS
NEW YORK LONDON

THE GIRL WHO WROTE LONELINESS

Pegasus Books LLC
80 Broad Street, 5th Floor
New York, NY 10004

Translation was supported by generous grants from the Korean Literature Translation Institute and the PEN American Center.

First Pegasus Books hardcover edition September 2015

Interior design by Maria Fernandez

ISBN: 978-1-60598-863-4

10 9 8 7 6 5 4 3 2 1

Printed in the United States of America
Distributed by W. W. Norton & Company, Inc.

For my oldest brother; my cousin; all those who attended the Special Program for Industrial Workers at Yeongdeungpo Girls' High School from 1979 to 1981; my language arts teacher, Choe Hong-i; and for Hui-jae eonni, who, for as long as I remain in this world, will never become a part of the past.

THE GIRL WHO WROTE LONELINESS

ONE

There exists in every life and particularly at its dawn an instant that determines everything.

—Jean Grenier

This book, I believe, will turn out to be not quite fact and not quite fiction, but something in between. I wonder if it can be called literature. I ponder the act of writing. What does writing mean to me?

Here I am on an island.

It is night and light from the fishing boats, afloat on the night sea, pours in through the open window. Out of the blue,

I find myself here, in this place where I have never been before, contemplating myself at sixteen. There I am, sixteen years old. A girl with a plump face, as indistinct as any other anywhere in Korea. It is 1978, toward the end of the Yusin regime, when U.S. President Jimmy Carter, who had been in office only a year, has announced plans for a gradual withdrawal of ground troops from Korea, and Secretary of State Warren Christopher has publicly acknowledged America's keen interest in establishing diplomatic ties with North Korea and other nations, all creating quite a bit of distress for President Park Chung-hee.

And I, sixteen years old, sit on the wooden veranda of a farmhouse, as indistinct as any other around the country, and listen to the radio, waiting for the mail. What can I do, if you leave, just like that . . . The radio is playing the grand prize–winning song from the National College Song Contest, the lead singer's voice desolate as wasteland. This cannot be, no, no, don't go.

While a new wind is sweeping across the city in hope to change the world, somewhere out there, in our countryside home, a sixteen-year-old girl, unable to afford high school, is listening to "What Can I Do." The ripe spring has passed and summer is approaching.

Nowadays, compared to something like Seo Taiji's rap number "I Know," the song feels almost classical, but when I first hear "What Can I Do" on the radio, I almost shrink with shock and turn the radio off. It is completely different from the songs I have been listening to. But I, who am sixteen years old and positioned in a place utterly different from that of the voices in the outside world calling to put an end to the Yusin regime and Park's emergency rule, I, who have nothing else to do but listen to the radio all day, turn the radio back on. "What Can I Do" comes on again. Perhaps "What Can I Do" has conquered the entire city. On every station that plays music, they are playing "What Can I Do." After hearing the song a few times, I am singing along. How could you, you were once so loving, once so tender.

The girl sings along, her expression rather blank. The mailman comes at about eleven o'clock.

At the time, the girl's dream goes something like this: to leave this dull place and go live with Oldest Brother in the city. To meet someone there and hear from him that he is happy to be given the chance to know her. But today, once again, the mailman does not make a stop.

Here I am on the island Jeju-do.

It is my first time writing away from home. As far as writing habits go, mine has always been to head home to write, even if I was out. Even if I had just set out on a trip, I would impulsively lament the fact that I was not home when I felt the urge to write. Head on home, I would think, as I rushed to pack up, pushed along by the sentences springing to the surface in an unfamiliar place. Was writing home to me? Wherever I might be at that instant, these sentences, surging up through my body, pushed me to hurry back home. When I was writing, I had to have the things around that my hands found comfortable and that my eyes were accustomed to—cotton swabs to keep my ears clean and my toothbrush on its stand by the bathroom sink. I had to have, by my side, smells that did not feel strange, and to have nearby the T-shirts and pants that I always wore. Fresh socks that I could change into any moment. All of my daily routines in their respective places, like my tongue inside my mouth, like my plastic washbowl under the tap.

Some sentences are like ambushing soldiers, jumping out from behind the bushes inside of me on an autumn day like this one, while I am walking down the street to keep an appointment. They conquer reality in an instant and fill me up with an excitement that seems to be wrapped in light. I am willingly captured by these soldiers mid-ambush and turn my back on my appointment. I head home.

But this time I abandon my habits. I abandon home.

I abandon home and arrive here on this island, and think about home. About my childhood under the thatched roof, before the New Village Movement replaced straw with synthetic slates; my family in that house with the thatched roof; the springs and summers and falls and winters that circulated so vividly above that roof of straw.

I take a breath.

I, sixteen years old, am now down on my stomach on the yellow flooring of lacquered paper, writing a letter. Dear Brother, please hurry, come and take me from here. Halfway into the letter, I tear it to pieces. It is already June. Rice planting season out in the paddies. In the compost dump, barley straw is rotting. Sunlight lands on my neck, stinging hot. The rose moss growing by the gate already has its face sticking out, as if it were pouting. I am sick of sunlight and rose moss. I pull down the pitchfork from a wall inside the shed. At first I drag the pitchfork to the compost dump and poke at the barley straw. Sunlight pours down, stinging my forehead. My hands begin to move wildly. What has happened? I think I see the pitchfork flash in the sunlight, but then it strikes down all the way through to the sole of my foot, clumsily lifted from the ground and up into my foot. I am dumbfounded. I do not dare pull out the pitchfork stuck in the sole of my foot. My shocked sole does not even bleed. I collapse on the ground. I cannot quite register the pain and I am not crying, either. With the pitchfork stuck on my sole, I lay myself down on the barley straw. The blue sky pours down on my face. A while passes and Mom returns, shouting, "What happened?"

Mom.

Only when I feel Mom's presence do the tears start streaming down. Only then I feel scared; only then I feel pain. Mom is in shock as she shouts, "Close your eyes, close them tight." I close my eyes, close them tight. From my tightly shut eyes, tears stream down. Mom grabs hard at the pitchfork and shouts again. "Don't open your eyes until I pull out the pitchfork." My eyes open furtively and catch Mom's eyes. She must find it all dreadful: her eyes also close as she holds on to the pitchfork by the tip of its handle. Without hesitating, Mom grabs the pitchfork with force and pulls it out of my foot. My nerves must have been so shocked that there is no blood even after the pitchfork is out.

"What a viciously dogged girl you are." Mom throws the pitchfork aside and lifts me up. "Just lying there, with that thing in your foot! Not even shouting out for help!" Mom's huge hand lands on my back with a sticky slap. Mom lays me down on the wooden floor of our veranda and places cow dung on the hole in my foot, wraps it with plastic. I lie on my stomach on the floor with cow dung on my sole and start writing my letter again. Dear Brother, hurry, please, come and take me away from here.

The springs and the summers, the falls and, especially, the winters . . . the wide wintry fields, the assault of snow-blasted winds, and heavy snows that would go on for days—yet somehow I do not recall winters in the country as being cold. The mittens that Mom had knitted with yarn that she had unraveled from Brother's sweater were so worn they could not keep out the wind, making the tips of my fingers frigid. Sometimes Mom had no time to mend my socks, leaving me to go around with cold feet, in socks where my heels poked out like potatoes. So how is it that I have no memory of being cold? The winter chases everyone, male and female, the young and the old, from the wide fields into rooms. In these rooms, the winter makes them roast chestnuts in the brazier, makes them take out the soft, ripe persimmons from the rice jar, and fetch sweet potatoes from the pantry to throw them out the back door into the snow, to peel the skin off with a knife when they are frozen solid. It was during one of these winters that I saw them.

For some reason, I stand by the brook, gazing at the winter fields beyond the brook. Under the distant white snow, under the snowy wind again starting to blow from the direction of the railroad, which is the only path that lay open to other lands, the fields embosom flocks and flocks of mallards. Having lost the grass seeds and tree fruits and the invertebrate insects, these mallards now searching for ears of rice in the snow are so beautiful to me. These hungry flocks blanketing the wide open winter fields . . .

In the middle of writing my letter, with cow dung on my foot and my stomach on the floor, I lift myself up and drag myself toward the shed. Ever since I got my foot pierced, I feel as if the pitchfork is glaring at me wherever I go. I pull the pitchfork down from the shed wall. Still feeling as if it is glaring at me, I drag the pitchfork across the yard, to the well. Without hesitating, I throw it in. The water splashes. Much later, I gaze into the deep, dark well, which swallows the pitchfork then quickly goes quiet and still, welcoming in the sky as if nothing has happened.

Writing. Could it be that the reason I am so attached to writing is because only this will allow me to escape the feeling of alienation, that I, my existence, is nothing?

One day, standing outside Deoksu Palace, captivated by a sentence surging up my chest, I grab a taxi, and as I head back home I see a passage framed and set up on the dashboard that reads, "May today be another safe day." Right above these words, the infant savior, dressed in white, sits kneeling in a column of light pouring down on him, his palms pressed together. Next to the painting of Samuel, praying, "May today be another safe day," are photos of the taxi driver's family—his wife and children. This was surely not the first time for me to encounter such a set-up, but somehow, this day, the Samuel portrait and the family photographs press down my unrealistic sentences and fill up my heart with a sense of reality. Only then I start to wonder why I am hurrying back home, breaking my appointment with the person standing outside Deoksu Palace.

Having lost my sentence, I tell the taxi driver to turn around, back toward Deoksu Palace.

Last April, one day not long after my first novel was published, in the middle of a languid nap, I received a phone call. A woman's voice of substantial volume asked for me. An unfamiliar voice. I thought then that it was my first time hearing this voice. When she learned that the person on the line was the one she was looking for, she did a double take then expressed her delight, noticeable by the change in the texture of her voice when she asked if I remembered her, offering her name.

"It's me, don't you remember? It's Ha Gye-suk."

"Ha Gye-suk?"

On other occasions, even if I hadn't the faintest idea who it was after the person on the phone stated his or her name several times, if that person seemed to know me for sure, I would have mumbled, "Ah, yes," trying not to let that person realize that I could not remember him or her, but that day, I had answered the phone in my sleep and ended up blurting, "Ha Gye-suk?" She must have been dismayed by my being unable to remember her, but she acted as if she didn't mind and right away explained who she was.

"Back in school you and Mi-seo were friends, remember? And I was friends with Mi-seo as well. You know, I was kind of plump." Here she burst into laughter, perhaps because she was plump back then but had now gotten fat. "And was an hour late getting to school every day."

When she got to "an hour late getting to school every day," I was abruptly awakened from my stupor. When she first said "back in school," I had wondered if she meant middle school or college, but when she introduced herself as the one who was an hour late getting to school every day, a door had discreetly opened, the door to a classroom in Yeongdeungpo Girls' High School, behind Janghun High School in Sindaebang-dong, Yeongdeungpo.

This girl, Ha Gye-suk.

The class is already underway. The girl in uniform with the ribbon bow tie, the purple-red schoolbag placed on the hallway floor, her hips slightly pulled back behind her as she discreetly opens the door at the back of the classroom, the girl with the bright red lower lip. Her plump cheeks, the curly hair, her eyes that always seemed to say to us, "I'm sorry."

It was now 1994. It was 1979 when we first met. The girl had called me up, as if to chastise me for napping, saying, "It's me, don't you remember?" and was now sliding open the classroom door from sixteen years ago.

Our daily schedule comprised four classes. Ha Gye-suk's lower lip always appeared slightly redder than the upper lip, and when she arrived an hour late and opened the door at the back of the classroom, her lower lip would turn even redder. How red it looked. This girl, her eyes, nose, and mouth were all gone now and all that remained with me was her red lower lip.

Thanks to this lower lip, the girl, Ha Gye-suk, had now come back to life in my memory. One day, when, again an hour late, she discreetly opened the door and stepped inside, Mi-seo whispered in my ear. "She works for this really vicious company. All the other companies dismiss their workers in time for them to get to school, but this place always arranges the hours so that the students miss the first class. You know why her lower lip is always so red? It's because each time she gets to the classroom door an hour late, she stands outside the door biting her lip over and over." When I realized that the person on the phone was the girl who used to discreetly open the door at the back of the classroom, that she was one of the girls who had, between 1979 and 1981, gone to school with me, it was my voice that changed texture. "My, who'd have imagined I'd hear from you."

Here I am on an island; feeling as if I have reclaimed nature, from which I thought I had grown apart since my childhood. For several days I have been walking around the island. Walking around town the first day, I found a bookstore. Its humble storefront made me stop and smile. There was a sliding glass door with drapes hand-embroidered with tiny patterns. Because of these drapes, I never would have thought it was a bookstore had it not been for the sign. Pleased about encountering a bookstore in an unfamiliar place, I slipped inside, even though I was not looking for anything. I had to smile again. The shop was small, even for a bookstore, but in one corner, they were selling razors and school supplies—pencils, erasers, and fine-point pens—and in another, rice puffs and sweet chips were on display. The store's owner was, unlike what one would expect, a pretty young woman, which made me smile to myself.

And then I smiled yet again, for among some one hundred books on the bookcase, there it was—the book that had made Ha Gye-suk call me up. My novel.

I took down a hymnbook from a corner of the bookshelf and paid for it before leaving the store. I was not a churchgoer but I had wondered about the composition of hymns and wanted to investigate. But back in the city, it is never easy to get things done except things that need to be done right away. My days were always wrapped up in one hassle or another, and I always had a long list of books I had to buy. From time to time it would again occur to me that I wanted a hymnbook and each time I would tell myself that next time I was at a bookstore I should pick one up, but that was all. The thought had passed me by for several years, and in the end, this was where I finally purchased a hymnbook.

With the hymnbook under my arm, again I walked around the island for hours and hours. The landscape that I was used to was the plains of the peninsula's inland region, and its springs and summers and falls and winters, but now, I am standing before the island's unfamiliar oleanders, windmill palms and crinum lilies, and the endless rows of dark blue waves. What I realize, out of the blue, is that nature is, to all of us, a nourishing nutrient, that it is nature that pushes us to travel back in time, to a remote path inside our hearts. Back in the city, designed so that we never once have a chance to step on soil, I would once again have let several years go by before I bought this hymnbook, which I have no immediate need for.

Ha Gye-suk's phone call was the first I received from people from that time in my life. After her call, people from those days began to call from time to time, asking if I was that person from that classroom in that school. When I confirmed that I was that person from that classroom in that school, they said, "It's really you," and revealed who they were. It's really you, this is Nam Gil-sun. This is Choe Jeong-bun. I saw you in the newspaper ad. It was your name and the face resembled yours, but I didn't think it was really you. Still, I wondered and called the publisher. They wouldn't give me your phone number, so I had to plead, you know. Most of the callers said they had seen me in the advertisement in the newspaper. And they said they were happy for me, as if it had happened to them.

One of them, whose name, she said, was Yi Jong-rye, said she had pointed out to her husband my photograph in the newspaper ad and told him this was her friend, and she felt this sense of pride; but her voice turned teary in the end. "It was a school, all right, but since nobody keeps in touch, my husband asked once, 'You sure you went to high school?' He had brought it up casually only in passing, but it's funny, because it really hit me hard, you know . . . How could he say that, when I worked so hard to get that diploma? I felt hurt, left with this ache in the pit of my stomach, and for days slept with my back to him. So when I saw you in the newspaper and I was able to tell him, 'This is my high school friend,' imagine how proud I was."

Listening to her words coming from the other end of the line, I laughed, but after we hung up, I was also left with an ache in the pit of my stomach and remained sitting there for a while, caressing the receiver. It's not just you. I am not any different. That was true. I had once been a high school student as well, but I did not have a single friend from high school, either. When middle-aged women on some TV drama not even worth your time chatted about meeting up with high school friends, I would gaze at them blankly. Even now, when someone introduces the person next to her, saying, "She's a friend from high school," I falter and take another look at the two of them.

Pouting when a friend finds a new friend; pressing a fallen leaf dry and writing her name on the back; going biking with friends; writing a letter through the night and slipping it between the pages of her book—neither I nor the friends who had called me up, had ever experienced such times. No time to pout, no time to press leaves—we had none of that among us.

What did exist among us were assembly lines at sewing factories, electronics factories, clothing factories, food processing factories.

It is my destiny to leave my parents' care early in life. All sorts of signs pointed toward this, even an online fortune-telling service that I tried out for fun. It said I would leave the place of my birth and experience hardships in my early years. Sometimes I ponder exactly when one's early years end. I ponder this as hard as when I ask myself, "What is literature?" Then I conclude that thirty would be good. I am now thirty-two, so that would mean the hardships of my early years have passed. At sixteen, when I pierced the sole of my foot with the pitchfork, while sitting on the veranda of the house with the blue gate, waiting for Brother's letter, I got a vague sense that life was made up of vicious wounds. And that in order to embrace that viciousness and live on, I had to retain in my heart one thing that was pure. That I should believe in and depend on that one thing. If not, I would be too lonely. And if I simply lived on, I would some day, once again, pierce my foot with a pitchfork.

I am sixteen years old and on the last day of rice planting I take the night train and leave the house and the well that swallowed the pitchfork. At the edge of the village is the railroad, across from which Father runs a store. Mom tells me to go say good-bye to Father and to get on the bus there. Then she'll catch that bus when it comes through the village center. Before leaving the house, the sixteen-year-old sister gazes down at the face of her seven-year-old brother, asleep after an early dinner. From the moment he was born, Little Brother had been glued to his sister's back like a turtle and is always wary and full of fear that she might disappear. To Little Brother, who had grown up on Sister's back, breathing in her smell, she is still the only one. To Little Brother, school is the only place that he has to release her to.

When Sister says, "I'm going to school, be back soon," then Little Brother can say, "Yes, you will be back." Even when he is playing outside, as soon as the sun sets, he will call out "Sister!" and run back into the house. Anywhere he might be, he calls out, "Sister." When he is fetching eggs, when he is pooping, or picking persimmons. Once, out on the newly paved main street, he hit his head on a truck, and he still called out, "Sister, Sister, Sister" as he was being taken to the hospital.

"Sister, where are you? I want to go to Sister." Left without a choice, his fourth-grader sister heads to the hospital straight from school, carrying her schoolbag. She sleeps at the hospital with Little Brother, has her meals at the hospital, and goes to school from the hospital. The way things are, Little Brother is not at all ready to part with Sister. If she were to tell him she is heading out to the city, he would burst into tears, so she dare not tell him she's leaving and just gazes down at Little Brother's sleeping face. Little Brother opens his eyes slightly and looks at Sister. He must have found it strange that she is dressed to go out when it is nighttime, and demands an answer, even in his stupor.

"Are you going somewhere?"

Sister says no, she is not going anywhere. Relieved, Little Brother closes his eyes. Sister puts her hand on the scar, still visible on the head of her sleeping brother. What a fuss he will make when he wakes up in the morning.

I haven't even crossed the railroad tracks when I see the bus lights. I had spent too long gazing into Little Brother's sleeping face. I am sixteen years old, and suddenly anxious as the lights on the bus approach.

"Father!" I shout out. Father runs out of the store, at the same time the bus arrives at the stop. "Father, I am off!" And without a proper good-bye to Father, I board the bus. I hurry to the back of the bus and look out the window. Father stands vacant and still in the dark. His face is not visible; only his silhouette stands vacant and still.

Since then I have not had the chance to live in the same house as Father. Even with Mom or Little Brother, we have not spent five days together under the same roof.

Boarding the bus in the village center, Mom asks of her sixteen-year-old daughter, "Did you say good-bye to Father?"

"Yes."

But was that a good-bye? Shouting toward the store, "Father, I am off," and not even getting to see Father's face. I should have set out just a little earlier. Father's silhouette glimmered in front of my eyes, as he ran out of the store and stood vacant and still in the dark. The bus is already leaving the village. What happened five minutes ago has already become a thing of the past.

Mom is dressed in traditional *hanbok*, an orange outfit. It comes with a lined jacket over her blouse, which is fastened with a chrysanthemum-shaped brooch instead of with ribbon strings. When I gaze at the brooch, Mom says, "You got this for me when you went on that school trip." The thin white collar of her blouse is dirty. When she notices that I am glancing at her dirty collar, Mom says, "I'd meant to sew on a new one, but got too busy."

At the train station in town, we meet Cousin, who will be going to the city with me. Her legs long and slender, Cousin stands carrying a large bag next to Aunt, Mom's brother's wife, who has become bone skinny. Cousin is a slender nineteen-year-old. I smell the raw odor of fish as Aunt's hand caresses my cheek. Aunt takes her hand from my cheek to and touches Cousin's hand. As they say good-bye, the mother's hand intertwines with the daughter's.

"And don't you fight and argue."

As she lets go of Cousin's hand, Aunt's eyes well up with tears. When it's time to get our tickets punched, Aunt asks Cousin to write them soon. Leaving my haggard aunt behind in the waiting room, Mom, Cousin, and I enter the boarding area.

I press my palms on the window of the train car and look out at the platform. Good-bye, my home village. I am leaving you to fish for life.

Even on the night train, Mom does not speak. She would barely have had time to straighten her back all day as she finished up the rice planting, but Mom does not even doze off. From time to time she glances at me, sitting next to her. Farewells make one gaze intently into the other person's eyes. And make one realize things out of the blue—this was the shape of this person's eyes, which one had never noticed before.

For ten days I had been ordering lunch at the same table and the woman at the restaurant finally struck up a conversation. It was two o'clock in the afternoon. The busiest hour had passed. Somehow I had been coming to the restaurant at this same time each afternoon, and had begun to feel apologetic that, at this hour, when the woman would likely be ready for a break after the busy lunch crowd, I was pushing her back into the kitchen. The woman brought out my food, then after washing her face, she spoke to me as she applied lotion on her face.

"Where are you from?"

"I came from Seoul."

"A long way, is it?"

Instead of answering, I smiled. I had just put a slice of kimchi in my mouth, so I couldn't answer even if I wanted. The woman said that if I had told her from the start that I would keep coming back this often, she could have arranged a special menu with dishes prepared for her family for a cheaper price. I glanced at the menu on the wall. How much cheaper would she charge? The price was written below each item. A pot of kimchi stew for 4,000 won. Bean paste stew cooked with abalone, clams, or crayfish for 5,000 won. Spicy beef soup for 3,500 won.

"Have you come alone?"

To my relief, she did not add, A woman, all by yourself?

"Yes."

"Tourist?"

"No."

"That's what I guessed. A tourist would not stay here day in and day out."

I smiled again.

"Then are you here for work?"

Now I was lost. Could I say I was here for work? Had I come for work? Unable to answer, I said, "Well, kind of," then smiled again. The woman must have understood my smile as "yes, I have come for work." She brushed her permed hair back over her ears and brought out three clementine oranges on a plate.

"What kind of work do you do?"

I could not go on eating my lunch. I put down my spoon and peeled the skin off one of the clementines. The citric fragrance seeped into my nose, cool and fresh. The woman brought me the paper from another table. She probably remembered me reading the newspaper after eating each day. The spot on the paper where her hand had touched carried the smell of her lotion. Her hospitality made me feel embarrassed for not answering her question and I quickly said, "I'm a writer." Right at that moment, the woman's face, on which had age spots settled across her cheeks like a map, brightened up.

"Oh my, really? What an honor!"

Honor? Overcome with shyness, I let out a quiet laugh.

It was the first time that I had referred to myself as a writer to a stranger, to someone in an unfamiliar place . . .

Mom.

Mom's dark eyes, like a cow's. I had this thought for the first time that night. And it remains unchanged, then or now. How, even now, after raising us, her six children, Mom can still have such clear eyes. . . . There are times when Mom's eyes push me deep into thought.

It is early summer in my sixteenth year and on the night train, Mom's dark eyes well up with tears. This is Mom's second time riding the train to Seoul. A while back, Oldest Brother needed some papers for his college registration but for some reason his letter arrived only a day before the papers were due. It would be too late if they were sent by mail, so Mom took on the role of courier. She got on the night train with the papers.

The only thing on Mom's mind was that she must deliver that night these papers, which her son needed the following day. And the only thing Mom knew about Seoul was that her son worked at the Yongmun-dong Community Service Center.

Whenever she tells the story of her first visit to Seoul, Mom always says that there are plenty of good people in the world. There sitting next to me was this young man, about your brother's age, see, so I took out the big envelope from my bag and said, the thing is, my son needs this tomorrow if he's to start university, but I don't know where to go. What am I to do? This young man, he got off with me at the station and although it was late at night, he took me all the way to the Yongmun-dong Community Center.

Not even the taxi driver knew the way, but the young man asked around, here and there, and got me there. The building was dark, but the young man said, "This is it," so I banged and banged on the locked door and your brother came out, and that young man, he went to such trouble bringing me there, but turned around just like that, before I could give him a proper thank-you, and was gone.

Mom had handled her first trip to Seoul with such courage, but now, en route to take me to Brother, her eyes are filled with tears. Looking away from Mom's teary eyes, I stare out at the dark outside the window, orange with the reflection of the *hanbok*. I stare at Cousin, sitting there like a single transplanted blossom of rose moss. Mom reaches out her arm and caresses my hair. Having already bid farewell to Aunt at the station, Cousin looks away from Mom and me.

"You want some?" Mom takes out boiled eggs from her bag. I shake my head. As she accepts the peeled egg from Mom, Cousin takes out a book from her bag and hands it over to me to take a look.

"What kind of book is it?"

"It's a book of photographs."

With bits of the hard-boiled egg on her lips, Cousin speaks to me in a low voice.

"I want to be a photographer."

A photographer? I repeat her word. It occurs to me that the photographers I've seen in photo studios were all men. I turn to Cousin and say that the all the photographers I've seen are men.

Cousin lets out a laugh and says, "Not someone who takes *those* kinds of photographs but *these* kinds of photographs," as she turns the pages of the book she has placed on my lap, one after another. Each page Cousin turns to carries beautiful scenery. The desert, trees, the sky, the sea. When she arrives at a page, Cousin stops and whispers to me, Look at this. It is night, inside a forest, and stars have settled down atop the trees, white and twinkling.

"They're birds."

In awe, I push my face closer to the book on my lap. Upon a closer look, what were twinkling upon their perch atop the trees in the night forest turned out not to be stars but egrets. The egrets had taken up their narrow perch here and there on the high branches of the forest, covered in dark, shining white.

"They're sleeping. Aren't they beautiful?"

I nod. Under the distant night sky, the white birds slept, gentle and benign, a beautiful blanket over the forest.

"I want to take pictures of birds, not people."

Mystified, I gaze straight into Cousin's face. While she tells me that she wants to photograph birds, her cheeks are flushed, as if they have been smothered with the fresh fragrance from the thickets or the soil and the leaves of the forest where the egrets are sleeping.

"When I start making money, the first thing I'm going to buy is a camera."

The night train chugs on, carrying Cousin's dream. I am no longer listening to Cousin's whispers. Already I am promising my heart to the sleeping egrets, so gentle and benign, a beautiful blanket over the forest in the dark, under the distant night sky. Some day, I shall go and see for myself those white birds up on the high branches. I shall go and see for myself their beauty and gentility, as they sleep with their faces toward the stars.

I cannot forget seeing the Daewoo Building that day, in the early morning hour. The tallest thing that I had even seen since I was born. At the time, I did not know that the building had a name: Daewoo. Following Mom out to the plaza outside Seoul Station at dawn, I run to catch up with Mom, who is walking a few steps ahead of me, and attach myself to her side. As if that were not enough, I search for Mom's hand and grasp it hard.

"What is it?"

"It scares me."

I feel as if the Daewoo Building, standing over there like a gargantuan beast, would stomp toward us and swallow Mom and Cousin and me. Cousin, nineteen years old, appears dignified even in the face of a gargantuan beast. Seeing that I am frightened, Mom tells me it is nothing.

"It's nothing, I tell you. Nothing but steel frames."

Despite what Mom may have said, I, having taken my first step into the city at sixteen, glare in fear at the gargantuan and beastly Daewoo Building in the dawning light; at the iridescent lights that have already come on; at the cars speeding toward some destination at this early hour.

Oldest Brother still has no room of his own after all this time. That is why we have to come on the night train, because the only place for us to sleep in Seoul is an inn, which we cannot afford. Oldest Brother may not have a room, but he had skin so white. His nails are clean and his white shirt is radiant. Eyes, nose, and mouth, chiseled in shape, are positioned neatly on his long face of fair complexion. He works at the sanitation bureau of the Community Service Center by day and studies law at a night college, but one would never guess unless he brought it up. His appearance suggests that he knows nothing about the hardships of the world, exuding the air of a young man who had spent his childhood in a home that is materially affluent. This young man is now treating his younger sister, his cousin, and his mother, who have arrived in Seoul on the night train, to some warm bean sprout soup across the street from the community center. His quarters are the night duty room at the center. Ever since he started working at the service center, the center's staff no longer serves night duty. There is no need because Older Brother sleeps there every night. Soon he will take Cousin and me to the Job Training Center. Today is the first day of our training.

"It will be hard work."

Oldest Brother speaks as if befallen by a hardship larger than the hard future that awaits us.

"But after you finish your training there and get a job at the industrial complex, you will be able to attend school. Special classes have been established for industrial workers, to take effect next year."

What Oldest Brother adds sounds like an excuse.

"If you don't take that route, the only schools you can attend are vocational schools, which are for new arrivals from the country. Vocational schools are not regular schools."

The Job Training Center is located by the gates of the Guro Industrial Complex.

We leave the restaurant and take the bus to the gates of the industrial complex. On the athletic field of the Job Training Center, Cousin and I say good-bye to Mom. I remember the athletic field from that day. The color orange, this shade of orange growing distant. Mom's huge hand holds my hand. With the other hand, the hand that is not holding mine, Mom places a 1,000-won bill on Cousin's palm.

"When you get hungry, don't suffer with an empty stomach—get yourselves powder milk drinks."

Cousin's eyes well up with tears. Heading toward the steel gates of the training center, the three of us left behind her, Mom's steps keep turning back. Mom is an orange stain on that athletic field.

The stain grows distant, then comes back, making Cousin and me hold hands. We say we must depend on each other.

"You two are on your own now. Don't give Oldest Brother trouble, you must depend on each other, you understand."

The orange stain is growing distant again. One step ahead of us, my tall brother walks with his eyes on the ground. Standing among the crowd of people assembled for job training, I continue to stare at the orange stain and Oldest Brother's back, growing smaller and smaller. I stare at Mom and Oldest Brother, growing more and more distant. They grow smaller and smaller, until they are no longer visible. I pick at the ground with the toes of my shoes, for no reason. I am sixteen years old.

This was how my life in Seoul began. But it is still a long while to go until I meet Ha Gye-suk and the others. Meeting them was not easy.

What is it that lies between me and them, those whom I have yet to meet?

It was hard, but only at first, and Ha Gye-suk and I began speaking on the phone quite often. Then one day, she said to me, "You don't write about us."

I felt a familiar soreness again.

"I looked up your books and read all of them, except for the first one. The neighborhood bookstores did not carry it and it's hard for me to make time to get out to the big stores. So that's the only one I didn't get to . . . You seem to write quite a lot about your childhood, and also about college, and about love, but there was nothing about us."

I am silent.

"I wondered if there'd be anything about us, you know, and I kept an eye out as I read." I did not answer and Ha Gye-suk called out my name, her voice sinking deep and low. "Could it be you're ashamed? About that time in your past?"

I was nervous and moved the telephone receiver to switch ears. Ha Gye-suk mistook my nervous silence as reticence and her usual cheery, almost chatty, tone turned glum.

"Your life seems different from ours now."

If I had answered her right there, and said, That is not so, would that have made me feel better? But I could not give her that answer. I was unable to say, No, that's not true. I had never been proud, but I had not been ashamed, either. But I could not quite say it. Perhaps there had been moments when I did feel ashamed. But it was never a significant thought. Or it would be more accurate to say I never had the time to pay attention to these thoughts or feelings.

I did not have the luxury of perceiving my situation as difficult or painful. I could not give much thought to each passing day; I had to live from each passing day to the next. The day was always hectic, from morning to evening, leaving me no time to think about anything else but the most immediate and necessary tasks that had to be done before I had to quickly go to sleep or wake up again. It was only after I approached thirty that I got to thinking about how worn out and exhausted I must have been back then.

I was about to turn thirty and one day I felt extremely, utterly tired. I realized, right away, that my fatigue dated back to those years, that I had already turned thirty, or even thirty-two, many years ago. What made me realize this was none other than writing, which I was so in awe of.

Is that how it goes with writing? That as long as you are writing, no time is ever completely in the past? Is this the fate that befalls all writers—to flow backward, in present tense, into a time of pain, like salmon migrating upstream, swimming against the current back to where it started, struggling through waterfalls that break and tear its fins? It always returns, pushing through waterfalls, carrying a deep wound inside its belly, risking its own life. It returns, taking the same route back, tracking its own trail, traveling that singular path.

I am at the Job Training Center. I wake up at six A.M. in my dormitory room. Sometimes when I awake, I still think of the pitchfork that I threw into the well. What would it look like down there, sitting still at the deep bottom? But there is no time for idle thoughts. I hear the bell summoning us to the athletic field, where we stand in line and perform the health exercise routine to a merry melody. Then we clean our designated areas, wait in line to wash up, after which we have breakfast. I have never before seen this kind of dinnerware, a single tray with slots for your rice and soup and all the side dishes.

To my sixteen-year-old eyes and my sixteen-year-old tongue, the tray feels unfamiliar and the kimchi tastes odd. I have a hard time eating at first, because of the strange-looking tray and the odd-tasting kimchi. When Cousin asks me why I am not eating, I blame the kimchi: I can taste a strange kind of fish sauce in the kimchi; Mom only uses sauce made from yellow croaker. As for the tray, I cannot find the right words for what exactly is wrong with it, so I don't bring that up. Back in our country home, my rice and soup bowls would be sitting facedown on the kitchen shelf. Cousin buys me a pastry at the snack stall. She is nineteen years old and I am sixteen and she does her best to cajole me.

"You can't keep spending money on bread like this. We have very little money and we won't be making any until we find a job and get paid."

I relent and take a spoonful of the soup from the strange tray to my mouth. I am again reminded of my bowls on Mom's kitchen shelf, which brings tears to my eyes. Floating on top of the soup, inside the strange tray, I see my seven-year-old brother's sleep-soaked face the day I left home, asking, "Where are you going, Sis?"

I take a big scoop of my rice. I drink up the soup. I chew on the stringy and odd-tasting kimchi, and swallow.

The teachers all refer to us as the industrial labor force. Even in the middle of soldering classes, we are reminded that we are here as part of the industrial labor force. The doors of our dormitory rooms at the training center are each marked with a sign carrying the name of a flower, as in kindergarten classrooms. What was the name of my room? Rose? Lily? All I remember is that there were lockers attached to our wooden beds. Some years later, there was a popular comedy skit on TV, titled *Atten-HUT!* I used to watch closely whenever it came on because the interior of the military barracks in the show was very much like the dormitory room where I slept as a sixteen-year-old. The only difference is that our rooms have a loft, accessible by a ladder. Five of us sleep on each floor. Cousin and I help each other, as Mom told us to, and climb up the loft to our designated beds. Following roll call at nine P.M., lights must all go out. Nights when I cannot sleep and lie staring at the ceiling in the dark, I get to thinking about the pitchfork inside the well, just as I do when I awake in the early hours of dawn. The sole of my foot hurts when I think of the silence of the pitchfork, sunken deep under the water, which makes me toss and turn and reach my hand out to touch Cousin's forehead, her eyes. If she seems to be sleeping, I shake her awake.

"What is it?"

I almost bring up the pitchfork, then decide not to. But I do not want to lie awake alone, so I keep reaching for Cousin's forehead and eyes, until she slaps my hand with her palm.

Cousin is nineteen years old. She uses scented lotion on her hands. When I get back to the dorm room after washing my face, she uses cotton pads to dab skin toner around my skin, pressing gently. Then she speaks to me in a whisper.

"One of our teachers, Mr. Kim, isn't he dashing?"

I nod. Mr. Kim teaches liberal arts. It is from him that I hear about the life of words, instead of industrial labor force, something I have not heard about since arriving at the training center. He tells us life is beautiful. Did he also tell us what made it beautiful? I cannot remember. He simply said, "Life is a beautiful thing." What its beauty will bring us, and what its beauty will take from us, he does not say. Simply beautiful, is all he says.

Everything turns white inside my head. I think of the entrance of the industrial complex. I stand at the entrance of the industrial complex, with Cousin by my side. Where did everyone go, leaving only Cousin and me here? There were twenty of us sharing one dorm room, but I cannot recall a single face. Out of the blue, a pair of eyeglasses appears then disappears again. The only reason I remember this face is because it was the only one wearing glasses, not only among our roommates but in the entire dormitory. So it is the eyeglasses that I remember, not the face itself. A pair of black plastic-rimmed glasses placed on a pale face. And I only remember a single name: Kim Jeong-rye. In this case it is only the name I remember; the face has been erased. All I have left is a faint impression that her face was rather big compared to her body. Kim Jeong-rye. The name belonged to an orphan. Each Saturday, when we are given permission to spend the night outside the dorm, this name leaves the Job Training Center, saying she is going to visit her orphanage. On one of these Saturdays when Kim Jeong-rye has gone to the orphanage, a commotion breaks out in the dormitory.

"The bread is gone."

"I lost my wallet."

"My clothes!"

We open Kim Jeong-rye's locker. It has been emptied out. Was Kim Jeong-rye really an orphan? Whichever the case, it turns out Kim Jeong-rye has also taken Cousin's lotion and she does not return when roll call comes around Sunday night. She has deserted the training. Also gone are seven of my new panties and three of my new handkerchiefs, which Mom bought in town and folded up for me into small squares to be packed with my other things.

Even when the weekends come around, Cousin and I have nowhere to go. We do not even know which roads lead where on the other side of the center's walls. Those who don't have anywhere to go play volleyball on the athletic field. Cousin and I join them in chasing after the ball. When we get tired, Cousin and I take a shower at the shared washroom inside the center, scrubbing each other's backs clean. On other days, we have to finish washing within a given time, but after the trainees leave for the weekend, we can take things slow and easy. After the shower, Cousin lies on her stomach on the hardwood floor of our dorm room, her face smothered with facial cream, and writes a letter to Aunt. I lie next to her and stare up at the ceiling while playing around with my feet. My foot keeps poking at Cousin. Irritated, Cousin suggests that I try writing a letter as well. I roll over on my stomach and whisper into Cousin's ear.

"I am going to write something other than a letter."

Cousin stares at me, the tip of her ballpoint pen still on the letter pad.

"Like what?"

I whisper into her ear my secret, something that I have not told anyone in all of my sixteen years.

"Like a poem or a novel."

Cousin's eyes grow wide.

"You mean you want to be a writer?"

Scared that Cousin is going to throw cold water on what I said, I keep speaking, trying hard to explain that this is what I have wanted to do for a long time, and that there is nothing else I'd rather do. Cousin tilts her head, lifting her pen from the letter pad to her chin.

"I thought those kinds of people were born different, you know?"

I am so distressed to think she might say, "That is why you will never be a writer," so I keep talking. "They are not born different. They think different."

Cousin does not say anything and is lost in thought. I pull myself closer to her, my face red with the fear that she is unable to understand what I am saying.

"It's no different from your wanting to be a photographer, taking pictures of those birds."

Cousin folds up her letter and puts it away in her locker, then lies down next to where I am stretched straight on my back, my eyes on the ceiling. Cousin lifts her legs toward the ceiling, crossing her slender ankles.

"What are you going to write about?"

For a moment, the pitchfork at the bottom of the well passes in front of my eyes.

"That I don't know yet."

Cousin is tender toward me, more so than usual, and I get to talking about how I struck my foot with the pitchfork. I even show her the sole of my foot.

"Look. It's all healed now but it still hurts when I walk too long, as if my tendon's being pulled."

Cousin gazes at my foot.

"What does this have to do with wanting to write?"

I cannot find the words to answer her question. How do I explain to her, that if do not keep something pure inside my heart, I will inevitably strike down at my foot again with a pitchfork? Instead, I say to her, "Only this will protect me."

I feel silly about my overly emphasized words and so I add, "No need to worry anymore about the pitchfork, because I threw it in the well."

Cousin sits up.

"What did you say?"

"The pitchfork. I said I threw it in the well."

Cousin stares at me as if she's completely clueless.

"Deliberately?"

I nod.

"Why would you do that?"

I cannot answer. I do not know how to explain that I was scared. I was scared that one day I would take it down from the shed again, intending to turn the barley hay over, and hurt my foot again. Cousin still looks puzzled as she speaks to me in a dignified tone.

"When we go home for a visit, you should tell Uncle so that he can pump out the well."

I could not speak.

"The water is probably all tainted by now. Did you think about the fact that people drink from the well?"

The water? I am speechless, never having thought about how the pitchfork would have tainted the water.

When Oldest Brother comes for one of his visits and takes us to a bakery near the entrance of the industrial complex, Cousin announces in a loud voice, pointing at me, "She says she's going to be a writer."

"A writer? You?"

Oldest Brother looks at me so dumbfounded that I throw Cousin a mean glance.

"What's the matter? It's not like it has to be kept a big secret."

Oldest Brother takes us to a Chinese place for *jajang* noodles and walks us back to the Job Training Center, sending us in with a bag full of milk and pastries and things. Then he walks across the athletic field with his eyes on the ground and his towering back hunched, and disappears through the center's gate.

At last, my sentences begin to take shape. Short, very simple. The past in present tense; the present in past tense. Clear like a photograph. Lest the door to the lonely room close again. Let the sentences convey Oldest Brother's loneliness as he walked toward the center gate, his eyes on the ground.

When I heard Ha Gye-suk say, clearly, "Your life seems different from ours," I realized that it was my heart that was sore. My heart ached. There was another person who had said this me, not exactly in Ha Gye-suk's words, but in the same vein: *You are different from me.* It was my mother.

Sixteen years after my sixteenth year, I am a writer and I am working on something to meet an urgent deadline. Mom is visiting me in Seoul and she keeps talking to me. I take down one of my books from the shelf and hand it to her.

"Why don't you read this for a while. I'll be done soon."

When I am finished, I find Mom sleeping, her face covered with my book.

"Mother!"

She seems apologetic that she fell asleep instead of reading my book, and says, as she hands the book back to me, "You are now different from me." Her words, at the time, seem natural and indisputable. Of course we're different: Mom was born in the 1930s and I was born in 1963. By "different," I gather that Mom is referring to generational gap. But this is not the case. There is something that I have never known. That the only letters Mom can read are the letters in her prayer book, and that although she may be praying with the book open on her lap, she has all the prayers memorized. I learn from Youngest Brother only the following year that he has been teaching Mother to read and write.

Over spring and summer, my sentences left me and there was only this voice, dripping like drops of water, into my heart.

"You don't seem to write about us."

"Could it be you're ashamed? About that time in your past?"

"Your life seems different from ours now."

Whenever I awoke from a cozy nap, her voice would without fail turn into icy water and fall in drops from the ceiling, drip,

drip, drip, down on my forehead. Y. O. U. D. O. N. T. S. E. E. M. T. O. W. R. I. T. E. A. B. O. U. T. U. S. C. O. U. L. D. I. T. B. E. Y. O. U. R. E. A. S. H. A. M. E. D. A. B. O. U. T. T. H. A. T. T. I. M. E. I. N. Y. O. U. R. P. A. S. T. Y. O. U. R. L. I. F. E. S. E. E. M. S. D. I. F. F. E. R. E. N. T. F. R. O. M. O. U. R. S. N. O. W.

⁂

Oldest Brother has come to visit and is staring into a piece of white paper. Written on it are names of factories that we are eligible to apply for upon completing our training. After staring for a long time at the factory names, Oldest Brother puts a circle where the name *Dongnam Electronics, Inc.* is written.

"At an electronics company, the work shouldn't be too messy, at least." As Oldest Brother hands me the paper that he has circled, I, sixteen years old, look up at him.

"I heard that I'm too young to apply, so I have to submit the papers under someone else's name."

"You're how old?"

"Sixteen."

"Sixteen," Oldest Brother repeats, his expression turning glum. "Don't worry. I'll take care of it." Oldest Brother lifts himself up from the chair at the snack stall, dusting off his clothes with his hands.

⁂

Among the trainees at the center, some twenty or more have chosen Dongnam Electronics, Inc. We share no previous ties, but the fact that we got our training together and will leave for the same place gives us a sense of intimacy. Our group of twenty-something sits around together and thinks about Dongnam Electronics, Inc. What kind of a place it is, what kind of things will happen there.

On the day we leave the Job Training Center, our teacher, Mr. Kim, writes down a poem on the blackboard in the auditorium. How beautiful, to behold from behind, one who goes, knowing clearly when it is he should go. He has curly hair. He holds the chalk in his right hand, his left hand supporting it from underneath. Such a sad poem. Cousin's eyes well up with tears. Mr. Kim recites the poem for us and says his good-bye. "You are the hope of our nation's industry . . ." Mr. Curly Hair, even he, in the end, lets out the word "industry" from his mouth. The hope of our nation's industry.

"Now you shall leave this place and start your lives on the job. Your workplaces will be the foundation of your lives . . ."

We have lived together as trainees for only a month but we swap our names and the names of the companies that we will be working for. We part. Repeating to ourselves, How beautiful, to behold from behind, one who goes, knowing clearly when it is he should go.

Dongnam Electronics, Inc., is located inside Guro Industrial Complex No. 1. Those of us assigned to Dongnam Electronics, Inc., some twenty trainees in all, now take our step from the entrance of the industrial complex onto the grounds of the complex. After being assigned the companies, we are given a week-long break. Oldest Brother takes Cousin and me to the room he has rented in the residential block of Industrial Complex No. 3, near the subway station.

Is the house still there? The house that I have never been back to since I left. The rooms in that house. I have never been back, not to the house, not to the room, not even in their vicinity, but the house is as vivid as a well-preserved photograph and emerges so vividly in my mind. The room in that house.

After passing through the subway station in this neighborhood, the Suwon-bound train enters Gyeonggi Province. If you are headed for Suwon on the subway, this subway station is the last station in Seoul. This is what I wrote down six years ago. The subway station where the Suwon-bound trains pass through is where the neighborhood starts. From the subway station, the road splits into three. Yet although the road split into three, whichever road you took, it took you to the industrial complex. The one road to the left, which led to the house, branched into an alley between the photo shop and the Barley Field Teahouse, and there were houses, with the alley between them. But when you got out of the alley where the houses stood, and crossed the elevated walkway that led to the market, on the other side of the market you again found yourself at the industrial complex. The house with the thirty-seven rooms, all located inside a labyrinth. Up the stairs and take the winding path deeper into a corner where, it seemed, nothing more could exist, there was yet another room, with a small kitchenette attached, inside this three-story red brick house.

"This is it."

Oldest Brother takes Cousin and me through the open gates. *This is it*—Oldest Brother's voice flows into my ears now, just as it did then. That was it. One of the thirty-seven rooms, our lone, remote room. The house was surrounded, to the front and back, by other houses with just as many rooms, but when we opened our window, we could see a countless number of people pouring out of the subway station. The path or the elevated walkway that led to the corner store or the market were always crowded with people, but why is it that, both then and now, whenever I think of that room, the first thought that occurs to me is that it was so very isolated? We would live in this lonely place, remote and alone.

I am writing once again. I envision three meters from the staircase to the second floor, in the middle of a courtyard, and I see that the surface, when seen from above, was covered with cement. There was a tap planted directly in the ground. To the left of the staircase were two yellow wooden doors. The windowpane on the wooden doors is thick with dust. Underneath that dust was written, in white paint, the Chinese characters for male and female, 男 and 女. Each morning, the people in the house, awkward in one another's presence, acting as if they were each there for some other business, would stand around the tap. This was the only time they could see one another's faces. Without smiling, without acknowledging one another, they washed. Behind the door second from the right . . . Hui-jae lived there, alone.

Hui-jae . . . the name that, finally, pops out. Cousin and I, along with Hui-jae, make up a genre painting of the industrial labor force from the late years of the Yusin regime. I am looking at a collection of Kim Hong-do's genre paintings. It is fascinating how, when Kim Hong-do takes up a seat facing the streets or the ferry point, the schoolhouse or the pub or the wrestling grounds or the laundry spot by the stream, and simply lifts his brush, the people of the eighteenth century are rendered more real in his paintings than in reality. How does one reach that level of artistry, everyone is said to have lauded, applauding in awe. I wonder—how would he portray Hui-jae?

The characters in this genre painting will mostly be captured in motion, but Hui-jae will be captured as a faint smile. I think of genre paintings from back in the ancient kingdom of Goguryeo. The tomb murals and the paintings that depict scenes of hunting, of battles, of dancing, of wrestling matches, of acrobatics. And of grain mills, butcher shops, stables and cow houses. We, or Hui-jae, cannot be placed inside an air of dynamic movement, within powerful brush strokes. We, along with Hui-jae, positioned in front of the constantly moving conveyor belt, or in front of the needle, always threaded, on the sewing machine, our eyes weary, never round or wide. We will always exist, not as the delightful and loving sentiments of everyday life, soaked in merry humor, but as pale shadows, barely able to afford a chance to bask in the sun on rooftops at lunch break. From the perspective of fashion history, we will be dressed in blue work clothes, the back of the shirt gathered in a yoke.

Unable to bear it, I stand from my seat.

I am running. I catch myself as I run. Sit down, you can no longer run. Then or now, and always. Sit down now.

During those solitary days, I would often, with difficulty, conjure up in my mind the birds in the books of photographs that Cousin showed me the night we came to the city. The birds, asleep facing the stars under the distant night sky, high and beautiful. I would make a hard effort to promise myself that there would be a day when I would go and see them with my own eyes, as I lived my days inside this genre painting. Later, even when I became devastated by loneliness amidst the exhaustion of everyday life and the absence of meaningful ties, I never abandoned the thought that I would one day go see for myself the birds from Cousin's photo book.

I would see the egrets in the forest, the forest after nightfall, the flocks of egrets leaning close together in clusters, blanketing the entire forest beautifully with their sleep, as if they had forgiven everything in this world. One day, I promised myself, with even more desperation on days filled with despair and loneliness, I would make my way beyond the ridge that was blocking my view, my arm rattling on the windowsill of my train car.

It has been sixteen years since this promise.

I still have not made my journey to see the birds. It is not that I have forgotten. On the contrary . . . with the passing of each year, there were even more days when I reminded myself of the promise, the white egrets emerging even more splendidly in my heart. Even when I massaged my tired feet, I would think about the forest that I had yet to visit and the flocks of egrets asleep with their faces to the stars, and somehow I could maintain composure in the face of the weariness that my fatigue brought me, and even in the face of the rare joys that found their way to me. Even the bitter miseries, the cold solitudes that fell for days like rain—they would somehow feel insignificant and ephemeral, giving me the strength to greet the new day and live on.

But now, this name, Hui-jae, haunts me—have the flocks of egrets flown into the distant sadness from all those years ago, from that time when her absence came to be? Was I able, back then, to remind myself of my promise to someday go see the forest?

I am sixteen. I step inside the lone, remote room. I open the window. My eyes turn round and wide. Had the train arrived just as I opened the window? The window, the size of a wrapping cloth, looks out on the subway station across from the vacant lot, and an uneven flow of heads, nothing else but the heads of these peoples' bodies, is pouring out. As the people move up the stairs of the subway station and rush out, like an incoming tide, to the fork in the road, only their heads and nothing else are visible. In less than five minutes, however, the people have seeped away somewhere and the fork in the road is completely empty. All those people, where have they gone? It seems it was a dream, these people, who in just five minutes crowded in and emptied out. I stand looking, listening to Cousin open the small window in the kitchenette. Cousin and I sweep and wipe down our room. We sweep up the traces that the former tenant left behind into the dustbin; pick up a shard of red brick that seems to have been used to level the cupboard; throw out scattered pieces of tissue paper from the attic, and the old, abandoned kerosene stove.

Oldest Brother places some money in Cousin's nineteen-year-old hands.

"Ask the landlady for directions to the market and go buy the things we'll need to cook food."

After Oldest Brother leaves, Cousin and I lie on the floor on our stomachs and write on a sheet of white paper the things we will need to cook food, just as he said. A pot, a strainer, a large bowl for rinsing rice, three small bowls, three sets of spoon and chopsticks, three plates, a kerosene stove, three rice bowls, three soup bowls . . . Cousin and I follow the alley all the way out to the market, which we are told is located on the other side of the overpass, and buy the kitchen items on the list. Older Brother's belongings are delivered from the night duty room at the Yongsan Community Service Center to our lone, remote room. A desk and a chair. *The Complete Compilation of Six Major Laws* and books on criminal law are inside his suitcase. I open a small bag to find a bundle of Older Brother's underwear, which needs washing. After looking around the room and the kitchen, Older Brother leaves again then comes back with a newly purchased vinyl wardrobe, a small cupboard, and a sack of rice. He connects metal beams to set up the wardrobe next to the desk and tells us to hang up the clothes in our bags. We leave once again to buy our bedding. Older Brother walks to the market the way he crossed the athletic field to leave the Job Training Center, his eyes on the ground. An intermittent sigh, *phew*, drifts out from his mouth. We buy floor mattresses, acrylic mink blankets, and three pillows, and divide up the load to carry. Older Brother says only what is necessary and does not even smile. "Let's eat out tonight." He takes Cousin and me to the alley outside our lone room and treats us to pork rib barbecue for dinner. He does not eat. He looks like he is extremely angry, or perhaps enervated; he just sits there watching us eat the ribs.

One does not always age according to conventional number sequence. One can go from sixteen to thirty-two in one day. It was that day at the restaurant that I, then sixteen years old, suddenly turned thirty-two. That day when I saw Older Brother sitting there, weary inside the smoke of pork ribs, treating Cousin and me to a barbecue dinner but not taking a single bite himself, I believe that I turned thirty-two, the age that I am now.

Out of our week-long vacation, we spend five days back in the country. It is our first time traveling back to the country from Seoul. Since Cousin and I only know our way around the route between the training center and our lone room, Older Brother comes along to get us our tickets and takes us to our seats and buys us an armful of pastries and soft drinks for us to eat on the train.

Here in the present, outside of my writing, I feel an ache in my heart.

Back then, eating was such a major issue; Older Brother, back in that time, is continuously treating us to food. At the restaurant across from the community center, he treats us to bean sprout soup; at the Job Training Center snack stall he treats us to pastries and milk; and outside our rented room he treats us to pork ribs . . . He is a mere twenty-three-year-old. A youngster already with a lot on his plate, working at the community center by day and attending law school by night. Cousin boards the train first, and Oldest Brother places some money in his sixteen-year-old sister's hand. Tells her to get a carton of cigarettes for Father, a slab of beef, and cookies for Little Brother to take home.

Mom is on her way out, carrying a lunch pail for Father working on the other side of the railroad. When Mom sees me walk in the gate, the pail falls from her hand. Hearing his sister's voice from inside one of the rooms, Little Brother pushes the door open. Sister!

Running outside in his bare feet, the seven-year-old brother clings to his sixteen-year-old sister's arm.

"Where have you been?" Mom's eyes well up with tears. "No more going away, promise?"

Little Brother jumps up and climbs his sister's back. "Get down, you're going to hurt your sister's back." But Little Brother is persistent.

"No more going away ever again, okay?"

Little Brother wraps his baby arms tight around his sister's neck. Mom picks up the lunch pail.

"After you left, he made a big fuss crying and whining, asking where you've gone. How are we going to go through that all over again?"

I head out after Mom with her lunch pail to see Father, carrying Little Brother on my back.

"After you left, he closed the shop for three days, just lying in his room."

That was what Father had done? I am reminded of that night, seeing Father standing blankly in the dark, which makes my nose sting. But Father shows none of this when he sees me. "It's you," is all he says. With this, the sting I felt in my heart is relieved. In the evening Father returns home near the center of the village. Mother has gone to town to her sister-in-law's house for the memorial rite for Grandmother. Father is a good cook, although he does not cook that often. According to Mom, Father's cooking tastes good because he is generous with the seasoning, making no attempt to be frugal.

"Whenever your father enters the kitchen, ten days' worth of seasoning disappears. How could his cooking possibly not taste good, when he uses so much seasoning."

Father dips long strips of pork into a red sauce made with scallions and garlic and red chili powder and sesame seeds and sesame oil and cooks them on the grill for us. Second Brother is now a military cadet and Third Brother is staying at a boarding house in Jeonju. Like baby swallows, Younger Sister and Little Brother and I nimble and chew the sauced pork that Father has grilled for us. Father says tomorrow he will cook *jajang* noodles for me.

"That's okay," I say.

And Father says, "But your face is all sunken."

He, whom I met sixteen years later, would not know, that once when he was making fried rice with kimchi in my kitchen I had thought of Father. He took out some soured kimchi from my fridge, chopped the lettuce into fine strips, then melted a cube of butter on a heated pan. Putting two fingers together, he said, "I need just this much sliced beef." As I took out the beef from the freezer, I let out a frail giggle behind his back, and in the middle of frying the beef on the pan, he stopped and asked what I was giggling about.

I answered, "Just because. It's just that I'm happy."

Only when he was cooking did Father stop thinking about what other people thought about him.

Right now, right this moment, writing this makes me happy.

Only when he was cooking, Father stopped thinking about what other people thought about him, I write, and I feel happy. For I am probably the only one in my family who can describe Father like this. If Mother found out that I had described him this way, she might throw me a sidelong scowl.

"Wouldn't people look down on your father if they heard he was in the kitchen cooking?" she would say.

I head down the very narrow trail of our family life in the village, a life typical to rural villages anywhere around the country. On this trail, I encounter an odd sense of calm. At no time do I think that my family is poor. I have never felt we were affluent, but we are not poor, either. The farther down this narrow trail I go, the less poor I am. On holidays, Mom always took out new clothes that she had prepared for us (there were many children who did not get new clothes for the holidays); always bought us new sneakers to wear (many children went around in rubber flats); kept me out of the fields (many children worked in the fields, their faces tanned dark); did whatever she could to let us continue with school (many children attended only elementary school). Because of this, other mothers in the village sometimes called Mom absurdly lavish in her ways, saying she had no grasp of her lot in this world. Nevertheless, making an effort to provide these things to us was Mom's own terms of happiness and it took a lot for her to give up trying.

It was always me who brought her despair. But this was neither Mom's fault nor mine. It was just that when I graduated from elementary school and wanted to go on to middle school, Second Brother happened to be entering high school, which placed me in a situation where we had only enough money to cover tuition for one child. Even then, Mom put me through school. By selling the only ring she had on her fingers. When it was time for me to enter high school, this time Third Brother was preparing for his college entrance exam and Younger Sister was about to start middle school.

Oldest Brother, after much deliberation, announces that he will take me to Seoul. That since other younger siblings will soon be coming to Seoul for college, it will be good to get settled early, so he shall start out by living with me . . . At the mere age of twenty-three, Oldest Brother has discovered how to prevent Mom from giving up her happiness too soon.

All through my vacation, whenever I get the chance, I linger around the well. Resting my arms on the edge of the well, I gaze inside. The well is deep, so deep, I cannot see the pitchfork that has sunk under the water. I cannot shake off what Cousin said, about the water becoming tainted, but I cannot bring myself to tell Father that I threw the rake in the well, that the water needs to be pumped out.

Little Brother instinctively notices signs of my imminent return to the city. He trails behind each step that his sixteen-year-old sister takes. Looking for Mom, who is out in the vegetable fields, I take Little Brother and head out to the mountain. Fresh from a rain, the mountain is overflowing with the smell of trees. Hazel trees, pine trees, oak trees, chestnut trees. Yellow soil sticks to the soles of my shoes.

I grew up at the foot of this mountain. Facing those plains. I grew tall amidst the torrential rains of summer and the heavy snows of winter. Even now, I cannot fully comprehend it when someone speaks about how facing nature makes one's heart free and peaceful. To me, nature is, to an extent, exhausting, and, to another extent, frightening. Nature was right under my skin. When I dug for potatoes, worms crawled out and when I climbed a chestnut tree, caterpillars stung. Scrub trees poked my arm and the stream in the valley made my feet slip. I liked caves or tomb mounds but when I entered the caves bats opened their wings with a sinister look and if I lay on a tomb mound for too long, the sun scorched my face, making it sore.

Nevertheless, I preferred to be amidst nature rather than out on the streets or at home. This was because there was more that made my heart pound in nature than at home. There was more that was forbidden in nature than at home. In a forbidden place, wounds, along with a sense of allure, always lurked. An elbow or a knee might grow accustomed to wounds but never to nature. Typhoons and torrential rain would wash away in a matter of minutes the paddies and fields that Mom and Father planted, and heavy snows would easily crack and break the imposing trees in the mountains. Human capacity instantly turned powerless. The vicious rotting smell flowing through nature's triumphant spirit. The fear that remains within me, unable to completely free my heart in the face of nature's solemn scenery, pulls me down as I strive to soar only upward. Nature reminds me that I am human. Nature reminds me that I am a weak being, standing with my feet, upon this perilous Earth.

Nevertheless, I love to walk through the paths toward the cornfields and valleys, through the slivers between rocks. I'll never know when I might run into a venomous snake, but my arm remembers the refreshing sensation on my skin when the wind passes through the sesame fields.

I offer my back to Little Brother, whose feet are still small, but he shakes his head. He refuses, however, to let go of my hand. He seems to think that if only he follows me everywhere, he will never part with his sister again.

There stands Mom, beyond the wind. Mom is planting pepper seedlings in the fields at the foot of the steep mountain. Nature must be afraid of Mom. Even when a storm leaves the roots of young rice plants exposed overnight, once the rain clears, Mom pulls and lifts and ties them up one by one to get them upright and balanced again. No matter what awful rotting stench they might emit, Mom hacks and breaks them up with a pitchfork, then dries them in the sun to use as fertilizer. No matter how strong the sun might pour down on her, Mom endures the glare, picking the peppers that have ripened red.

The day I set out to go back to the city, Mom takes Little Brother, adamant not to part with me, to Aunt's house.

"Stay here a bit. Mommy will go bring Sister." Mom leaves Little Brother behind at Aunt's and comes to see me off. "Hurry and go on now." And I head back to the city, carrying the luggage that Mom has packed for me. I glance once toward where Chang lives, the air now awkward between us.

Perhaps the reason for this awkwardness was not because I had suddenly moved out to the city but because of my status in the city. In the country, our household had so many memorial rites to host and thus had plenty of food around, more than any other. Our house was in the center of the village and had the largest yard in the neighborhood, the largest number of chickens, bikes, ducks, and sauce jars out on the terrace. But out here in the city, I am the lower class. Placed within this contradiction is Oldest Brother, and now I will step inside this contradiction as well.

•◆•

The company is vast. There seems to be more than a thousand employees. Viewed from the main gate of the grounds, the buildings stand in the shape of the vowel ㅠ. The three-story structure that resembles a school houses the TV Division and the single-story structure houses the Stereo Division. The new workers from the Job Training Center are grouped into the two divisions as well. Cousin and I are lined up one behind the other to prevent being separated. Before our positions are designated, the operations chief announces that the head of the administration department will offer an official greeting. The administration head, a man with a large build, adds at the end of his greeting that we must not join the union. He also says that we should report it to him if one of our colleagues joins a union.

Union? I have never heard this word before but, perhaps because of his tone, this word brings me fear. What is it that they do there that makes him say we must not join and that we should report it if someone joins?

As we hoped, Cousin and I stay together, both of us sent to the Stereo Division. There are three production lines at the Stereo Division: A line, B line, C line. And there is also the prep line. Cousin and I, determined not to be separated to different lines, again stand hand in hand. We are assigned to A line. Even as we stand holding hands, the conveyor belt keeps turning endlessly. I am given the number one spot on the A line. Cousin is number two. The foreman sits next to my chair and teaches me what I need to do as number one. My job is to bring the plates for the core parts of the stereo system from the prep line and use the air driver to insert the seven screws that will hold the PVC cover in place. Because each hole requires a screw of a different size, I have to memorize where this screw and that screw goes. Each time the screw is inserted, I am startled by the gush of wind bursting from the air driver, which further slows down my already slow work speed. Only when I finish my job at number one can the number two down the conveyor belt do her job. There is about a two-meter distance between me and Cousin at number two. I have to adjust my pace so that the plates with all the screws in place will keep flowing through that distance without stopping, Foreman tells me. On my first day, I try so hard to maintain the pace and to get the right screw in the right place that I do not even hear the bell at the end of the day.

Because I work slowly and often put the screw in the wrong place, one of the skilled workers on our line, who has to connect another part to the screws that I insert, keeps bringing the plates that I have finished back to me, pointing out the wrong screws. Foreman gets impatient and frequently stands behind me. With him watching from behind my back, my work slows down even more. Getting impatient, Foreman takes the air driver from me and attaches the screws himself, or brings over the plates from the prep line and piles them next to me, but at least ten fewer stereo systems make it to the test division that day compared with other days. Because our output is less than that of the B line or the C line, at the end of the day those of us on the A line receive, from the operations chief, words of admonishment.

A letter arrives. It is from Chang in the country. When I see that the sender is Chang, my face blushes abruptly. Chang is the boy who lives at the end of the newly paved road back in our village. Outside Chang's gate, different flowers blossom each season. Forsythias, azaleas, clavillias, cosmos. Chang writes:

> I learned from your younger sister that you moved to Seoul, that it has already been two months, and that you have already visited once. I noticed that I haven't seen you around but had no idea that you had left for Seoul. If you had told me you were leaving, Ik-su *hyeong* and I would have arranged a farewell party or something—it's a pity. I realize you will be surprised by my unexpected letter. I asked Ik-su to go over to your house and find out your address. Your mom doesn't like me but she's friendly with Ik-su *hyeong*. And since you and Ik-su are related, I guessed she would give him your address. I hope we can exchange letters. The things that happened in the past are now bygones, and I hope we can stay good friends from now on.

I am so happy to receive Chang's letter that I can't sit still. The bygones that Chang mentioned in the letter went like this. Chang and I have been friends since we were young, but when we got to middle school, each time we saw each other, our faces flushed for no reason. Mom dislikes my befriending Chang. I do not know why she does, but since Mom disapproves, I find Chang dearer. Because he knows that Mom disapproves of him, Chang does not even come by to offer a bow to my parents for New Year. I might go over to Chang's, but Chang never comes over to our house. One night coming home, I run into Chang. Chang is on his bike and I am walking. Chang gets off his bike and ties my schoolbag to the back of his bike and we walk together. On the bridge where the lights in the village come into view, Chang stops the bike and says, Let's talk here for a bit. Let's talk a bit, he says, but Chang is quiet in the dark. Stars twinkle in the sky. It occurs to me that the starlight is blue.

"Do you know why your mom dislikes me?" Chang's voice is gloomy.

"No."

"It's because . . ." Chang is about to say something but stops. He stops, then begins again.

"It's because of my father."

"What about your father?"

"My father's alive."

I glance across at Chang in the dark. In the thick darkness I cannot see what kind of expression Chang has on his face. Chang lives with his mother. I have never heard anything about his father but have assumed that he had passed away. When people pass away, they cannot live with you.

"Where is he?"

Chang answers, Gyeongsang-do. Gyeongsang Province? Where can he mean by Gyeongsang-do?

"Where in Gyeongsang-do?"

"That I don't know. Mother would not tell me. She just said Gyeongsang-do."

"Why doesn't he live with you?"

Chang says nothing. I say nothing. When the silence starts to feel awkward, Chang speaks again.

"Father cannot live with us."

"Why not?"

"He has an illness that prohibits him from living with us."

Illness? I grow more and more puzzled and say nothing. I remembered, out of the blue, what Mom once said, trying to express her disapproval of my befriending Chang—that illness is inherited. Chang pulls out a white envelope from his pocket.

"Would you keep this for me?"

"What is it?"

"It's a letter from Father . . . It's been weird. I keep thinking about him, and I can't focus on my studying. I might flunk the high school entrance exam if I keep this up. Would you keep this for me and give it back when I'm in high school?"

I say nothing.

"Mother promised me that if I pass the test, she'll tell me where Father is and pay for my trip so that I can go see him."

When I reach out my hand and take the letter, Chang speaks again.

"Please keep it safe. You mustn't lose it. It's very important to me."

I nod.

"Can I read it?"

Chang says that I may. We start walking again slowly and arrive at the village. Mom is waiting for me out by the new paved road, and when she sees me walking side by side with Chang, she snatches my hand, as if Chang is not even there. When we get home, Mom presses me about Chang, asking exactly where we started walking together.

"We met on the bridge."

"You arranged to meet there?"

"No," I said. "We ran into each other. He was riding his bike and I was walking home."

Mom sighs and says, "Don't start befriending Chang again." Mom's being so unreasonable . . . How embarrassed he must have been when Mom snatched my hand out on the road. I feel apologetic and sorry for Chang. When I do not answer her, Mom raises her voice, saying, "What stubbornness!" But I still refuse to answer.

Late that night I open the letter that Chang handed me. He must have carried it in his pocket for a long time, for the letter is all crumpled. I find the stains on the paper endearing, thinking that they were made by Chang's hands. Old writings on an old sheet of paper. Tear stains, made either by one who wrote the letter or one who read the letter—it is impossible to tell. Because of the smears, the letter is unintelligible save for a single sentence. The sentence goes, Let's try and make a lot of money to live together happily in one place. I fold the letter and slip it inside the pages of The Sorrows of Young Werther and put the book inside the bottom drawer of my desk. Without knowing about the letter inside, Younger Sister lends the book to a friend and the friend loses the book. Ever since the book has been lost, each time I run into Chang in the street my heart collapses. Chang's voice follows me around, asking me to please keep it safe and never lose it, telling me that it's very important to him.

I keep avoiding Chang even after the high school entrance exams are over. Finally one night on the railroad tracks I confess to him that I have lost the letter. As soon as I finish talking, Chang starts walking away, taking big strides, leaving me on the tracks. He'll come back, I think, but Chang does not come back. Things become awkward between us; even when we run into each other out on the new paved road, we look away. This was how things were when I moved to the city.

Inside the genre painting, the air driver in front of me hangs in mid-space. When I hold the screw that will attach the PVC cover in my left hand, then pull the air driver and press, the screw goes in with a gush of wind: *shhk*. Cousin, at Number Two, also has to insert more than ten screws. The only difference is that my air driver hangs midair while Cousin's is attached at her side. In other words, I attach the screws in the center and Cousin attaches the screws in the front. At first, Cousin keeps her mouth shut tight and stares down at the conveyor.

She is displeased, for she feels this business of pulling down the air driver hanging midair and attaching the screws is vulgar.

"I'd rather be soldering. This looks like man's work."

I do not respond. I hate solder smoke just as much. As Cousin and I turn into skilled workers, our names disappear. I am Number One on the Stereo Division's A Line, and Cousin is called Number Two. This is what Foreman shouts.

"Number One and Number Two, what are you guys doing? You're holding things up."

Even if I am not called Number One, my name no longer exists. The name that I have been called for sixteen years cannot come work with me at the company because I am sixteen years old. Being a sixteen-year-old disqualifies me to be an employee at Dongnam Electronics, Inc. One has to be eighteen years old to be hired as a worker. I don't know how he arranged it, but somehow Oldest Brother got my documents filled out in the name of an eighteen-year-old Lee Yeon-mi, so at work even if I am not called Number One, I am Lee Yeon-mi. Miss Lee Yeon-mi! When someone calls me this, I do not realize it's me they're talking to and fail to respond. Only when Cousin pokes me on the side do I lift my head, with a slow "Y-yes."

Whether it is hanging midair or attached to the side, Cousin and I are poor at handling the air driver and no matter how we try to hurry things along, the number three position on the conveyor is empty. In the evening as we walk from Industrial Complex No. 1 to our room at Industrial Complex No. 3, we massage each other's shoulders.

"I feel I'm developing hard muscles."

Cousin looks as if she's about to cry.

Cousin and I earn a daily wage of 700-something won. After three months on the job we will get a 500-won raise, Foreman says, which makes about 1,200 won. Another three months will bring a 200-won raise, then after another three months . . .

It is clear that was how much we made, but thinking back today, I cannot quite believe it and doubt my memory. Manufacturing jobs were paid by the day, so excluding Sundays and half of the Saturdays, the amount would have come to, let me see, 1,280 multiplied by 25 or 24, then take away the lunch costs—so how much did I actually make?

Could I be remembering things correctly? With that money, the workers paid rent, sent some home, and even supported younger siblings who lived with them . . . Unconvinced, I do some research here and there about the labor conditions of 1978. The Labor Administration had set the minimum wage for trainee factory positions, which were mostly held by young girls, at 24,000 won, but after deducting the costs for lunch and transportation, the average monthly wage was only 19,400 won, according to records. We walked from Industrial Complex No. 3 to Industrial Complex No. 1 so we did not have to spend money on transportation; we received overtime allowance for extra hours, all-nighters and Sundays; so does that mean we made at least a little more than 19,400 won?

Over spring and summer, ever since the day Ha Gye-suk's voice turned into icy water and fell in drops down on my forehead, my body began to feel sick for no reason. At first I felt as if hot lumps of charcoal were burning inside my chest, then the lumps would shoot all the way up to the back of my tongue, come close to rolling out of my mouth, then crawl back down again. My insides were burning but my forehead was covered with sweat. One morning after a night spent fighting four or five of these attacks, I could not take it any longer and visited the hospital. The doctor hung up my chest X-ray and said there was nothing wrong. He said nothing was wrong, but as days passed, the burning was replaced with phlegm, surging up my throat. I switched to a different doctor, who concocted a week's supply of medication for me, but the phlegm did not go away. Taking the phlegm with me, I set out for home.

In my bag is another packet of medication to last four days, which my younger sister, also a pharmacist, put together for me. Since I had been painfully coughing up phlegm every time Younger Sister called, she asked what was wrong. When, after hesitating, I still failed to answer, she waited to close up the pharmacy at nine o'clock and then, carrying her one-year-old baby on her back, came to see me with her packet of medication and her diagnosis that my symptoms were stress-related.

"What's eating you? You have what people in the old days called 'heart's anger disease.' Let it out, only that will make you better."

In order to avoid Ha Gye-suk's voice, I pack my bags and leave home. I think of the farthest I can get away from home within this country. I get on the plane. But in the end, here I am, sitting here gazing at the lights from the fishing boats floating on the night sea. And I write, This book, I believe, will turn out to be not quite fact and not quite fiction, but something in between. I wonder if it can be called literature. I ponder the act of writing. What does writing mean to me?

I wonder if it could be called literature. I ponder the act of writing, what writing means to me. That is what I write. Would I be able to open, with words, that opening of my sixteenth year, that door which I have kept closed for so long? Especially here, where I have run to, away from the sentences, away from my habit of heading back home from wherever I was when a sentence came to me. Here, where all the daily routines are utterly unfamiliar, nothing like the tongue inside my mouth, here where I have never been before, here facing the crashing, splashing night sea, here where a dark hallway lies behind the door, where not even a single towel is my own.

I ceaselessly collect certain moments with words, in an attempt to lock them up like photographs, but the more I try, the more despair I feel. Life flows outside of words. The more I write, the more pain I feel at the difficulty of concluding that literature moves toward hope and what is right. If hope would well up from inside of me, allowing me to speak of hope in a heartfelt way, it would make me happy as well. Literature, however, is destined to be rooted in the problem of life, and the problem of life has less to do with hope and what is right, but more with unhappiness and what is wrong. After all, isn't life about living on even when one is trapped inside unhappiness without hope?

At times this recognition makes me give up my surgical knife. And in the end, I choose the many-layered web of meaning over a single point. And I tell myself that I should approach and confront that thickness; that it is not the writer's, but the readers' part to unravel every single layer and observe what she finds. Would it be best if what I write would lead ten readers into ten different directions of thought; that life is supposed to take varied forms and shapes; aren't there some lives that do not allow literature to intercept them?

That day, after Ha Gye-suk said to me, "Your life seems different from ours now," if I had told her, "The reason I had not been able to write about you is that my heart was still aching," would that have made a good excuse? That I had not been able to write about them because just the thought would fill my chest with pain? If I had told her that I was sorry, that I was only sixteen years old then? It was not that I was ashamed of them. It was that I had not walked out of that place in a natural manner. I had run from that place, aghast at the turns of a fateful life. I had run and had never taken even a step toward that direction ever again. Without realizing what I was doing, I stepped over the other side of the stepping stone. But I could not say I had really crossed to the other side.

Wherever I was, at whichever point in time, the loneliness lived inside of me, taking up the same amount of space as the village where I was born and grew up, but opposite in meaning. The only reason I was not able to directly address them through my writing was because it allowed not even a glimpse into the sense of happiness that I get when I think of the village where I was born. It only allowed memories of the crammed room that I had to share with Brother and Cousin, of the feeling of desolation, like being locked in the attic, or the sound of heavy footsteps that one makes when the only thing that keeps them walking is the determination to live on—and finally, there would be Hui-jae, blocking my way.

As long as Hui-jae was there, looking the way she did, I could not figure out how I could go back to that place or how I should approach these girls who had been my friends.

I was sixteen years old when I walked into that lone room and nineteen when I ran out from it.

I could not quite find a way to make peace with those four years of my life. I did not know how to accept the fetters of life that had bound me, who had walked out of nature directly to the factory without any connecting bridges in between. Nor could I accept the young women, around my age, some perhaps five or six years older than me, whom I saw there . . . and this city, where nature's breath could no longer reach.

I remember lunch break on our first day at work. One by one, Foreman hands out meal tickets stamped with the word "Lunch."

The cafeteria is located on the roof. Cousin and I walk side by side up the stairs. People in blue uniform shirts form a queue that starts from inside the cafeteria all the way out on the roof. A spicy aroma spills from the kitchen. After a long wait, I receive a food tray containing a lump of rice with a strange substance poured over it.

"What is this?"

"It's curry."

Cousin pronounces the word aloud, "curry," and glances at me with eyes that seem to ask what the problem is. Curry? I have never heard of this food before. What kind of food looks like this? I am doubtful about its dull yellow color. I spoon up a small amount and take it to my mouth. It's nauseating.

"I can't eat this." I put down my spoon.

"It can feel that way at first, but you'll learn to like it after a few tries. Try to bear it."

I try another taste but I feel like I might lose my breakfast. "You'll have to finish on your own."

Unable to sit through the meal because of the smell, I empty the tray into the food trash pail, return the tray and leave the cafeteria. I stand around on the roof for a while and come back to the assembly line. At the number one seat, I rest my head on the conveyor belt, which has come to a stop for lunch break. Then Cousin shakes my shoulder.

"Have this then."

A pastry bun with red bean filling.

"Where did you get this?"

"Where do you think? I went outside and bought one." Cousin opens the wrapper and puts the bun in my hand. "You sure are strange. Making a fuss about nothing at all."

A life different from ours. A person different from me. When I heard Ha Gye-suk say the words, Your life seems different from ours now, I felt blank, thinking of Mom. Could it be that I had been ashamed, as Ha Gye-suk asked, of my high school years or my illiterate mother? Perhaps I had known earlier that Mom could not read. I probably made no effort to really find out because I did not want to know. Saying to myself, "See, she has a sutra open in front of her," or "She's reading the Bible." All the while perplexed or hiding her in the mothers that appeared in my writing.

Meanwhile, in real life, I would pour tender affection on Mother, enough to puzzle her, as a means of offering my apology. Perhaps that was what I was doing. At least with Mother, I was making an effort as I continued to open up and shut down my heart, but what about my high school years? The manner with which I handled those past years in real life was rather odd. Actually, I did not even realize I was being odd until a certain moment would approach and announce, "You are being odd."

When a poet friend who was a few years older, after reading the bio in my first book, said to me, "Hey, you graduated from Yeongdeungpo Girls' High, I had no idea. I went there, too. We're alumni," her delight was genuine, but I got nervous. I was worried that she might start asking which classes I was in, whom I studied language arts with.

As soon as I got the chance, I left. My high school years made me treat myself as someone who had a big secret to keep, and changed me from a natural-born optimist to a withdrawn introvert who refused to speak about those years except with those who were very close. And now Ha Gye-suk was flatly reprimanding the gag order that I had imposed on myself. Telling me, You don't seem to write about us. Your life seems different from ours now.

After we hung up, I paced the room, letting out my anger toward her. How dare she treat me like someone who had shut the door on her first true love in order to live a different life. Ha Gye-suk was right, however. I did not write about them. Only once had I made an attempt. It was published as the last story in my first collection, the one book that Ha Gye-suk had not yet read.

But even if she had read it, she would not think it was about us from back in those days. I was not honest. I was trying as hard as I could to feign innocence. About my youth, about my own being. An omission committed by vivid pain, which was all that prevailed in the absence of the self. This is fiction, I told myself, but all the while my heart ached enough to kill me. In order to appease this aching heart, I concluded with a rushed ending, fast-forwarding to what happened ten years later. Unsure that I could confront it face to face, I quickly closed the lid and that was when I realized the truth. That those years had not completely passed for me. That I was carrying those years on my back like a camel's hump. That for a long time, perhaps for as long as I was here, those years would be part of my present.

Six more years have passed now, and during that time, whenever those years tried to leap out through my sentences, I took a breath, pushed them back down, and closed the lid. It was not because I was now living a life different from the people I knew then. I had not even known what kind of life they were living. It was that, even if the years were pulled out somehow, I had no idea where I should stand amidst them. Whatever you do, once you lose your confidence, it is difficult to recover.

When closing the lid no longer worked, I fled home, but Ha Gye-suk's voice persistently followed me here, dropping icy water on my forehead—drip, drip, drip—and whispering, Whatever excuse you might come up with, the truth is that you are ashamed, you are ashamed of us. Even now, trying to lift the closed lid as I gaze out at the fishing boats on the night sea, my confidence does not return. I cannot tell what shape this writing will take when

I am done. Here I am, sitting face to face, but even as I write I have a feeling that I might continue to run. I have a feeling that every chance I get, I might try to cross over into another story. See how I am already letting go of conventional narrative form. What am I trying to do by abandoning the most approachable form of storytelling? The truth is, I am not actually trying to do anything. All I can guess is that as I keep attempting my escape and then come back, I escape again, and then come back again of my own accord, as if the writing might somehow be completed in the meantime.

This is something that has been fermenting inside of me for such a long time that I have nothing to add or take away from it. In the time that I do stay seated between my escape attempts, I imagine that the weft and the warp yarns will somehow weave together.

For a long time I contemplate the present. In these times, when things as simple as songs are so fast it is almost impossible to sing along, what is the present that I should hold on to? I would like to get past things, but could I really get past anything? Unless one has her mind set from the beginning to write a story set in the future or an imagined world, isn't writing always about looking back? In literature, at least, aren't all memories that came prior to this moment subject to examination? Isn't literature about excavating the past that flows through to the present? To find out why I am here at this moment in time; to find out what it is that I am trying to do here and now? Today will again turn into yesterday and flow through to tomorrow. Isn't that why literature is able to keep flowing on?

History is in charge of putting things in order and society is in charge of defining them. The more order we achieve, the more truth is hidden behind that neat surface. Truth, for the most part, lives behind the orderly surface. I believe that literature flows somewhere behind order and definition. Amidst all that remains unsolved. Perhaps literature is about throwing into disarray what has been defined and putting it into order to make it flow anew for those in the back of history, the weak, the hesitant. About making a mess of things, all over again. Is this, in the end, an attempt at order as well? Is it now my time to look back?

The first payment we received at the end of our first month, which was actually a few days short of a month, was a little over 10,000 won, I recall. Cousin and I went to the market and bought thermal underwear for our parents and mailed them to the country.

It is September. Cousin and I are now quick with the air driver. Sometimes, after hurrying through our share of the work, we can even afford to chat while Number Three finishes. We have become skilled workers.

Cousin whispers in my ear. "We are so lucky we weren't assigned to a soldering position."

I have no idea what she means and ask, "Why is that?"

"Look at Number Thirteen's face."

I stretch my neck and glance at Number Thirteen, who was assigned to Dongnam Electronics with us from the Job Training Center. Smoke rises over Number Thirteen's head with a sizzle. After three months at the job, Number Thirteen's bright complexion has given way to a dull yellowish pallor.

"I wonder if it's lead poisoning."

I check my face in the mirror. Your complexion has turned lighter since you started drinking tap water here, our landlady had said. As I look into the mirror, Number Thirteen's dull yellow face glides over my light-toned face. I agree with Cousin that we are lucky we were not assigned to lead soldering.

After work Cousin and I stop by the market to get groceries and, after returning home, we start dinner on the kerosene stove. Today is my turn to cook and tomorrow will be Cousin's turn. The person who is off cooking duty does the laundry and cleans the room.

Breakfast is the only time we get to eat with Oldest Brother. Before leaving for work in the morning, Cousin and I clear the breakfast dishes and set the table again for dinner. Oldest Brother goes straight to school from his job at the Community Service Center and has dinner upon returning home late at night. No matter how exhausted he is, he enters the room only after washing his face and feet with a bowl of water in the crammed kitchenette, then washing his socks in the same water and hanging them on the laundry line. Even when I offer to wash them for him, he refuses, saying, "It's a habit for me," already rubbing the socks with soap. Habit. Washing his socks every night and hanging them to dry is a habit that Oldest Brother acquired in the city, while refusing to eat a meal without soup is a habit that Mom instilled in him back in the country. Mom's meals always included both a stew and a soup.

Having to choose between the stew and the soup, Brother was unable to give up the latter. He will do without stew but will not eat his meal without soup. When Cousin and I cook stew, we make sure to cook soup as well and serve it to Oldest Brother. On days when this feels like too much of a hassle, Cousin grumbles, "Brother is a soup fiend."

At night Cousin sleeps next to the window, Oldest Brother next to the wall, and I in the center. Cousin and I usually fall asleep first while Oldest Brother sits at his desk until he also retreats to the floor, although I never know exactly when. Oldest Brother pays the rent, which is 20,000 won a month with a 200,000-won deposit, and also gives us money to pay for food and expenses. We try to be as frugal as we possibly can, but there is never enough money. Cousin and I take out some of our earnings and contribute to household expenses as well.

More and more workers leave the job because of low wages, which results in more and more new employees and frequent changes in the people sitting at the conveyor belt. People leave just as I am beginning to get familiar with their faces, and new faces are hired. Whenever new employees start work, the head of the administration department offers them a word of warning.

"Make sure you don't join the union. Union fees are used for no other purpose but to keep the wheels rolling on the chairs of the union leaders," he says.

The words low wage spread an ache through my heart. Low wage. Low wage . . . Could my memory about our wages be correct?

When the restaurant owner learned that I was a writer, she said she would ask me just two questions. "Just two," she said, which made my heart sink. What was it that she wanted to ask? And why this condition: "Just two?"

"The first question . . ."

Of her two questions, the first was about what level I write at. What level?

"I'm sorry I don't quite understand," I said. The restaurant owner tilted her head to the side, then made an earnest effort to explain.

"You see, I got a book as a present once, the only time someone ever gave me a book. It was a relative who gave it to me and I tried really hard to finish it, since it was a present. But I just couldn't read it. I didn't get it at all. It's been four years since I got it and I still haven't finished it. It must be that some books in this world are reserved only for educated, knowledgeable people. That's why I was wondering what level you write at. I was curious if you wrote things that someone like me can read, or things that are at a higher level."

The woman looked at me, waiting for my answer. It seemed I should offer her a prompt answer, but I simply stammered, "Well, what can I say . . ."

When I kept repeating "Well," the woman said, "My other question is," and continued with the remaining of the two things she would ask. Now I was nervous. I have to be able to answer this time. I hope she asks me a simple question, one that I can answer.

"Do you decide on the title first, or just start writing first?"

I sighed in relief. "Sometimes I have the title then begin writing, and sometimes I can't think of a title even after I am finished writing and have to agonize over it for a long time," I told her.

The woman nodded, saying, "Can't think of a title, is that so? Nowadays novels are so hard to follow. I just can't understand what they're saying. I wish writers would make them easy so that people like me can read them, too."

Easy? Now that was a difficult order.

Yu Chae-ok. She is forewoman of the prep division and will be portrayed in my genre painting in a dynamic style, using powerful brushstrokes. One day Miss Choe on the C Line is stopped from getting to work. She is held back because she went home without working extra hours the night before. The head of production demands that Miss Choe submit her resignation. Yu Chae-ok steps up to Miss Choe's defense, saying it is unreasonable to demand a resignation for not working extra hours. That extra hours and overtime lie outside regular work routines. Isn't that why we get extra pay? Sometimes employees cannot work extra hours due to personal circumstances. It is nonsense that she should be made to hand in her resignation for this. Yu Chae-ok and the head of production start raising their voices over Miss Choe. The head of production hurls abusive words at Yu Chae-ok.

"What kind of ill-bred horse bone are you? This is a production line. What happens here is under my jurisdiction. Who do you think you are, telling me to do this and that?"

Yu Chae-ok shouts at him in a similar tone. "Are we machines? Why are you mistreating us like this? Does it make any sense that you demand a resignation from Miss Choe because she went home with a nosebleed after five days of overtime?" She continues to shout, "We formed a union to protect our rights, in accordance with the labor laws. No matter how the management tries to interfere, we will go ahead with the inaugural ceremony."

While the production head and Yu Chae-ok fight, thrusting fingers at each other, Miss Choe bursts into tears. The head of administration jumps in and yells at Yu Chae-ok, "You ungrateful bitch."

Yu Chae-ok throws him a furious look. "I haven't received a single favor from you!"

Miss Lee from the prep division calls Cousin and me to a corner. Miss Lee, with her not-your-usual-short but very short height, always keep her hair in a short bob. Always scurrying about in busy, mincing steps. Her busy walk always draws attention. Her busy walk always makes her appear as if she is delivering a message, which makes people stop even at a distance and follow her with their eyes. Even when she is simply heading for the bathroom in her busy walk. Miss Lee greets us with an amiable smile and pulls out a document.

"This is the union application form."

I take the sheet of paper in my hand.

"We already have two hundred twenty-seven people who plan to join."

I am silent.

Miss Lee continues. "The company always says they're in the red, but this is a huge export manufacturer. We have to join hands and claim our rights and interests. We have to secure raises and demand compensation allowance for menstruation leave. They have that under unpaid leave. But it's our rightful leave, spelled out in the labor laws. We should get paid for working on those days. When we're just a minute late for work, we get a late stamp on our time card, which results in an hour's pay cut. No wonder so little ends up in our hands, after all the deductions here and there. And that's because we let the company do whatever they want without resisting."

When Cousin and I say nothing, Miss Lee speaks again.

"The union is for all of us. You think Yu Chae-ok is speaking up only for her own good? We need organized power. We must join the union and help Yu Chae-ok."

While we are sitting together for a late dinner that night, Cousin tells Oldest Brother about Yu Chae-ok and Miss Lee. When Cousin is done talking, Oldest Brother lets out a groan-like sigh.

"What should we do? Join?"

Oldest Brother asks how the management is responding.

"They're going berserk. Like they're going to fire people the minute they join."

Oldest Brother gazes at the union application.

"So what should we do?"

After a long time, Oldest Brother finally speaks.

"You're going to start school and things might get complicated if the management starts thinking ill of you . . ."

The next day, we sense an unsettling air throughout the factory. We whisper to one another.

"Yu Chae-ok was called in by the company president."

"What for?"

"According to what I heard, he said he's got connections everywhere, the Labor Administration, City Hall, and the Central

Intelligence Agency, the Labor Supervisor's Office, the National Security Headquarters, and that no matter how desperately we might try, it will be hard to form a union, so we should give up."

"Then what happened?"

"When Yu Chae-ok would not give in, the president threw his ashtray at her, yelling, 'Well, you can't have a union without a company.' If we go ahead with the union, he said he would close down the company."

Scurrying, Miss Lee approaches Cousin and me.

"Have you thought about it?"

Cousin and I are unable to answer.

"Almost everyone on the A line has submitted their union applications. What about the two of you?"

". . ."

"We notified the management of the date of the inauguration. The management acts the way it does because of workers like you. We must act in perfect unison. If we come together as one, we will have the courage to hold the inauguration ceremony right here on the company lot and put up our plaque on the main gate of the grounds."

After Miss Lee asked us to think it over one more time and turned back, Foreman steps in in front of us.

"What did Miss Lee say?"

My heart pounds as if I have done something wrong while Cousin manages, with difficulty, to tell him that she did not say anything to us. Foreman, his arms crossed, gazes dumbfounded at Cousin as she feigns innocence, saying, Honest, she didn't say anything.

"You two were talking with Miss Lee just now, and you say she didn't say anything?"

Cousin gives it another try. "Just asking if we didn't find the work too hard . . ."

"Well, if you did, what is she going to do, make it easy for you? Is she going to pay you out of her pocket?" Foreman then turns to threats. "Union? What a laugh. A union will never be permitted. The president has already spoken to various authorities. No matter how hard Yu Chae-ok tries, running about like that, it's no use. If the two of you don't want the management to get the wrong idea, don't even think about joining the union! Union members will never get a pay raise, the president said."

When Foreman is gone, Miss Lee comes over again, and when she goes away, Foreman comes back again. After a whole morning of being hassled by the two, at lunch Cousin whispers into my ear. "I'm going to join the union. What about you?"

I gaze at Cousin. "If you join, I will, too."

"But you're going to school, aren't you?"

"And you aren't?"

"I'm not going."

I fill out the application form next to Cousin. Cousin takes our applications to Miss Lee. Then she lets out a breath: *Phew.*

Several days went by as I tossed and turned, without returning to what I had been writing. My heart burned with pain, as if it had been scraped with a broken shard of porcelain. I kept doubting. Will I be able to finish this? Where are all the people now and what are they doing? Yu Chae-ok, Miss Lee, Foreman, the head of administration? The company had more than a thousand employees, so there would be people who have already departed this world because of one accident or another.

Here on the island, I have been eating only one proper meal a day. Just now, I was sitting with an order of abalone porridge at a restaurant by the sea after a walk. When I was about halfway into my meal, a shabby looking man, who looked about sixty, walked in.

The shabby man asked if the spicy meat soup on the menu was cooked with pork or with beef. When the restaurant owner answered that she used beef, the man ordered the soup. When he was served his soup, the shabby man pulled out a bottle of *soju* from inside his coat. When the owner glanced at him, he said, I hope you don't mind. The owner responded, We have alcohol, too, but it seems you brought your own. The shabby man replied, I thought you might not. Whoever heard of restaurants that don't serve *soju*? The owner snubbed the shabby man.

I wonder if he's a seaman.

Even after being snubbed by the owner, the shabby man chatted with her about boats. About the boats that used to sail the seas off Jeju Island long before modern ferries, possibly even before I was born. He talked about how on windy days like today, these shabby and dangerous boats would overturn in the middle of the sea, taking many lives. They seemed to have completely forgotten about the new ferries sailing the sea today, about the fact that they were sitting in a restaurant, so singularly focused on their conversation about the dangerous and shabby boats of the old days. They were so focused on these shabby, dangerous boats of the past that I felt as if they were sitting on a distant island that I could not get close to, even though I was sitting just a few tables away.

Right then, I was hit with a sense of confusion. Could it be that the lone room has now become a distant island that I can no longer go near?

As I sat there in this unfamiliar restaurant, eating an unfamiliar meal and listening to unfamiliar talk from unfamiliar people, I thought that I should leave now. But this is not something I should run from. I should not regard my life inside that lone room as something any different.

Ever since the union was formed, the management is left without a single peaceful day. They promise that they'll do anything if the members break with the union. Then the next minute they threaten that they will not leave the members alone if they continue with union activities. They offer Yu Chae-ok a promotion to chief of production if she steps down as union leader. They also offer to hand over a company snack stall to Yu Chae-ok for her to manage.

We turn to Yu Chae-ok all at once.

Now even Cousin and I are anxious that Yu Chae-ok might change her mind. Yu Chae-ok. Despite the slander and verbal assault, despite all the conciliatory offers, she receives an official stamp of registration from City Hall for the labor union's Dongnam Electronics chapter. Now the management criticizes her as a blind pursuer of powerful positions and demands that she step down as union leader to make way for the head of production or chief of production. The union requests the formation of a labor-management joint committee, but the management refuses. Foreman paces the production line with his hands folded behind his back.

"So the two of you also joined the union, I hear?" he asks. Foreman sounds cold as he gives out orders to hurry on with our work. "You people don't know your place in the world," he spits out.

Then one day, the union launches a campaign to enhance production quality and quantity. Yu Chae-ok gives out ribbons that read *Production Enhancement* to all the union members and makes everyone wear them on their chests. Cousin gets her cheek slapped by the head of administration for wearing the ribbon on her chest.

"Why did he hit me?" Cousin gazes blankly at the administration head's back as she rubs her assaulted cheek. All through the day, people wearing ribbons that read *Production Enhancement* get insulted or kicked. Scared of getting hit, I quickly take off the ribbon and hold it in my hand. The union leaders said that taking off the ribbon meant defeat and urged the members to keep the ribbons on their chests, but the following day the union leaders are the only people still wearing the ribbons. They might have taken off the ribbons, too, but they are no longer individuals. Persecution always brings them together, the rule goes. Because if they don't stay together, they feel insecure.

Then it is time for the civil defense drill. The head of production holds in his hand a list of union members who were dozing off during the drill. He urges them to hand in their resignations.

Resign? For dozing off during a civil defense drill? When the members do not comply, the management transfers them to different divisions to split them up.

Then there is news of a union fee of 300 won. This causes yet another ruckus. The union requests that the company management deduct the fee directly from the workers' wages but the request is turned down. On payday, the union leaders try to collect the fees on the spot but fail, due to interference from management. In the end, a fight breaks out between Yu Chae-ok and other union leaders trying to collect the fees and the company's management staff. The following day, one of the management staff is lying in a hospital bed. The head of administration again tries to persuade Yu Chae-ok to leave the union. When Yu Chae-ok refuses, the administration head starts to shout.

"In that case, as of now, you are fired."

An argument breaks out between the head of administration and Yu Chae-ok, the latter protesting that it's unjust, which again starts a fight between the management and the union members, grabbing one another by their collars. The head of administration, who was seized by the collar during the whole ruckus, checks himself into a hospital room, claiming that he was assaulted by Yu Chae-ok and the union members. Now the managing director steps forward. He offers that if Yu Chae-ok leaves the union, he will cancel her dismissal and promote her to a managerial position. When Yu Chae-ok declines, the management announces the dismissal of union chief Yu Chae-ok and some fifty union members, citing the management staff lying on their hospital beds alongside the head of administration

I write a letter to Chang. I write, Today the management halted production and handed out applications for a new union, insisting that a management-friendly union is needed. Only a few people filled it out, though. Those who didn't were scolded. They told us we're going to regret this. They said that members in the new union will get a raise of 100 won in their daily wage. I describe Yu Chae-ok in detail to Chang. About how brave she is, how reliable. She is as reliable and trustworthy to me as Oldest Brother, I write. But I think she's been defeated by the management, I write.

Even without Yu Chae-ok, however, the union forms a Countermeasure Committee for the Dongnam Electronics Chapter of the Korea Metal Workers Federation, kicking off with a general meeting attended by various notable figures. A letter of appeal is sent out to various circles. The letter calls for the following actions.

1. Immediately allow the union chief, who has been unfairly dismissed, to return to her job.
2. Bring the dismissed union members back to work and stop the persecution of rightful union activity.
3. Return all workers who have been transferred for participating in union activity to their original positions.
4. The management should immediately accept the labor union and guarantee union protection for all members.

Miss Lee comes to see us again to get our signature. The petition, which almost every employee in the production division has signed, calls for a 50 percent raise in wages. For fundraising for dismissed workers. For putting an end to the oppression of workers. For compensation for working on legal holidays and annual leave. For ending discrimination between administration staff and factory workers. After submitting the petition to the management, the workers collectively refuse to work overtime in protest. As the issue begins to create a stir outside the company, the management, which has never accepted the union up to this point, finally agrees at the joint labor-management conference to raise the minimum daily wage to 830 won. They agree to permit a labor union signboard to be hung at the company; to pay a 200 percent bonus within the year; to provide an office for the union staffed with two full-time workers; and to follow the pending decision by the National Labor Relations Commission regarding the dismissed union chief's return.

However, Cousin and I do not get to see Yu Chae-ok again. She does not return to work. On the same bulletin where the list of dismissed workers was announced, a new notice is posted, inviting applicants to special high school classes for industrial workers. It says interested workers should pick up forms from the administration office, fill them out, and hand them in to the administration staff at their respective division. Cousin goes to pick up the forms for me from administration. Oldest Brother tells Cousin she should send in her application as well. Cousin says she does not want to.

"How come?"

Cousin says nothing.

"How come you don't want to?"

"How can I go back to school at this age?"

"How old is that?"

"Nineteen."

"That's not so old."

"That is old. All my friends are graduating." Oldest Brother looks at Cousin without saying anything. Frightened of Brother's gaze, Cousin loses her nerve.

"You mean you want to be a factory worker all your life?" Cousin shuts her mouth tight. "You like people calling you factory girl?"

Cousin shuts her mouth even tighter.

"You can't get out of that life if you don't go to school."

Still Cousin's tightly shut mouth does not open.

"Is that what you want?" Cousin bends her head low. "Is it?"

"Well, everyone else lives that way!" was Cousin's response to Oldest Brother's question.

"Everyone? Who? You might live that way, but everyone else goes to high school and goes to college, pursuing the things that they want to do."

As Oldest Brother presses on, Cousin is now on the brink of crying. Yet Oldest Brother does not relent.

"So you mean to tell me you're going keep living here like this forever, is that it?"

"What do you mean forever? I'm going to save up to buy a camera, and get married, too."

Oldest Brother softens his tone and lets out a little laugh. "What do you want a camera for?"

I answer, after watching the two of them speak. "She wants to be a photographer."

Oldest Brother says, "Some grand dream," then adds, sounding apologetic yet firm, "It's the same with marriage. If you work at a factory, you can only find someone on that level. To live a decent life in this country, the first thing you need is schooling."

When Cousin still does not say that she will go back to school, Oldest Brother raises his voice again.

"Then why move all the way out here in the first place? Why not just go work at a factory near home? If you don't plan on going to school, pack your things and go back home." Cousin turns all sullen, but left without a choice, she picks up an application form form.

She turns to me. "Why are *you* going to school?"

I go blank at Cousin's question. I have simply thought that is what one has to do. Cousin is the first person to ask why that is. Unable to answer why I'm going to school, I say to Cousin that it would be nice if we could attend school together. "Besides, if we get admitted, the company is going to pay the tuition."

Cousin snorts. "You think the company is trying to do us a favor? They're doing it for tax benefits. And if we go to school, we won't be able to work overtime. Actually, we'll have to leave work an hour earlier than regular hours and the company is of course going to cut an hour's pay from our daily wage. So when will I ever save up enough money for a camera?"

After filling out her application only at Oldest Brother's insistence, Cousin gets even more worked up about getting in. They're admitting fifteen students but 160 people have applied. Another notice is posted, that the selection will be made on the basis of the applicants' work history at the factory and a separate test. The test will be supervised by the union leader.

I still can't figure it out. How did the management ever get the idea to delegate the student selection process for the special industrial workers' class to the union? I wonder if it was a conciliatory gesture to make up for their adamant opposition to letting Yu Chae-ok back to her job.

Despite Cousin's earlier reluctance, when we are notified of the large number of applicants and that work history will be a major factor in the selection, followed by the announcement of the test date, Cousin seems anxious.

"What are we going to do? We've been working for less than six months now."

"Doing well on the test will help."

Cousin turns glum. Saying that she doesn't think she can, Cousin asks again, "What are we going to do?"

It's not like I have an answer. I said we should do well on the test—but we can't even study for it. We don't have the books.

"What are we going to do if we fail?"

"We won't fail."

"But it's been three years since I graduated middle school. It's different for me!"

I try to calm her anxiety. "Other people graduated five, six years ago. We're two of the youngest applicants. They're all twenty-three, twenty-four, twenty-five, even."

Still not convinced, Cousin mumbles, "But it'll be so embarrassing if we fail." Then, after thinking awhile, she suggests that we write a letter.

"To whom?"

"To the union chief!"

Union chief? In return for getting rid of Yu Chae-ok, the management set up a union office on the roof next to the cafeteria and the newly elected union leader now works there full-time.

"What would we say?"

"That we badly want to attend school."

"Yeah, like other people don't."

"Other people are other people, and we have our own reasons. If the test results are close, they will pick us because of our letter."

When I think about it, she seems to have a point. Cousin seems convinced by her own words, her sullen eyes beginning to sparkle.

"You write it. You said you wanted to be a writer."

"We should each write our own. People don't write letters jointly."

"What does it matter? You write it, and we'll both sign it. Makes perfect sense."

The day before the test, I sit at Oldest Brother's desk and write down how badly we want to attend school. At first I have no idea what I should say, but the letter quickly becomes long. I write that wearing uniforms is a big dream for us, and that if we are given a chance to finish school, I hope to become a writer and Cousin a photographer. That we will never forget the grace we received from the union chief if we are given this chance. At the bottom, we write the date and our names, and we seal the letter. Cousin will be in charge of delivering the letter to the union chief's desk at the office the next morning.

Oldest Brother comes home at night carrying taffy sticks rolled in white powder, for good luck.

"Hope you do well."

The taffy that Oldest Brother got for us is sweet. We point and laugh at our cheeks, smothered with taffy powder, and help each other wipe if off. Oldest Brother tells us to brush our teeth and go to sleep early, but we have a hard time getting to sleep, tossing and turning as we listen to Oldest Brother's tired breathing. On the day of the test, we have to get to work an hour earlier than usual. Cousin and I have to get there even earlier, to put our letter on Union Chief's desk. While we are taking the test, Union Chief glances at me. He checks the name on my answer sheet and grins. He brings up Cousin's name and asks where she is sitting. I point to where she is sitting way over in a different row. Union Chief pats my shoulder and moves on.

When the list of admitted students is posted in the cafeteria, I see that I made first place and Cousin second. When we go to the union office to receive our admission notice, we thank the chief, to which he replies, "You don't have to thank me, you two had the highest scores," and adds, "I appreciated the letter."

One day, I am called into the office by Union Chief. He sits at his desk wearing a gray uniform and when I step inside, he tells me to approach the desk. "How come your company documents and the school admission papers do not match?"

I, still sixteen years old, hesitate, unable to answer.

"Tell me, why is that?"

"Well, actually . . ."

I stammer as I tell him that actually I am sixteen and not eighteen, and that my name is not Lee Yeon-mi.

"Sixteen?"

Union Chief looks unconvinced as he stares at my height. I had grown to my adult height at fourteen. I am the same height now as I was then.

"Then who is Lee Yeon-mi?"

I didn't know anything about that. All I knew was that because Dongnam Electronics employees had to be at least eighteen, which disqualified me as a worker, I had submitted the paperwork that Oldest Brother prepared for me. Oldest Brother would know who Lee Yeon-mi is. I had simply received the paperwork from Oldest Brother and had not asked who Lee Yeon-mi was. Union Chief speaks again after a long silence.

"We're short on staff at right now, so there shouldn't be a problem for the time being. Besides, you've already been working here for several months. But you can't attend school under Lee Yeon-mi's name, so bring in your real paperwork."

He speaks kindly, but I feel as if I am being questioned. Perhaps he's noticed how I feel, because he adds, "You make sure to work hard in school," and continues to say that there are only so many chances to study in one's life.

Thanks to Union Chief, I get my own name back on the company records. Thanks to him, my payment envelopes carry my own name instead of Lee Yeon-mi's, a name I know nothing about. Thanks to him, I no longer have to get lost when someone calls me "Miss Lee Yeon-mi?" and I answer a beat later, "Yes, yes!" People now call me by my own name. The name that belongs to me.

Union Chief. If I had not forgotten his name, I would like, just once, to write his name with my own hands. His name may have been forgotten but his appearance hasn't. Short height, gentle voice, rough skin on his hands.

He commuted on his bike. On his bike, he took the same route that Cousin and I took to walk back to our lone room, and when we met on that route, he would get off and walk his bike next to us. Sometimes he invited Cousin and me up to his rented room on the second floor of a house near the market, where he lived with his wife and their three-year-old son, for some fruit or hot citron tea. Sometimes, though rarely, he gave us a ride on his bike to help shorten the distance to our single room. Cousin would ride in front of him and I in the back. At work, when I felt someone tapping on my shoulder, I would look back to find him standing behind me and, seeing my tired eyes, he would unconsciously reach out his hand as if to rub them for me then pull his hand back.

A warm soul, but one that I betrayed.

It is winter and Third Brother, who did not get accepted to one of the first-tier universities, visits Seoul to take tests for second-tier schools. In the crammed room where the three of us live, Third Brother sits with his back against the wall and glances at me, turning glum. Oldest Brother pleads to Third Brother to apply to a night program at a second-tier university and take the civil service exam, like he did. Third Brother, his hair still in his high school crew cut, does not answer. He takes only the university test and goes back home without saying good-bye. He never answered if he would do as Oldest Brother said, but Third Brother's name makes the list of students admitted to the night program majoring in law. When he comes again for the physical exam at the university, Third Brother still does not smile. At the dinner table, Third Brother ignores his food and complains about how four people will now live in this room, his tone gruff, as if everything is Oldest Brother's fault.

"I can sleep in the attic," Cousin offers.

"Me, too," I add. Oldest Brother says there's no need to do that. When the next room becomes available, we will rent another room. But Cousin and I know too well that we cannot afford to rent two rooms. When spring arrives and Cousin and I start school, we will no longer be able to work overtime and our earnings will be even less. Our offer to sleep in the attic seems to have made Third Brother even angrier and he glares straight at Oldest

Brother. My heart sinks with a thump. It's not like anyone forbade us to do so, but nobody among my siblings has ever glared at Oldest Brother in defiance like this. Nobody told us we couldn't, but somehow we had grown up thinking we shouldn't. Even Second Brother, who was only two years younger than Oldest Brother, never set himself against Oldest Brother, not even once. Not in childhood, not then, not now. Oldest Brother has that about him. He is not a fighter or someone who uses force the first chance he gets, but despite this, he has something about him that keeps people from behaving childishly or picking a fight. He was overly proper, to the degree that it seemed like a flaw. Even when he was young, he was polite to Mother and Father, sociable with other people, and always focused on his studies. Additionally, he was neat and noble in his looks, so when Father or Mom chided, "Why don't you try to be more like your oldest brother," we simply felt small, unable to refute or give excuses. He was someone who always tried his very best. Not only in schoolwork but in his courteous attitude toward Father and Mom and his brotherly attitude toward his younger siblings. He had always done the best he could from where he stood.

But now Third Brother is glaring at him.

Oldest Brother holds Third Brother's steady glare and says, "Go on and eat." Then he says, "Your sister is going to attend night classes after her shift at the factory." He even adds, "And you know what? She says she wants to be a writer." Only then Third Brother looks away and lifts his spoon to eat. A shadow of gloom covers his face. We finish eating in silence.

After the dishes are done, I feel awkward about going back into the room and so I head to the roof, where I find Third Brother standing by the railing. He gazes down at the jagged rows of factory chimneys. Third Brother had a strong sense of pride. He would not lose to anyone. Rather, it would be more accurate to say he was good at many things. In the country, there was no kid who did not fear him. He was a good athlete, had an intimidating presence, and was an avid reader, which made him knowledgeable. Wherever he went, he was a leader. But now he had failed to get into a first-tier university and is about to become a student at a night college. When I turn back down, not wanting to intrude on his thoughts as he gazes down at the factory chimneys, he calls out my name. I approach and Third Brother strokes my head.

"Is it true what Oldest Brother says?"

"About what?"

"That you want to be a writer?"

Because it is Third Brother who is asking, I lose my confidence. It is he who should be a writer, not I. It was he who read with a scary intensity, while I had only been glancing over his shoulder at his opened books. It was he who had introduced me to almost all the writers I'd come to enjoy and the books that I'd read up to that point. As a matter of fact, he was not only an avid reader but was just as good a student as Oldest Brother and a far more outgoing one, surrounded by friends. He always came in first in school marathons, played the bass drum in band, played varsity handball, and was appointed president of the student council year after year. If there was one aspect of him that was different from Oldest Brother, it was that he was not your typical model student. He was a mischievous troublemaker as well. Father never used his cane on us, but Third Brother was the sole exception. For he would take an entire box of instant *ramyeon* noodles from the store or steal our neighbor's chicken with the neighborhood boys.

But at the same time, every chance he got he was writing in his notebook, endlessly erasing and writing and erasing again. Wherever you opened in his notebook, the page was filled with small letters, hazy like fog. His love of writing was so strong that it made me wonder why he had chosen to major in law and not in literature. Because this was who he was, I did not have the confidence to say to him that I wanted to be a writer.

"You have the composure." When I don't answer, Third Brother begins again. "You have the composure. So you will make a good writer. I want you to take over my aspiration as well." Third Brother continues. "I'm going to be a prosecutor and help lift up our family."

One Sunday, Cousin and I go to a tailor shop near the school we're going to attend and order our uniforms. Cousin has a very slender waist. I try to steal a glimpse of Cousin's slender waist but she catches me looking. Cousin gives me a scowl and I panic, then we break into laughter. Being the older one, Cousin takes me to the market in Garibong-dong and treats me to a bowl to *ramyeon* noodles with a generous topping of rice cake slices to celebrate our new uniforms. I was the one who was so eager to go to school but now I am the cool one while Cousin, who had not cared much, has gotten all excited about ordering new uniforms, her cheeks flushed red as she slurps down the broth.

"After our welcome ceremony at school, let's go home for a visit. Wearing our uniforms."

When I don't answer, Cousin asks again, "Okay?" She keeps pressing me, so I agree to do that. But I wonder if we will find the time.

I turn seventeen and Cousin turns twenty. It is now January 1979, and with the new year life gets busy. Oldest Brother graduates from university and Third Brother begins his first year. Third Brother takes the civil service exam, as Oldest Brother had asked him to, then makes his test results invalid by refusing to show up at the physical exam. Instead, he makes a promise to Oldest Brother. He is going to focus only on his studies so he can get a scholarship and pass the bar exam. Oldest Brother, who will soon be entering his military service, gazes with a tired look at Third Brother.

"I will now be serving the military as a commuting soldier. I will no longer be able to contribute to our rent. All I ask is that you get by on your own until I am discharged."

The union and the management seemed to be getting along well for a while, but with the arrival of the new year, the union is going one direction and the management in another. Miss Lee tells us, "You should check out our commercial on TV. It's really something."

We don't even have a radio, let alone a TV. On Sunday, while the two of us are at the store to buy laundry detergent, Cousin, suddenly pulling my arms, screams, "There it is!"

On the TV screen in the room behind the store, a pretty woman with long hair, wearing a leather jacket and headphones, sings along to a foreign song. Then she smiles, saying, "Dongnam Stereo, Dongnam Stereo." As the words "Dongnam Stereo" reverberate, creating an echo effect, the stereo system that we have soldered and assembled with screws fills the screen in its full splendor.

As she opens the detergent packet, Cousin says, "You know that song just now?"

"What song?"

"That song that the woman in the headphones was singing just now advertising our product."

It's now become a habit for us to say "our product" instead of "stereo." "What about that song?"

"It's by Smokie. 'What Can I Do!'"

"Who's Smokie?"

"This group that I like. They also have this other song, 'Living Next Door to Alice,' which is so sad. There was this girl named Alice who lived next door and the man loved her in secret for twenty-four years. He just watched her from afar, unable to tell her how he feels, but one day a fancy limousine came and took Alice away."

Cousin puts the detergent down on the floor and shouts out, like the woman in the commercial saying, "Dongnam Stereo. What can I do!"

Our payment keeps getting delayed. At first, payday is delayed by two days, then the following month by five days, then by ten days the next. The management blames sagging production. Miss Lee gets upset.

"Sagging production—do you agree?"

We don't. Every morning, the chief of production lines up the workers in the production division to assign the day's production target and every day the target amount has been going up. In order to reach the target, the speed of the conveyor belt has been increased and we have cut our morning and afternoon ten-minute breaks by half. I, a skilled worker now, am diligently pulling the air driver and attaching the screws, without a moment to look up. But they say production is sagging.

"It's not because of sagging production, but because the management is launching a subsidiary. That's what's delaying our pay. Launching a subsidiary's fine, but why do they have to put our pay on hold to do that?"

Nobody knows why. All we know is that if our pay is delayed, everyone's life turns into a mess. Because our pay is our entire living allowance. If our pay is delayed, our rent is delayed and we are left with no money to send back home, no money left to scrape to put away in our savings.

The union starts discussing the possibility of a collective refusal of overtime.

Miss Myeong at Administration. The one Cousin envies the most in the whole company. Instead of soldering, instead of pulling down air drivers, Miss Myeong is always going about the factory carrying documents under her arm, or checking our punch cards. Inside her desk drawers are keys to our supply room. She has curly hair that falls gently over her shoulders, clear eyes, and lustrous skin. When Miss Myeong stands in the sun and smiles, her vivid eyebrows raised, her teeth glitter white. When Miss Myeong walks past the flower bed, carrying her yellow document folder under her arm, her smooth calves move with vitality below her skirt. Cousin admires everything about Miss Myeong. Especially the fact that she is managerial, not production, staff.

This same Miss Myeong asks to see Cousin and me one day. I have no idea why this person whom we have never spoken to and only watched from afar wants to see us, but still my heart churns.

"It's not like we've committed a crime or something." Cousin tries hard to appear composed. "We've never been late in the morning. And we've never once left work early."

Miss Myeong smiles sweetly and asks Cousin and me whether we handed in our union application. Only then I realize why my heart churned when Miss Myeong asked to see us.

"Are you union members as well?" Miss Myeong puts on that sweet smile again. Cousin and I have a hard time answering. "And you two still plan to attend school?" Miss Myeong asks next.

Cousin and I gaze back at her, thinking, What is she talking about? Are we planning to attend school? But isn't that a done deal? We already had our uniforms made. Miss Myeong speaks again in a low voice as she flips through her documents.

"The president feels that the company cannot provide money for union members to attend school."

We just stand there staring at Miss Myeong's face. Quite some time passes until Miss Myeong speaks again.

"Which means, you should quit the union if you want to go to school."

Cousin and I leave the Administration Office and walk toward the production division, our heads low. As soon as we step into our division, the many people sitting at the production line all gaze up at us at once. All of a sudden Cousin and I are regarded with suspicion by the production line staff. Scurrying Miss Lee, who persuaded us to complete our union applications, scurries over and asks Cousin and seventeen-year-old me, "What did Miss Myeong have to say?"

Cousin and I hesitate to answer. As we hesitate, Cousin and I are both thinking about Union Chief, whom we had written to. There was nothing that Cousin and I have done after joining the union. Nothing but writing our names and address on sheets of paper. We had yet to learn what a union is and what it is trying to do, but we did know from a gut feeling that quitting the union would mean betraying Union Chief.

By calling for us out of the blue, Miss Myeong has made us feel guilty in front of scurrying Miss Lee and Union Chief.

It is terribly cold to walk home from work. Our factory is located in Industrial Complex No. 1, so many workers rent rooms near the No. 1 Complex, but our lone room is located near Industrial Complex No. 3 because that is where the subway station is. Because Oldest Brother and Third Brother have to take the subway, to get to the Community Service Center, to get to the university. On this day, the way back to our lone room seems longer and colder. Union members will begin refusing overtime the following day, so what are we supposed to do? Cousin and I shiver. Miss Myeong's words, asking whether we still plan to attend school, strike our ears like the wind hitting against the power poles. If we join the union members in refusing overtime, does that mean we cannot go to school? We only have a month until school starts. My head feels all tangled and my heart distressed. Cousin pulls her hand out from deep inside her pocket and holds mine. She lets it go, to pull off the scarf from around her neck and wrap it around mine, then takes my hand inside her pocket, big and roomy, and holds it tight.

"Where are your gloves?"

I do not answer. I am thinking, What do they matter in the middle of all this?

"You lost them?"

I barely nod.

"Is your head in the right place or what? You already lost your scarf and now the gloves, too?"

I gaze at Cousin in the icy wind, looking like I am about to cry.

"Always crying at every little thing."

So are you, I want to say right back at her, but I hold it in. After walking for a while, tightly grabbing my hand inside her pocket, she takes me to the market and buys me a pair of gloves, and pulls them over my hands.

"Now don't lose them. When we start school, we will feel cold into March. Because we'll be walking home at night. We might need to wear gloves through April."

On the overpass, which we have to cross to get to our lone room in Industrial Complex No. 3, Cousin, shivering and shaking, puts the question to me in the end. About what we should do the following day. I, seventeen years old, breathe into my twenty-year-old cousin's scarf and answer. I address her as sister, which I never had done before.

"I am going to do as you decide, *eonni*."

Cousin goes on, still shivering in the icy wind.

"I don't know what we should do, either."

All through the following morning, Cousin and I are anxious and restless. Miss Lee comes over to deliver the firm message.

"No overtime starting today."

When we get to the cafeteria at lunch, we realize that we are not the only anxious ones. All fifteen of us who have been accepted for school have anxious looks on our faces. We ask one another what we should do. Cousin and I have the number two and number one positions, respectively. If Cousin and I do not start work, the conveyor is left empty. If Cousin and I refuse to work overtime, people will notice right away. The managerial staff from the administration and the production division, having caught on to the union's plan, whirl around the production line all afternoon like a flock of black kites.

Foreman, far friendlier than usual, says to Cousin and me from behind us that we are getting paid the following day. They say that if the workers refuse overtime, we will not be able to meet the amount required for the buyers' examination on the weekend, and that if that happens, the exports scheduled until March will come to nothing. And if that is the case, not only will the company suffer great loss, but the workers' pay for the following month will be affected as well. And since we are starting school the following month, leaving work at five, an hour earlier than the regular finishing time at six, at that point we will no longer be able to work overtime even if we want to.

If we are to work overtime, we should have dinner, but Cousin and I cannot bring ourselves to either refuse overtime or eat dinner. When the bells rings to announce the end of regular work hours, the union members head to the lockers, instead of to the cafeteria, to change out of their uniforms and leave the factory. Cousin and I, unable to leave with them, stand on the roof.

The union members glance at us and ask, "Aren't you getting off work?"

When Cousin and I return to the production line, it's empty. The few people remaining in their seats are those who will be starting school and who are close to Foreman. Despite the fact that the conveyor belt is moving, and that Cousin and I are in our number two and number one positions, there aren't enough people to keep the assembly line going. There is nothing for those remaining to do but to watch the conveyor belt move in silence.

"This is what shame is." Cousin, who maintained composure even in the icy wind, wells up with tears as she says, "This is what shame is."

The following morning as we walk to work Cousin and I feel as if our footsteps weigh a thousand *geun*. For the first time since we started working here, our punch card is stamped with red letters that read *Tardy*. When we arrive at the production line, those who refused overtime glance at Cousin and me all at once. I feel ashamed. Yes, this is what shame is. Unable to bear the stinging glares, Cousin and I go stand in the bathroom instead of sitting at our workstations. The mirror above the taps reflects our faces. Out of the blue, I blurt out, "I'm going to be a writer."

The bell rings to kick off the workday, but we remain standing there, gazing at each other in the mirror. I continue.

"I don't care about anything else but writing. Even right now, I'm not a bit ashamed. Not a bit!"

Cousin says to me, "Don't bite your lips. Doesn't it hurt?" Then she steps closer to the tap, turns on the water and, cupping the water in her hands, splashes it on the mirror. Then she wipes the mirror with her hands, making squeaky noises. Until Foreman calls from outside, "Number One! Number Two!" to drag us out of the bathroom, Cousin keeps cupping the water and splashing and wiping the mirror, over and over.

Father, who has come to attend Oldest Brother's graduation, bringing with him Third Brother's tuition, which he has struggled to put together, sits at one end of our room wearing an agonized look. Father asks Oldest Brother various questions. Are we renting the room on full deposit or monthly payments? How much is the monthly rent? After sitting for a long time with his agonized face, Father leaves for Cheongju to ask for a loan from his uncle, seeking to get a full-deposit rental contract on our current room, at least, even if he cannot get us another room, so that he can ease the burden on Oldest Brother, who won't be able to earn money for the time being.

He returns that evening. Having failed to secure a loan, Father is now in even deeper agony. Mom sits next to Father and expresses her bitterness toward the uncle in Cheongju who refused the loan. Saying that when the uncle, the son of a widow, was attending school away from home, Father sold the rice he had harvested to send him tuition, that this is why people say goodwill is all useless. Oldest Brother tells her not to worry. That we will manage somehow. Third Brother, who has been staring at the floor, stands up abruptly and walks out of the room. Father lies down with his hand over his forehead and lets out a moan, while Oldest Brother sits at the desk next to the vinyl wardrobe with his back erect, staring intently into the pages of his textbook on criminal law.

When Mom, overcome with disappointment and sorrow, starts to cry, I squat down next to her and cry with her. Cousin starts crying as well.

Unable to forget to this day, Mom recalls what happened sixteen years ago each time Father's uncle from Cheongju comes to visit the ancestral grave, each time she has to prepare food for a memorial rite in his wife's place.

"You wouldn't know what it took for your father, considering what kind of a man he is, to go all the way to Cheongju. Just the thought of that day turns the back of my neck stiff."

Until school begins, each time the union decides to refuse overtime, Cousin and I sit at our number two and number one workstations at the assembly line, our heads hanging low.

The third time Miss Myeong summons us, she calls us in to the managing director's office. All of those who will be starting school are summoned there. Managing Director says, "The company is on the brink of collapse because of the union." He jerks himself up from his swivel chair, his body in a pose that seems to say he can no longer stand it.

"I cannot believe that, in the middle of all this, you, who will be going to school with support from the company, remain members of the union. If you do not sign these withdrawal forms right this minute, your admission will be canceled!"

We sit with our backs against one another and fill out the withdrawal forms. Our withdrawal forms are posted on the company bulletin board. Next to it is a list of benefits for those who have withdrawn from the union. They will have priority in receiving payment, they will get a raise . . .

Cousin and I now avoid Union Chief. There is no way we can look at him. When I am overcome with the shame of looking away from him, I think of the hungry mallards searching for ears of rice on the snowy fields of winter. I remind myself of the promise I made one day to go see the white birds asleep with their faces toward the stars . . . I, seventeen years old and in no position to refuse overtime, pull out a sheet of paper on the conveyor belt and write to Chang.

I don't care whether I joined the union or not. I don't care whatever went on with the withdrawal forms. If only I could join others when they refuse overtime, I think I would be satisfied. I cannot look Union Chief in the eye, a man who treated me so kindly. If we see him standing over there, Cousin and I stop or turn around without getting done what it was that we had to do. When we see his bicycle at the market, we quickly turn toward another street. At lunchtime up in the cafeteria, when we seem him standing in line, Cousin and I give up eating and walk back down . . .

I exert pressure on my pen and press down hard as I write.

> Some day, I am going to see the beautiful birds asleep with their faces toward the sky. No matter how people look down upon us, I will never abandon this hope. I will live on with the pledge that I will someday go see them with my own eyes. The birds sleeping in the forest with their faces toward the stars will forgive me, won't they. They will forgive everything that went on in this world. I will go and see with my own eyes the flock of egrets beautifully blanketing the forest with peaceful sleep. Do you want to come with me?

No matter what promise I make to Chang on the conveyor belt, going to school, for me, at seventeen, going to meet Ha Gye-suk and the others, is an act that makes me betray people, and makes me look away from them in shame. It leaves me with nothing else to do but to follow Cousin's footsteps and crawl into our lone room.

In the country nature could wound, but in the city, people are wounding. It is my first impression of the city. Just as there were many prohibited areas in nature, in the city there were many prohibited areas between people. People who look down on us, people who are too frightening to go near, people who turn venomous when you meet . . . but those who are missed nevertheless.

I returned home from the island. Twenty days have passed since arriving home. After making my flight reservations for the following morning, as I headed out for my last lunch on the island, I stopped by the bookstore that had made me smile when I discovered it upon my arrival. If my book was still on the bookstore shelf, I wanted to give it as a present to the restaurant owner who, for twenty-five days, provided me lunch and I never got sick. The book was still in the same spot. It felt odd, paying for a book that I'd written.

After finishing the kimchi stew that the restaurant owner had cooked, she brought out some coffee and I handed her the book, which made her face light up.

"Goodness . . ." The owner uttered only this exclamation, "Goodness," three times.

"I don't know if I can accept—a book is quite expensive."

I was worried that she might leave it sitting on her shelf for four years, unable to read it. When I said I was leaving now, the owner asked if I had finished what I was writing. I answered that I hadn't. That I was leaving because I couldn't rein in my mind. The owner seemed genuinely sorry about my departure and invited me to come back for dinner. Saying she was going to prepare a very nice meal, she urged me to please come once more. Since arriving on the island, I had been substituting my meals, with the exception of lunch, with simple snacks like fruit, bread, instant *ramyeon* or soup, and had no plans to come out for dinner but nevertheless I said, "Yes, I will."

When evening came, I remembered the owner's heartfelt invitation and thought for a minute that maybe I should go, but didn't. Instead, I pulled out the book of hymns that I'd bought but hadn't even flipped through yet, and opened it. Printed on the inner flap of the black cover was the Lord's Prayer. I gazed long at a line from the printed text. Thy will be done, on earth as it is in heaven.

My young mom, who escorted sixteen-year-old me to Seoul, had no interest in learning a prayer or anything like it. Mom always had a mountain of work waiting for her. She had perilla seedlings to bed out; memorial rites to prepare; rice fields to weed; soup to cook for my older brothers' meals; younger children to raise; food to take to the workers in the field; floors that needed mopping. Now my old mom can memorize everything from the Lord's Prayer to the Apostles' Creed. Give us this day our daily bread. And forgive us our trespasses, as we forgive those who trespass against us. And lead us not into temptation, but deliver us from evil.

I turned to the next page and saw that the book was probably intended as a gift edition, with a line marked To______ and another for the date. Without thinking, I took a pen and filled in the space to read, "To Hui-jae *eonni*," then change it to "To Mom." Then I added, "October 3, 1994."

From the plane carrying me back, I gazed out at the world and saw a water route. The stream was flowing into the river, and the river was flowing into the sea. This was actually taking place. I thought, if only today's hours could flow into yesterday, and yesterday into the day before yesterday, if time could keep flowing back like that, back, back to that room of 1979 and place this book of hymns on Hui-jae's lap. If only that could be, then I would feel less lonely about living on.

TWO

My soul preached to me and showed me that I am neither more than the pygmy, nor less than the giant. But now I have learned that I was as both are and made from the same elements.

—Kahlil Gibran

It's been a month since I returned from the island. When I opened the window upon my return to this empty home, foliage was descending the mountain ridge in the distance. I turned on the radio out of habit. Navigating through zapping static, I adjusted the channel to an FM station that was playing, in the middle of autumn, Schubert's song cycle *Winterreisse.* At well-side, past the ramparts, there stands a linden tree. While sleeping in its shadow, sweet dreams it sent to me. I listened to the song as I wiped the dusty window frame and replaced the lightbulb in the refrigerator, its filament disconnected. And in its bark I chiseled my messages of love: My pleasures and my sorrows were welcomed from above. Today I had to pass it, well in the depth of night. Its branches bent and rustled, as if they were calling to me: Come here, come here, companion, your haven I shall be. I plugged in the phone, washed my hair, and dabbed lotion on my face.

I took the box from outside my door, containing a pile of mail that my next-door neighbor had collected for me, to the small table out on the balcony and sorted outdated correspondence. Letters, postcards, and bills fell from the pile. Amidst them, a familiar script. It was the handwriting of a woman named Kim Mi-jin, who had been writing to me from time to time since last spring. The reason I recognized her handwriting was because her letters were written with a nib pen dipped in ink, which is quite rare these days.

Opening the envelope with a pair of scissors, I pulled out the letter and as I read on, my heart stopped. She had written that she was going to kill herself. That she was writing the letter at work; that the time was nine o'clock at night; that she was going to take the finished letter to the mailbox, return to the office, and kill herself. This letter she sent me was her final note in this world.

I checked the date on the postmark. September 19. The letter had been mailed a month ago. The letters that I had received from her up to that point were all dark and full of despair. But because she had written nothing about why she was in despair, there hadn't been anything I could do. It was the same again this time. She said she was going to kill herself, but there was nothing about why she was going to kill herself. Nor was there anything about why she was sending her suicide note to me, of all people.

When I woke in the morning, the foliage had descended slightly further overnight; then when I woke again the next morning, the foliage had descended still further. A month went by like this. When the foliage had reached the foot of the mountain, up on the mountaintop the leaves began to fall. The leaves that had changed color fell and scattered at the slightest wind. I changed the lace tablecloth on my balcony table to a green hemp cloth for the winter.

As I headed home late at night, on the bus or walking down an alleyway, I thought about Kim Mi-jin. Did she really die?

1979. My body remembers that year through the memory of the taste of *soju*. The stinging smell of the distilled liquor going down my throat.

Miss Lee is talking to Cousin. "You should watch out."

Cousin is silent.

"Foreman has his eyes on you."

Cousin looks at her with confusion.

"Once he gets his eyes on someone, you know how tenacious his pursuit is? And when he doesn't get his way, he starts getting all abusive. That's the kind of guy he is."

Cousin still looks at Miss Lee blankly.

"Crazy jerk, at least he's got eyes that see properly."

Cousin still says nothing.

On that one day, it is Cousin that Foreman has his eyes on, according to Miss Lee, but for some incomprehensible reason he hands me a present. I unwrap it to find a box. When I open the lid, there is a fountain pen inside, along with a note. It says no overtime is scheduled that day and asks me to meet him at the Eunha Tearoom at the entrance of the industrial complex. It also says that I should keep this a secret from Cousin. I am flustered all afternoon. When Cousin asks me what is wrong, I stare at her face or look away. On our way home from work, I walk close behind Cousin. I get so close that our feet bump into each other. We arrive at the market like this. Cousin stops and turns me around.

"What is going on?"

"What do you mean?"

"Hey, come on—!"

Frustrated, Cousin lets out a holler.

"What is it, I asked!"

"What are you talking about?"

"You mean to tell me you're acting normal? Why are you getting so close behind me that I can't even walk? Is anyone coming after you? Look at you, you're trembling. You've been like this all afternoon!"

I am silent.

"What is it?"

Only then do I take out Foreman's present for Cousin to see.

"What's this?"

"A fountain pen!"

"Fountain pen?"

"Why would Foreman Lee give you a fountain pen?"

I have no answer.

After reading the note from Foreman Lee asking to meet him at Eunha Tearoom, Cousin throws the note and the pen into a trash can outside the marketplace.

"What a crazy jerk. Let him wait all he wants."

Cousin takes a few steps, then, as if she's thought of something, Cousin turns back to the trash can and picks up what she threw in there.

"I have an idea."

I look at her with confusion.

"Let's go meet him together."

"I don't want to."

"We'll show up together and rip him off."

"Off what?"

"Ask him to buy us tea and take us to dinner and beer."

"Then what do we do?"

"What do you mean what do we do? That's how we're going to make him pay, that's what."

Cousin drags me back the way we came. It is already thirty minutes past the time that he asked to meet. Foreman Lee is sitting behind a haze of cigarette smoke. Cousin said the plan was to rip him off, but as soon as she sits down in front of Foreman Lee, she pulls out from her pocket the fountain pen and note that she had retrieved from the trash can. My heart sinks as I watch her.

"Do you even know how old she is?"

Silence.

"She's only seventeen."

More silence.

"She didn't even get her period yet."

I do a double take.

"Don't you have a little sister of your own? You have some nerve meddling with her."

"She's like a little sister so I wanted to treat her to dinner, since she's starting school and all. Why are *you* making a fuss over it?"

"We have our own brother to treat us to dinner." Cousin takes my hand and leads us out of Eunha Tearoom.

"Maybe he just wanted to treat me to dinner like he said."

"You are so clueless. He's now making a move on you because he couldn't get his way with me."

"He did the same to you?"

"Well, he didn't give me any fountain pen, that's for sure. Instead, he tried to kiss me!"

"When?"

"The other day while we were working overtime, remember the girl from Administration came saying Foreman is calling for me?" I stare at Cousin in shock.

"Jerk."

"So why didn't you tell me?"

"If I did, then what would you have done?"

I could not answer.

"Don't even acknowledge him. You know Miss Choe who used to work on the C line? He even got her pregnant and she got into a whole mess, with his wife coming after her and grabbing at her hair."

"So what happened to Miss Choe?"

"How would I know? She handed in her resignation and left."

On our way back, we hear a song playing from a marketplace cart peddling music tapes. My dear beloved, are you really leaving me.

"The shameless bastard could have kept things quiet, sending her away, but no, he even accused her of stealing needles."

"Stealing needles?"

"Remember Miss Choe was stationed next to the quality control staff from the inspection division, in charge of inserting the turntable needle and waxing the stereo systems after they passed inspection?"

I recall Miss Choe's movements, working hard as she polished the assembled stereo with flannel cloth applied with white wax. Miss Choe, with her hair parted neatly and braided in two plaits.

"Where did you hear all this?"

"You're the only one who hasn't heard. We all know."

I'm the only one who hasn't heard? From the marketplace, wrapped in a swirl of smells, of fish cake soup, sticky pancakes, and rice puffs, Lee Myeong-hun's song keeps playing. My darling, please tell me one thing before you leave. That you loved me, no one but me.

"Why did you have to tell him such a thing?"

"Tell him what? That you didn't even get your period yet?"

I just look at Cousin.

"Well, you didn't, am I wrong?"

"Whether I did or not, why tell him such a thing?"

"It's not like I gave it much thought. Just kind of blurted out."

"I was so embarrassed."

Looking as if she has already forgotten all about Foreman Lee, Cousin dips her hands inside her pockets and is singing along to Lee Myeong-hun's song, when she pokes my side and speaks in a surreptitious voice.

"I wonder why you're not getting your period yet. I started when I was in my second year at middle school, you know."

Cousin is twenty years old and I am seventeen. One day in March 1979, at five P.M., Cousin and I, number two and number one on the A line at Dongnam Electronics, get on the bus outside the factory and continue beyond the entrance of the Industrial Complex to Yeongdeungpo Girls' High School in Singil-dong. As we step inside the school gate, we see a white statue in the flower bed at the end of the slope, facing the athletic field. I approach closer and gaze at the statue. It is of a girl in a summer uniform, her hair cropped straight right below the ears. I am assigned to Class 4 for first-year students, and Cousin to Class 3.

We stand in line on the athletic field in the sunset for a beginning-of-the-school-year ceremony. I get into a solemn mood for no reason as we sing the national anthem. I caress the tulip-shaped school badge on the collar of my winter uniform. For the past year, my dream has been to be a student in uniform once again. The principal stands on the podium, against the backdrop of the three-story main building and the lilac trees planted in the flower bed, and speaks about the president. This Special Education Program for Industrial Workers was established because of the president's special affection for our industrial warriors.

In honor of his great spirit . . . The old principal's address continues on, long under the light of the setting sun. When we get to the classroom, our homeroom teacher writes his name, Choe Hong-i, on the blackboard in Chinese characters. 崔弘二. His glasses glitter under the fluorescent lights. The attendance chart lists our names, student numbers, and company names. As he calls out each of our names, student numbers, and company names, he looks up intently at each of our faces. After he is done with attendance, he gazes down at us, leaning on the lectern with his arms. Out of the blue, he says that everything the principal said is wrong.

"The person you need to be grateful to is not the president but your parents."

I crane my neck from where I am sitting far at the back and watch him cautiously. Why is it that his words feel like a precariously thin layer of ice? Vivid eyes, nose, and ears. Medium height. Lean build. He adjusts his glasses sitting on his steep nose. A lean finger lands on the black rims of his glasses. His mouth speaks again.

"You have been working all day at the factory: That alone is sufficient qualification for you to attend this school."

What woke me was the phone ringing from the room with my piles of books. H, who had fallen asleep at my side at dawn around the time that I had, opened and closed her eyes, her body curled up tight. She would not know that she always sleeps either curled up or completely flat. Her long, wavy hair seems to cry, "It's cold, so cold," even while she's asleep. I suppose the caller will hang up if I don't answer. I had unplugged the phone in the bedroom, so in order to answer, I would have to open the door and walk over to the study. I pulled up the covers for H and curled up in the same position. The ringing persisted.

"Who is it at this hour?"

Stretching out her tightly curled body, H pushed me away. As if to plead to me to please do something about that sound. As I struggled to lift myself up and pull the doorknob, I bumped my head against the face of Simone de Beauvoir, reading a book, in the photo that I had pinned to the door. I was still not quite awake when I picked up the receiver in one hand, rubbing my cheek with the other.

"Are you still in bed?"

". . . ?"

"Did I wake you?"

It was Oldest Brother. What was he calling about at this hour? I switched on the fluorescent light with my free hand and checked the clock. It was seven A.M. After asking if he had woken me up, Oldest Brother did not say anything. I felt a chill on the back of my neck as the cold November wind slipped in through the crevice of the door.

"*Oppa*?"

Silence.

"*Oppa*, what is it? Is anything the matter?"

There was something uncanny about Oldest Brother's silence. What could it be? I felt something inside my chest sink all of a sudden. A call from your family in the very late or early hours always makes one's chest sink. News that one family member has to deliver to another at such an hour is bound to be ominous. Perhaps Father has fallen ill?

"*Oppa*?"

Silence

"What is it? Where are you calling from?"

"From home. You're in the paper."

". . ."

"I called while I was reading the paper."

So Father is okay. Once I regained my calm, it suddenly hit me. What had he read in the paper that made him call me at this hour? Not having read the paper yet, I could not say anything. He had called several times before to tell me he had read about me somewhere, but never at this hour. His voice was clearly not like those times, when he had sounded proud. When my second novel was published and I began to be talked about as a writer,

Oldest Brother had been all smiles. He said he had seen my book even in the tiny bookstore in the building where he worked and had even introduced himself to the storekeeper as the author's brother, asking her to push the book. Saying his coworkers wanted to meet me, Oldest Brother took me hiking with them one Sunday, wearing a big smile all day long as he showed me off. I had felt perplexed as I watched Oldest Brother, nearing forty, snapping photographs, handing me slices of grilled meat, picking a leaf from my hair that had fallen from a tree.

Imagine, I could be someone that Oldest Brother wanted to show off to people.

I had smiled along with Oldest Brother. I posed for the camera standing next to him in a field of reeds, and when his coworkers asked me this and that, I did my best to answer this and that. But now Oldest Brother's voice on the end of the line was not the same as when he had been all smiles.

"It sounds very realistic."

As soon as he said this, these were the words that burst out of my mouth, without time to think.

"*Oppa*! I don't know what it said in the paper, but that's not how I wrote it."

"It's not like I said anything."

After we finished talking, I couldn't hang up and just stood there for a while, listening to the hang-up signal go *beep, beep, beep*. That wasn't how I'd written *what*? The words that had burst out of me fell not on Oldest Brother but on me. What was it? What hadn't I written that way?

I opened the front door, picked up the paper, and came back in the room. H had fallen back to sleep in a flat position. I opened the paper. *Books and Issues*. My face, looking swollen, was printed on the page, my name next to it in a large font. *Author Publishes Autobiographical Novel About Teenage Years*. While I read the article, I was nervous that H, asleep on the bed, might wake up. When I finished reading, I pulled out the page with my photo, folded it to make sure H could not read it, and pushed it under the bed.

It is lunchtime. Coming down from the cafeteria with me, Cousin admires the sunshine and sits down on the bench outside the TV division. In the athletic field male workers are playing soccer. I, seventeen years old, walk to the assembly line to get the book I left on my workstation. The assembly line is dark, with all the workstation lights turned off. At the end of the C line is the inspection division. I am plodding along when the inspection division door opens and Foreman walks out. I walk in his direction and he walks toward me. I greet him with a nod and am about to walk past him when he calls, "Miss Shin?" Just as I turn around, he walks up to me and pushes me against the wall of the storeroom stacked with packaging styrofoam, lifting up my face with his hand under my chin.

"What is it? The fountain pen wasn't enough? You're writing something down all the time, so I thought a fountain pen ought to do it."

I feel a fearful chill all over my body.

"What are you doing to her!"

Arriving at the scene, Cousin thrashes Foreman's back with a block of styrofoam.

"Who do you think you are?" Foreman turns around and strikes Cousin on the cheek, just before she turns to flee.

Cousin, twenty years old, squats down in the fifth-floor locker room and cries after getting hit on the cheek and on her ear by Foreman, all because of me.

"I want to die."

I, sitting right next to her, stare at the floor. The work hour bell rings. I rise and start taking off my uniform.

Cousin, with swollen cheeks, stops crying and asks, "What are you doing?"

"I'm going home."

"What then?"

"I'm going."

At midday, there are no traces of people on the roads of the industrial complex. Only black smoke surging up to the sky. I trudge along the factory walls. I miss Chang. If only I could see him, all this might feel like nothing. I walk past the open gate, beyond which lie thirty-seven rooms, and head to the store. When I pick up a bottle of *soju* from the shelf, the storekeeper stares straight at me.

"You didn't go to work today?"

"I got off early."

"How come, someone visiting?"

"Yes."

"Who?"

I just smile and pay for the *soju*.

I am soon squatting on the kitchen floor, opening the cap and pouring half the bottle of *soju* into a rice bowl. I am drinking it down, my eyes shut tight. A nauseating taste crawls up my throat, making me collapse into a kneeling position. The chill from the cement floor seeps into my knees. I am still kneeling as I put the cap back on the bottle, slide it into a brown bag and place it inside the bottle cabinet of the cupboard.

The phone rang again. Not wanting to bother leaving the room, I plugged the bedroom phone back in and picked up. A woman with an unfamiliar voice asked for me. When I asked who it was, she asked back, "Are you her?" The voice mentioned the name of a women's magazine and requested an interview. When I did not say anything, she asked again if I was the person she asked for. When I did not answer, she said that she had read this morning's paper and that she would like to interview me. I said I was leaving on a trip. She asked when.

"Right now. I was just on my way out."

She asked when I was coming back.

"I'll be gone about a month."

"A month? That makes it difficult."

I quickly wrapped it up.

"I'm sorry. Good-bye."

I hung up and turned on the answering machine. H, awake now, asked in a hoarse voice what it was about. After gazing at H, still under the covers, I pulled out the paper that I had pushed under the bed and threw it in front of her.

"A women's magazine is calling me after seeing this."

"What is it?"

"Read it."

I was staring at the hair fallen on the back of her neck while H read the paper when the phone rang again. Please leave a message, I will get back to you. As soon as the beep sounded, the voice of someone at another women's magazine was heard. I would like to request an interview. Please get back to me at this number. While the tape was still reeling, I walked to the machine and turned off the volume.

"Folks found something to talk about."

H lets out a little snicker.

"Actually I was afraid you'd read it and hide it under the bed."

"So how did the writing turn out?"

"How would *I* know?"

After closing the paper and sitting still for a while, H asked, "Do you know Hyeong-su?"

"Who?"

"He's Gap-tae's friend."

"The painter?"

"Yeah. Guess what. He had an operation for stomach cancer."

"..."

"His wife had stomach pains so he took her in for tests and he thought he might also get some tests done since he was there, and it turned out the wife was fine but he had stomach cancer."

"..."

"He had his entire stomach removed."

"Really," I said and glanced at H, sitting there blankly. Hyeong-su, this name out of nowhere. A slight laugh escaped my mouth. It had come out of nowhere, but while I was listening to H, my heart had become simple. H opened her mouth again.

"Don't answer your calls for the time being. It never makes a good picture when a writer is talked about for something other than her writing."

All day long, the faces of twenty-year-old cousin, seventeen-year-old me, and everyone from the Special Program for Industrial Workers at Yeongdeungpo Girls' High School in 1979 would not leave my mind. The bloated faces of those sitting pale under the blue fluorescent lights in the evening hours, dozing as we took classes on abacus calculation, typing, bookkeeping, and business English. And of Hui-jae.

At the corner of a street outside the subway in Industrial Complex No. 3, on our way back after work from the factory in Industrial Complex No. 1 to our lone room, is a marketplace. Every day after work we would stop by the market to get new ingredients for soup and on the day of our welcome ceremony at school, we again stop by to shop. To do so, we have to get off the bus one stop before home. It's a hassle, but Oldest Brother will not eat unless the meal includes soup. The marketplace near closing time is a desolate place. There are piles of trash here and there. Empty plastic bags swishing around in the wind. An old woman is sitting not inside the market but on the street outside with pollock on an apple crate. The fish have protruding eyes and bursting guts, and the last two are available for a bargain price.

"Do we have some radish at home?"

"Yeah."

"Then let's get the pollock."

"Doesn't it look like they've gone bad?"

"They look okay to me."

Cousin pays for the pollock, gets her change, and hesitates for a minute. Then she takes my hand and sets out hastily.

"What is it, slow down."

Out of breath, I shout at Cousin's back. Only when we've gotten far from the fish vendor does she slow down her near-sprint stride. The plastic bag holding the pollock must have split somewhere because there is water dripping on the ground from the bag. Cousin picks up an empty plastic bag rolling on the ground to use over the torn bag. Then she leads me by the hand to one of the many snack stalls lining the market alleys. It's been a while since we got our monthly allowance from Oldest Brother. Our payday is nearing, which means that we are running out of money for this month.

"Let's come back when we get paid instead."

Cousin giggles.

"It's my treat. To celebrate the start of school."

Cousin puts her bag down on a long bench and orders *ramyeon* noodles topped with slices of rice cakes and stir-fried potato noodles. The stir-fried noodles cost twice the amount of a bowl of *ramyeon*. I poke Cousin's side.

"Why are we getting the stir-fry? It's expensive."

Cousin says it's okay. She asks for an extra plate and splits the stir-fry into two servings and we slurp down the noodles with the warm *ramyeon* broth. Cousin's cheeks, frozen taut in the night wind in March, turn soft and pink. When we leave the market and reach the overpass on our way back to our lone room, Cousin confesses to me.

"Actually, what happened was that when we bought the pollock . . . I gave her a one-thousand-won bill but I think the granny thought I'd paid with a ten-thousand-won."

". . . ?"

"She should've given me five hundred won in change but instead gave me ninety-five hundred." Cousin spins the plastic bag that contains the pollock. "The granny suffered a big loss today," Cousin blurts out in a nasal twang as she runs off, leaving me behind on the overpass.

Third Brother, now a university student studying law, comes to live with us in our lone room. When the four of us lie down for the night on two sleeping mats, there is no room to spare: our heads butt up against the desk and the vinyl wardrobe. In our lone room, our small low table is always set for a meal. Ever since Cousin and I started night school, the four of us never get to sit down together for dinner except on Sundays. Cousin and I eat dinner at the factory cafeteria before leaving for school, so we prepare dinner for my brothers each morning. We rearrange the breakfast leftovers, wash the spoon and chopsticks and set the table again with clean rice bowls. We keep the steamed rice beneath a blanket in the warmest spot of our heated floor, but it always gets cold.

After school, as soon as we get home, either Cousin or I head back out to the corner store, where they sell a hot briquette for twice the price of unlit charcoal. There is a long line of people like us holding tongs in front of the store at this late hour. But when Cousin or I show up, the storekeeper offers us a hot briquette before our turn, skipping over everyone else in line.

If anyone protests, the storekeeper says, "Hey, I'm in charge here," then mumbles these words, as if to himself, "Looks like she just got back from school and that room's icy cold, no parents there welcoming them with warm floors."

The storekeeper has a scar from an old cut under one eye. On one arm, he bears a tattoo of a snake. Whenever I see the scar or the tattoo, I get a creepy feeling, but then, when I catch him sculpting ceramic figurines of the Virgin Mary or cherubs, I am charmed. Back in our room, while I slip the hot briquette inside the fuel hole and add a fresh briquette over it to stoke the fire beneath the floor, Cousin clears the table of dinner dishes and rinses new rice for breakfast. She also prepares ingredients for our next morning's soup, so that all we have to do when we wake up is bring fresh water to a boil. When the hot briquette is in the fuel hole and I fill the boiler with water, the water circulates beneath the floor and heats the room. Once the fire is going strong, the floor gets scalding hot, but when the fire dies, it feels like sitting in a cold tub, much more frigid than any other kind of floor.

Cousin has skin like a chicken's, prone to bumps and cracks. When her legs are exposed to cold wind, her skin gets chapped. She used to wear pants all of the time, but our high school uniforms only come in skirts. Now Cousin washes her legs and feet every night and rubs them with Tamina lotion. I wait for my turn to use the bathroom while she takes her time with the washing, but I'm tired and I often fall asleep before she's done. No matter who goes to sleep first, in the morning we always find Third Brother against the wall near the desk; Oldest Brother lying next to him; me next to Oldest Brother; and Cousin between me and the opposite wall. My sleeping habits were formed back home in the country, where I slept in a big room by myself, taking up all the space I needed. Ever since Third Brother came to live with us in Seoul, I tend to whack Oldest Brother in the face, or accidentally kick his legs in my sleep. One of those nights, Oldest Brother bolts upright in the dark. I must have slapped him in the eye again while turning in my sleep. His hands shield the assaulted eye as he roars.

"What kind of a girl are you, with such wild sleeping habits!"

After that reprimand, I restrain myself, holding one arm across my forehead and one arm across my tummy. I try so hard to be still in my sleep that now I wake up in the exact same position.

One morning, I wake to find a blister on my ankle, right on the knobby, peach-pit bone.

"I think the floor burned me."

I show Cousin my blister.

"How do you get a burn from the floor? Couldn't you feel it happening?"

Cousin has no idea how much I struggle at night not to turn in my sleep.

⁂

The body remembers. Sixteen years have passed and I no longer have the need to sleep perfectly still, but there are nights when I go to bed wrapped up in that same guarded pose only to wake in the morning, unmoved.

⁂

Mom comes from the country to visit us. In her pocket she carries the money she made off a litter of pups.

"That dog turned out to be quite prolific. Produced seven little ones. I fed them well for two months till they were chubby and sold them for a good price on market day."

Mom takes the money she made from the puppies at the country market to the market in the city and buys an electric rice cooker and a thermos. It makes me so happy that we no longer have to cook rice on the kerosene stove. As she heads back home, Mom warns us not to get friendly with the storekeeper.

"Why not? He's so nice to us."

"Don't you see that scar on his face? Doesn't it scare you?"

"Not really. He makes pretty figurines."

"What difference does that make? Don't you go making small talk or anything like that with the man. When you're away from home, there's nothing you should fear more than people."

"But you said people who make things with their hands are never bad."

"I never said that."

"Don't you remember, Mom? That time when I was little and that beggar stayed with us a few nights. The one who wove us a straw basket! I was scared of him and asked you to make him go away, and you said you can always trust people who make things with their hands."

"The things you remember! That was ages ago. Why must you dig up ancient history as old as the Goryeo Kingdom?"

After Mom leaves, I stand there, marveling at the rice cooker and thermos. Now all we need to do is rinse the rice, add water, and plug it in. Every morning up to now, at the crack of dawn, Cousin and I had to light the circular wick on the stove to steam rice, then breathe in the smelly burning kerosene that made our heads ache. We love the electric rice cooker that Mom bought. And the thermos that keeps boiled water hot for us all day long.

Oldest Brother graduates from college and prepares for military service. He files for leave from his job as a clerk at the district office. When he returns, he casts a despondent gaze toward his desk, toward his statute books, with titles like *Criminal Law, Civil Law.* I watch as he lets out a single sigh.

"If someone could support me for just one year . . . two years at most, if only someone would, I might have a shot."

But there is no one to support him for a year, not even for a month. He has no choice but to put on the froglike camouflage uniform and the froglike camouflage cap and commit to one and a half years as a soldier. My tall brother fills my sight. Why am I so young? Why wasn't I born his older sister?

Oldest Brother waits, and looks out toward the subway station, his towering height blocking the entire window from my view. At other times, arms across his chest, he gazes down from the roof of our building, absently watching the chimneys of the No. 3 Industrial Complex. Then he hands over his desk and its stacks of statute books to Third Brother and settles on the floor.

He says to Third Brother, "I am going to do whatever I can to back you up, so . . ."

He pauses. "So focus on your studies and nothing else, consider yourself deaf and blind."

Third Brother hangs his head and does not answer. Oldest Brother keeps going. "I know our country is troubled. And I know how hard it is for a young law student to shut up and keep his head down these days. Nevertheless, keep your eyes and ears shut, don't think too much . . . There will be plenty to do later on, once you have some power."

During the bus ride from Garibong-dong to his school in Myeongnyun-dong, Third Brother turns into a hardcore activist. He goes everywhere in his campus military drill uniform, saturated with a dense, smoky odor. His eyes sink like the inside of a well.

Cousin wears makeup and knows exactly what colors and styles flatter her shape. She finds it awkward, after all this time, to put on a school uniform and go out with an unmade-up face. Wearing the round-collared uniform blouse now, not her V-neck shirt, she stands before the mirror, lipstick in hand as usual. She seems tempted. She hesitates, then replaces the cover and slips the lipstick in her pocket.

Five o'clock any afternoon of the year 1979. This was the hour that I loved. For this was when I could leave my station at the conveyor belt. For this was when we could walk off the production line, drenched with the roar of the conveyor belt, the buzz of air drivers, the zap of smoky soldering irons. As we wash our hands under the tap beside the men's bathroom and change into our school uniforms in the locker room, the national anthem plays on the PA system, signaling the lowering of the flag. Five o'clock, 1979, when we stop and place our right hand over our hearts as we face the flag . . . May Heaven look after us /until the East Sea goes dry /and Mt. Baekdu wears away. Five o'clock, when we are served cold leftovers for dinner at the cafeteria then take the bus out of the industrial complex to head for school. Five o'clock, when the bus conductor would open the door at our stop in Singil-dong, holding in one hand a mini English vocabulary book the size of a die.

To leave the conveyor belt at five o'clock, Cousin and I spend every single moment of our workday attaching screws to PVC boards, without uttering a word. We begin our work half an hour earlier than the others because we have the number one and number two positions, respectively, on the A line of the stereo section; because production cannot continue seamlessly without us; because we must stack enough PVC boards next to the number three workstation before five o'clock in order for the production to go on once we leave for school. At lunchtime, we eat quickly, then immediately resume our places along the conveyor belt.

"I can't lift my arm."

One day during lunch break, Cousin tries to lift her chopsticks but gives up. Her job is to operate the air driver that hangs above her head, pulling it down repeatedly to attach the screws. She is now in tears. I mix the hardened rice into her soup of bean paste and marshmallow leaves, and bring the spoon to her mouth. Then, with chopsticks, I feed her the fried anchovies. At first, Cousin refuses to be fed, but I hold the spoon to her mouth and wait, then she relents.

"You're acting like an older sister."

"Then treat me like one. Call me *Eonni.*"

Cousin tosses a sideways glance at me, then chews her anchovies.

We are out on the roof and I massage Cousin's arm as we sit in the sun. Something glimmers white on the roof of the factory building across the street, which we both notice at once.

"What are those people doing?"

They are women. Naked women. They are lined up along the railing at the edge of the rooftop, as if they are about to jump. All of the workers leaving the cafeteria stop and watch. The naked women seem to be shouting something down toward the people on the street, but no sound reaches us. Policemen swarm in on them from behind. I close my eyes as I wrap my arms around Cousin, who is so young but unable to lift her own arm. When I open my eyes again, the police officers are dragging the women in off the roof, grabbing them by their arms, heads, necks.

All afternoon, our production line is abuzz.

"The production supervisor pressured a female worker to quit the union but when she refused, he forced her into the warehouse and raped her."

"The female worker reported everything to the union."

"But management sued *her*, accusing her of trying to frame an innocent man. That's why the union leaders took their clothes off and went up to the roof. They were daring the managers to act out in the open where everyone can see, not in some dark corner of the warehouse."

In the meantime, Cousin must have recovered the use of her arm because she reaches up for the air driver and pulls it toward her without any problem. She compresses her lips for a moment, then whispers in my ear.

"I'm getting out of here, no matter what."

To attend school, Cousin and I work through the lunch break and the two ten-minute breaks at ten thirty and three thirty. Miss Lee from the union comes to find us working on the line.

"Why don't you ask for a transfer to the preparation line?"

Cousin and I did not join the others in protest when they refused to work overtime and we had to quit the union so we could go to school. Nevertheless, Miss Lee is friendly toward us. The one that Cousin and I worry about is Foreman. It doesn't matter to us whether we switch to the preparation line or not, all we ask is that Foreman, who is now also Chief Manager, continue to leave us alone.

"There is no conveyor belt at the preparation line, so it should be less stressful for you there."

Cousin and I can't bring ourselves to look at Miss Lee—Scurrying Miss Lee, we call her, for her busy, hurried walk. She seems to realize how sorry we still are, and she pats our backs."Hey, it's not as if what happened was your fault." But her kind words make us hang our heads even lower.

"At least the two of you had an excuse. You didn't have a choice if you wanted to start school. But so many people are quitting the union now. They say being a member has brought them nothing but harm."

Scurrying Miss Lee lowers her eyes, as if weighed down by the disappointment.

"We're up against so much, we would be overpowered even if we stood in solidarity."

Cousin takes the lipstick from her pocket and offers it to Miss Lee.

"What's this for?"

"I don't need it anymore. You said you liked the color, remember, and asked me where I'd bought it."

Cousin's lips are pale, now that we are students and not allowed to wear lipstick. Her long, slender calves are encased in black opaque tights instead of flesh-toned sheer stockings. As she works all day, reaching for the air driver that hangs in midair to attach screw after screw onto PVC boards, it seems as if photography is the furthest thing from her mind. But in my mind, albeit on rare occasions, the egrets appear again, the birds in the photographs that Cousin showed me on the night train. In the book, the egrets sleep in the treetops with their wings tucked in. Beneath the dark night sky, the egrets dot the forest, sleeping peacefully like the stars.

At seventeen, I am the youngest in our entire school. Most of the other students are three or four years older. Kim Sam-ok, who occasionally skips school to attend rallies, is a whopping twenty-six years old. She wears her hair in the required schoolgirl style, cut straight right below the ear, wears the same flat shoes, carries a schoolbag as well, but her face still looks like that of a twenty-six-year-old. On her, our uniform, with the tulip-shaped school badge, looks awkward. The uniform and the face do not quite match. The uniform is so girlish, while her face is soaked with exhaustion.

In class, I sit beside a girl named An Hyang-suk, a lefty who works at a confectionary factory. I have met other left-handed people before, but she is the first person I've seen actually write with her left hand. The process looks so easy for her, as if she has been writing this way for ages. When she's not watching, I hold my pen in my left hand and give it a try, but my writing feels utterly inept. When we both take notes during class, her left elbow bumps my right arm. Each time she bumps my arm, her mouth spreads into a slight, apologetic smile.

"What's wrong with your hand?"

One day I reach for her other hand, but immediately release it. Her right hand feels solid, nearly rigid. The awkward abruptness of it all makes me take her hand once again, then let go, again. Left-handed An Hyang-suk smiles, as if she knows exactly what's going through my head.

"I wrap candies at the factory. The work hardened my skin."

"How many candies do you wrap?"

"About twenty thousand a day."

Twenty thousand candies is more than I can imagine.

An Hyang-suk touches my hand. "Such soft skin. Must be they're paying you for no hard work at all."

Her palm feels like the sole of a foot against the back of my hand.

"At first, the job was fun, you know, it didn't even feel like work. After a few days, though, I began to bleed, right here where you squeeze the plastic wrapper then twist." She shows me both of her thumbs and index fingers. I didn't notice it before, because she mostly keeps her hands out of sight, but now I see that one of her fingers is crooked.

"The skin's callused now, so there's no more bleeding, but a couple of years ago, this finger stopped working. That's why I write with my left hand."

She quickly hides her right hand under the desk again, and looks me in the eye.

"You can't tell anyone about my finger . . . Promise?"

I nod.

One Friday in April, Cousin and I head back to our lone room with the groceries for breakfast the following morning. When we reach the edge of the marketplace, Cousin stops under the overpass to the No. 3 Industrial Complex and gazes through the window of a hat shop, still open at this hour. As if she has just remembered something, Cousin grabs my hand and pulls me into the store. She tries on several different berets, the kind with a tiny felt stem in the center, before settling on a white one. She stands before her image in the mirror.

"How do I look?"

The white beret goes nicely with the round collar of our spring/fall uniform. When I tell her it looks pretty on her, Cousin puts the hat on my head. She grins.

"Let's both get one."

"What for?"

"We'll each get one, come on."

"But where will we wear them? It's a waste."

But Cousin's mind seems to be made up already. No matter what else I have to say, she's at the counter, paying for two berets. As we follow the alley that leads back to our room, Cousin is all smiles.

"We're going home tomorrow, remember? Now that we've started school, we have to show everyone there's something special about being a student in Seoul."

I look at her quizzically.

"Look at our uniform. Too ordinary. No different from the uniforms the girls wear back home. It doesn't stand out. That's why we need berets!"

". . . What?"

"Of course hats are part of the uniform at lots of schools, but not in our town, lucky for us. So if we show up at home wearing these berets, we'll definitely be noticed!"

Out of the blue, I think of Chang. Of the look on his face when he sees me in my uniform and new beret.

The next afternoon, Cousin and I board the train. We skip school for our visit home. Oldest Brother is in military training now and Third Brother is on a school field trip. The two of us wear the white berets Cousin bought the day before. Mine keeps slipping off so Cousin uses a hairpin to make it stay in place.

We get off the train back home and split up. Cousin lives in town but I have to take the bus a little farther to the village. As luck would have it, Chang is on that day's last bus to our village. When I board the bus, his eyes grow wide. The moment I see him, my hand instantly reaches for the beret on my head. I try to take it off, but the hairpin keeps it in place. Chang smiles awkwardly, or so I think. We both stand silently, holding the passenger handles, swaying this way and that, and then get off at our village's stop. Chang speaks as we walk in the darkness along the paved road.

"Want to go for a hike tomorrow, to the mountain spring?"

"Where is that?"

"On the trail that leads to Gyoam."

When I don't answer, Chang speaks again. "I'll see you tomorrow around two, at the Gyoam trail entrance."

Chang runs toward his house, leaving me in the dark of the paved road.

The braided-twig gate to the side of our house is open. When I step through the gate, the animals in the yard all stir. The dog crawls out from under the house, where she had settled for the night; the flock of ducks flaps their wings by the flowerbed; the pigs in the sty oink and heave, trying to get on their feet; the baby chicks of spring go cheep-cheep in the coop; even the nest of swallows beneath the eaves rustles with activity. I drop my schoolbag in the yard, gather the laundry from the clothesline and call out to Mom. "It's Sister—"

Little Brother hears me first and bolts out the door. Only then does the dog wag her tail and let out a bark.

"You didn't tell us you were coming."

Mom, wakening from a deep sleep, fetches the schoolbag that I left in the yard to take in the laundry.

"I wanted to surprise you."

"Sister, you're a student again!" Younger Sister finally opens her eyes and grabs the beret off my head, yanking out the hairpin, trying it on herself.

"Students in Seoul wear this kind of hat to school?"

I snatch the beret off her head and hang it on a hook on the wall.

"It's so pretty, let me try it on one more time, ple-ease."

Mom silences Younger Sister, saying the hat is not a toy. Then she looks at me in my uniform, and her eyes well with tears. In the middle of the night, Mom grills fish fillets that she kept pickled in a salt crock out on the terrace, and serves me dinner.

"If you'd told me you were coming, I would've made something nice."

Little Brother rests his head against my right arm as I lie down for the night in Mom's bloomers. He calls out to his other older sister, the one who is younger than me, "Second Sister, come over here." When she gets closer, Little Brother makes each of us extend an arm. We hold our arms side by side while he examines them. "Oldest Sister's arm is whiter! Second Sister is so dark!"

"That's because she drinks tap water!"

Younger Sister hides her arm behind her back and pouts.

"Whatever, Oldest Sister's arm is prettier!"

My little brother and sister tug the blankets, slapping each other on the back, kicking, making a ruckus. Then, one after the other, they crawl into my arms, each settling around me, and fall asleep.

What about the pitchfork in the well, the one that I threw in there, so many months ago, before I left home? For a while I lie awake thinking about the well outside, on the other side of the door, across the hall, across the yard, until I, too, fall into a deep sleep.

When I head for the trail to the mountain spring, Little Brother tags along. I tell him he can't come, but he won't quit nagging and whining. I have no choice but to give in. I hold his hand and whisper secretly.

"You can't tell Mom that we're going with Chang! Understand?"

Little Brother has no idea why he shouldn't tell, still he swears that he won't.

"Really, you must never tell. Promise me."

Again, Little Brother gives me a pinky swear, without knowing why.

Chang stands awkwardly waiting at the Gyoam trail. The three of us head for the mountain spring, taking turns in the lead. As we go deeper into the mountains, Little Brother's excitement grows and he runs far ahead of Chang and me, shouting, "Squirrel!" He chases the squirrels, then loses interest after a while and returns, saying, "They're so fast, Big Sis." As we pass a cairn built up over the years by well-wishing hikers, Chang hands me a stone that he has found along the trail. I place the stone on the top of the cairn. On the way back, when we return to this spot, Chang finds another stone for me to add. Little Brother watches us, then finds a stone to give me. I place his stone on the cairn, too.

While Little Brother runs ahead to chase more squirrels, Chang pulls a book the size of his palm out of his pocket and hands it to me. Dongseo Pocket Books. *Saban's Cross.* A novel by Kim Dong-ni.

"I wanted to give you something but couldn't make up my mind. I found this book in the pile on my desk. I remember you always liked reading books."

Do they still run the midnight train to Seoul? That last train leaving for the city at 11:57 P.M.? Whenever I went home for a visit, I always returned on the 11:57. Each time Mom came along to see me off at the station, carrying the heavy care package she had prepared for me.

How did Mom make it back to the village all those times, walking the mountain roads well past midnight?

On my way down the train platform, I turn and see Mom standing near the gate. She gestures for me to go on, to keep walking. I walk on, turn around again and she waves again. I look again and again. She gestures for me to go, again and again. As I walk along the platform, I see Chang standing on the other side of the fence, his face against the fence of the train station.

Chang just stands there. He does not wave.

After protests on several occasions, refusing to work overtime, the amount we are paid at the end of the month is paltry. To make matters worse, only non-union workers get paid.

The union members, with no money in their pockets, flock to the office on the factory grounds. The office is empty, except for Chae Eun-hui, who sits with her head hanging low. She used to work on the C line, but was promoted to a desk job in the production department. When Miss Lee asks Chae Eun-hui what is going on, she says she has no idea.

"I went to pick up this month's payment envelopes at accounting and it turns out that more than half the people are not getting paid at all. So I asked what's going on and they said everyone who didn't get paid should go see Miss Myeong at administration."

"Who told you that?"

"Head of Accounting."

Miss Myeong at administration, whose skin is light and fair, hands a sheet of paper to each person who rushes to her office.

"The company president has sent orders that only those who have signed this form will get paid."

At the top of the paper that Miss Myeong hands out, the heading reads "Statement of Withdrawal."

> May 10, 1979
>
> On (date), I stamped my seal on a document at the urging of a friend, with no knowledge I was joining the labor union. When I stamped my seal, I had no idea what was going on. Since I had no intention of joining the union and think that being a union member will not do me any good, I wish to formally withdraw from membership.

The workers fix their gaze on the union leaders.

"How could you do this?" Miss Lee turns her anger on Miss Myeong, who in turn sinks down at her desk.

"How could you?"

"What do I know? I was told to pay only those who have put their name and signature at the bottom of the page. I'm just doing as I've been told."

"Where are the envelopes with our money?"

Frightened by Miss Lee's shrill voice, Miss Myeong shrinks in defense, reflexively extending one hand toward a file cabinet against the wall then just as quickly pulling her hand close to her chest.

"So it's in here, huh?"

Miss Lee pushes Miss Myeong out of her way and opens a file drawer. Regular pay. Overtime. Special shift. Compensation allowance for menstruation leave. A stack of envelopes fill the drawer, lettered in fine print, tiny like sesame seeds.

"You can't do this!" Miss Myeong yells, trying to block the file cabinet with her body.

"No, *you* can't do this. Get out of the way."

"If you want to get paid, all you have to do is write down your name and sign, right here."

Someone shoves Miss Lee and pounces upon Miss Myeong.

"Get out of the way, you."

Miss Myeong falls to the floor and a flock of hands grab the envelopes out of the drawer. Lifting herself to her feet, Miss Myeong shouts.

"What do you think you're doing? This is outrageous!"

Someone yanks on a handful of Miss Myeong's hair.

"Outrageous? We aren't stealing. We're getting paid for the work we did. What you're doing is outrageous!"

Miss Myeong's sleek, wavy hair, which Cousin has always admired, is getting even more disheveled as more hands join the assault, clutching her hair, clawing her face. Miss Lee tries to pull all those hands off Miss Myeong.

"It's not her fault. Stop it, stop this right now."

A list of names is posted on the factory bulletin board, a notice of dismissal. The names belong to those who stormed Administration that day. Miss Lee's name is on the list. At the bottom, big block letters in aggressive red say:

> **THOSE NAMED THREATEN THE LIVELIHOOD OF OVER 600 PEOPLE. WE WILL NEVER ACCEPT THE UNION, EVEN IF WE HAVE TO RISK CLOSING DOWN THE FACTORY.**

Ever since the dismissal notice was posted on the factory bulletin, there hasn't been a single day of quiet at the factory. The union confronts the dismissal with a strike and a list of demands:

1. Immediately withdraw the dismissal.
2. Accept our legitimate and democratic union.
3. Immediately halt all attempts to destroy the union.
4. Deliver payments on time.
5. If the management refuses to sign an agreement to the above conditions, we will enter a strike.

In deciding on the strike, opinions are torn between the TV division and the stereo division. The TV division, with its large number of male workers, is adamant in its support of the strike. When production does not meet even half the usual amount because the union members have already taken their hands off work, the management overcomes the strike crisis by ignoring the dismissed workers continuing to come in to work.

I am writing. It was spring of that year that I first saw Hui-jae. I remember the blouse she was wearing as she washed her school uniform at the tap in the center of the cemented yard of that house. I don't know whether fall and winter had gone by without our ever running into each other while living in the same house, or whether Hui-jae had moved in that winter, or early that spring. Even if there had been only one person living in each of the thirty-seven rooms, for a total of thirty-seven people, I had only run into three or four of them when spring arrived. That there was no way of knowing who lived in which room. The front gate was always open, and when I stepped inside the gate, the first thing I saw were the locks on the doors that faced the yard. Sometimes, I would gaze at the back of the person opening one of the locks as I walked up to the third floor.

It is Sunday. After Cousin leaves for the bathhouse on the other side of the overpass, carrying her basket of toiletries, I, seventeen years old and finding it awkward to sit around the room with two older brothers, take off the covers sewn onto our comforters and walk downstairs, carrying the covers inside a large washbowl. At the tap at the center of the yard sits a woman doing her laundry. I, deciding to wait for her to finish, put down the washbowl by the tap when I notice that the clothes she is washing are the same uniform as mine, and I look up at her face.

A small, expressionless face. A small, nonchalant face. A small, quiet face.

This is all I have written about the day I first met Hui-jae *eonni*. That it was a day of pleasant sunlight. That although the two- and three-story buildings were shading the yard, the sun shone down on the center, where the tap stood. That I would have been delighted that Hui-jae's laundry happened to be the same school uniform as mine. That I waited with my washbowl by the tap for her to finish. That I had never run into her before, not at school nor in the street. That it occurred to me that perhaps the uniform that was being washed belonged to her sister. That without regard to what I was thinking, as Hui-jae was busy rinsing her laundry, the tiny flower patterns on her blouse, tucked into a wide skirt, were pulled and distorted by her movements. That after watching, rather precariously, her thin waist, not much bigger than a fist, and the flower patterns that kept getting messed up, my eyes directly met hers, as she lifted her head with a gourd dipper in hand. A nonchalant face, devoid of expression, like sunshine.

Yes, that's what I have written. That it was "a nonchalant face, devoid of expression, like sunshine."

If she had not put on a faint smile right then, I, embarrassed, would have either clasped my hands, run up to third floor, or stepped outside the open gate for a walk to the end of the street and back. Wearing a faint smile, Hui-jae's face had a smudge of laundry detergent, like a scab. She pulled my washbowl under the running tap and headed to the roof. When I went up to the roof as well, still wearing my rubber gloves after washing the covers, she was sitting by the railing, enjoying the sun after hanging her uniform and socks and handkerchiefs and underwear on one side of the laundry line. Hui-jae did not take her eyes off the subway station until I was done hanging all the covers, turning this way and that, with a bustle.

"Your towel's on the ground."

When I was done hanging up my laundry, the sight of her was blocked by one of the covers. Only her voice reached me from the other side. On the ground, a towel that I had washed with the covers had fallen, and while I picked it up, went back down to rinse it, and returned to hang it again, she remained seated in the same spot. I was standing there fidgeting, unable to simply turn back downstairs, when she stretched out her arm and pointed somewhere, saying, "Look at that."

I approached closer and looked at where she was pointing, to see black smoke soaring, surging like clouds from one of the factory chimneys across the street from the subway station.

"Isn't that something."

She pulled back her hand and laughed meekly. I noticed for the first time as she rubbed her palm on her skirt, wrinkled from sitting crouched to do the wash, that the back of her hand was unnaturally swollen, as if from soaking in the water too long. She must have felt me gazing at her hand because she laughed faintly again.

"I got my hand pierced by the sewing machine needle, and it's now swollen because I got it wet. Which room do you live in?"

"On the third floor."

"You're in Class Four, right? I saw you on the bus the other day. And once at school as well . . . I didn't know you lived here."

"I haven't seen you before."

Hui-jae laughed yet again, faintly, at my words. Perhaps she thought I looked young, addressing me as she would a younger sister, and I responded using polite honorifics.

"One thing good about this house . . . No one would know even if someone died."

Don't you think? she then seemed to ask, looking at me with rounded eyes. The smudge of detergent was still on her cheek and a wart, unusually flat, sat next to her nose.

That day she and I carried a pot of scallion flowers, which had been sitting abandoned by the sauce jar terrace, and placed it under one of the drying covers so we could squeeze water on the plant.

Was it because of the sun? I made an effort to find some reason to linger on the roof a while longer without letting her see how I felt. I liked her. Even now, when I think that she would have felt the same, I still well up with tears. That day we were happy for a short while because we liked each other. That moment when my heart felt peaceful, with a touch of melancholy, though I don't know about hers, I felt that my heart had turned infinitely benign.

This was especially true when we played the "sure game." "Sure game" is a name that I made up. She was the one who proposed it, although it's not much of a game. When Hui-jae *eonni* said something, all I had to do was say "Sure" without any objection. To shift turns, when I said something, all she had to do was say "Sure, sure." I don't remember what I said back after that. But what remains vivid is her voice, like water . . . to me, her voice felt like five o'clock in the afternoon when she said "Sure, sure," giggling intermittently, sometimes clapping her hands.

"I am going to sleep. I will sleep soundly without waking for three, four days."

"Sure."

"My brother wouldn't say he wants to go to college after he graduates, would he?"

"Surely not."

"But if he says he wants to, I guess I will have to send him."

"Sure."

"Nonsense. I can't work any longer than I do now. A day is only twenty-four hours long."

"Surely not."

"This is all I can do."

"Sure."

"Foreman is going to install a fan in the work room tomorrow, won't he?"

"Sure."

"He saw all that dust rising from the fabric with his own eyes, so how could he not."

"Surely not."

"Will I someday be able to live in a two-story house with a garden?"

"Sure."

Her lips, fleshy and with barely any color except for a faint touch of her skin tone, happily opened and closed. Sure, Sure, Sure. During this short time, when nothing was impossible for us, Hui-jae *eonni* asked, vaguely, "Could I give birth to a pretty baby?" and I answered, "Sure." During this dreamlike time, she had overturned all of reality.

In our "sure game," she was not a seamstress; she did not live in one of the thirty-seven rooms; and her brother was already a college student. At first I was pressing the soil inside the scallion pot with my finger as I answered, "Sure, sure," then later found myself scooping out the soil, a fistful at a time, as I answered,

"Sure, sure." The dim, wary feeling that gathered in thick clouds as all that had loosened packed in taut again each time I walked into that house completely disappeared while we played the sure game. Like two little girls walking far into the distance, we continued to play this game, devoid of ups and downs, until the comforter covers were dry. Minute by minute she turned clearer and brighter; from time to time I felt a choking in my chest.

I do not remember how old she was. She looked three or four years older than me, so perhaps nineteen, twenty, twenty-one. Prone to blushing from time to time, she seemed like a young girl, I now think, but then again, she might really have been just a young girl.

This girl, whom I now dearly miss, suddenly looked up at the sun's direction, as if she'd just come to her senses, got to her feet, shaking off.

"I must sleep."

"Sure."

"I'm not playing the game anymore. I'm really getting sleepy."

Suddenly putting on a cold air, she hurried down from the roof. After she left, I sat squatting on the roof, digging the dirt from under my nails. Her blouse, her skirt, her hand gestures, the veins on her slender neck stayed with me, trickling like a brook into some part inside of me, making me ask myself, "Is it a dream?" and turn around with a swirl. The comforter cover flapped like a curtain drawn over some secret, and one of her handkerchiefs had been pushed by the wind down to the ground. I clipped her handkerchief back on the line with a clothespin and descended from the roof.

Cousin, back a long time ago from the bathhouse, is clipping her fingernails when I come down from the roof and she gazes straight at me.

"Where have you been all this time?"

I don't answer.

"Where?"

"On the roof."

"Roof? What were you doing there all this time?"

I am unable to give her an answer.

"You sound like a fool all of a sudden. What's going on?"

"What are you talking about?"

"You're acting weird."

"What do you mean?"

Cousin looks right at me. "What?"

Cousin rolls up the tissue with the nail clippings and throws it into the trash can, as if she can't figure it out.

"I don't know. Let's just go get groceries."

Cousin brings it up again as we're crossing the overpass.

"You got a scolding from Oldest Brother while I was out, didn't you?"

"No, I didn't."

"What is it then?"

"What are you talking about?"

"You seem all down and drained, as if you got a bad scolding."

Stammering, I tell her about Hui-jae *eonni*. About how we played together on the roof.

"Sound like you had fun. So why so down?"

"Don't know."

"You're not making sense."

Ever since the first chapter of this novel was published, it seemed that I had become a subject of gossip. Every call I answered was from a women's magazine. I answered and told them that I was not home. If they asked who I was, I said that I was my younger sister, and that Older Sister had gone to the country and that I didn't know when she'd be back. It was also difficult for me to listen to the messages left on the machine, and I kept the phone line unplugged for about two weeks.

I plugged it back in, thinking that should have done it, and when the phone rang, far past midnight, I answered it in my sleep. The caller was looking for me and I answered, "This is she," without thinking. Only when the caller named her magazine, I said to myself, "Ah," but it was already too late.

"You're back from Germany." She sounded glad. I must have told her that "Older Sister" had gone to Germany.

When she said she wanted to see me, I began, "Well, actually . . ." and told her the truth. That it was me who had answered all the previous calls, that I had answered her call and told her that I was in Germany.

"But why?"

"Because I didn't want to do the interview."

She laughed instead of getting upset.

"You've put your name out in the world, so how can you always do only the things that you want?"

I did not reply.

I pleaded with her. I pleaded, to this woman whose face I'd never seen, that I'd only just begun the serialization and that I'd like to focus on the writing without other distractions. Asked her to please leave me alone. She was a pro. She had already begun throwing me questions and before I realized it, I was answering her. I can't let this go on, I thought, and said I was going to hang up when she retorted, in an affable manner.

"Then why did you do the newspaper interview?"

I pressed the receiver hard to my ear.

"Just because I did an interview with a newspaper, does that mean I have to say yes to you as well?"

"Well, in whichever case, we will make our decision and get in touch again."

I was dumbfounded. It was my business and I was saying no, so who was going to make what decision? It looked like she was going to write her article based on this phone conversation and print it with a photo from another occasion.

"I have made it clear that I'm not doing an interview. I am going to look closely through your magazine next month and I will be very upset if you have a story on me in there."

"I'm not in a position to decide, you see. I will have to speak to my editor at work tomorrow and then I'll be able to give you an answer."

"But this is my business. Who's going to give what answer? Let me tell you once again, I said I'm not doing an interview. I ask you to not ignore my words. Or I'll be very upset."

I quickly hung up and pulled out the phone cord.

I could not sleep. I tossed and turned, again and again, hearing the phone ringing in my ear even when it had been unplugged. I remembered a familiar face who worked at the same women's magazine that the caller worked for. I shall call him in the morning, I told myself, but my unsettled heart took no comfort.

When I awoke, I put on a CD of Lee Oskar's harmonica album and pressed play. My chest felt congested and my head throbbed. I opened the window halfway. About thirty minutes into the music, I finally felt calm. At first I didn't even notice the cold wind and only then did I feel a chill on my forehead and the ridge of my nose. I pulled up the covers and sadness came over me for no reason. What am I doing, here and now?

I rose to pick another CD and gazed into the face that belonged to Chet Baker, holding his trumpet. What am I doing, here and now? What? Chet Baker held his mouth closed, looking hollow, the wrinkles on his face carrying his yet incomplete wanderings. I pulled the Lee Oskar out, put the Chet Baker in, turned up the volume and took out the liner notes to read.

"Chet Baker's landmark album recorded two weeks before his death." Released in 1988, this album is a historical recording of the concert that took place two weeks before the death of this legendary musician.

1988? He must have recorded this album while we were hosting the Olympic games in Seoul. I continued reading producer Kurt Geise's reminiscence. "The stage was completely filled up with two orchestras and Chet Baker, standing alone between them, appeared very small . . ." Geise wrote, "Two weeks later, he was found dead . . ." And that the Amsterdam police . . .

I programmed the player so that this man's voice, which turned out to be his last words, would keep playing over and over in my room even if I fell asleep, and lay down again.

There were times when I would encounter, on the bus or from storefront speakers on the street, the voices of people who were no longer on this earth. Of singers like Kim Jeong-ho or Cha Jung-rak or Bae Ho or Kim Hyeon-sik . . . The reason I flinched the moment I heard their voices, the reason I fell into silence, as if time had come to a stop, was that I thought the only thing these deceased people left behind was their songs.

Some time ago, I used to work as a scriptwriter for a radio program that played Korean oldies for an hour. The DJ was a news announcer nearing his retirement. He was a fan of Bae Ho. On Tuesday mornings we recorded the show for the coming Sunday, and when we wrapped for the day, the old man would sit me, a young woman, down to share a midday drink. Singing Bae Ho's "Turn Back at the Rotary."

Dark rain here at the rotary as this lonely man, sighing and soaking in the rain, longing for the love that he has lost, arrives at the rotary, sad and forlorn . . .

One day the old man asked me, sitting there with my glass of *soju* untouched, "Do you know what kind of a singer Bae Ho is? I mean, do you know why his songs still live in the hearts of so many fans?"

"Well, he's a good singer."

At my pointless answer, he responded, "No, it's because there is death permeating his voice. Because these are songs that he sung in his sickbed, nursing his nephritis, out of breath as he shifted back and forth between life and death. Because these were songs that he spit out from a chair, unable to even walk. That bastard . . ."

Tipsy from his midday drink, now he was referring to Bae Ho as the bastard. "You know what he said upon his death at twenty-nine? 'My dear fans, thank you. But I think I am beyond hope . . .' That's what he said. Crazy bastard, thankful for what? He had no clue that it was the damned songs that killed him."

I once asked him, "What do you feel like when you listen to a dead singer's song?"

The winter tree branches outside the window of the coffee shop where we were sitting were lit with twinkling lights that reminded us of Christmas. The twinkling lights on the branches, luminescent in the dark, stirred inside of me some deep instinct to return home. I wanted to go back if only I could. But to where? Perhaps he felt it was an odd question, because he simply gazed at me across the table.

"There's nothing different, it seems, when we encounter a work by a dead writer or a dead artist, but isn't it a strange feeling to listen to a dead singer's song?" When I asked my question again, he lifted himself up from his comfortable position, sunken deep in his chair.

"Probably because it's their actual voice. Because it's too real. And it's not just songs. I once heard the voice of a colleague of mine who had died reciting a poem and it was quite bizarre. Perhaps *eerie* is a better word. A person's voice is like a part of his body. Like that person is alive right there in front of you."

Could it be that Hui-jae still remains with me in body? For whenever I think of her, I suddenly fall silent, just as when I hear songs by those who are no longer here on this earth.

The following day after school. When classes are over, Cousin always comes to my classroom to head home together, so I am sitting there waiting for Cousin when, unexpectedly, Hui-jae *eonni*'s face appears in the hallway window instead of Cousin's.

Can't be, I think, and stay seated, and Hui-jae gazes toward me through the window. When I just keep sitting there blankly even after I see her, Hui-jae comes in through the door at the back of the classroom and puts her hand on my shoulder.

"Aren't you going home?"

Before I can tell her that I am waiting for my cousin, Cousin comes running down the hallway and taps on the window. She's signaling me to hurry and get going. When I glance toward Cousin, tapping on the window, Hui-jae glances that way as well. Perhaps noticing something's unusual, Cousin comes into the classroom.

"What are you doing? Let's get going."

I introduce Hui-jae to Cousin, saying she's the person I met on the roof the day before.

"Ah, I see." Cousin gazes blankly at Hui-jae for a moment, then asks, "I heard you live on the first floor, right?"

Hui-jae answers, "Yes," looking at me as if to ask who this is.

"This is my cousin. She lives with us."

We walk out of the night campus, feeling awkward. Cousin, who on other nights offered me her arm, walks next to me at a distance. I am about to take Cousin's arm when it occurs to me that Hui-jae might feel left out, so I pull back my hand and I, with Cousin in front of me and Hui-jae behind, walk between them in an awkward stance.

Cousin sits at the conveyor belt looking sullen. She is frustrated about something. She doesn't answer even when I ask something. Cousin leaves me behind and goes to lunch by herself. I trot along and line up behind her but Cousin, who on other days would hand me a tray and a pair of chopsticks, picks up only hers. I try to guess what's bothering her. Have I done something wrong? I search in my mind but can't figure it out. Being a slow eater, I haven't even put down my spoon when Cousin stands up and leaves the cafeteria with a chill. I quickly put down my spoon and follow her. Cousin is alone at the tap, washing her hands. I approach and poke her on the side, as if to ask what's bothering her, but Cousin doesn't even acknowledge that I'm there.

Afternoon arrives and still Cousin doesn't acknowledge me. She pulls down the air driver and attaches the screws, her lips pressed tight. Resenting her now, I also look away. I feel nauseated and dizzy for no reason. At five o'clock, Cousin once again walks out of the assembly line by herself and heads to the locker room. I, having chased behind her all day, now give up and leave the assembly line much later, wash my hands at the tap, and head to the lockers. As I walk into the locker room, Cousin, already changed into her school uniform, is on her way out. When Cousin looks away, putting on a prim air, I look away as well. When I find Cousin having dinner in the cafeteria, I, seventeen years old, walk past her and head down the stairs. Only then Cousin calls to me.

"Aren't you going to eat?"

The first thing Cousin's said to me all day. At least she hasn't turned mute. I throw my schoolbag on the floor and yell, "Why are you acting this way? What have I done?" Overwhelmed by the frustration of having been ignored all day by Cousin, I break into tears.

"What are you crying for, you're causing a scene."

"Why are you acting like this?"

The students arriving for dinner glance our way, wondering what is going on. "You're causing a scene," Cousin says as she comes over to lift me up but I push her away.

"Why are you acting like this?"

"Why do you call her *Eonni*?"

"Her?"

"Hui-jae or whatever her name is."

I still don't quite understand.

"You never call me *Eonni*, but you're following around this woman, who you barely know, calling her *Eonni*, *Eonni*."

"You refused to talk to me all day because of that?"

Cousin lets out a laugh, as if she's embarrassed.

On the bus to school, Cousin stammers and offers me a confession, which is not at all like her usual self.

"I don't like your being friends with that woman."

". . ."

"I don't like it when you smile and hold hands and walk arm in arm with that woman."

"You stopped talking to me for a whole day because of that?"

"What am I to do, I was so angry."

"I was dying from frustration all day."

"So are you going to keep it up with her?"

"Keep what up?"

"Keep calling her *Eonni*?"

"I could call you *Eonni*, too, then."

Cousin lets out a slight laugh. Perhaps she's forgotten our squabble earlier in the day, or perhaps she's embarrassed about how she behaved, because when classes are over, Cousin is the first one to greet Hui-jae, who arrived at my classroom ahead of her. My cousin, she talks to Hui-jae more than I do and walks closer to Hui-jae than I do.

After that, I call Cousin *eonni*. Anywhere we go, any time, I call out to her, *Eonni—Eonni—*.

Today I received a letter. It would be more accurate to say I found it rather than received it. On my apartment door hangs a sack to receive milk deliveries, which was left behind by the previous owner. This afternoon, as I was leaving for the supermarket, I turned the key and put it in my pocket, but worried I might lose it, I put it inside the milk delivery sack. Walking down the stairs, I considered retrieving it, thinking perhaps I'm being too careless with my key, but in the end, I kept going, telling myself I would be back in thirty minutes. An hour at the longest.

When I returned and put my hand inside the sack to get the key, I pulled out an envelope along with the key. It was a letter with 840-won worth of stamps attached, posted via express mail. The mailman had probably come in my absence and when nobody came to the door, he must have left it in the milk sack, since the mailman knows that I live here. The sender had posted the letter via express mail, but if I had not put my key in the sack, I still would not know that there was a letter inside. But who was it that had news so urgent they had to deliver it via express mail?

The envelope read: Han Gyeong-sin, Faculty, Yeongdeungpo Girls' High School, Singil-dong, Yeongdeungpo-gu, Seoul.

> How do you do? I teach at the Special Night Program for Industrial Workers at Yeongdeungpo Girls' High School. I am writing this letter after reading an article about you in the paper. I wanted to extend an invitation for you to come for a talk with my students, as a writer and as a graduate of our school. From what I read in the paper, I did get the impression that perhaps you are not yet ready for such an occasion. But at the same time, I also thought that you might not be aware that night programs still continue to be offered, and that perhaps if you knew, you might gladly accept our invitation.
>
> When I mentioned that you are a graduate of the same program, my students showed great interest and said they want to read your autobiographical novel when it is published. My students

> are your future alumni and at the same time readers of your work. If you decide to come, my colleagues and I, also your readers, will be just as thrilled as the students.
>
> This past February, after attending my students' commencement, I contributed an article to *The JoongAng Ilbo* newspaper. When I read the published piece to students, they were so happy. Recently one of the students asked, "Aren't you going to writing something else for the newspaper? It will be nice if you wrote about us."

I stood frozen for a while, as if I under a sudden siege.

Special programs are still being run for industrial workers. I had not known. Ever since I left, I had never again been in the area. Perhaps my subconscious preferred to get far away from that time and from that space. Perhaps I had attempted to brush off every trace of factory smell that I was smeared with.

But all of a sudden, halfway through the 1990s, the sounds of the conveyor belt moving is suddenly in my ear.

There is a girl who reads Hegel. She is Mi-seo, class president and my desk partner to my right. She opens the Hegel when she gets to school in the morning and during breaks, pulls out the Hegel that she has pushed under her desk and reads it. While Mi-seo is gone to the teachers' office, I, seventeen years old, open the book to the page Mi-seo was reading. I read the part that she has underlined in pencil. I can't understand what it means, so I read it out loud. But I still can't understand it. Mi-seo, upon her return, snatches the Hegel from me and shows her anger as she pushes it under the desk.

"It's my book."

I stare into her face. Why is she getting so mad—it's not like I stole her book, I just took a peek. When it's almost time to go home, I put a question to Mi-seo.

"You know, about that book, do you understand everything it says?"

"Why do you ask?"

"Because it looks like a difficult book."

"I don't get it, either."

I look at her blankly.

"Why are you looking at me like that?"

"How can you keep reading the book so intently when you don't understand it?"

Mi-seo takes out the Hegel from under the desk and puts it in her bag. "It's none of your business."

She picks up her bag and abruptly leaves, as if I'm being ridiculous.

Much later, when she and I have become close, Mi-seo brings up the Hegel. "Only when I am reading this book do I feel different from all of you. I don't like you people."

It is now the 1990s. Is someone still reading Hegel in that classroom today?

We have music classes. When we are arriving at school around dusk, our music teacher is washing his car. His car is visible even from a distance, glittering in the setting sun. It seems he once aspired to be a classical singer. When someone says to him that his voice sounds like that of Eom Jeong Hang, the famous tenor, he laughs with jovial delight. The song that he had us sing, after our school anthem, which went, Heirs to a tradition of cultural splendor, gazing out at the dignified flow of the blue Han River, was the song "Nostalgia."

When flowering April comes around again, my heart fills up, my beautiful beloved waiting around the mountain path, beyond the bright green hills . . . We are required to sing "Nostalgia" to his piano accompaniment for music test, so when we are walking back from one of our music classes, the sound of singing relays between the front and back of our throng. Where is my home of the old days, its mountains covered with azaleas, owls hooting in the distance. Where is my beloved . . . The music room is on the first floor of the annex, past the main building.

In the main building, nightly cram sessions are underway for senior-year students from the daytime program to prepare for college entrance exams. We have to pass the lilac tree by the main building to get to our classroom. Tell me you love me, my dear beloved in my heart. If not for you spring will never come . . . Suddenly a window opens with a screech in one of the classrooms in the main building and the daytime students, in the middle of a cram session, shout.

"Hey, keep it quiet."

One of those who were singing retorts. "Do I hear anything? I don't hear anyone making noise."

"We're trying to study here."

"So who's stopping you?"

"We can't concentrate with all the noise you're making. Keep it quiet when you're passing by."

"Aren't we even allowed to sing?"

"You're no better than beggars!"

In an instant, everything turns quiet. The taut relay of words spirals into silence with that single line, "You're no better than beggars." The singing that had continued quietly comes to a halt as well. "You're no better than beggars," they said, but perhaps the words alarmed them as well. When this side keeps silent, the other side gently closes the door as well. Only the lilac tree stands between this side and the other. We stand still like that for a while, then someone starts out for our classroom. Quiet, gentle steps brush past the lilac tree. Our calves, after moving about restlessly all day long, churning out goods at the assembly line, walk in muted motion under the brightly lit window on the other side.

After this we never again sing as we leave the music room. Thus the song is still vividly carved in my chest. When flowering April comes around again, my heart fills up.

One night, while opening the door to the attic, I get a scare. Something from inside the door falls at my foot with a plop and it is dark. Utterly shocked, I've already let out a scream, which makes Oldest Brother look. The thing that has fallen at my foot is, unexpectedly, a wig.

"A girl, making such a big fuss."

Oldest Brother picks up the wig and hangs it on the inside of the door. He must have hung it on a nail on the other side of the door and I had pulled the door too hard, making it fall.

"What is it, *Oppa*?"

He doesn't answer. When I ask again what it is, the noise of the passing train cuts in. As we're turning in for the night, before Third Brother is back, Oldest Brother explains.

"Starting tomorrow morning, I'm going to be teaching at a private tutoring center in Anyang."

I am silent.

"I need to get there by six so no need for the two of you to wake up and get busy."

". . ."

"After the class, I'll stop by home to change, so if you can have some lunch packed for me, it'd be great."

This time Cousin asks. "What will you be teaching?"

"English."

At dawn, I open my eyes at the sound of Oldest Brother, cautiously turning on the light. When he sees that I'm awake, he signals with his eyes for me to go back to sleep. If I get up, this tiny room will only feel more crowded. I close my eyes, pretending I'm falling back asleep, then through half-open eyes, watch Oldest Brother's movements. He quietly opens the attic door and, standing in front of the mirror hanging by the window that looks out to the subway station, puts on the wig on his naked head. He takes it off and puts it on again, as if something's not right. He tries it this way and that. When he turns around to pick up his bag from the desk, I get a glimpse of his face with the wig on and break into a giggle. The wig, parted in the middle, is a slapdash production: anyone could tell it's a wig.

"Do I look funny?"

Oldest Brother brushes the bangs away from his forehead. But since it is a wig, and the bangs were designed to fall on his forehead, it is no use and the bangs fall back down in an instant. He looks in the mirror again.

"Do I look too weird?"

"You don't look like you."

Oldest Brother turns serious in front of the mirror. "Do I look like a Seoul National University student?"

I let out a laugh, still under the covers.

"I told them I was a student at Seoul National University. I mean, who would sign up for my class if they knew I was in military service."

Taking care not to step on Third Brother, who had returned while we were sleeping and was now asleep with his face turned to the wall, Oldest Brother turns out the light.

"Get some more sleep now."

As he opens the door to leave, I see the darkness outside through the gap. He takes down his shoes from the shelf in the dark and walks down the stairs, his footsteps making thick stomping sounds.

I hear the sound of Oldest Brother opening the wooden bathroom door at the bottom of the stairs; the sound of Oldest Brother coming out of the bathroom and pushing the gate to leave; the sound of Oldest Brother running down the alley toward the subway.

It's five o'clock in the morning. His stomach is empty. The train that comes at dawn is as empty as his empty stomach. After teaching his class, he comes back by the same route he took at dawn, takes off his wig and hangs it on the inside of the attic door, takes off his suit and hangs it in the vinyl wardrobe, has his breakfast, set on the table in the empty room, dipping his rice in the lettuce soup, and leaves for duty at the Community Service Center, carrying his lunch box. One day he announces with a bright face that he has been asked to teach an evening class as well. Now he is in a circular line. At dawn he puts on his wig, puts on his suit, heads to the tutoring center, teaches his class, then comes back, eats his breakfast, puts on his military uniform, sets out with his lunch box, then comes home again, puts on his suit, puts on his wig, and heads to the tutoring center.

From the mudflats deep inside me, something lifts its head with great effort and shouts, What are you trying to do? What are you trying to achieve by digging out obscure little details? Don't try to make a summary, lining up events in chronological order. That will only make it more and more unnatural. You're not under the illusion that life is a movie, are you? You're not thinking life can have a linear plot, are you?

He told me, It was after my father passed away. I remember I was at the sink, he said, brushing my teeth. My father, he used to clear his throat with a dry cough, you know, in the middle of brushing his teeth, and it was after his death and I was brushing my teeth and I found myself clearing my throat with a dry cough. I stopped brushing. Unable to think the sound had come from me, I looked around for Father. Only a while later I said to myself, Ah, that's right. Ah, that's right. Father has passed away. I resumed brushing, feeling quite strange. That was the moment I actually felt Father's absence for the first time. The feeling of absence, I think, can manifest itself in such unexpected places. Absence by death is especially difficult to feel at first. Gradually, we realize in our everyday lives that the person is no longer here, that we cannot see him again. Through things like a chair that he liked to sit in when he was alive; the spot where he used to keep his soapdish; the way he wore his socks—things like that. These things are not included in history. Or in chronology.

Third Brother grows more and more gaunt. I secretly put 3,000 won in his pocket, then Cousin says we are out of briquettes.

"What will we do, we've used up our living allowance."

I retrieve the 3,000 won from Third Brother's pocket and give it to Cousin.

But he grows more and more gaunt. When I take out the empty lunchbox from his schoolbag, along come handouts printed with the words "Down with Dictatorship, Abolish Yusin Constitution." He returns late at night, takes off his clothes, drenched with the smell of teargas, lies down next to Oldest Brother and goes to sleep. He does not say much about anything. One night we are heading straight home without having to stop for groceries. We get off the bus and are walking down the tree-lined street amidst the factories when Cousin calls out, "It's Third Brother!" On a bench under one of the trees, Third Brother is sleeping with his schoolbag tucked under his head. I shake him awake.

"*Oppa*, what are you doing, sleeping out here?"

"I thought I'd lie down for a minute, but fell asleep."

He slowly stirs himself up. Then one morning I am packing his lunch but cannot find his lunch box.

"Get your lunch box for me."

Still, no lunch box appears. I open the door and ask him again to get it.

"I lost it."

"Your lunch box?"

"I was sleeping on that bench yesterday and someone took my bag."

"Why would you sleep out there? You should come back to the room and sleep."

Brother smiles shyly.

"The room's crammed as it is and if I'm back that early, you two will feel uncomfortable, changing and washing up."

•••

One day, Oldest Brother brings to our lone, remote room, a woman with a face like a doll's.

"This is my sister and this, my cousin."

This doll-like woman's name is Mi-yeong. She has huge eyes. She has long lashes, a small build, and a yellow gold necklace dangling on her long neck. She has delicate fingers, wears high heels and a short skirt. The woman stays for a while, sitting there in the room, then leaves.

"Who is she, *Oppa*?"

". . ."

"Your girlfriend?"

". . ."

"What did you bring her here for?"

"Why, you don't like her?"

"Well, that's not the point."

"What is it then?"

"You should have taken her somewhere else instead of bringing her here. That's stupid. If I were your girlfriend, I'd run away."

"How come?"

"I don't know. It just occurred to me."

Oldest Brother says, "Why, you little. . . ." and laughs. He tells me she wouldn't do that but I start feeling anxious that she will someday bring him sadness.

•••

I arrive at school one day to find a daytime program student waiting for me.

"Did you happen to take my PE uniform from the locker?"

I shake my head.

"Where did they go?"

Number fifty-six. She and I share the same desk and locker. She slams the locker shut and stomps out, carrying her schoolbag.

"I can't wait to move on to our second year."

In her second year, she would not have to share her classroom with us. She will move to the main building. Since our program has only a few classes, we will not move to the main building even in our third year. The student comes back and fires stinging words.

"Please keep your hands off the locker."

When she's gone, I step in front of the mirror. My eyes appear blank. Mi-seo walks over and asks what's wrong.

"Her PE uniform's missing."

"And she says you took them?"

". . ."

"Why are you standing there doing nothing when you've been wrongly accused?"

"I'm not just standing here doing nothing. I'm very upset right now."

At my brusque response, Mi-seo, who works at a pharmaceutical company, once again pulls out her Hegel and reads.

I don't want to go to school. I don't want to do abacus calculation and I don't want to take out my bookkeeping notebook. I tell Cousin that I'm not coming to school anymore.

"What are you talking about?"

"I don't want to go to school."

"You? Not wanting to go to school?"

Cousin laughs as if she can't believe me.

"Starting today, I'm not going to school. You go on alone."

Cousin just smiles, as if she were hearing a joke, but when, at five o'clock, I turn onto the street that leads to our lone room instead of to the bus stop, she pulls my arm.

"What's wrong?"

I just stare at her.

"You're really going to quit?"

I nod.

"Stop joking now, we're going to be late."

"I'm serious. I'm not going."

"Oldest Brother's going to get very upset, you know that."

"How will he find out unless you tell him?"

"What is it all of a sudden?"

"I don't like school anymore."

"What don't you like about it?"

"I don't like abacus calculation, I don't like bookkeeping. There's nothing I like. So you go on. I'll get the groceries, do the cleaning, have everything done."

"What if Oldest Brother happens to come home early?"

We part and I walk slowly along the streets of the industrial complex and back to the lone room. It looks like Oldest Brother just now changed out of his military uniform and into his suit, put on his wig and left again. I hang his uniform on a nail and sit around idly. Unable to quite grasp the fact that I am alone in this room, which has always felt crowded, I sit, then stand, then try lying down. I lie on my stomach and read a few pages of *Saban's Cross*, the book Chang gave me, then lie with my eyes to the ceiling, then turn over again and start writing a letter to Chang. I no longer want to endure everything. What I wanted to do at school was not abacus calculation or typing. I wanted to read books and write. In order to do that, I thought I had to go to school. But it seems this school has nothing to do with any of that. I stop here and open the window to look out at the subway station. Each time a train makes a stop, a mass of heads surges up, then they disappear in an instant. I step out to the kitchen and take out the bottle of *soju* from the bottom shelf of the cupboard, pour a small amount and drink. I come back and continue to write.

. . . There are only horrible people around.

I head out to the subway station and squat down to wait for Oldest Brother. It is almost midnight when he walks out the exit from afar.

"*Oppa*!"

His eyes, sunken deep from fatigue, turn wide with wonder. Seeing him out here, wearing his wig, I feel as if he is a stranger, not my family. I burst into giggles, as if I've run into some comical character. He seems to find it funny as well, and when we turn into the alley, he takes the wig off and carries it in his hand.

"How come you're out here? How come?"

"I was bored."

"You have time to be bored?"

Oldest Brother, walking ahead of me, breaks into a hollow laughter.

The next day, upon returning from school, Hui-jae *eonni* comes up to the third floor and opens my door. It looks like she hasn't even stopped by her own room because she's carrying her schoolbag in one hand. In the other, she's carrying a white paper bag filled round and taut with something. She does not even ask why I wasn't at school. She puts down the paper bag and just smiles faintly before heading back down the stairs. The sound of her footsteps tapping down the stairs to the first floor. I look inside to find sweet chrysanthemum buns, still warm inside the bag.

It has been about a week since I've stopped going to school. Returning from school, Cousin opens the door and calls me quietly.

"Your teacher's here."

I stare blankly at Cousin.

"He said he wants to pay a home visit, so I brought him."

I'm anxious that Oldest Brother might come home and see him, but Teacher Choe takes his time looking around the room. He asks me to walk with him to the bus stop. I put on my shoes and jacket and follow him out. Outside in the alley, he gently taps my shoulder.

"So what is going on?" I stare silently ahead.

"I noticed you're a reader and that you seemed to enjoy school, so why is it that suddenly you've stopped coming to school?"

". . ."

"Was I wrong?"

". . ."

"The school makes it a rule to report to the company if a student doesn't show up for class."

I guess they would. And when a student quits work, the school would probably be notified. One qualifies to attend school only if she is working. If I don't go to school, I will not be able to leave the conveyor belt at five o'clock. At the bus stop, Teacher Choe urges me to come to school the following day.

"Let's talk further once you're back at school."

As he gets on the bus, he waves his hand at me. Behind his hand, rows of factory chimneys stand tall and jagged. I feel as if I've met a person at the factory for the first time. After the bus has left, I stay standing there. Putting my hand on my shoulder, still warm from Teacher Choe's touch.

The following day, Teacher Choe calls me to the office and tells me to write a self-examination about missing school.

"Write down everything you want to say and hand it in in three days."

To write the self-examination, I buy a college notebook at the student supply store across from the school. Just as I had written such and such about why Cousin and I must attend school to the union leader, this time I write such and such about why I do not want to go to school to my teacher, and as I write, things start pouring out from my heart.

I write that this was not the city life that I had in mind, and that this was not the school life that I had in mind. That I don't want to do abacus calculations or bookkeeping, that the only thing in my mind right now is Little Brother and that what I want is to go back and live with Little Brother. The self-examination turns out long, almost one third of the notebook.

After reading my self-examination, Teacher Choe says this to me.

"Why don't you try writing novels?"

This word, writing, fell on me. This was the first time someone ever said this to me. Try writing novels.

He went on. "You don't have to do abacus calculations if you don't want to. Just come to school. I'll talk to the other teachers. Do whatever it is you want to do. But you must not miss school."

He hands me a book. "This is the best novel I've read recently."

On the cover is written, *The Dwarf Launches His Tiny Ball.* I return to the classroom and open it.

The math teacher walked into the classroom. The students noticed that he was not carrying his book in his hand. The students trusted the teacher. He was the only teacher in the school whom the students trusted.

My teacher Mr. Choe Hong-i. Now I go to school in order to see him. All the longing that had been locked up inside my heart after making an uneasy move away from home finds new direction and heads toward Teacher Choe. I, seventeen years old, carry *The Dwarf Launches His Tiny Ball* with me always. Wherever I go, I read *The Dwarf Launches His Tiny Ball.* I almost know it by heart. Hui-jae *eonni* asks me what kind of a book it is.

"A novel."

"Novel?" she asks, just once, and turns her head down, looking uninterested. Teacher Choe fills my heart completely. Even when I don't work on my abacus, the abacus teacher passes me by. Even when I don't write balance sheets in my bookkeeping notebook, the bookkeeping teacher does not make a case of it.

In abacus class, I open my Korean class notebook to the last page and copy down *The Dwarf Launches His Tiny Ball.*

> People called Father a dwarf. People saw right. Father was a dwarf. Unfortunately, people were right only about how they saw Father. They were wrong about everything else. I am willing to risk everything that belongs to the five of us in our family—Father, Mother, Yeong-ho, Yeong-hui and me—to say at any given time that they were wrong. When I say "everything," it includes the lives of the five members of our family.

I now transcribe *The Dwarf Launches His Tiny Ball* onto my notebook even when I am sitting at the conveyor belt. People who lived in heaven did not have to think about hell, I write. But the five of us lived in hell and thought about heaven, I write. Not a day went by that we did not think about heaven, I write. For each day of our life wore us down, I write. Our life was like war, I write. We lost every day in that war, I write.

Mother, however, endured everything, I write.

If Teacher Choe had suggested that I write poetry instead of suggesting that I write novels, then I would have dreamed of becoming a poet. That was how it was. I needed a dream. In order to make it to school every day; to not be bothered as I brushed Oldest Brother's wig; to endure the smoke from the factory chimneys; to live on.

This was how novel writing came to me.

I carried the letter from the teacher at the factory school, Han Gyeong-sin, with me in my bag into mid-December. From time to time I pulled out the letter and read the part that said that I could call this phone number from five thirty to nine in the evening. 842-4596. After pulling out the letter and reading it, again and again, I now had her phone number memorized. But in the end, I was unable to call her. Time kept passing and the weeks between early and mid-December, which was when Han Gyeong-sin had wanted me to visit, were gone. When I got to thinking, They should be on winter vacation now, I took the letter from my bag and put it inside a drawer, counting the years since I left that school. It had been thirteen years. I had thought I would have gained objective distance by now. When I had decided to write about them, it had seemed that I had overcome that time in my life. That was why I had decided to write in as much detail as I could about that time. To restore my memory from that time so that I might open up, so that my footsteps, which had been cut off at the closed gate of my life, might be reconnected.

But it turned out my wounds had yet to harden. It seemed I had not been able to overcome anything. It seemed that my desire had triumphed even before the wounds had hardened. My desire to write something about that time before I grew too distant from it, before I had nothing to say about it, had moved on beyond me. If not, how could I be so anxious, so ashamed, so scared that I was surprised at myself? How could I let myself be won over by my wariness of others, focused singularly on self-protection? If the wounds had hardened, if what had happened had been overcome, then why would my eyes keep welling up with tears?

If someone said to me that he had read the first chapter that had been published, I would no longer want to be with that person all of a sudden. I wanted to quickly get away from the person and be alone.

As December came and went and New Year arrived, I became extremely passive. I felt either too upset or too numb. I did not read or listen to music or turn on the television. I would either be standing or sitting or lying down when I would happen to notice something like a strand of hair stuck on my soap and have a fit. After undergoing an internal uproar, like picking up every single breadcrumb from the floor by stamping each one with spit on my finger, I ended up feeling dazed. I would go to sleep at any time of the day, which meant there was never a time when I could sleep soundly. I had an annoying headache on any given day, and when someone talked to me, I would cling to some small random thing they said and interpret the meaning in the worst way possible.

One early morning, I opened the front door to get the paper, pushed the paper inside, then walked outside. It was the kind of morning where the snow overnight had formed soft, thick heaps on the cars parked in the plaza. Standing between other people's cars, I looked up at the window of the apartment that I had just left. My window was the only one that was brightly lit; everyone else probably still asleep. I had a strange feeling, gazing at my own window from the outside. I walked past the closed dry cleaners, the art studio, the pork-and-potato stew place, and on and on. I hesitated for a while when the road came to a fork, then headed toward the hills. The hills, both near and far, were covered with snow. I had made it about halfway toward the temple that I had often hiked to before winter came. At a distance four or five hikers were gathered around, looking anxious. In a corner next to where the people were standing lay a man in blue hiking gear, I would say in his mid-forties, his body twisted and foam at his mouth.

"Looks like a seizure."

The mountain path, covered with snow, was cold and narrow. It seemed no one among the crowd had been hiking with the man.

"He's going to fall down the valley. What'll we do?"

Some five minutes passed like this. Then in an instant the man's body stopped its twisting. His arms and legs went limp, like they were drained of all energy, then the man gently lifted himself up. His eyes were still hollow. The man seemed dazed for a moment, like he did not know why he was lying there, then quickly got to his feet. He brushed the snow off his clothes and wiped the foam off his mouth with his sleeve, then set out trudging down the hill. The people who had gathered, on their way up, not down, the mountain, headed up again, glancing back at the man. I stood on the spot where the man had lain twisting his arms and legs and gazed at the man's back as he descended the hill. There were still lumps of snow on his clothes. When he disappeared from my sight, as I put my palms together to warm my cold hands, I was once again surprised at myself. While I was gazing at the man's back as he walked down the snow-covered path after recovering from his seizure, my nerves had calmed, surprisingly.

Hiking Path Closed. A wooden sign hammered into the winter mountain path. A forbidden road. As I stood gazing down the road where I was prohibited from, my listlessness lifted and my senses came alive again. I stopped in my path and turned around. I felt a longing. For myself. For the person writing at the desk. This longing swiftly whipped up inside my head. I even missed the sense of distance that I had so feared. I saw in front of my eyes myself, sitting at the desk, just as I would when I was thinking of someone else. I wanted to hurry back home and be captivated by writing once more. I ran. I got into a taxi that was waiting at the start of the hiking path.

My headache finally lifted. No internal turmoil, even with six strands of hair on the floor; when I got to thinking about the uncertainty of my future, I said to myself, Well, there's nothing I can do about it. While I am writing at least, it seemed that nature, which I lacked, seeped into me. Mountain paths and water routes and plains.

With only a few days to go until summer vacation, Kim Sam-ok, the oldest student in our class, who sits in front of me, comes over to Mi-seo as she's reading Hegel and tells her that she will not be able to come to school starting the following day.

"How come?"

"There's going to be an all-night sit-in."

Kim Sam-ok is in the same grade and same class as we are, but we use honorifics when we talk to her since she's six years older. Mi-seo closes the Hegel and asks, "They will let you stay in school even when you participated in sit-ins?"

"The company closed down without prior notice."

We are mute with shock.

"They closed down the dormitory and the cafeteria as well. . . . If we do not come and collect our retirement allowance and severance pay, they're going to deposit the money with the court."

"What about school, then?" Mi-seo asks.

"I don't care about school. I have to work. How can I survive if the company closed down without any plans? I also have to send money back home to the country."

I gaze blankly at Kim Sam-ok as she talks with Mi-seo. How much money does she make, if she can send some of her earnings back home? Mi-seo must have thought the same thing.

"You've been sending money home all this time?"

A meek laugh escapes her lips as Kim Sam-ok spits out her answer. "I made a single tube of toothpaste last three years. Get the picture?"

Summer. An intense heat wave. Third Brother goes back to the country for summer vacation and Cousin's older brother, who attends college in Jeonju, comes to Seoul. Hui-jae invites me over to sleep in her room, worried that our room might get too hot with four people sleeping in there. I ask Oldest Brother and he flares up.

"How can a girl think about spending the night outside of home?"

"But it's only Hui-jae *eonni*'s room."

"Enough of this nonsense!"

Oldest Brother buys some *chamoe* melons and puts them in water inside a rubber bucket under the tap in the kitchen. When I get back from work and open the kitchen door, I see the melons floating on the water. When he gets back late from the tutoring center, Oldest Brother exclaims as he slices a melon.

"I can't believe that a fruit can taste this good!"

One Saturday, Oldest Brother suddenly sits up in the middle of the night. He jerks himself up with such force that I, who was asleep next to him, stir awake as well. I'm soaked in sweat from the heat and my back feels sticky. The summer moonlight pours in through the window and I can see the attic door without turning on the light. Oldest Brother speaks as if he's shouting.

"Jae-gyu, I want you to leave tomorrow."

Our male cousin Jae-gyu, who had just come to stay with us for the summer, jumps up from his slumber. Cousin, who was facing the wall, wakes up as well. Jae-gyu is her brother.

"Please leave, will you?"

He does not respond.

Oldest Brother's voice is firm. At the break of dawn, while Oldest Brother has gone up to the roof, Cousin Jae-gyu gets dressed and leaves the lone room. Cousin sets out after him. Returning from the roof, Oldest Brother asks where everyone has gone. When I tell him that Cousin Jae-gyu left, saying he's going back to the country, and Cousin went to see him off, Oldest Brother gets mad.

"He left without even staying for breakfast just because of what I said?"

When I, having been on my toes all night, well up with tears, Oldest Brother yells again.

"What are you crying for? Did someone die?"

It's almost noon but Cousin still isn't home from seeing her brother off. Scared of Oldest Brother, ranting angrily about how Jae-gyu could just leave like that without even saying good-bye just because of what he said, and about why Cousin, who had gone to see him off, was so late getting back, I, seventeen years old, sit crouched next to the kitchen cupboard. I've served him breakfast but Oldest Brother is too upset to eat. I open the bottom cabinet of the cupboard and see the bottle of *soju*, wrapped inside the yellow paper bag. I take it out and, after filling a rice bowl halfway, drink it in sips.

"Come in here." Oldest Brother calls a while later. I stay sitting there stubbornly. When I don't come in, Oldest Brother pushes open the door. He pushes it so hard that it hits the hot water tank installed above the fuel hole and bounces shut, then opens once again.

"Why aren't you coming in?"

As I lift myself up, I feel my head spin. I walk into the room and sit with my back against the wall. Oldest Brother sits at the desk and speaks with his back to me.

"I wasn't being angry with you."

As soon as I hear these words, I break into tears, overcome with anguish. Surprised at my crying, Oldest Brother looks back at me in confusion.

Once I start, I cannot hold back my tears. I even start getting hiccups in between tearful gasps. Oldest Brother gets down to the floor and shakes me.

"What is this smell? Have you been drinking?"

Dumbfounded, Oldest Brother wets a towel, squeezes out water and wipes my face.

"You must be crazy."

After crying myself to exhaustion, I fall asleep.

"Crazy, that's what you are."

I keep waking up and falling asleep again as the hiccups return in between sobs. When Cousin returns at night, Oldest Brother talks to her in the kitchen.

"I didn't say what I said because I have anything against Jae-gyu."

She does not answer.

"It was just too hot . . . Would I have acted that way if we had two rooms?"

After this, Oldest Brother says nothing when I sneak away to Hui-jae *eonni*'s room and spend the night there. Cousin, who dislikes Hui-jae, never comes to her room. When I ask why not, Cousin says that Hui-jae has a strange smell.

"Smell? What smell?"

Cousin, unable to find the right words, mumbles, "She's got this smell, she does . . ."

I remember the room Hui-jae lived in. The kitchen, with barely enough room for two people to stand and turn around. The first thing you see when you open the kitchen is a shelf. A pair of purple high heels sit on the shelf. She would have worn these heels before she started school. Each time I enter her room, I bump my head on the shelf with the pair of purple heels. One would think I'd be more careful after a few times, but I still bump my head every time. The first time I bumped my head on the shelf, Hui-jae said, wearing her faint smile, "You're tall." But it has nothing to do with height. Hui-jae, who is a handspan shorter than me also bumped her head on the shelf from time to time. Each time I bump my head, this is what she says.

"You'll get used to it. I also used to bump my head every single time, but now it happens only once in a while."

The windowsill is her dressing table. The scenery that the window possesses is one of a red brick wall from the house next door. She never opens the window. After I got to know Hui-jae's room, I realized that our room was the brightest, at least among the thirty-seven rooms in this building. From our room, we can see the vacant lot outside the window, the last stop for the number 118 bus, the factory chimneys, the subway station, and the sky, but from Hui-jae's room, the scenery outside the window is the wall. Then one day, I see that her lotion bottle has been taken down from the windowsill to the wooden floor table and the window is open. I look down from her window. It seems that the rain gutters on both houses spout down this wall and the ground at the foot of the wall is soggy. It looks like a swamp, deep enough to reach one's shins. The surface is scattered with a dizzy clutter of cigarette butts, empty packs of *ramyeon*, and chewing gum wrappers.

"Looks like it's never been cleaned," I mumble.

She approaches and says, "Look at that," pointing to the ground under the window. I look to find a chopstick sticking straight up in the mud.

"It looked so soggy so I tried shooting a chopstick, like shooting an arrow. That's how it ended up like that." Smiling faintly, she closes the window and puts the bottles of lotion and toner back on the sill. Next to them, also the jar of moisturizing cream. The seascape vinyl wardrobe; wooden floor table; small radio; the seashell necklace hanging on the wall; the brand-new iron, which she got for ironing the collars for her uniform, still inside the box.

When I think of Hui-jae *eonni*'s room, I seem to remember more about the objects than the person inside the room. Things like the photograph pinned on the wall of her younger brother or the plastic dish the size of a hand, filled with hairpins. The yellow laminated paper flooring, the sugar scoop. Probably because it was so new. I remember the iron more vividly than any other object in her room. "I bought it to iron my uniform collars"—her voice from back then is also just as vivid, as if she were talking to me here by my side.

Vivid, I write, which is a surprise for me. To think, I have come to use the word "vivid" to describe her. She was always faint. All of her routines were mute, like freckles hidden under the chin or under the ears. The reason that Cousin, frank and outgoing, felt uncomfortable around her was probably because of her quiet ways. She was so quiet that at times it made people nervous.

And it did, even for me. When she sat on the roof enjoying the sun, or was in her room, unmoving, I was compelled to approach and shake her. Thinking back now, her quietness might have been her balance, but at the time, when I saw her small body captured by this quietness, it seemed as if her soul had left her body and I would feel compelled to shake her to get her to come to her senses.

I shake her up and we play the Sure Game.

"I want to be a phone operator."

"Sure."

"I want to be a certified operator and work at a bank."

"Sure."

"What do you want to be?"

"Sure."

"No, what do you want to be, I asked."

"What?"

"I want to be a novelist."

She echoes, "Novel?" And dozes off in the heat of the summer night.

She awakes from her dozing and murmurs. "The first factory I worked at was in Bongcheon-dong. I was fifteen or something. And the factory was tiny. We made bags, less than forty of us in all. We ate and slept in the rooms at the factory, where I met So Yong-tak, this boy from Jin-do Island. It was really nice to have him around. I unstitched seams in the attic and he worked on the sewing machine in the room. He was a guy but he was very good with the sewing machine. He looked like a girl. I liked that about him, but he seemed to hate his girlish looks. He consciously tried to act tough and manly but I knew everything. The attic where I unstitched and picked seams had ceilings so low that it touched my head when I stood. We had just come back from summer break and he climbed into the attic and handed me something wrapped in white paper. I opened it to find a seashell necklace. He had made it out of shells he collected on the beach back home on Jin-do. We got a room at the top of the hill in Bongcheon-dong and lived together for about four months."

"Are you surprised?"

"I am."

She stops her story and says nothing.

"Then what happened?"

"What? . . . I ran away."

"Ran away? How come?"

"You see, I have a younger brother back home in the country. He was coming to visit me. I was scared. I didn't want him to see me that way. No, that's an excuse, I felt like I was suffocating. I had the feeling that if I continued to live there with the boy, I would never again be able to come down from that hill. Never again. So one Sunday, while he was napping, I said I was going to the store for some *ramyeon* and never went back."

". . ."

"I took nothing with me when I walked out. Nothing but that necklace in my pocket."

I, seventeen years old, gaze at the seashell necklace on the wall.

"You never saw him again?"

"No. I can't say for sure, but he probably wept terribly. He's no taller than me."

"Don't you miss him?"

"It was all years ago."

After talking in a faint voice, as if she were mumbling to herself, Hui-jae looks right at me and asks, "Can a story like this make a novel?"

Our summer vacation is almost over. We are suddenly told that we have to ship more than a thousand stereo systems at the end of the month. Overtime and all-night shifts continue day after day. One day as we are about to have our late-night snacks, I tell Cousin that I cannot possibly pull another all-nighter.

"But vacation's almost over . . . What can we do, everyone else is going to work all night . . . They won't allow any exceptions."

"Really, I'm not just saying I can't. I'm dying here."

"Are you sick?"

"It's like my back is about to snap and my tummy as well."

"I wonder what the matter is, out of the blue."

"It's not out of the blue. I felt bad yesterday and the day before as well, but it was bearable. But now it's impossible to bear."

Cousin stands up and goes to talk to Foreman.

"He wouldn't hear it. . . . Just hold on a little longer. He said after tonight, the really urgent stuff will be done."

Dawn arrives. Grasping my aching, twisting tummy, I rise from my workstation and head to the bathroom, and Cousin sets out after me, following close behind.

"What can this be?" I ask, leaning my painful back against the bathroom wall, Cousin bursts into a giggle.

"You must've been having menstrual cramps. Stay right here. I'll go and get a change of clothing and pads from the locker room."

After Cousin leaves, I turn back to look at my hips in the mirror. Startled, I collapse to a squat. Worried that someone might come in, I lock myself in one of the toilet stalls.

Summer vacation is over, but Kim Sam-ok does not show up at school. Every time he checks attendance, Teacher Choe Hong-i glances at Kim Sam-ok's seat. He asks those of us who work at the same factory as Kim Sam-ok to raise our hands. Without raising her hand, someone says, "The company went out of business."

"Which company is it?"

"It's YH."

The entire class turns silent. Teacher Choe calls Mi-seo, the class president, to the office. Would he pay a visit to Kim Sam-ok's home as well? Back from the teachers' office, Mi-seo once again opens the Hegel.

"What did he say?"

"He asked me to find out what happened to her."

"Will you be able to do that?"

"I don't know. There's someone in our company who used to work at YH, so I guess I'll try asking her."

"What kind of a company is it?"

"It's a wig factory. Haven't you heard of this woman who jumped off the New Democratic Party headquarters building? Kim Gyeong-suk! Hey, they have the same name."

"Kim Sam-ok worked there?"

"Yes."

"How did this woman die?"

"From the fall, but the artery on her left wrist was slashed. She cut it with a soda bottle shard."

The next day when I meet her at the shoe locker as we're arriving at school, Mi-seo suggests that we go get a snack at the stall.

"You know, about Kim Sam-ok."

I stop in the middle of drinking my water and gaze straight at her.

"She's missing."

"What are you talking about?"

"It sounded like things got pretty intense while school was out. Kim Sam-ok was also at the New Democratic Party headquarters. Even the lawmakers and the reporters were soaked in blood, so imagine how the protesting factory workers got treated."

"How?"

"The police raided even the party chairman's office. Saying they're going to kill everyone if they don't behave. Kim Sam-ok also got beaten up and was taken away by the police . . ."

"And?"

"She was released, but she was going about crying day in and day out, that it was she who should have died, not Gyeong-suk, the younger one.

"She was taken into custody, then was deported back home to the country."

"So she's home now, then?"

"That's not it." Mi-seo puts down her pastry.

"Why aren't you eating?"

"I don't feel like eating, thinking about Kim Sam-ok. When they were taking her away, she tried to resist by jumping out of the window of the riot police bus and hurt her leg, which made her limp.

"Now her younger brother is in Seoul looking for her. When she was sent back home, she sat crouched in the attic day after day, then one day she disappeared."

"Where could she have gone?"

"The girl who told me all this said we must keep it a secret. Whether you participated in the sit-ins or not, if you ever worked for YH, nobody will hire you now. That girl sent around her résumé, trying to get a job somewhere else, but failed for no clear reason. She found out that a list of those who had been at the New Democratic Party headquarters, and anyone who had participated in the sit-ins, had been handed over to all the other companies."

"Then how was she able to get a job at your factory?"

"She covered it up by submitting her sister's papers."

Upon returning from the snack stall, Mi-seo once again starts reading the Hegel. I, seventeen years old, stretch out my neck toward her and ask.

"How old was Kim Gyeong-suk, the girl who died?"

"Twenty-one."

While the parts that I could overlook, I remember in great detail, some parts that should resurface naturally are in a void, like a street in ruins. What became of Kim Sam-ok after that? No matter how I hard I try to find her, she is nowhere to be found.

All I can find now, in the archives at the *Dong-a Ilbo* or *Hankook Ilbo* newspapers, is this:

> A car horn tooted three long honks. This signal launched the so-called Operation 101. With six fire engines lighting the scene, the fire squad laid out mattresses outside the party headquarters to prepare in case the factory girls attempted to jump off the building, while the police raided through the main entrance and over the wall behind the building, gaining access into the fourth-floor auditorium and the chairman's office and press room on the second floor using two tall ladder trucks. The police clashed with the New Democratic Party's administrative staff, who had built a barricade with chairs and desks, and the building quickly turned chaotic as the police moved up to the second floor, throwing tear gas bombs. Inside the fourth-floor auditorium, where the factory workers were staging the sit-in, a group of plainclothes policemen were the first to pour in, shutting and blocking the windows, after which hundreds of riot police entered, wielding their clubs as they dragged out the factory girls one by one down the staircase and into the police bus parked outside the main entrance of the building to take them away. Chairman Kim of the New Democratic Party had dissuaded the factory girls from leaping to their deaths, but they panicked when the police stormed in, crying and resisting with broken soda bottles, and several tried to break the windowpanes with their fists and jump

out, but were stopped by the police. In just ten minutes, all the protesters were pulled out of the building. In the course of the raid, some of the factory girls attempted suicide, using shards from the broken windows and soda bottles. Kim Gyeong-suk, the deceased, was found collapsed by the basement entrance at the back of the building, her left wrist artery slashed, and was taken to the Green Cross Hospital across the street. In teams of four, the police carried the female workers by their hands and feet, taking away every single protester in ten minutes.

On August 13, a funeral was held for Kim Gyeong-suk at the Seoul Municipal Gangnam Hospital's funeral parlor, attended by three family members including Kim's mother, YH Trading staff, and the police. The ceremony took three minutes and her remains were cremated.

In the vacant lot that the window of the lone room looked out on, lettuce leaves are sprouting. Who could have planted them? Whichever way the world turns, the lettuce grows. However, they simply grow bigger; their insides do not fill up. The green lettuce leaves are covered with black dust from the factories.

It was five fifteen in the morning. My doorbell suddenly rang for a long stretch. Who could it be, in the middle of the New Year holidays, at this hour? I jumped to my feet, pushed the door open in the room, and called out toward the front door in an exaggerated voice.

"Who is it?"

Nothing but quiet. My heart pounded with surging fear.

"Who is it?"

Nothing but quiet. My ears perked up and I struggled to listen for any signs of movement outside the door, but nothing was heard. It could be my aunt from the country. This aunt, widowed while young, lived alone those young years, in a house with a garden that faced the newly paved main road. It was through her that we could hear the stories about the generations of our family that came before Father. Your grandfather, he ran a traditional herbal medicine shop . . . And your grandmother . . . During the days of the Korean People's Republic before the war . . . When we passed a ditch along the rice paddies, she would say, All this used to be your family's land, from there to there . . . When we passed a house with piles of firewood, she would say, Back then, yours was the only family in the village that kept piles of firewood . . . Aunt used to help out Grandfather in his shop in her childhood, measuring the medicine on a scale and wrapping it in white pouches, and whenever someone complained of an ache, she would come up with names of this or that medicinal herb, offering an endless concoction of prescriptions . . . Boil it with this or that, but don't drink it right away, expose it to morning dew.

My aunt the young widow. Whenever I was with her, I didn't feel like it was just the two of us but that we were there with Grandfather and Great-grandfather, Grandmother and Great-grandmother, and all of Grandfather's siblings, who I heard had died in a mass killing during the war. I liked this feeling and disliked it at the same time. When my aunt, the young widow, heard someone outside, no matter how late at night, she would fling open her door, shouting "Who is it," and gaze out at the garden.

I could not bring myself to open the door. I knew that my aunt could not possibly be the one there. I wanted to open it to check who had made the sound, but I was too afraid, so much so that I felt a chill on my forehead. The best I could do was come back to my room, pushing the door closed as hard as I could, so that the sound could be heard loud and clear. Even after returning to my room and sitting back at my desk, my ears were focused on the sounds outside the door. Had I heard wrong? It was clearly the doorbell, but at this hour, in the middle of the night? I was rubbing my chest when I felt someone's presence behind me. I looked back, startled. My shawl, which I had left on the backrest of the chair, had slipped down to the floor. As I reached down to pick it up, a sigh of relief escaped from me.

It seemed that someone entered this room.

It seemed that someone, who, even if I were to ask, Who is it? was incapable of saying out loud, It's me, was standing behind me, gazing down at the back of my neck.

That's it. I turned out the light and got into my bed. This presence followed me and crouched down beside me.

Is it you, Hui-jae *eonni*?

Is it you?

You startled me.

How did you come all the way here?

I have a very good life, you're thinking, right?

I'm sorry.

At first, wherever I was, I would break into tears. You would weigh down on me, making it impossible for me to sleep. I don't remember the dreams I had. But I would wake from a dream and realize that you are dead, and then each time, I would break into tears.

You'd already know even if I don't tell you, you probably saw everything. That for a long time, I cried and had dreams. For a long time, I kept track of the passing time with you. When spring came around, I told myself, *My first spring without you.* Then spring came around again, my second spring without you, then spring came around again, my third spring without you, then my fourth spring without you. Then little by little it faded.

What did you say?

Eonni? What are you trying to tell me?

I can't make it out. Speak a little louder, what?

What?

I can't hear you—I can't, what did you say?

No matter what you might say, I am going to write you. I'm not sure if I will be able to bring you back to life exactly the way you were before. I used to think, sometimes, that one day, when I can call them my friends, I would like to make a place for them, and for you—a dignified place of your own. A dignified place, socially or perhaps culturally. In order to do that, I would have to closely follow the truth, and my truth about you. It was not when I was gazing into my memories, or into the photographs that remain, that I was able to be truthful. Those things were empty. Only when I was writing down this and that, lying on my tummy, I was able to understand myself. I am trying to reach you through my writing.

What was that?

Speak a little louder. What are you saying?

Huh?

Stay outside of literature? Is that what you are telling me?

Where is outside of literature?

Where are you right now?

October. Outside the window of our lone room, in the vacant lot by the bus stop at the end of the route for the number 118, the lettuce leaves finally grow green. October, when the lettuce, attended by no one and covered in dust from the factories, had grown to the size of a hand. Each time she looks out at the lettuce patch, Cousin whispers that whoever this person is, he must be very rich.

"He'll get fined if he leaves the lot unoccupied, so he just scattered some lettuce seeds, to make it look like a vegetable plot."

"Next year, houses will go up over here and there. No more view of the lot then."

One day in October, we stand on the athletic field where dusk is falling, listening to the old principal's teary speech. This is what he says. That the president has passed away. That the man who presented us with so much opportunity passed away from a gunshot. The old principal speaks in a choking voice, then starts weeping, standing there with his back to the setting sun. All those years of hardship, he devoted himself to national salvation . . . We stand at ease and gaze at the old principal's grief. The old principal, taking out his handkerchief and wiping his tears. With the handkerchief in his hand, the old principal goes on about the dead president, then weeps, then goes on talking again, then wipes his tears. At first we gaze blankly at his tears, then someone starts sniffling. When one person starts sniffling, another sniffles. The sounds of sniffling here and there mingle together.

I, seventeen years old, am unable to sniffle and just stand there, looking down at my feet. I feel sorry that I cannot weep when everyone else does. A few years ago, when his wife was shot at the August 15 Liberation Ceremony, I cried and cried, but this time, no tears would come to me, only the sound of gunshots in my ears. I had heard the news of the president's wife being shot amidst the midday heat. Someone said, Yuk Young-soo was shot dead. It was too unexpected and I couldn't believe it at first, thought it was a joke.

How can someone so beautiful die? I had no particular feelings for the president, but his wife I liked. Her hair, always done up in an elegant chignon, her neck long like a crane's, the stylish hem of her traditional blouse, her smile, which reminded me of hydrangeas . . . It seemed as if she would always be there, in that style, in that image. But now she's been shot? The First Lady resembled a magnolia blossom but her favorite flower was the chrysanthemum, they said. Chrysanthemums began piling up as high as a mountain and the radio played Handel's *Sarabande* for days on end. The villagers neglected work and spoke in whispers. The First Lady is dead. She was shot by a North Korean spy. The miller who lived at the edge of the village had a TV, and a straw mat was laid out on his yard. The villagers sat around, row after row, gazing at the screen of the TV set in the main hall of the miller's house.

The screen showed the president wiping his tears as he watched the First Lady's hearse, decorated with a mound of chrysanthemums, leave Cheongwa-dae. It was heart-rending to watch the husband who had lost his wife to a bullet. The villagers wept. I, a child, wept along with them. After this I saw from time to time First Daughter Geun Hye taking her mother's place next to the president. She had a beautiful and delicate profile. I felt a sting at the tip of my nose, to think such a beautiful person has lost her mother. First Daughter Geun Hye looked just like my beloved First Lady. Her smile like a magnolia blossom, her neck long like a crane's. And now she has lost her father, she has now been orphaned. I gaze down at my feet and think about this person, who is now alone.

We have returned from the athletic field and are sitting in our classroom. Teacher Choe Hong-i seems dumbfounded at the students, their eyes red from weeping along with the old principal.

"What, may I ask, are you crying about?"

Silence falls on the class. Teacher Choe speaks in a low but firm voice.

"A regime that came into power through a coup d'état has now come to an end, in the hands of one of its subordinates. A corrupt dictatorship that has continued for eighteen years has collapsed. Now the Yusin regime will come to a close and a better world will arrive. A world where something like what happened to Kim Sam-ok will not occur again, where your rights will be respected. The dictatorship had continued too long. Eighteen years too long."

Eighteen years. I, seventeen years old, repeat his words inside my head. Eighteen years. It turns out he was already president a year before I was born. That is probably why even now, when I think of the president, it is President Park Chung-hee's face that comes to mind. There was a time when getting a new president was unthinkable for me, for he was the only president I had known. They said that upon being shot by Kim Jae-gyu, the president, the subject of the old principal's grief, had said, even as he bled in the arms of a songstress, "I'm all right."

He had said the same thing on May 16, 1961, two years before I was born, as he crossed the Han River at the break of dawn. When the military police, on a mission to suppress the coup, launched fire on Park's squad from the northern end of the First Han River Bridge as they crossed the bridge to head north, Park had said to his brigadier general, who was trying to stop him from moving forward, "I'm all right, I'm all right."

Feeling scared after hearing the news of the president's death, on our way home we skip our trip to the market to pick up groceries for cooking soup for next morning's breakfast and head straight to our lone room. No one speaks. Complete silence. Will the program really close, now that the president who provided us with the opportunity to attend school, as the principal had said, is dead?

Hui-jae *eonni* is the first to disappear into the first floor, then Cousin and I into the third floor. The next morning at dawn I, seventeen years old, slip out the front door carrying a knife inside the plastic bowl we use to rinse our rice. I look around as I enter the lettuce patch on the vacant lot. The lettuce leaves are covered thick with night dew. The dew feels cold on my fingers but I turn red below my ears. Even though I am bending low, and even though there are few people out at this hour, I feel as if someone will show up any minute. Show up to scold me for entering someone else's lettuce patch. I also get the feeling that the owner of this lettuce patch, although I've never seen him before, will show up right there in front of me and scream, "Thief!"

I suppress my fear and pick as much lettuce as I need for cooking soup in the morning. Right as I step inside the front gate with the bowl containing the lettuce I picked, Hui-jae *eonni* opens her door and steps out. I quickly hide the bowl behind my back and walk up the stairs. Cousin is on her way out the door when she lets out a laugh.

"You and I were thinking the same thing. I was worried about what we should make soup with then remembered the lettuce, so I was just now on my way to pick some."

Only when I put down the bowl with the lettuce that I secretly picked, my fear subsides. "A president sure is a big deal. Making us come straight home without even stopping at the market. We could say the president ordered us to steal, right?"

When this writing is complete, will I be able to make it wholly to the other side, into another passion? Could I be released from the violence and savagery, the chaos and frailty, which, by fits and starts, had been tormenting me from inside?

Martial law is declared following the president's death. Third Brother does not return to our lone room even at night. It is a crime for just five people to get together to talk, Mi-seo whispers to me while reading Hegel. When we find ourselves sitting around in groups of three or four, we scatter in the middle of a conversation. The streets are blanketed by a quiet restlessness, as if a pack of wolves have ransacked them.

"I just hope he's okay," Oldest Brother says, scanning the room for Third Brother as soon as he gets home late in the evening, wearing his wig.

One day while Oldest Brother is out to teach his early morning tutoring class in his wig, Third Brother walks into the room. He must have stayed out in the night dew, for his shoulders are damp. Before we have a chance to talk to him, Third Brother starts packing his clothes and books.

"Are you going somewhere?"

Cousin brings in breakfast and Third Brother sits at the table, his nose sharp.

"Tell Oldest Brother that I'm going to be away in the country for a while."

"What about school?"

"The university's been closed."

"So you're going home?"

"No, not home."

"Then where?"

Third Brother is unable to answer.

When I keep probing where he's headed, he only asks me to tell Oldest Brother not to worry and once again walks out, through the same door that he just walked in.

Cousin, twenty years old, has a fancy for the handsome engineering high school student interning at the inspection division. Sitting behind Cousin, with her heart on the high school intern, I am copying *The Dwarf Launches His Tiny Ball* onto a notebook. I have very little to go before I am done.

> "Don't cry, Yeong-hui."
> "Please don't cry, someone's going to hear."
> I could not stop crying.
> "Doesn't it make you mad?"
> "I'm asking you, stop crying."
> "Any scoundrel calling Father a dwarf, I want you to kill him."
> "I will. I'll kill him."
> "Promise me you'll kill him."
> "I will. I promise."
> "Promise."

The name of the new president elected by the National Council for Reunification is Choi Kyu-hah. On the center wall where a photograph of Park Chung-hee used to hang in the production department office, a photo of the bespectacled new president goes up. President Choi Kyu-hah. Choi Kyu-hah the president. It feels odd. Until then, the president had been Park Chung-hee and Park Chung-hee had been the president, therefore it feels odd to say either President Choi Kyu-hah or Choi Kyu-hah the president.

The new president appears mushy. The slant of his chin is not sharp like the dead president's; his ears, on which his glasses rest, are not pointy like the dead president's. He looks like a regular old man around the neighborhood. A man like him, as president. Had it been because he was neither steely nor sharp? On a December night, not even seven days into his presidency, gunshots are heard out of the blue around Hannam-dong, Samgak-ji, and the Gyeongbok Palace. Someone must be trying to threaten someone in secret. Or is someone trying to kill someone once again? The following day, the Ministry of Defense issues a short statement that in the course of investigating President Park's assassination, charges were brought against Martial Law Commander Chung Seung-hwa and that he was arrested by the Joint Investigation Headquarters.

Then what about the gunshots?

It was Sunday. I had gotten together with Third Brother's family for dinner. Ribs were cooking on a charcoal grill. My nephew, who had just turned five, was playing with his ball, throwing it against a wall. A waitress had come over to cut up the grilled ribs with a pair of scissors when all of a sudden, Third Brother asks, "The novel you're writing, is it about the time we lived in Garibong-dong?" My face flared up, like the ribs on the charcoal fire.

Anxious about what he was going to say, my heart pounded, but he brought up something unexpected.

"You know, the 12/12 Incident, they're saying it will be ruled as a military coup brought on by revolt against senior ranks, and yet they're saying they will not prosecute—does that make any sense?"

"Please, are you going to get into all that, with your sister?" Sister-in-Law must have heard it too many times at home and interrupted him, complaining that he was at it again.

"All has failed now, but . . ."

Brother took the bottle of *soju* and poured some into his glass.

"What I wanted to do was write." It seemed this was an unexpected answer to Sister-in-Law.

"If you wanted to write, how come you majored in law?" Brother picked up his drink and swigged it down.

"I concluded that I could not change anything through writing."

"What did you want to change?"

"Society."

I scooped up a spoonful of clear juice from the bowl of radish kimchi on the table.

"The novel you're working on is set in those times and I just want to say, this country can never change exactly because a revolt like 12/12 can succeed. Where will we ever find order if this is what goes on in the military, where the law is upheld to a frightening degree?

"Chun Doo-hwan was a man Park cultivated as his protection to sustain the Yusin regime. The incident was Chun's coup, staged in response to talks within the military following the assassination to eradicate soldiers involved in political activity, and with Chung Seung-hwa replacing the major command positions in the metropolitan area with his own men as soon as he took office as Martial Law Commander. Chun was a mere major at the time. A mere major throwing out the Army Chief of Staff without even a nod from the supreme commander. If that kind of thing is acceptable in this world, what isn't? If 12/12 goes unpunished by the law, no matter what the state might say, the public will never accept it. What follows will be an endless cycle of upheaval, deception, betrayal, the same old topsy-turvy . . . Try writing about that kind of thing."

I simply sat there listening.

"If you're a writer, you must not look away from such things. That coup in the end caused what went on in Gwangju. It's a frightening thing."

I poked at the ribs on the grill with my chopsticks.

"What good is a civilian government? They conclude that it was a military coup brought on by revolt against senior rank, but they can't even prosecute . . . And what good is having a civilian president in office? The man who gave the order to open fire during Gwangju has a seat in the National Assembly as if nothing ever happened. The least he could do is stay away from public office, his conscience should at least do that much. Don't you think?"

I don't know, *Oppa.* To me, worrying about whether our briquette fire was still going, or whether you had to sleep on the streets after packing up and leaving, things like that feel more important. Like why it was so cold back then. When I took and sliced a strip of kimchi, set it on a plate and served it on the table, a thin coast of ice would form and the plate would slide all the way across and down. The plate would break and the kimchi would scatter all around. *Oppa.* What I really hated back then was not the president's face but things like the knife refusing to slice through the radish that we had bought to make soup because it had frozen solid. Like on a snowy morning when I turned the tap. I loved it when the water gushed out unfrozen, and hated it when it was frozen and refused to come out. I wanted to write not because I thought writing would bring about change. I simply loved it.

Writing, in itself, allowed me to dream about things that in reality were impossible to achieve, things that were forbidden. From where had that dream seeped in? I consider myself as a member of society. If I can dream through my writing, doesn't that mean the society can dream, too?

Oppa. When I think about writing, I think I am reminded of the penetrating eyes of a dog gazing at his master. The beauty of the fate in those eyes, the sadness that comes from submitting to love, the silence that comes from having seen what it should not have.

It is a Sunday in November. Hui-jae *eonni* is making glue. On the briquette fire, a pot of flour glue is boiling and bubbling.

"What is it for?"

"To put up new wallpaper."

"Wallpaper?"

"Too many stains on my ceiling."

Hui-jae asks if she can borrow our chair. She props up her pillow on Brother's desk chair and puts up the wallpaper. Even with me assisting her, there are spots that neither of us can reach.

"Hold on a minute."

I go up to our room and bring Oldest Brother. He climbs on the chair with a sheet of wallpaper that we have brushed with glue, puts it up on the ceiling, rubs his palm back and forth, then heads back up to the third floor. When he's gone, Hui-jae tilts her head quizzically.

"That's your brother?"

"Uh-huh."

"But he's not the brother you talked about that other time."

"When was that?"

"That time, the other night."

I suppress a giggle. When I told her last time, "That's my oldest brother," he was in his teaching attire, and she seems to think that the person who just helped her out with the wallpaper is a guy from one of the rooms upstairs who commutes to military service. When I explain about the wig and the suit, Hui-jae spreads into a broad smile, the first I have seen.

"That's funny!"

Hui-jae often breaks into giggles after this. When we're coming home on the bus, each time she starts to giggle as we approach the market, I ask, "What is it?" and she says, "I was thinking about your brother," and giggles again.

Another day in December, I pull out Chang's card from the mailbox. I had stayed behind in the classroom by myself and snow was pouring down. I went over to the window and as I gazed out at the athletic field, I felt as if he would be walking toward me in the snow. I read, over and over, the words written on Chang's card. When I think about Chang, my heart brightens up, making me think I want to give him something of mine that is good. The most precious thing to me, as a seventeen-year-old, is the notebook into which I'm copying *The Dwarf Launches His Tiny Ball.* I start thinking I should give the notebook to Chang. My hand moves faster as I transcribe the novel.

> "I have a question."
>
> It was a student from the very far back. "What is it?"
>
> "I once heard that the phenomenon of UFO or alien spotting is the result of self-defense in moments of social stress. How should we look at it in your case?"
>
> "I ask you to believe that, when the western sky brightens up and flames soar up, I have left for another planet with an alien. There can be no

elaborate explanation. The only thing I am not sure of is what I will be faced with on the moment of my departure. What will it be? Silence, as in a cemetery? Or not? Is it only the dead that shout out loud? Time is up. Whether we live on earth, or another planet, our spirit is always free. I hope everyone will be accepted with good scores to the university of your choice. Let us spare one another other parting words."

Attention!

The class monitor called out as he rose. Salute!

The teacher bowed in response, lowering his torso, and stepped down from the podium. He walked out of the classroom. His gate was strange as he walked out. It would be how an extraterrestrial walks, the students thought.

With the winter sun already setting, darkness was settling in the classroom.

I close the notebook and buy a card to send to Chang. "I'm giving you this notebook," I write. "Please keep it for me, something to replace your father's letter, which I lost way back when." I gift-wrap the notebook with my copied-down pages of *The Dwarf Launches His Tiny Ball* and mail it to Chang.

The day I mail the notebook to Chang, I take out the *soju* bottle from the bottom shelf of the cupboard as if I just remembered, and pour what is left down the drain hole in the kitchen floor.

Christmas. Oldest Brother's girlfriend, who, we heard, said she'd come by eleven o'clock, does not come. When afternoon arrives, Oldest Brother suggests to Cousin and me that we go to the movies. The movies? As we are leaving, I glance toward Hui-jae's room and find the lock on the door. Could she have gone to work on Christmas?

Oldest Brother takes us on the subway. The train is packed with people. Cousin searches for my arm amidst the tangle of the crowd and grabs it. We get off at City Hall, slip out of the underground walkway and walk the street. It's our first time going to the movies in the city. Myeongdong. Korea Theater, next to Cosmos Department Store. *Jeux Interdits*. Oldest Brother checks the tickets and saying we have some time, takes us to a bakery on the basement floor of Cosmos Department Store. Cousin gets a long loaf and I get a cream-filled choux puff.

"Aren't you getting anything, *Oppa*?"

"I'm just going to get a glass of milk."

A while later, Oldest Brother, Cousin, and I are inside the theater.

On the screen, a carriage and a car make their way along the river. It looks like there is a war going on. A little girl does not even know that her parents have been killed by an air raid, but when her dog dies, she starts weeping. Peasant boy Michel. The two children quickly become friends. Rather, Michel follows Paulette's words and does anything Paulette wants.

Oldest Brother seems very quiet, so I turn around in the middle of the movie to take a look. Oldest Brother has fallen asleep.

After learning from Michel that when someone dies, a funeral is held and a grave is dug, Paulette becomes fascinated by a game of graves and crosses. When Michel says you cannot make a grave unless something dies, Paulette says then she could just make something die and continues the game by killing bugs and animals. When Paulette wants a real cross, Michel goes to the graveyard and steals a cross.

This time, Cousin seems very quiet, so I take a look at her. Cousin has fallen asleep as well.

By the time Michel's parents start thinking it will be big trouble if they let Paulette stay in their home, relief workers come and take Paulette away. Led by a nun and wearing her name on her chest, Paulette arrives at the train station where, amidst the bustle of the crowd, she hears a child call out, "*Maman*." Paulette shrinks back and her lips quivering, calls out, "Michel." She misses him. Michel . . . Michel. Before we know it, the name Paulette calls out is changing, from Michel to Maman.

Outside the theater, Oldest Brother says that way is Myeongdong Cathedral and suggests we stop there before heading back. Cathedral. Back in the country, Mom used to take Oldest Brother to a cathedral in town when he was a young boy, the Myeongdong Cathedral. We walk up the stairs and find a display reenacting the birth of Baby Jesus. The model of the stable, made with hay, looks cozy. The Virgin Mary holds the newborn Baby Jesus in her arms. The Baby Jesus is adorable and the Virgin Mary is beautiful.

"*Oppa*, who are those men on their knees?"

Standing next to me, Cousin smiles.

"Don't you know? They're the Magi."

Magi? Oldest Brother has disappeared. I search the cathedral for him and come across a girl praying in front of the Virgin Mary, her hair covered by a chapel veil. Oldest Brother is standing next to her. My oldest brother. A young man brought his younger sister and kin to the movies instead of the woman who did not show up for their date on Christmas and he is now standing in front of the Virgin Mary with his head held low. What does he pray for? He looks so lonely in front of the Virgin Mary that my seventeen-year-old heart feels lonely as well. The way Oldest Brother looks at this moment, I shall never forget him in whatever future I am in. Cousin seems to disapprove of how clean the white veil looks on the girl's head.

"Is it like we're not allowed to pray without that thing?"

"I, I'm not sure."

Cousin gets behind the girl and, standing there with her palms together, winks at me to do the same. I just stand there fidgeting, my eyes on Cousin's back as she prays.

•

As soon as I opened my eyes, I went to the door, recalling the doorbell in the middle of the night. Only the newspaper outside. *Ill-fated Wrestler Song Seong-il Dies After Long Struggle.* Who is Song Seong-il? I pulled up the paper and read the article. Song had competed in the 100-kilogram division of men's Greco-Roman wrestling at the Asian Games in Hiroshima last October, without knowledge of cancer cells gnawing at his body, and won the gold medal, overcoming immense stomach pain, emerging as a true symbol of fighting spirit. He was unable to defeat the demon of his illness, however, and at the young age of twenty-six, had departed on the road to eternal sleep, the article read. I stared into the ill-fated wrestler's photo. Tomorrow would be Lunar New Year.

•

On the last day of December, Oldest Brother buys a small television set for our lone room. He turns it on for us and heads out to Yeongdeungpo Station to catch the night train to our home in the country. The factory is giving us only one day off on January 1, saying they will give us a longer break at Lunar New Year to make up for the missed holiday. Cousin, who has now befriended the high school intern, heats up water to wash her hair, applies a drop of her treasured perfume under her ears, puts on her boots instead of the school shoes and heads out.

"Where are you going?"

"Some of us are getting together to hang out in the intern's room. You know, I think he really likes Yun Sun-im *eonni*. Didn't you notice?"

"But Sun-im *eonni* is what, twenty-three?"

"Well, still whenever he sees me, all he talks about is her."

Cousin slaps my shoulder.

"Tell me what you really think. Am I prettier, or is Sun-im *eonni* prettier?"

"You're prettier."

"You mean it?"

"Well, Sun-im *eonni* is pretty, too, isn't she?"

"You're right, she's real pretty. She's got that long hair and her eyes are always smiling. Just seeing her makes *me* feel good, so of course the guys go for that, right?"

Hui-jae *eonni* and I stay in our room all day, watching TV. New Year specials. Martial artists come on and demonstrate marvelous feats. They collect energy and turn out lightbulbs with their eyes, lay out seven, eight dozen eggs in containers and lie down on them. Even when a man with a huge build places a wooden plank on the man on the eggs and climbs up and presses down on him, the eggs underneath do not break.

Then one moment, Hui-jae *eonni* goes, "Uh, that man . . ."

I look at the man she is pointing at. The host asks how he got into these dangerous sports.

"I was teased a lot, because I had a slight build and girlish looks."

As he answers with a smile, dimples form on his cheeks.

"So I took it up, to look more manly, one thing led to another and here I am."

I tap at Hui-jae *eonni*, who is gazing blankly at the TV screen.

"So who is he?"

"It's him."

"Who?"

"The guy I told you about."

Aimlessly, I turned on the TV. A singer named Park Mi-gyeong is singing a song with a strong beat. When you tell me you loved me, I feel it's only an act. Subtitles run at the bottom of the screen. "No

Excuse." Must be the title of the song. If your heart's changed, don't give me excuses. I tried stretching my neck to Park Mi-gyeong's dizzy movements, then leave the room, the TV still on, and opened the fridge. Nothing to eat but apples. But it's Lunar New Year tomorrow, I should at least make myself a bowl of rice cake soup, I tell myself and get my wallet, while Park Mi-gyeong goes on singing. No going back for me now, no. At the bottom of the stairs, I found a card in my mailbox. I pulled it out and checked the sender's name. Handwritten with a nib pen dipped in ink. The same handwriting of the person who had sent me the suicide note back in September. Well, she clearly wasn't dead if she could send a New Year card.

Standing there, I tore open the envelope. There's no this or that, not even a single word about the suicide note that she sent me. I feel fortunate that I was able to feel your presence this past year. I wish you all happiness. That was all it said. I put the New Year card into my pocket, put my hand inside next to it, and stepped outside, pushing the door open. Cold wind brushed back my hair, which had been let loose from the ponytail. In the cold wind, I was suddenly overcome with solemnity. Felt my presence, she'd said? My presence?

THREE

Our skin cracked by different winds
We breathe
We sleep because we're lonely
We cannot meet even in sleep
We see only another's crown
Or show ours, only time to time
Our blistered soles colliding
Each of our heads in a different direction again we lay
breathing weary.

—Hwang In-suk, "Circle Dance"

This alley, where snow would not melt. This alley, where a snowfall would turn into an icy path overnight. The world has many hidden alleys inside. Unlit windows. Cold telephone poles. Broken bricks. Tiny, labyrinthine rooms on the other side of the fence. Odor from the sewer. The smell of frying sticky sugar-filled pancakes. The long exposed hallway of an inn . . . The smell from the kerosene stove. A young factory worker with a boil on his head staggers drunk. Life's anxieties seeping into the booming blare of his sad song. The gates that cannot never be locked, with so many people passing through. Piles of briquette ash. Frozen trash. The drunk young factory worker falls on his knees, holding on to a power pole. Dry vomit surging against the current, up his multiple innards.

Oldest Brother's woman would have disliked this alley. Would have disliked the wig that he had to wear over his naked head, and also me, adjoined to him like a tumor.

Perhaps that is how it's set out to be. The women of the world will disappoint the men and the men of the world will disappoint the women.

On top of that, Mom disapproves of the woman's slender waist. The woman also disapproves, of Mom's thick waist. The woman greets Mom with a head-to-floor bow when Mom arrives in Seoul. Mom turns her back. In Mom's eyes, this frail, slender woman is not the kind who will stick to household work. While Oldest Brother goes to see her off, Mom makes a fist and pounds her chest.

"She come over often?"

"No." The woman does not come over often. Since some time ago, she often does not show up after saying she would.

"With a waist that tiny, no way she'll handle the work around our house!"

The work around our house? I ponder the country. Come to think of it, around our home in the country, there are no women with such a slender waist. Nor women with such smooth fingers, such silky hair, such big, dark pupils.

When Oldest Brother returns, Mom sits him down.

"You know you are the eldest grandson of this family. Will she be able to serve up a single meal with a waist like that?"

"She's a good cook." Cousin lets out a giggle. "Cooking isn't all of it."

Mom does not even open the gift box that the woman brought. When Oldest Brother asks her to open it, she pushes it far away.

"She's a good woman."

Whatever Oldest Brother said, even if he called a bus a train, Mom would believe him, but this time she does not budge.

"Your feelings for her are deep, I can tell, since you met her out here, lonely and away from home, but no way I can allow it. Say you were a second born, maybe I might just let it be, but you're the eldest. If I let her in to our family, it looks like I'm going to have to nurse her for as long as I live! I can't allow it, never, you hear me now."

Chang does not write back. I open the mailbox every night and face disappointment.

At any point in history, there would be furtive secrets; even if one were not living on but dying, there would nevertheless be tender memories; just as a plump child, his eyes glowing blue, continues to grow in that alley filled with wretched stench, just as our chests grew firm like white taro corms under our weary blue uniforms, at any point in history, there would be furtive memories to keep.

> Will you remember me
> and that I was at your side
> even if one day I am gone, gone away . . .

Halfway into that alley, in the labyrinthine house with thirty-seven rooms, Hui-jae *eonni* turns twenty-two or perhaps twenty-three. Three or four days later, the day I turn eighteen, twenty-one-year-old Cousin invites over Hui-jae, who just had her birthday, and sings a song with a slice of castellan cake in front of us, decorated with a matchstick. My beautiful, born in the middle of winter . . . my lovely one . . . Happy birthday to you. Happy birthday to you.

The Ministry of Education announces new guidelines on hairstyle codes, giving students freedom to choose how they wear their hair. Until then, we wore our hair in braids. How busy it kept us, brushing and braiding each morning. As soon as the new code is in effect, Cousin and I head to the hair salon at the Garibong-dong Market and have our long locks cut. Cousin gets a short cut and I a bob. Back after having our long locks cut, Cousin and I gaze into the mirror. All we got was a haircut, but it seems like we are strangers. Cousin turns glum, saying that she looks like a guy.

I called up J.

"Wanna come over?"

"Finished with your writing?"

". . . No."

"Then I can't."

"If you come, I'll go get some blue crabs and steam them."

"I can't."

"I'll make you pancakes with garlic chive."

"No thank you."

"Then what about we meet outside and have lunch?"

Silence.

"I'll head back, as soon as we finish eating."

A laugh escaped from J's mouth at the other end of the line.

"Stop looking for distractions, just stay put and write."

"I'm going to head back right after lunch."

"I have a lunch appointment."

"With whom?"

"No one you know."

"What time?"

"I have to leave right now."

I hung up, then tried calling her again thirty minutes later. When I said, "It's me," J answered with a scream.

"Stop calling!"

Silence. She quickly softened and began to coax me.

"Call me when you've sent in the next batch of your manuscript, okay?"

She hung up. Mighty J.

1980.

We are alive. Even if the life we lived in that alley had resembled a makeshift lodging, what is important is that we are alive. That we keep old numbers in our address books even if we let an entire year go by without a single phone call. That I can reach out and hold the hand of another. Even if I had no memory of your existence in this world, if you were alive, waking each morning, breathing and bickering amidst the air of this world . . . then I would not have kept on avoiding the time and the spaces between my sixteenth and twentieth year. Even if I remembered, even if I remembered them forever . . . even if I did . . . what would be the use? What can memory change?

I did not know what happened afterward; it was still a long way to go until life would be over. I once saw her stagger down a long wall, some man by her side. . . . These expressions could be used only if she were alive.

From the scene where the most powerful man of the Yusin regime was assassinated, an endless series of stories spring up, like conspiracies in ancient royal courts, about women and alcohol, about the debaucheries and secrets feuds of those in power. That year, 1980, the flower trees in Seoul would have been caught by surprise upon blossoming. Slugging from under the frozen earth, out into the world, they would have found that spring had already poured out all over—it was spring in politics, spring in Seoul. A sense of liberation spreading fast to the person next to you, and the next, brought on by the death of an absolute dictator. In spite of the emergency martial law still in effect, spring in Seoul that year, likened to the Prague Spring, spreads hope in the air, together with the fresh, beautiful flowers blossoming around the mountains and rivers. Amidst this wave of democracy, surging high and proud like a river flooding over, Reverend Moon Ik-hwan returned from prison to his home in Suyu-ri. Startling the flowers, the wind, the branches.

Even in the middle of winter, even in the cold and the snow, forsythias are bound to blossom, like mad.

In that alley where the ice would not melt even after spring arrives, the girl stands by the power pole, waiting for Oldest Brother. I, now eighteen years old, am on my way out the gate with a pair of tongs to go buy some hot briquettes when I stop with a flinch. From a distance Oldest Brother is approaching, looking weary in his wig. The footsteps of a weary eldest son. The footsteps of a poor young man, carrying the weight of his entire family on his back at twenty-five. Oldest Brother's footsteps come to a stop when he sees the girl.

Silence.

Soon the girl takes off her necklace and hands it to Oldest Brother, standing there with his head low.

"I came to give you this."

"You don't have to do this."

"But you gave it to me."

Pushing the necklace into Oldest Brother's resistant hand, the girl turns around. My eighteen-year-old neck hangs low as I stand behind them with the briquette tongs in my hand. Poor *Oppa*. The girl with the slim waist turns around and walks away, her heels clicking hard the ground, but Oldest Brother, in his wig, runs after her and stops her.

"Do you really have to do this?"

"I'm tired."

The girl turns back around and walks away. As she disappears into the night wind, Oldest Brother stands there watching, his shoulders sunk low but his face raised upright. After standing like that for a long time, Oldest Brother turns around toward our lone room and I quickly hide behind the gate. For some reason I feel he might get angry if he knew that I had been watching him from behind.

Oldest Brother's girl left behind clicking footsteps in that alley in order to leave him, but we left our footsteps in that alley, morning and night, in order to live. We all did. Cousin, Hui-jae *eonni*, and me.

Third Brother, who had packed his bags and left our lone room, comes back on the subway. Cousin and I, now in our second year at school, are home from school, making kimchi.

"How you guys been?"

"*Oppa*!"

Cousin is startled but happy to see him as she pulls out her hands, red from mixing the spices and the lettuce, from the kimchi bowl. I am wiping the room with a rag when I hear Cousin's giddy squeal and stick my head out to the kitchen. Third Brother is standing by the kitchen door and I notice that his hair is cropped very short.

"Where have you been?"

Third Brother does not answer, asking instead, "Where's Oldest Brother?"

"At the tutoring center!"

"But he teaches in the morning."

"He has evening classes, too. Doesn't get home until midnight."

Cousin pushes the large kimchi bowl to the side to make way for Third Brother. Even after stepping inside the room, Third Brother just stands there. His shaved head shines under the fluorescent light. He remains standing like this, with no intention of sitting, it seems. He puts down his bag only after a long while. He looks like he is about to head out again soon.

"Did you have dinner?"

Third Brother is still standing, as if he's taking a look around someone else's room. He stands by the vinyl wardrobe, gazing at the desk.

"Do you want some dinner?"

Third Brother still does not answer as he pushes his feet back into the sneakers that he just took off and heads outside.

"Where are you going?"

There was only the sound of him plodding down the stairs in the dark without giving me an answer. I stand there listening to the sound, then rush out after him. I jump down two, three steps at once. *Oppa*—When I catch up with him in a flurry, Third Brother looks at me quizzically.

"What is it?"

"Where are you going?"

"To greet Oldest Brother when he arrives."

"For real?"

"Of course, for real . . . What is it? You wanna come along?"

We were in the middle of making kimchi. There are dishes to be washed, the room has to be wiped, and now that Third Brother is home, we have to make him dinner even if it's late.

"You're not leaving again, are you? . . . You should know how worried Oldest Brother is . . ."

"I'm not going anywhere. Just on my way to greet Oldest Brother."

"Promise you'll come back with Oldest Brother?"

"I will."

Third Brother pats my eighteen-year-old head. "I'll be right there, so go on home," he says. Adding that he has something to talk about with Oldest Brother. Finally convinced, I turn around and head back. A while later Oldest Brother, in his suit and wig, and Third Brother, with his head shaved, walk in together. Oldest Brother looks cheerful. Only now do I feel relieved.

"You made new kimchi?"

"Uh-huh."

"Smells good."

Oldest Brother's compliment puts a smile on Cousin, who made the kimchi. Oldest Brother is always saying Cousin's kimchi tastes good. That it tastes just like the way Mom makes it, that Cousin will make a good wife.

"Would you make some sauce to grill this?"

Oldest Brother hands over a newspaper-wrapped packet, which holds about a half-*geun* of pork belly. Third Brother pulls out a bottle of *soju* from the yellow bag in his hand and puts it down on the floor. While Cousin makes the sauce, Oldest Brother takes off his wig and hangs it on the inside of the attic door, then washes his feet, washes his socks and hangs them on the line in the kitchen. I head out to the store to buy a piece of hot briquette but Third Brother stops me and offers to go instead.

"Unless Cousin or I go, you have to wait in a long line!"

Still, Third Brother comes along. On the first floor, Hui-jae *eonni*, who has just finished washing her face after returning from her night shift, is about to close her door when she sees Third Brother and me, heading out to buy hot briquette.

"Who's that?"

"My third older brother."

Hui-jae whispers in my ear, her eyes on Third Brother as he steps out the gate ahead of me.

"You have many brothers."

"He's a university student."

I am surprised at myself for offering information that was not even asked. "You must be proud." Hui-jae slaps my shoulder upon my declaration. Only I feel apologetic and let out half a giggle. When the storekeeper sees me, he pulls out a hot briquette that someone else would have already asked for.

"Thank you!" I say. Noticing the unusually energetic tone in my voice, the storekeeper glances at me, saying, "Looks like someone's in a good mood today."

As Third Brother lowers his head to get the tongs into the holes of the hot briquette that the storekeeper pulled out, I see that his jaw line has gotten sharper.

"*Oppa*, where have you been?" I ask.

The cold February wind scrapes past my calves, creating a wave of red flames on the briquette.

"Oldest Brother was so worried, wondering where you could have gone since you weren't in Seoul or back home."

Third Brother walks ahead without answering, his hands clumsy with the tongs.

"Why didn't you get the heat going earlier?"

"It's not as cold these days, so if we put in a new briquette around this time, it lasts until morning . . . So where were you?"

I ask over and over where he has been as we walk down the alley. But Third Brother does not answer.

The four of us sit down together in our lone room in the middle of the night, the first time in a while. The pork, grilled in a chili paste sauce with chopped scallions and minced garlic, is served on a plate with flower patterns. Oldest Brother pours *soju* for Third Brother in a small glass placed in front of him. Third Brother empties the glass in a single shot. Oldest Brother places a slice of the grilled pork in front of Third Brother as he puts down his empty glass and reaches for the kimchi.

"Eat before it gets cold."

Oldest Brother's wigless, shaved head and Third Brother's shaved head, his jaw line sharper than before, appear tinged in blue under the fluorescent light.

"Better times will come. You should focus on your studies now. Don't forget that you're a law student."

As he offers his empty *soju* glass to Third Brother, Oldest Brother seems to be either in a good mood or slightly melancholy.

"Anyway, it's a relief it's not any worse than this."

Cousin looks at me with eyes that seem puzzled what this is all about. I have no idea, either. What it is that he is relieved about for not being any worse

Early spring. The mountain path that I sometimes take for walks has turned soft and mushy.

Yesterday I took a trip to Chuncheon. This "she" who lives in Chuncheon was to be featured in a special section in the upcoming issue of *The Writer's World Quarterly.* When I received the call asking me to serve as the guest writer of the feature "A Visit with the Writer," I had at first waved it off.

Love has many faces.

Because I admired her as a writer, I possessed an illusion about her even though I did not know much about her. I was twenty years old when I first read her stories. She was like flash of light. The tragic air emitted by the objects in captivity of her gaze pulled me in instantly. I am going to be like her, I thought. I am going to become beautiful in order to get closer to this beautiful person. My attachment to her turned more and more adamant. However, then or now, my adoration of her became the reason I could not readily go to her.

But yesterday, at last, I was sitting in the car driven by an editor from the magazine.

The first time I went to Chuncheon was also on an early spring day like yesterday, like today. I had just entered the college, which lay at the foot of the Mount Namsan, but I was doing nothing but sitting on the benches on campus, unable to fit in. I was twenty years old, and I had finally gotten away and was alone, having become a college student. We had moved to Dongsung-dong and Oldest Brother was now married. Could it be mere coincidence? The place that Oldest Brother now headed for work every morning as an employee after ending his years as a civil clerk was Daewoo Building, which had loomed over me like a gigantic beast that day I first got off the train at Seoul Station. Cousin had left her job at the Community Service Center and now worked at a trade agent's office on the floor above Mountain Echo Coffee.

I was in a shop in Namyeong-dong. That spring, unable to adapt to the changes taking place around me, I was doing nothing but sitting still. Oldest Brother's wife washed everything for me, even my socks, and hung them in the sun until they were fresh and dry. Suddenly there was nothing for me to do. At school, people who were complete strangers to me, the kind of people I had never even come across until then, introduced themselves, dressed in colorful outfits and full of vivacity. It seemed they were about to set out on a picnic.

When I was with them, it felt unfathomable that somewhere in this world there were still factories, that somewhere in this world there were thirty-seven rooms and a marketplace with dim, dark alleys. Suddenly I felt I had become the odd one out. After living for so long in our lone room, it had become the only place that did not feel awkward to me. I would sit awkwardly on a bench at the school that I had worked so hard to enter and when I got tired, I walked all the way to Namyeong-dong where Cousin worked. Then I would wait at Mountain Echo Coffee Shop until she got off work.

One day that March, I set out for school, and only Oldest Brother's wife was still in the house. But my feet would not head in the direction toward school. I couldn't possibly go and wait for Cousin at Mountain Echo Coffee Shop at this hour. I walked around here and there. Then I got on the bus, then the subway, and the place I got off was Cheongnyangni Station. I bought a ticket to Chuncheon but had no plans, had never been there before. The train sped on as mountains and fields, rivers, streams and housing lots swelled up then grew distant outside the window.

I began to heave. The sunlight was blinding.

As soon as I got off at Chuncheon Station, I stopped by a pharmacy and emptied a bag of motion sickness reliever into my mouth. But the heaving still would not stop. After wandering aimlessly around Chuncheon Station, I looked at the clock. If I got back now, I guessed I could make it there by the time Cousin got off work. I bought a ticket to take me back to Cheongnyangni Station, hurrying as if some urgent business had come up.

That was the day when Cousin screamed at me. Her voice was louder than the shouting, "What can I do," in the Smokie song that the DJ was playing. "Stop coming here," she said. "Go to school and work hard," she said.

When I got into a huff and rose from my seat, Cousin took hold of me and led me to a food court across the street from Seongnam Cinema in Namyeong-dong and bought me spicy *jjolmyeon* noodles. Mixing the red sauce into the noodles for me, Cousin corrected what she had said. She said I could come by once in a while, but that I really should work on my studies. And that she wished she could, even if it were only in her dreams, just spend one single day as a college student.

Before I got to know her, the writer, the name Chuncheon only reminded me of that day when I almost got sick. And of Cousin's gloomy voice saying that she wished she could, even if it were only in her dreams, just spend one single day as a college student. But ever since I began carving her name inside my heart, Chuncheon became for me, from the place of my sickness that spring day, to the place where she lived. She was, since my twentieth year, the jewel embedded in my heart. After spending the entire night awake with my face buried in her writing, a white stack of moth carcasses were piled under my lamp. Only then the night's fatigue would come rushing in.

There had been times when I made rash attempts to plunder her. If only I could, I wanted to rob her, without hesitation. If I had not encountered her after leaving the despondent neighborhood of Yeongdeungpo, what would I have done, I wonder.

She had comforted and lightened the barrenness inside of me, leading it into compassion. I had passed through the dark tunnel of the 1980s with her as the firefly illuminating my path.

She, who had been my firefly, spoke, in front of me. She said that for a long time she had felt solitary, her days spent in doubt that her yearning to write had vanished; that there had been many days when she sat blankly all day, wondering if she was going to spend the rest of her life only *saying* that she would write.

Her solitude.

One blue dawn, I read "The Old Well" in *Literary Joongang*, her first publication in five years. Returning after plowing through her solitude, she was like a dried coral sprinkled with water drops. If "The Old Well" was the product of a writer's fears and intimidations, it seemed to me that those fears and intimidations were the requirements of a writer. Once again she was leading women into the realm of myths, women who had turned squalid from fumbling around the cold truths of being human. Flashes of light that pierce through life, the layers of images that pass through then turn blue as they are reflected on the well. She was heated up, taut. Anonymous women, each dressed in the wardrobe of language that she had woven, came into life then grew hard into a golden carp inside the well, transcending femininity and humanity.

This muddle of emotions that swirled up in my heart that morning as I read "The Old Well"—do I dare call it jealousy? How does she manage to stay utterly unchanged like this? I paced the room back and forth. It seemed that she had returned after reaching the very bottom of the blue well, inside a bucket with its rope cut.

"'The Old Well,'" she said, "'The Old Well' was the result of my desperate struggle to return to fiction writing."

The vision of a golden carp soaring up toward life's surface from the deep bruise of loss, from the abysmal depths of darkness, shaking off blue drops of water.

⁂

It is Sunday. Oldest Brother calls for me.

"Go and get some sea salt from the market. Get an ample amount. And you know those rice sacks? Get one of those, too."

"What for?"

"Just go get them."

Oldest Brother puts on his socks but before setting out, he calls me again. He pulls out some money from his pocket and places it in my palm.

"Buy several heat patches as well."

"Do you have an ache or something?"

"Put them on Third's back. He could barely sleep last night."

I head up the overpass to the market with Cousin, who had been hanging up laundry on the roof. When I tell her what Oldest Brother said, Cousin tilts her head, saying, "Maybe that explains it."

"Explains what?"

"Third Cousin. In front of us, he acts like he's fine, right? But I saw him on the roof yesterday and he was walking with a limp."

"A limp?"

"When I asked him if he's in pain and he said he's fine and walked down without showing his limp. But it seemed like he's in pain."

When we return with the heat patches, Third Brother is asleep, lying prone against the wall of our lone room. Oldest Brother is out. I tear the cover off the patches and lift up Third Brother's shirt.

I lift it gently, but Third Brother is startled and shouts, "What is it?"

His pupils are like those of a fawn being chased by a hunter. His back is bruised black and blue all over. Shocked at the sight of the bruises, Cousin covers her mouth with her palm. When I crawl backward with my hands on the floor at Third Brother's absurdly loud voice, only then he fixes his wide-open eyes on me, saying, "It's you."

"Oldest Brother told me to put this on you."

Third Brother lies back down, entrusting his back to my eighteen-year-old hands. What had happened to him? The bruises are the darkest around his waist. I feel sick looking at them. I put the patches all around his waist and give him a massage. I try to rub gently, but he flinches with pain.

"Does it hurt?"

He buries his head in his arms and does not answer. Who has done this to him? I recall what Oldest Brother said the night Third Brother came back. When he said, "It's a relief that it's not any worse than this," was he referring to the injury? Third Brother, who was impressively tall and broad-chested, was now lain prone in front of me, crouched up like a baby eagle, his body black and blue all over, his fearful eyes shut. My eyes well up with tears from the stinging scent of the heat patches.

When Oldest Brother sees the salt that we bought from the market, he tells us to heat it until it's sizzling hot, then pour it into the sack and place it under Third Brother's back.

"But how did he get like that?"

Oldest Brother does not answer. Cousin glances at me with suspicion. I have no idea, and shake my head. Who in the world did this to *Oppa*? Cousin, twenty years old, follows Oldest Brother's instructions, placing a stainless steel washbowl on the kerosene stove and lighting it. She pours the salt into the washbowl and sits down by the stove, stirring the salt. The salt makes crackling sounds as it heats up.

Third Brother was a marathoner. Back in the country that we left behind, a festival was held each May to celebrate the

Donghak Peasant Army Uprising. For three consecutive years, Third Brother was chosen for the role of Donghak leader Jeon Bong-jun to carry the matchlock gun, and for three consecutive years came in first place in the local marathon, winning a pile of notebooks as prizes to take home. That was the Third Brother that we knew, but now he had come back black and blue all over like this—where in the world could he have been? The ankles below his long, long calves, with which he used to run like a stallion, lay in the threshold of our room.

New first year students begin the Special Program for Industrial Workers, which used to be only us. We move up to a classroom on the second floor. Classes are rearranged, so we part with several of the familiar faces and encounter new ones. Mi-seo, who reads Hegel, left-handed An Hyang-suk, and Ha Gye-suk, who always opened the classroom door apologetically, arriving an hour late, are once again in my class. Cousin is once again in a different class. Hui-jae *eonni* no longer comes to school. Ever since the new year started, I have rarely seem Hui-jae. In the bus on our way home from school, or on the overpass as we head back to our lone room after stopping by the market, it is actually Cousin who often brings up her absence.

"Have you seen Hui-jae?"

I shake my head.

"I wonder if she's quitting school." Cousin's voice sticks in my ears. Many students have given up moving on to their second year in the program. There had already been quite a few students who did not return to school after summer break during our first year. At night, as we head up to our lone room, we find the lock still attached on Hui-jae door.

My teacher, Mr. Choe Hong-i. With the start of the new school year, he is appointed to another class. With this shift in teachers, I lose interest in school right away, as if I had been attending school only for the purpose of seeing him.

I receive a box of candies from left-handed An Hyang-suk. What are these for, so out of the blue? I glance at An Hyang-suk with a curious expression. She whispers to me apologetically.

"Let's be desk partners again this year."

Left-handed An Hyang-suk is four years older than eighteen-year-old me. I do not answer, since I wanted to sit with Mi-seo, who was only a year older than me, rather than with An Hyang-suk.

"It's that I feel bad, you know. You're used to it now but if I have to share the desk with someone else, I'll have to go through it all over again, like my elbow bumping into hers each time we write, and being stared at."

Our new homeroom teacher teaches physics. He does not assign seats to us. He tells us to sit where we would like as we come, the short students in the front and the tall ones in the back. Ha Gye-suk takes the seat at the very back, next to the door. This makes her feel a little less apologetic in the second year. Even when she arrives to class late, the seat is left untaken. There are even times when someone leaves the door ajar so that she can sneak in more easily. When I take the seat at the last row at the other end of the classroom, with a view of the flower bed, An Hyang-suk hesitantly comes to sit next to me.

From my new seat, I have a distant view of the music teacher's room and the bench and the statue of a student in summer uniform. I think of Teacher Choe. Now I get to see him only during language arts. Sometimes during break I go to the teachers' office and take a peek inside. I catch a glimpse of Teacher Choe, sitting in a far corner with his back turned, then I walk back.

One day, Hui-jae *eonni*'s homeroom teacher asks to see me. According to other students from Hui-jae's factory, every day at five in the afternoons she says she's going to school and after changing into her uniform, she leaves work with everyone else, but she never shows up at school, he says, then asks me what is going on.

"It's been a long time since I last saw her." I am curious to know what is going on as well.

"I heard you live in the same house?"

It is difficult to understand. I don't know how it is, either, that we live in the same house but do not see each other. I live in the same house with many others, but I barely recall making eye contact with other tenants. The only memories that I have are of people walking out of their doors or fastening their locks. Of the sound of the radio heard from time to time, or of people chatting in a group; of the smell of cooking instant *ramyeon* noodles late at night; of people lined up outside the bathroom each morning, their heads hanging low in silence; of lamplight flowing outside from their rooms, or of unlit windows.

Among the numerous kitchen doors in that house that opened up to the street, Hui-jae's door was the only one that I, eighteen years old, walked in and out of, out of intimacy. But ever since then, this door was locked. It was locked when I checked as I arrived home at night, or when left for work in the morning.

"Does she seem to come home at night?"

I am not sure of this, either. All I have seen is the lock on her door. The teacher says that if she keeps missing school without notice, he has to report it to her factory. According to regulations for the Special Program for Industrial Workers, students cannot quit their jobs while they are at school. In other words, one can attend school only when one is working. If a student attended school after leaving her job, the factory retaliated by submitting to the school a petition seeking the student's expulsion.

When she hears about my meeting with Hui-jae's teacher, Cousin's looks worried.

"Hui-jae's homeroom teacher is the type to stick to principle, I heard. They say he actually expels students when the factories petition for it."

For three days after this, past midnight, I head down to the first floor to check. Hoping she'd be back at this hour. But Hui-jae *eonni*'s door is still locked.

Unexpectedly, it is Oldest Brother who brings word of spotting Hui-jae. He grimaces as he tells me he saw her return at dawn, dressed in her uniform. Saying she didn't seem that way, but perhaps she's prone to bad behavior.

"That's not true." Right away, I wave him off. "She's not like that."

Cousin gives me a sideways glance as I adamantly defend Hui-jae. One night I try to stay awake and listen for the gate. Could it be around four A.M.? I hear someone gently push the gate open. I get up quietly and go downstairs. Hui-jae is inserting the key to her lock and I expect her to be surprised, but she merely gives me a faint smile. Her braids, oily from going too long without washing, cling heavily under her ears. Looking at her under the light, I notice that her face is bloated like dough raised with baking soda. Bits of loose thread stick to her braids. If the school reports to her factory that she hasn't been coming to school, will she be fired? Not knowing what to say to her now that I've seen her, I just stand there gazing at her back as she washes her face.

The next morning, she is standing in the early morning air. Her hair braided and wearing her uniform, her schoolbag in hand, she stands there waiting for Cousin and me. For the first time in a while, we set out into the alley together. Only when we reach the overpass I deliver her homeroom teacher's message.

"Things like school don't matter anymore."

She breathes in the morning air and takes her first steps up the overpass.

"You're not coming to school anymore?"

"No."

"Why not?"

"I need to make money."

Cousin repeats, "Money?" Cousin asks why Hui-jae is still in uniform then.

"Because I have to leave work at that hour."

"Where do you go to make money?"

"I found this job."

I come to a stop on the steps up the overpass. The sky is somber and soaked with water. Job? But she already has a job at the factory. What other job?

"Are you saying . . . ?"

Cousin tries to ask, but Hui-jae cuts in. I only now catch what Cousin is trying to say and poke her on the side. There are people like that at work sometimes. People who leave their assembly line workstation chairs for a new job. They leave their workstations for teahouses or bars. When Cousin asked, "Are you saying . . . ," that was what her words implied. Cousin tries to add to her question, but Hui-jae cuts in.

"It's at a place called Jinhui Tailoring by the entrance of Industrial Complex Number Two. I signed on to work from six to eleven o'clock at night, but there's too much work recently and many times we had to pull all-nighters. Even when we wrapped around two in the morning, I couldn't get off because of the curfew." Her voice was like she was drifting in shallow sleep.

I don't remember what measures the school took regarding Hui-jae. Or the reason why she had to give up school and work two jobs. I think she mentioned she wanted to bring her younger brother to live with her, who was currently in the care of her stepfather, that she planned to find a room for the two of them, but I don't recall the details. I do think I heard her say something like, "Phone operator" or something like that. It is laughable that all I remember of her dark, difficult days was her faint voice. All that remains is her voice, feeble like a flower petal left between the pages of a book I read long ago, dried so crisp that it brittles away the moment you find it.

I decide to get up an hour early out of the blue, around the time when Oldest Brother opens the attic door to get his wig, to make time for a trip to the bathhouse. It is either a Tuesday or a Wednesday morning, following a weekend when I had to miss my bath because of an extra shift. I am rubbing myself with soap under the shower when I feel her reach for my shoulder. A smile. That smile of hers, the faint smile in my faint, faint memory.

"I dozed off and ran the needle into my hand . . . at the break of dawn."

She soaks her red, swollen hand in a basin and again gives me a faint smile. I feel a dizziness erupting. When I catch sight of her swollen hand, it is as if I can hear, amidst the sound of the sprinkling water, the rattle and rumble of the sewing machine that drove the needle into her hand. The water drops that fall on my body feel like drops of water bursting out. I rub soap on her back and see a spot in faint blue spread wide in the small of her back toward her hips. Like a nameless, deserted island on a map, the spot, resembling an ink stain, extends into a faint trail, all the way to her belly.

"You know what my childhood nickname was?"

She turns around and asks, as if she felt my stare.

"What was it?"

". . . Miss Spots."

It's nothing very funny, but she and I giggle aloud, spilling the water in the wash basin. Miss Spots . . . Miss Spots . . . Together we burst into laughter, then I laugh, latching on to the tail end of her laughter, then she laughs, latching on to the tail end of my laughter. We giggle until our jaws feel stiff, as if there were nothing funnier in this world. Has she come straight to the bathhouse from Jinhui Tailoring? She is wearing her uniform when we're walking back home. While I cook breakfast, she lies down in her uniform and sleeps.

When I wake her up to go to work, her eyes are as red as her hand that the needle drove into.

⁂

The Seoul Spring. The union leader wears a bright expression. So does Miss Lee, who often eats lunch with him. Union members wear ribbons that read, "Stop destroying the union," and participate in protests. In the mirrors by the tap or in the bathroom, when Cousin sees them adjust their ribbons, as if they've just remembered, after washing their hands or combing their hair, she turns glum. The Seoul Spring pushes the union leader once again to stage a fight with those who ride in black sedans, on the freedom to refuse overtime and extra hours, on paid vacation, eight-hour shifts, severance pay, pay raises. Miss Lee's face turns dark when she sees us. She says there's so much we don't know. That our ignorance is a fortunate thing for those who ride in black sedans. Miss Lee's voice is gloomy but clear. Her voice carries faith, and despair as well.

"If you don't start looking after yourselves, they'll just keep imposing on you to make sacrifices," Miss Lee said.

⁂

A writer friend called me up.

"You been doing good?"

"Yes."

"So good you're all smiles?"

"Should I cry instead?"

"What are you doing?"

"I'm answering the phone."

He laughed out loud. I laughed along. It seemed like he had something to say, but was hesitating, which was unlike him.

"So let me have it."

"About what?"

"Seems like you have something to say to me."

"I'll talk if you promise me you won't get upset."

"What is it about? If it's something upsetting, I'll get upset."

"Then I won't."

"Hey, that's not fair, after getting me all curious."

"Then promise you won't get upset."

"Do I get upset that easily? . . . Do I?"

"Whenever I discuss your work, you get all upset and sullen."

"My work?"

"Yes."

"That's not getting upset. I just get embarrassed."

"Whichever!"

"Go on, I'll hold it all in. No getting upset or sullen."

"I just read the second chapter of your book."

My heart went into a sulk. Already I had turned sullen. What did you read that for, I wanted to say, but my words sank deep down my throat and once again I was flustered.

"Try to remember now. The movie you saw that day, was it really *Jeux Interdits*?"

The movie we saw that day was not *Jeux Interdits*. It was *Comme un Boomerang*, with Alain Delon. Boomerang. I had forgotten how the story went exactly. It was about a father and a son. About the father rescuing his son, imprisoned for a criminal offense, and taking him across the border. Alain Delon played the father and he rescued his son on a plane.

"It was *Comme un Boomerang*."

"Then why did you write that it was *Jeux Interdits*?"

"It's a novel!"

At my insistent voice, he was silent for a while. Of course he knew. How could he not. That the sentences that make up a work of fiction can never move further ahead of the flashes that come and go throughout life. The limitations of the sentence, which can only exaggerate, lock out, and expose without universality.

The movie that I saw with Oldest Brother and Cousin that day was *Comme un Boomerang*, but I did not like it. Perhaps that itself functions as a problem for my current self. The way I refuse to even sit in the same spot with something that is not of my disposition. The way I refused to even discuss why it is not of my disposition or to be persuaded by it. Perhaps this closedness was blocking me from viewing life from a different perspective. The sole reason I had inserted the film *Jeux Interdits* in the anecdote where *Comme un Boomerang* should have been was because the latter did not suit my taste in film. My friend, now aware that I was upset, tried to make amends, and became even more flustered than I was.

"Yes, I know, I didn't mean anything by what I said. It's just that I know *Jeux Interdits* was in theaters for only a single run back around 1960. Which was before you were even born. So when I read that the movie you saw that day was *Jeux Interdits*, it kind of threw me off, personally. That wouldn't have been the case if a similar thing came up in another novel. It's hard to explain, but in this novel that you're writing now, I thought it would be better if you didn't do that, so . . . just write about things as you saw them . . . but think that I'm asking you for reality. You know what I mean, right?"

He was pointing out my quick resignation, that no matter how I obsessive I was, fiction merely follows the trails of life. One cannot move ahead of life, no, one cannot even move side by side with life, through writing. The decorations and the directions and the exaggerations just fill up the place that is occupied by my resignation.

After hanging up, I boiled some spinach for dinner. Fresh, crisp spinach. To keep its color from fading while the spinach cooked, I put a pinch of salt in the boiling water. I rinsed the cooked spinach twice in cold water. I placed the leaves in my hand and wrung out the water. Yes, this was all I could write. That I placed the leaves in my hand and squeezed out the water. There was no way I could express, through my sentences, the texture, the smell, of the spinach in my hand before it was squeezed. Despite the fact that its truth was perhaps buried inside that which I was incapable of expressing. The spinach's crisp green color calmed my prickly heart. In a bowl I often served cold noodles in, I spread out the spinach leaves in light, fluffy layers. I minced two cloves of fresh garlic. I took out a bottle of sesame oil and one of sesame salt, and then chopped some scallions, on the slant.

. . . On the slant?

Third Brother's wife was a Seoul native. Having worked for quite a number of years as a flight attendant after graduating from the same university as my brother as a fashion design major, she was an optimistic soul and laughed a lot. She was so friendly, so much so that at first I thought her attitude was a remnant of her former profession that she had not quite shed yet. But six years after the birth of her child, she had not changed at all. While still a new bride, she was assisting Mother for the first time in the kitchen one day while they prepared for a memorial service.

Mother had told her, "Chop them on the slant now," pushing a basket full of scallions her way. She approached me, skewering together taro stems to fry them in egg batter, and asked quietly. "What does 'on the slant' mean?"

I wouldn't know myself what it meant but I did know what it looked like so I placed one of the scallions on a cutting board and chopped it diagonally for her to use as a model, pushing the cutting board toward her.

"This is on the slant."

As she tried to chop them into the same shape as my model, she would break into a smile when our eyes met. Her eyes red and teary from the stinging scent of the scallions.

We are on an overtime shift. In the middle of pulling the air driver toward herself, Cousin hangs her head low.

"What is it?"

"My eyesight has grown dim."

She says that the tiny holes for the screws seem to be flickering. I walk over to her, sitting on her workstation chair with her head hanging low.

"I'll take over for a while. Go to the bathroom and sleep for just a minute."

Cousin gets up, saying she would.

It's time to get off work.

At the security office, the guard carries out a body search. The search is to check for anyone trying to sneak out parts from the assembly line. Seo-seon, from the packaging section, tears the guard's hand away as he lifts the pocket on her chest to search it. We are "Grade 1 Staff." The administrative staff are called "Official Staff." Official Staff do not have to go through a body search. They punch in their time on their cards and walk leisurely past the security office. Those who have to endure the bag and body search are the Grade 1 Staff. After refusing the body search, Seo-seon is pushed to the side without a chance to punch in her time. The Grade 1 Staff next in line all follow suit, handing over their bags but refusing the body search.

Section Chief Ha comes running from the administration office. "What are you hiding under your clothes? You know how the saying goes—a thief is bound to feel a prick in his foot!"

We have greeted the Seoul Spring, however, and Seo-seon shouts with confidence that she refuses to have not just her bag but her body searched by a male guard!

The might of the Seoul Spring makes one of the cafeteria women come down to the security office every day when we get off work. Now the Grade 1 Staff no longer have to endure a body search by a male guard. Seo-seon wears a bright expression. So do the other female Grade 1 Staff who now get their bodies searched by a cafeteria woman, a fellow female, thanks to Seo-seon.

Increasingly often, Third Brother sleeps out. He does not come home for two, three days in a row, sometimes for an entire week. This is something Oldest Brother cannot stand. He says a person might take their meals in various places but should sleep in one place. And that a family is made of people who sleep together under the same roof. But Third Brother does not comply. His back has not recovered, Cousin says. She is concerned about Third Brother's injury. One Sunday, Oldest Brother questions at Third Brother, who has returned all haggard after several days away.

"Where did you sleep?" A whiff of chilly air circles the room.

"At Changgyeong Gardens."

The campus at Third Brother's school is adjacent to Changgyeong Gardens, with only a wall in between. *Down with dictatorship! Abolish the Yusin Constitution!* Chased by riot police, Third Brother probably climbs over the wall and infiltrates the flower beds at the Changgyeong Gardens.

Oldest Brother jumps to his feet from his chair.

"Do you have to do this! How can I make you understand! This is no time for you to be going around staging protests!"

Third Brother, who has never rebelled against Oldest Brother, abruptly shouts out loud, "It's time to be doing what, then?"

"You're a law student!"

"So you're telling me I should be a coward like you, running and hiding in order to study."

Oldest Brother pushes Third Brother against the wall, screaming like a beast.

"Bastard!"

Third Brother's head bumps against the wall with a loud thump. "Beat me up, go on and kill me!"

Third Brother lashes out, his eyes ablaze. His voice and movements are full of fury. It seems that he wants to be beaten up, by Oldest Brother or anyone else, for that matter. Oldest Brother has his chair in his hands. The chair is thrown against the window. Books are thrown at Third Brother, *The Complete Compilation of Six Major Laws, Civil Law, Criminal Law,* all of them.

"Why must I live like this!" The anger and frustration that Oldest Brother has kept suppressed for so long finally explodes. Why in the world must he live like this? At the height of his youth, his shoulders bear the responsibilities as the eldest son as if it were a divine punishment. His pent-up anger—as the eldest son obliged to take care of his younger siblings on behalf of his parents in the remote country, to work for money while serving his military duty and to sleep in discomfort in a tiny room with a sister and a cousin—sets off a bloody eruption on Third Brother's nose. Oldest Brother shouts at Cousin and me, trembling in the kitchen.

"Get lost, right now! All of you!"

Oldest Brother's threat sends Cousin off to the roof. But my feet will not budge.

"You get out of here as well! . . . Get out, I said!"

Third Brother, his nose bleeding, shouts at Oldest Brother. "Leave her alone!"

Oldest Brother throws his fist at Third Brother and hits him under his ear.

"You bastard, you get out of my sight! Get out!" Just as Third Brother's anger was not really targeted at Oldest Brother, Oldest Brother's anger is not targeted at Third Brother, either. It was just that they happened to vent their anger on each other at that moment. Things get out of hand if all that anger and frustration is held in for too long. The vinyl wardrobe collapses. The attic door is about to come unhinged. I grab Oldest Brother's legs as he lifts the desk, this time to strike down at Third Brother.

"*Oppa*, please don't!"

When I open my eyes, everyone is asleep.

Through the broken window of our lone room, the warm spring sun shines in on my brothers. And on Cousin, lying prone with her back in the sunlight. It is such a peaceful sight that I wonder if it was a dream, all that anger exploding all at once. Oldest Brother's hand is wrapped in bandages and Third Brother has a cut on his lip, swollen red. On my forehead sits a cold wet towel and I can smell medicine on my lips. The door opens slightly and Hui-jae *eonni* peeks in. I, eighteen years old, shut my eyes. Hui-jae's eyes linger on my closed eyes and I don't open them again until she looks away. She closes the door and quietly walks down the steps. Only after I hear her arrive at the bottom of the stairs and close the door behind her, I sit up. Cousin hears me move and sits up as well.

"Are you okay?"

"It was scary, wasn't it?"

"But who would've thought you'd actually faint?"

It was May. The Seoul Spring was over. The Seoul Spring that lasted two hundred and three days.

I took my seven-year-old nephew out to lunch. He had been swimming at the pool over the winter and now looked fresh and alive, enough to make the spring weather seem unremarkable. I'd heard he was a handful for his family these days. Whatever caught his eyes, he would inquire about, nitpick, double-check, over and over, making his parents laugh, or feel trapped, or so I had heard. When his mother noticed him passing gas anywhere he went, she told him, "Please don't pass gas everywhere you go."

Then one day, his mother was napping and he shook her awake to ask, in all seriousness, "Mommy, may I pass gas now?"

When his mother said, "You may," and closed her eyes again, this time he pulled up her eyelids and asked, "Mommy, how come after I pass gas I want to go poo?"

He was now beginning to read, and he was hiking in the mountain with his father when he asked, out of the blue, "What's *sudoegal*?"

"Sudoegal?" His father, my third oldest brother, was clueless, and my nephew said, "Sudoegal, over there." He was pointing to a signboard outside a restaurant by the hiking route, listing the menu, from boiled beef and barbecued ribs to pig's feet. The boy had read the list vertically, creating a nonsensical jumble of syllables. Even as I listened to my brother tell the story and burst into laughter, the boy's expression reflected a curiosity. He had to know what exactly this thing was called *sudoegal*.

Sweat gathered inside my young nephew's hand as it held on to mine. The willow trees lining the street were slender and supple, and the distant mountains were tinted in a mild shade of green. The boy looked up at me as we passed under a gingko tree grown thick with new leaves.

"Auntie?"

"Yes?"

"Are leaves clothes for trees?"

Although we were holding hands, I had not actually been paying attention, my eyes scanning the flowers that had lost their petals overnight in the rain, and this question caught me off guard. It's finally coming, I suppose.

When I could not quite answer, the child shook off my hand and asked again, "Auntie, are leaves clothes for trees?" Leaves? Clothes? Well, I suppose leaves were the first clothes for mankind. I gave him a vague yes. Wearing a sunny smile, he was just like a soap bubble. We walked on for quite a while longer.

"Let's turn out the lights and get to bed"—this was his parents' routine line each night at home. The expression, "turn out the lights," seemed to have taken on a profound significance in the child's mind. One day I was leaning back on the sofa with my eyes closed and he had shaken me with his hands.

"Auntie, why do you turn out your eyes?"

Recalling this, I let out a small laugh as he found my hand again and resumed his questions like some philosopher.

"But then why do they take off their clothes in the winter?" He was talking about trees again.

So young, and impatient as well. When I stammered, "Well . . . ," unable to come up with an answer, he pressed me hard, asking again why they take off their clothes when it's so cold. "Well, that's because . . ." I was at a loss when he finally produced his own answer, his voice exploding with a clang. "It's because they're going swimming, right?"

Swimming? Since leaves were clothes for trees, and since he took off his clothes when he went swimming, he had probably found his answer in that. When I just smiled, unable to respond whether he was right or wrong, he kept on asking, "I'm right, aren't I? It's because they're going swimming, right?"

Suddenly in my mind a tree performed a handstand.

I let go of his hand and ran off, bursts of laughter escaping from between my lips. He was just as worked up, tailing right behind me and asking, "Right? Right?" What persistence! I turned around and yelled. "Hey! You *Sudoegal*! I don't know—I don't know, either."

May comes around every year. Just as it did back in the days of the poet Yeongnang's days, when he would cry for three hundred and sixty days, dismayed at the peonies falling in May. Just as it did in 1980, the year I was eighteen years old.

May, the name of our grievous wound.

May that year comes at us as a wound, vanquishing all of the usual vigor that May spurts out at the world. Wherever we were back then, whatever we had been doing, as long as we live on in this land, May will always be May of that year.

May that year. One weekend in May, left-handed An Hyang-suk gets on the train to Gwangju to visit her hometown

Hwasun, famous for the statue of the reclining Buddha. She said she'd be back by Monday but she does not return. One, two, three days . . . It's only on the seventh or eighth day that she arrives back at school, out of uniform.

"What are you doing out of uniform?"

While checking attendance, the homeroom teacher takes notice of An Hyang-suk's attire.

"Come see me at the teachers' office!"

An Hyang-suk returns from the teachers' office with a pale face. Upon closer observation, I see that both her face and her body have turned visible thinner. We are in the middle of our abacus calculation class. The teacher instructs us to work on ten level three problems from our workbook and paces up and down the aisles. The classroom turns quiet, except for the rattling of the abacus beads. When the teacher walks past us, down the aisle, An Hyang-suk whispers to me.

"It's complete chaos . . . People have died in great numbers!"

I look at her with confusion.

"Phones don't work, trains have stopped running, guns are going off—it's madness."

"Where?"

"In Gwangju. Nobody will believe me. Not even our teacher. My uniform got all torn up, pushed and pulled by the crowd . . . I made a narrow escape, I tell you."

The abacus teacher turns around at her desk and heads down our aisle again. An Hyang-suk shuts her mouth and begins working on her abacus again with her left hand. After the teacher has moved on past us, An Hyang-suk whispers again.

"I'm so scared."

"You said the trains are not running. How did you get back?"

"On a tractor."

"Tractor?"

"My uncle took me on his tractor through back roads along the highway, to the train station in Iri . . . Gwangju is completely closed down. It's turned into a sea of blood. No one can get in or out."

"Who's killing who?"

"The soldiers are killing citizens."

"The soldiers, how come?"

". . . I don't know. Uncle told me to keep my mouth shut . . . Keep this to yourself."

An Hyang-suk gazes deep into my eyes, which are sparkling as I listen to her story.

"How can it be so quiet here in Seoul?"

The Seoul Spring, the forsythia that had blossomed out of the blue in the dead of winter, is trampled over by the armored vehicles of the New Military Group. Perhaps armored vehicles were invented for the purpose of trampling over spring. It was the Soviet armored vehicles that shoved away the Prague Spring. Or were they called tanks back then?

The subway train speeds past our lone room with a loud thump. People split off into separate directions in fear, lifting their fingers to the lips to gesture, "Hush." Oldest Brother sees off Third Brother as he leaves for a farm in the mountains, carrying a bag full of law books.

The conveyor belts slow down. After the trampling of the Seoul Spring, we no longer get overtime shifts and work slows down visibly as well at the stereo section's preparation line. Sometimes work stops for two hours straight. Even the foreman's gait has slowed down as he moves back and forth between lines. There's talk here and there that the stereo section might be closed down. That export deals have been cut off. The engineering high school student interning at the inspection division sits at the line opposite from us, making scribbles on the conveyor belt. Cousin steals a glance at the back of his neck. Only when he lifts his head, yawning with boredom, Cousin takes her eyes off him and dips her head. The intern's eyes are now on Yun Sun-im *eonni.* Cousin looks at Yun Sun-im as well. As she gazes at Yun Sun-im's wavy curls, Cousin's eyes well up with sadness.

Whenever I encounter a middle-aged woman with an amethyst ring on her plump finger, I am reminded of our landlady, who owned the house with the thirty-seven rooms. She did not live in that house. The only days we see her are the three days around the weekend toward the end of each month. She stops by in order to collect the rent and utility bills. A black sedan parked in the alley is the sign that she is there. Her chauffeur is always dozing off in the car after parking it in the alley and we have to walk sideways to squeeze past the car whenever we have to go through. The bridge of her nose, powdered white, is as shiny and smooth as the amethyst ring on her finger. This woman is exacting in her calculations where her interests are concerned. The utility bills that she divides up among the tenants each month are accurate down to a single won.

Hui-jae *eonni.* Just once, I saw her get angry.

Her anger was aimed at the landlady, wearing bejeweled rings on three of her fingers, including the amethyst one. Hui-jae, venting her anger at the landlady's car parked in the alley, saying she should let out all the air from her tires.

"Listen to this. She tells me my electricity bill comes to two thousand and twenty won. So I hand her two thousand won and she asks me 'where's the twenty won.' So I hand her a hundred. But she doesn't give me back eighty won."

I let out a little laugh. Hui-jae's cheeks are flushed with anger.

"That's what happened last month, and the month before that as well."

Cousin, solid as a rock, never lets this happen. She makes sure she has enough change and counts up the exact sum to hand to the landlady.

Union Leader. I remember the things he said. "I wanted to make you realize that while you are working your night shifts, somewhere in this world, there are people soaking inside tubs full of warm water, in the bathroom attached to their rooms. I wanted you to at least realize that you are being sacrificed and that you seek out your rights, to learn to cherish yourself."

Union Leader. He is tantalized by our inability to assert our rights, by our fear, which keeps us from fighting against low wages and low allowances. Rather, we worry we might lose our extra shifts and overtime work and have to do without the extra allowance. We do not know how to cherish ourselves. As he said, we are incapable of thinking that we are being sacrificed.

Miss Lee's face is a pale yellow. "It's all over."

Seo-seon, who rejected the body search during the Seoul Spring, hands in her resignation.

"These people will grind up worms into our soured kimchi if they have to."

Cousin whispers to me, "People say the world has gotten scary. They take you away for just opening your mouth. Send you off somewhere to be re-educated. They are the ones who took away Union Leader as well."

On the factory bulletin board, the layoff list is announced. Most are union members from the stereo section. The hard-working Miss Lee's name is on the first row of the list. Neither the production supervisor nor the chief production manager is ever seen again. The foreman is promoted to production supervisor. The foreman holds an assembly, taking over as supervisor. He explains that because exports have been cut, the three assembly lines will be reduced to one, which makes the layoffs and transfers inevitable. The number one from Line B and the number two from Line C are assigned in to mine and Cousin's place. Due to the transfers, the students and union members lose their positions. We come to work in the morning, but have no workstations to go sit at. The foreman, now supervisor, assembles those of us pacing between the lines and once again explains that we will be assigned positions each morning according to how work is progressing. Cousin and I, twenty and eighteen years old, respectively, who used to occupy the number one and number two positions respectively, on Line A, can no longer stay together. One day Cousin is sitting at the preparation line and I'm sitting next to an inspection division staff member waxing stereo cabinets with a flannel cloth. Another day Cousin is soldering, her movements clumsy. Smoke from the lead rises over Cousin's head. On another day we are both sent to the TV section in another building to provide backup. Or so they say. There's nothing to do once we get there. We stand around aimlessly, trying not to get in the way.

My heart hurts each time I pass the conveyor belt at Line A. Even when I hang my head low each time I pass it on my way to the restroom, the chair I used to sit in enters my vision. My workstation as well. The seat where I used to write letters to Chang each time the conveyor belt came to a stop. The spot where I used to place my copy of *The Dwarf Launches His Tiny Ball*, with a cover made from drawing paper. Ever since we lost our places, Cousin and I have been feeling glum. We keep circling the industrial complex on our way to work. Naturally we are often late. Our lame gestures, reminiscent of old day laborers standing around by the fire at a completed construction site. Things were better when we were complaining that the conveyor belt was moving so fast, protesting that we're no machines. Back then, if our biceps turned hard and sore, all we needed to do was massage them.

As we pace around, our workstations lost, an awareness grows inside of me of the ignobility of human existence. When I had to sit at the workstation and insert screws all the day, pulling down the air driver, I had no room for distraction. Now there is just one thing on my mind: that I be given a place to sit at work.

My heart was wounded by the sense of lameness, of not knowing where to go. Even after many years, when I am obliged to be somewhere crowded with people, the first thing I think about is this. Will there be a place for me there? If I feel things will not work, that I will once again be made lame, I would end up not going, thanks to my unconscious that has stopped growing.

My cousin, ice stuck between her toes, her hands red. My cousin, quick to turn sulky, or cheery, who would bawl out in fury at anyone, then hang her head low, gazing at the hole at the bottom of the power pole, hollowed out yellow by someone's piss, pulls out the camera that was engraved in her heart, as if she has suddenly lost her sense of direction, throws it into the piss hole, and whispers to me. "I'm going to be a phone operator."

"Phone operator? That's Hui-jae *eonni*'s dream, not yours. Remember the night we left home? The night we said good-bye at the station to Auntie, who smelled of fish, you told me that you're going to take pictures of the white birds sleeping in the forest."

"Fat chance. You have to be born for that kind of thing."

"That's not true. You will get to do it one day if you never let yourself forget. If you forget your dream then it's over. If you keep holding on to that longing, to get closer to your dream, you can do it. Keep getting closer and closer and some day you will be able to get to that forest. Even if you don't get there, you will be near it."

Furious, Cousin shouts at me. "Stop patronizing me. You think you're so well read and smart? I can't stand the sight of you. How dare you!"

This girl, my cousin. Even in the summer heat that called for sleeveless shirts, her arms would be covered with goose bumps.

Her twenty-one-year-old arms always appeared cold. Now those arms seem to rise up high, then fall with a slap on my cheek.

"You don't know what you're talking about!"

I shout back. "If you stop going to school, I'll tell Oldest Brother!"

"Go on, tell him! He's *your* brother, not mine."

"Oldest Brother is going to break your legs."

Cousin is gasping hard as she glares at me. "He's going to pack up your stuff and send you back to the country!"

My cousin leans back on the wall and starts to cry. "He doesn't want me because I'm a factory girl."

I, who had just been bawling and screaming, stand there with a blank expression.

"He says Yun Sun-im is a factory girl with a pretty face but I'm a factory girl and one with a homely face at that."

A jerk, this student intern.

"And *he's* not a factory guy?"

"He says he's only interning. He's going to college. So I'm going to be a phone operator. And I'm going to take the entrance qualification exam and attend college like him." Cousin wipes her tears and bites her lips. "You won't tell Oldest Brother, will you?"

I shake my head. Cousin has already signed up for courses at the Jongno Phone Operator Training School.

"When you take the exam and earn a certificate, you can get a job at the bank. At places like post offices, too."

. . . Ah, places like banks or post offices.

Miss Lee and other laid-off workers continue coming in to work. They have submitted a petition to be reinstated on the grounds of wrongful dismissal, and stage protests. Each morning a scuffle takes place between the laid-off workers trying to get in through the main entrance and the security guards trying to keep them out.

"What makes you think you can come to work when you don't even have time cards!"

Those who sympathize with the petitioners for reinstatement on the grounds of wrongful dismissal are fired as well. From inside the main entrance of the factory, Miss Myeong gazes out at Miss Lee with her armed crossed. Arriving at work, Cousin looks away from the petitioners for reinstatement on the grounds of wrongful dismissal by glaring sideways at Miss Myeong.

I am now on my own. Hui-jae and Cousin have both grown distant from school. We leave work at five o'clock but I head for school and Cousin heads for the phone operator training school. I return alone to our lone room on the night roads, stopping by the market on my way.

Oldest Brother has no idea that Cousin is attending the training school to earn a phone operator certificate instead of going to school. Just as before, he heads out to the tutoring center each morning, donning his wig, but he is growing increasingly gaunt. Inside his desk drawer sits the gold necklace that the woman left behind, twinkling and unmoved.

"This necklace belongs to Mi-yeong *eonni*, doesn't it?" One day Cousin finds the necklace in the drawer and swings it in her hand. Even in our lone room, the gold necklace shines with a twinkle. "Why is it here?" Cousin puts on the necklace and looks into the mirror.

"Put it back!"

Recalling the night that the woman came and gave my brother the necklace back, I start feeling cross. I keep thinking that I hate her. Her white face. That pretty face. Twinkling eyes. I cannot stop thinking that her prettiness has brought misery to Oldest Brother. I feel sorry for him as I imagine the future commitments that would have glimmered inside his heart when he presented her with the necklace. He was not the kind of person who would give a necklace to anyone. He was not the kind of person to commit his heart to anyone.

Cousin puts on a smile as bright as the twinkling necklace.

"Can I wear this when I go out, just once?"

I throw a fierce glance toward Cousin, wearing her twinkling smile. Cousin seems like she really wants to wear the necklace and keeps asking me to look the other way, saying, "Just once. Why did she have to give back the necklace? Mean of her. She should've just kept it or thrown it in the river or something, what does she expect *Oppa* to do with it. And what's *Oppa* doing, keeping it here. Right where we can find it with the pull of the drawer."

I am overcome with anger for no reason, and snatch the necklace from Cousin and put it back where it was, closing the drawer with a bang.

Ever since the necklace has been in the drawer, Oldest Brother is unable to sleep deeply. He tosses and turns, again and again. Sometimes he sneaks out the door in the middle of the night. His footsteps heading up to the roof. One night I follow him. He pushes his way through the laundry on the clothesline that someone left hanging overnight and sits by the railing, simply sits there.

Oldest Brother, who had not even taken up smoking. What is he thinking, sitting there then? What is he looking at, sitting there? I fear that the chimney at the Design and Packaging Center factory, soaring high into the night sky, might collapse toward him. If only I could, I wanted to go see the woman and tell her about Oldest Brother's suffering.

Deep in the middle of the night, Cousin and I are startled awake by Oldest Brother's scream. He is sitting blankly in the dark. When I try to turn on the light, he says, "Don't."

"What is it, *Oppa*?"

He says he has pain in his chest, that he feels short of breath. He rubs his chest, sitting there in the dark room. As if she should do something about it, Cousin turns on the light and gets a cup of water from the kitchen for him. Oldest Brother stops short of taking a sip and puts the cup down, as if he cannot manage even a drink of water. His hand is still rubbing his chest, but he tells us he's okay, that we should get back to sleep.

On the radio playing in the inspection division, people are talking about eating lettuce wraps. The show is *Requests at Noon*. They are talking as if they see a scene from the countryside right in front of them, enjoying lettuce picked from the fields with rice and freshly prepared paste. "Adding chopped green peppers to the paste will enhance the taste of the lettuce with its zesty flavor," the host said. To this, Cousin added, "Fresh garlic as well!" What catches my attention is not the green peppers or the fresh garlic. It is when the host says, "But make sure you don't eat too much lettuce. It will make you sleepy!" Sleepy? Lettuce will make you sleepy?

One day, Oldest Brother stares blandly down at the dinner table. The table is practically a field of lettuce. Lettuce salad with spicy seasoning, lettuce wrap, lettuce soup.

"How come all you're giving me is lettuce these days?" He tries a spoonful of the soup and asks what kind of soup it is.

"Lettuce soup!"

"First time I've tried soup made with lettuce."

". . ."

"Have we run out of money?"

Only then, Cousin lets out a laugh. "No, it's because we heard that lettuce helps you sleep . . . You haven't been sleeping well."

"That's why you made lettuce soup?"

"That's right."

Oldest Brother bursts into cheerful laughter. His laugh subsiding, he is about to put a lettuce wrap into his mouth when he asks, as if he's just remembered. "By the way, where were you coming from yesterday?" He is looking at Cousin.

"Me?"

"You were getting off the subway . . . You didn't seem to hear me call and kept on walking." The phone operator training school that Cousin is attending instead of school is located near the Bell Pavilion downtown. She takes the bus there from the factory and returns home on the subway.

"Yesterday, well . . . I had something I needed to do."

"I don't want the two of you going around alone at night. Even if one person runs a little late, wait so that you can come home together. The same goes for when one has something to attend to."

Cousin quickly answers that she'll do that. Sitting there next to her, I feel my heart pound.

My professor from college was staying at a place called Mureung, deep in the mountains. I visited him there last April, after publishing my first novel. A friend who came with me was busy weeding the garden and filling the fridge with side dishes for our professor, who had to handle his meals by himself, but all I did in Mureung was doze off into sleep here and there. I was caught dozing on a chair looking out at the river, then again while squatting outside the doghouse where a Jindo breed dog was lazing about, even while we had a conversation with our mentor.

Following them down the riverbank, I plopped down on the grass and dozed off again, only to be awakened by a baby goat pooping right next to me. Sleep coming over me, so intense I could hardly keep my head up. Finally, my professor said, "It's you who needs a rest, not me." I returned to the city, nodding and dozing.

This same professor called me on the phone.

"Professor!" I burst out. I was in the middle of washing my hair. Drops of water dripped onto the receiver from my hair, wrapped up in a towel in a rush. What could he be calling about? I got to thinking that I hadn't called or visit again after that visit to Mureung. Pulmonary emphysema. My professor had rented the house in the mountains to recuperate from pulmonary emphysema.

"Are you in Seoul?"

"No, I'm calling from Mureung. I called the day before yesterday but there was no answer."

He had called the day before yesterday as well. What could it be about? I started getting nervous.

"I was visiting the country."

"I see. That's good. How long were you there?"

"About ten days."

"So it was a pretty good stay?"

"Well, I managed."

"That's good. I was going to suggest that you come here for a few days and get some rest, but I guess there's no need."

I said nothing, waiting . . .

My professor continued a little later. "You seem to be writing too much these days . . . I was doing that at one point as well. Writing as if my life depended on it."

"I am? Writing *that* much?" Without realizing it, I was speaking in a sullen voice. On the other end of the line, my professor once again stopped speaking. He had noticed my sullen voice.

"Well, a writer should write a good amount, but not in your case. For you, to write is to dig up your own flesh to eat. If you dig up too much, it will make you ill."

Drops of water continued to drip, drip, from my wet hair.

"Is it disheartening, what I said?"

In the middle of the night, a flutter of anxious footsteps is heard from the alley. Doors banging shut here and there. Cousin is the first to wake up from the noise.

"What is that sound?" Cousin shakes me awake.

"What?"

"That sound."

Oldest Brother wakes up as well.

The old shopkeeper woman is pleading, asking what this is about. Screaming, "Let go!" The sound of the bathroom door being torn off. The sound of a roller shutter pulled down in a hurry.

"Tell us what is going on!"

The crowd buzzing. Fearful screams exploding here and there. No one dares look out the window. Inside our lone room, Cousin and I pull each other close. What could be going on? When the stomping of military boots fades away, silence instantly falls on the alley, which seemed about to burst any moment.

In the morning, Cousin goes out to get a cube of bean curd, but comes back empty-handed. The storekeeper, who used to go off on his bike each morning to pick up a whole plate of bean curd, was taken away in the night, they say.

"For what?"

"They don't know."

"But he must have done something wrong to be taken away."

"People say they took not just the storekeeper but also a man pissing in the alley."

"Where to?"

"I don't know. Remember he had a scar from an old cut under his eye. And a tattoo on his arm. He was kind of scary."

"What do you mean, scary? He used to give us the first briquette that was ready even before our turn."

"That's true . . ."

The storekeeper, whom Mom warned us not to get friendly with, disappears that night and does not return. The granny at the store sits there days on end, as if she has let go of her spirit, then closes up the store. She wanders here and there looking for the people who stomped in in the middle of the night and took her son. The store reopens and inside, the Virgin Mary figurines, which the storekeeper shaped out of clay whenever time allowed, lie on the shelf, broken and fallen over.

"What about *ajeossi*?"

"He's gone to some social purification training. I'm told that I should wait and he'll be back."

Left on her own, the granny no longer sells hot briquettes, even when winter arrives. She leaves the brazier, piled high with white ash, out on the street and sits there, gazing out toward where the alley ends.

A rite of blood, called on by lack of legitimacy.

One day as I was walking . . . It was 8 P.M., August 9, 1980. On my way to work I was taken into custody on the road by Dadaepo Beach by six police officers in combat gear, armed with carbines. Beaten up with clubs and bamboo sticks and kicked with boots, until I was close to death, I was taken to a Samcheong Training Camp in an army division somewhere in Changwon, with a serious injury on my back . . . This memoir, of a man who was taken away to a social purification program during that time and was now a pastor, opened with an introduction that began with the words, One day as I was walking . . .

One day as I was walking, I happened to come across a poster announcing a "showing of Gwangju incident videos." The place I headed to, clasping my pounding chest, was the Church Without the Camp in Yeongdeungpo.

How I wept, watching on the screen the atrocities of the Gwangju incident, which I had only heard of. The distorted faces of the numerous corpses, fallen at the hands of the soldiers under martial law, cracking down mercilessly on the citizens, as if engaged in a street battle . . .

I was taken into custody not for a criminal act but merely for having a criminal record, and the places where I was interned for two years and six months—the Samcheong Training Camp, the Samcheong Labor Service Camp, the military correctional facilities, the Cheongsong Protective Correctional Facility No.3—were nothing less than human slaughterhouses, unthinkable in a democratic state.

Nam-hong, who was taken at the age of seventeen to a valley somewhere near the frontlines in Gangwon Province, where he was shot in the side with an M16 while protesting his prolonged detention, meeting a bitter, regrettable death as he called out for his mom, his intestines pouring out of his body; Inmate Kim who was hit in the head by a gunshot from only several meters away, departing this world without a single cry; the desperate voices of fellow inmates begging to be spared, for the sake of parents and family back home, as they rolled in the sea of blood, beaten up mercilessly with boots, hoes, baseball bats, coming at them without control, without reason. These brutal memories . . .

When I came out alive of this hellish valley of death, blessed by the grace of God, I tried to erase from my memory the nightmarish past, never wanting to recall them ever again, and to forgive and forget all within the love of the Lord.

He wrote on. *However, however,* he was saying.

The images from the video of the Gwangju incident that I happened on that day presented me with great shock and helped me realize what it was I had to do for the people and history on the road to democratization. Numerous people were taken by force under the guise of social purification and struggled to survive for three, five years at the Samcheong Training Camp, a scene of bloodshed brought about by an unjust law that served to create a social atmosphere of fear in the course of the birth of a new regime. I plead, and pray, from deep in my heart that a campaign as tragic as the Samcheong Training will never take place again in this land, the way it did in 1980, a year when humanity, morality, and democracy were obliterated. I truly hope that this book will be read by many around the country, to ensure that there will never again be another case where a great number of people are unjustly sacrificed for the glory of a single individual. I also hope that this book will contribute, in some small way, to restoring the honor of my many peers who died in that valley in the frontlines, unable to overcome the pain of being accused as a criminal without trial; those who were befallen by machine guns while engaged in bloody resistance; and the ten thousand men who endured the Samcheong Training Camp, coerced into sacrificing their dignity while suffering in silence.

. . . Kyungnam University student Kim, dragged away like a dog while shouting for democracy; office worker Sin, taken in while making a drunken ruckus at home only a month into his marriage; high school graduate Lee studying for his second attempt at college entrance, accused as a gang member while on an outing; labor worker Song, taken in by the police while demanding overdue wages; seventeen-year-old high school student Nam, taken in while heading out to greet his mother; Lee, a chef taken in because of a tattoo on his arm while getting off work; street vendor Bak taken in while selling his wares at the market; newspaper reporter Yi dragged in like a dog, beaten and covered in blood after being dismissed from his job; old bachelor Hwang dragged in while badgering his parents to find him a wife; sixty-year-old Kim . . .

Did the storekeeper, taken in while making ceramic figurines of Virgin Mary, make it back? I did not see him again, not even after leaving the alley.

I am wiping the floor of our lone room with a rag. While wiping Oldest Brother's desk, I quietly open the drawer. Finally, he's gotten rid of it. The woman's necklace is not there. I am now relieved.

As summer vacation approaches, Oldest Brother plans out a new schedule. Enrollment has increased at the tutoring center, so he will be able to make quite a bit of money over summer break, he says. Saying that the director has promised to give him another hour-long class over the summer, Oldest Brother seems cheery. But how will he find the time when his mornings and evenings are already full?

"The class is scheduled from six thirty to eight so I can go straight from my military service shift."

"What about dinner?"

"My next class starts at nine, so I can eat in between."

He says that after summer, his military service will be done and he'll be able to get a proper job again, then we will be able to rent a bigger place.

Our wages fall into arrears.

We receive the wages for the previous month only on the next month's payday. I miss Union Leader and Miss Lee and Seoseon. Those faces that were always carrying out discussion over lukewarm bean sprout soup poured over rice on the stainless steel serving tray, with some soured kimchi on the side. Those faces that used to shout, about the company president, "Even if he dies, we must not cry, no one." If only they were here, our wages would not be in arrears like this.

Suddenly all's quiet at work. There is talk that the stereo division will be closed down, and also that the president will hand over the company to the bank. As if to prove the rumors right, the conveyor belt at Line A, the one assembly line still in production, comes to a stop. Now there is no work to be done. We clean the facilities and sit around and chat. We never have to stand in line for lunch at the cafeteria. People have left the factory one by one and those who remain are mostly from the TV division.

School is about to let out for summer vacation. I come home from school to find Oldest Brother at the desk.

"*Oppa*, how come you're back so early?"

Instead of answering my question, Oldest Brother tells me to come sit as I head up to the attic to change.

"What's this?"

I, eighteen years old, adjust the buttons on my uniform.

"How come you're home by yourself?"

". . . Well actually."

As I stammer, Oldest Brother raises his voice at me.

"Why are you doing this? All of you going about doing whatever you want? . . . What is this, I asked!"

"Phone . . . to be a phone operator . . ." I stammer.

"When did she stop going to school?"

"About . . . a month ago."

"At least you could have told me, don't you think?"

"She asked me not to . . ."

"You didn't because she asked not to? You still have no idea what's important, do you!"

I, feeling cornered, start to weep. Cousin walks in the door, clueless, but noticing Oldest Brother's angry eyes as she put down her schoolbag, she quickly lowers her eyes, startled. I had been swallowing Oldest Brother's scolding but upon seeing Cousin's face, I burst into tears.

"Stop the crying!"

I try to stop but can't. Tears start falling from Cousin's eyes as well. As we both weep, Oldest Brother looks on, dumbfounded.

"You'd think I'd given you a beating or something."

We expected a huge ruckus, but Oldest Brother goes back to his desk and sits with his back to us. But his back carries an air of determination.

"If you're not going to stay in school, you should pack up and leave." Cousin's tears fall more profusely. "Will you go back to school or not?"

Cousin goes on crying without an answer. Oldest Brother looks back with a cold expression. "Will you go back to school or not?"

"I will." Oldest Brother sounds so firm it stops Cousin's tears. He sounds as if he will take her straight to the train station and buy her a ticket, telling her to leave for the country, if she answers that she will not go back to school. Wiping away her tears, Cousin goes up to the attic to take off her uniform.

We are lying down to sleep after washing our faces and feet in silence. Cousin is crouched with her face turned to the wall. From the other end of the room, Oldest Brother calls Cousin's name. Still crouching, Cousin responds in a feeble voice.

"Is that what you want to be, a phone operator?"

"No."

Looking confused by Cousin's answer, Oldest Brother asks, "Then why did you start going to the training school instead?"

"I don't want to work in a factory, *Oppa*." There is no hesitation in her answer. Oldest Brother seems taken aback.

"Is it that bad?"

"It is."

Oldest Brother asks again, as if he's had a thought.

"Then what about working somewhere like the Community Service Center?"

"I'd like that!" Cousin immediately sits up.

"There's nothing to like. If you ask me, working at a factory is better."

"Is there an opening?"

"For someone to run errands. Take papers to the district office, answer calls, things like that."

"That's fine. Anything's fine with me as long as it's not the factory." Cousin pleads with Oldest Brother to please get her the job at the Community Service Center. Saying that she feels even less like working at the factory nowadays. We don't have anywhere to sit, we don't get paid, and everyone says the company will go under soon.

My cousin, now twenty-one years old and about to leave the factory, is cheerful. Now in the morning, she takes the subway to the Yongsan Community Service Center. On the road leading to Industrial Complex No. 1, at the market entrance, on the overpass, I think of taking Cousin's arm and feel overcome with emptiness.

For the first time, I hear the word "lockout." Lockout? It was better when every day we had to work overtime and extra hours. When the conveyor belt churned on and on frantically. I hear someone behind me throwing a fit.

"How come every company I work for goes under! My darn luck."

In the evening I see Cousin at school. "Did they process my severance pay yet?"

I shake my head.

"I worked for them until my bones were loose, they should at least give me my severance pay."

"They say the company is going under."

"What?"

"There's going to be a lockout."

Cousin is left speechless as well at the gravity of this word, lockout. Mi-seo sends me a note while reading Hegel. The note reads, "Any vacancies at your factory?" None. Even my position's gone. An Hyang-suk glances at Mi-seo's note.

"Are they having problems at Mi-seo's factory?"

"Not sure."

An Hyang-suk walks over to Mi-seo.

"You want to come work at our factory? They're hiring."

Mi-seo, who has always shown disregard for An Hyang-suk, pushes her face into her Hegel again, as if it's a ridiculous suggestion.

"Did you see her being all snooty!" An Hyang-suk grumbles, returning to her seat. Mi-seo stays unmoved, her face buried in the book.

"Look into it for her, though. It seems you're the only one in our class who lives in a dormitory."

"Why, does Mi-seo need to live in a dorm? But she commutes from her sister's place, doesn't she?"

"She doesn't like her brother-in-law."

"How come?"

"He and her sister fight all the time."

"But isn't it a treat to live outside the industrial complex? After school, whenever I see Mi-seo cross the street alone to take the bus in the opposite direction from the rest of us, I get envious. At least she gets to see other neighborhoods each morning and night."

"You will look into it, right?"

"But why are you so worked up about it?"

"You will, won't you?"

"All right!"

The next day when I ask how it went, An Hyang-suk shakes her head.

"They said 'no students.'"

I received a letter from my publisher. I opened the envelope to find another one inside. The publisher must have forwarded me a letter that was sent to their address but meant for me. The envelope was thick, appearing to contain a long letter. I checked the name of the sender: Han Gyeong-sin, Faculty, Yeongdeungpo Girls' High School, Singil-dong, Yeongdeungpo-gu, Seoul.

Han Gyeong-sin? Ah! Teacher Choe Hong-i, no, Han Gyeong-sin. My heart sank. I had not been able to accept her invitation to visit her students at Yeongdeungpo Girls' High School, and on top of that, I had quoted her letter in my novel without her permission. There was a note written next to the postal code in neat handwriting, asking that the letter be forwarded to me. Someone with this handwriting would not reproach me, I told myself, trying to comfort my sinking heart.

March 6, 1995

Hello.

I read the second chapter of your novel a few days ago. There was more going on compared to the preceding chapter and I enjoyed it, finishing it in one sitting.

Enjoyed it?

It might be misleading to say I "enjoyed" it. It is my way of describing a compelling experience that gave me much to think about, not one that I found merely entertaining.

After publishing *The Dwarf Launches His Tiny Ball*, Cho Se-hui wrote one or two more linked stories for *The Literary Joongang*, but declared that he would no longer write fiction. Among his reasons, this is what I remember vividly. "Many people told me that they were moved by my story. But their faces appeared so bright and happy."

It occurred to me that you might feel the same way when people tell you after reading your novel that they enjoyed it.

It's been only two years since I began teaching at the Program for Industrial Workers, but as I read your book, there were so many things that I wanted to tell you. I wanted to explain to you the differences between the industrial scene that you experienced in the early eighties and one that my students are in today, and I wanted to convey the differences between the classroom scene of then and now; the inferiority that is still seizing the students despite the change; their wary relationship with the day students; their work environment that I have observed; the companies' method of managing the students; and so many other things.

March, 1979, the year you entered the Special Program for Industrial Workers at Yeongdeungpo Girls' High School at the age of seventeen, was a special time for me as well. That was when I was appointed to a faculty position at Jangchung Girls' Middle School, straight out of university. A couple of classes were set up there for industrial workers as well. But these students would arrive at school after we got off work, so the only time I got to see them was Field Day, which took place once a year. The students, who appeared two or three years older than the day students, and were taller as well, got to take the day off and participate in the activities, and they seemed excited.

What I remember about them was the three-legged race held on Field Day. You remember, two people racing with a leg tied to each other's? It's simple enough, if you just keep in step, one, two, one, two, but the students, older and taller, kept getting their feet tangled and fell behind the day students. I remember the teachers all saying, in surprise, "It's the power of education. Learning from social experience. It has nothing to do with age, does it?" Other than that, I was barely aware of the special industrial workers program, until after working at many different schools, I was appointed to Yeongdeungpo Girl's High School three years ago. I was going through a difficult time, having entered a PhD program late in my career, and was planning to take a leave of absence in a year, but the vice principal recommended taking an English teacher position for the special classes, mentioning that the schedule should allow me to pursue my academic work as well.

Going into the program, I was prejudiced, that these students, "pitiful and faced with such hardship," would require much care. My heart ached just thinking that they had to work all day and study at night. But when I read their self-introductory essays, my thoughts were changed. Their writings captured the same hopes, despairs, goals and the small, mundane joys of the everyday, no different from those of a day student. My previous position had been at a so-called "elite" school and I had spent the first year at Yeongdeungpo in the day program, so I was able to compare three different groups of students. And I had come to recognize the very ordinary truth that the quantities and the qualities of the dreams, hopes or despairs of the students in various environments were not different.

Of course, many of the students from affluent areas possess economic and material wealth. However, I do not believe that the dreams they write about, as in "I want to be a world-class designer" or "I want to be a doctor," are any different, in quality, from the dreams of the students in the industrial workers classes, like "I want to learn the skills to become a beautician," "I'm going to save up to open a small gift shop," or "I want to go to college, even if it's just a two-year vocational school."

There are students who have been damaged by parental negligence despite the material wealth that they were born into, while there are industrial worker students who say, "I couldn't stand my drunken dad and practically ran away to Seoul. But nowadays Dad has gotten his act together and I visit home with gifts on Chuseok holidays."

I recall the faces of students from wealthy neighborhoods, fatigued from academic pressure despite their affluence. One student, who looked like a doll with her round, twinkling eyes, always had on an anxious face, full of regret. She said her parents had both attended good schools but she would never get into a top university, so her mother was too embarrassed to leave the house, her heart always pounding.

When we have the physical fitness test for college entrance, every year I see a group of girls behind the current seniors, making their fourth attempt at entering college. How tame and good-hearted they seemed. They were in most cases students who had the lowest grades around. Their parents continued to send them to college prep cram schools because it was too scary to send a daughter overseas, but they still could not stand the idea of their daughter ending up a mere high school graduate. If these students had been born into a less well-off family, they would be enjoying a healthy work life. You wrote that you still wake up in the same crouched-up position as when you used to sleep in the lone room. These students might go to sleep in their soft beds, in their spacious rooms, but they would awake each morning to find their minds crouched up even tighter.

Perhaps I am able to make this comparison only because the industrial labor conditions these days have far improved from the eighties. Last year I had the chance to visit several of the factories where my students worked. At one factory, where a majority of my students worked, labor representatives participated in wage negotiations, including one of my students. Working conditions were clean and many of the procedures had been automated. On weekdays they worked from eight thirty to five and until one P.M. on Saturdays. At some divisions, workers took every other Saturday off. If you could see fabrics being cut by computerized controls and automated robots ironing shirts on mannequins, I think you would be astonished at how times have changed.

Other factories offer slightly less favorable conditions but in most places, the workers get off work on Saturdays by three P.M. After Saturday classes were pulled up to four P.M. from six, some companies made their student workers resume work from ten P.M. to midnight on Friday nights when they returned to their dormitories after school, which "infuriated" the teachers and the students, but this is the worst that can happen in the work environment of the nineties.

Once, when students were absent without leave, protesting the use of abusive language by a mid-level managing staff, the school mediated by arranging a meeting between the students and company representatives. Companies have various tactics to keep a close watch on the students. The worst kind has staff waiting outside the school and takes the students, almost by force. When students quit their jobs, unable to endure inhumane treatment, some companies issue official requests pressuring the school to expel the student. On the other hand, some companies try to guide the students when their work is unsatisfactory or when they have violated dorm regulations, and will fire them only when the efforts turn out useless.

But they will still say, "We will not notify the school, so do continue with your studies if you wish." The bigger companies can afford to do this, but as with individuals, humane consideration is not always proportionate to the company's wealth.

My first worker students, especially the first-year students, all seemed quite hopeful about the future. Many had come from the country, in hopes to make money and study at the same time. But as time goes by, they began to get weary. And about 30 percent of the students drop out. In many cases, they find it hard to overcome the hardships, the loneliness, and the fatigue they face living far away from home. But what I find more discouraging is when students get caught up in the glamorous temptations around them and leave the school for the entertainment district. Their parents, who should be disciplining them, are back in the country, while the students are so fragile, weary, and overwhelmed. Their work conditions might have improved compared to the eighties, but since their surrounding environment has become more decadent and affluent as well, their sense of relative poverty might also be heightened.

But the rest of the students charge on energetically with their lives. Those suffering from stomach ailments or backaches often miss school, but there are also quite a number of students who maintain perfect attendance. When I encounter students who appear no different from students who have received a good education in well-to-do families, my heart brightens.

Last time I wrote to you, I did get the feeling that you probably would not accept my invitation. Thinking that you would be averse to expressions like "labor" or "working by day and studying by night," I tried to "lure" you by trying to emphasize the occasion as a meeting between a writer and her readers, rather than one between an alumnus and current students, hoping it might appeal to your writerly sensibilities. But while I was reading the first chapter of your book a few days after mailing my letter, I thought, "She would not come. If I had read this first, I would not have written her."

When I read the first chapter, I was quite surprised that you were looking back on those times with such pain, after all this time. And I asked my students whether they also felt shameful or inferior about attending night classes. About half appeared unaffected and the other half answered that they felt the same. I asked what there is to feel inferior about, when they were working so hard, at school and at the factory, and I got an unexpected answer.

"People don't all think like you do. If you tell them you attend night classes, they'd look down on you, and if you tell them you attend night classes for industrial workers, they'd look down even more."

"If you have a boyfriend, it's better to say you just stay home, without a job. People think it's better to be idle and out of job than being a factory girl."

"Our teachers are always talking about how we 'work by day and study at night,' but I don't like hearing that expression."

All I could offer them was that they are acquiring skills that could support them for the rest of their lives, while three fourths of the day students will never make it to college, and then I gave them this quote from Eleanor Roosevelt: "No one can make you feel inferior without your consent."

One of the teachers, who has been teaching the special program for a long time, tells me that the students have an intense sense of inferiority, more than we think. They even think that only the most inferior teachers get assigned to the program, when the truth is that many of the teachers apply to the program in order to pursue their higher degrees and therefore are better educated.

Well, come to think of it, we had a big laugh hearing that a wife of one of our teachers was told this by a friend: "Is your husband still teaching the night program? You should make him study more and move to the day classes."

We teachers try to be as considerate as we can so that the students don't feel discriminated against. During school festivals when the day students stay behind late, we make sure to hold the music performances or film showings off campus to prevent any conflict. We hold special ceremonies to mark the beginning of vacation, which, I heard, was devised in order to prevent any misunderstanding on the first day of school, about night students leaving a mess behind.

Once I told my senior class, "Don't leave scribbles on the desks. You're sharing them with other students," and it started a clamor. They said, "We never write on the desks. We've been keeping our mouths shut until now, but you know what the day students write? Words like *bitch* we see all the time, and we get things like, 'You're factory girls, you should at least clean up your waste paper if you want to study at school.' Or even, 'If I were you, I'd rather die than work as a factory girl.'"

I was in such a fluster trying to comfort my students. "In any group, there are bound to be one or two people who lack character. I'm sure you have people like that at work as well, right? If the other students learned that their own classmates are writing such things, they will feel apologetic and ashamed," I said to them. "If you trip on a rock as you're walking down the street, say, 'Just my luck,' and keep going. What would people say if you shouted, 'You rock, why were you there?'"

At my words, the students answered, "They'd say you're crazy!" and burst into laughter. They were seniors, mature enough to laugh at this. If they were in their first year of high school, such scribbles would have hurt them more deeply.

The academic level of the students lags behind these days compared to when you were studying here. Back then, there were many applicants so the admission process was more selective, requiring a year or two of work experience. But nowadays, the number of students has dropped and because they start school immediately after getting hired, most are young, lacking determination.

"Is someone still reading Hegel in that classroom today?" Today, I asked my students if they knew who Hegel was. Most answered, "Sounds like a name that came up in ethics class, was he a scientist or a philosopher?" Come to think of it, such phenomenon is not restricted to night students in the Special Program for Industrial Workers.

A while back, I asked students at a so-called prestigious high school, "Do you know who Simone de Beauvoir is?" and no one could answer. So I asked if they knew what she meant when she said, "One is not born, but rather becomes, a woman," and they all just looked at me blankly, except for one girl who said, "Doesn't it mean that women should use makeup and take care of their looks?"

I know that you still feel pain, unable to brush away your memories of the weary and difficult years. But from where I stand, as a teacher, I think you have truly been "blessed." Among the hundreds of students in the industrial worker program, I have yet to find a single one who had siblings that were able to provide such a rich spiritual and cultural soil for growth. Meeting a teacher like Choe Hong-i was also a blessing, one that was possible only at that specific place and time. Nowadays, it is unimaginable that a student spends class time copying a novel in her notebook, in any class at any school. The reality in education today calls for students to stage a perfectly orchestrated, massive performance, don't you think?

This year, we accepted no new students in the program. The number of applicants has fallen sharply in the past few years. This is because living standards have improved and most parents are able to send their children to high school. In two years, the Special Program for Industrial Workers, which you have tried hard to leave behind and forget, will become history. We now have only 110 students, in all of the second- and third-year classes combined. As the number of classes decreases, I will leave the school as well next year.

Adapting to a new environment is never easy it seems, for adults or for children. On my first day here, due to the abrupt shift in routine, I felt awkward and anxious about being at school in the dark of the night, and the fatigue I felt was just as bad, despite the reduced hours, which made me think I should have just taken a leave. Heading home after classes ended at five past nine o'clock, I gazed out the window as I crossed Yanghwa Bridge. The lights along the river were emitting a beautiful glow, as if in a dream, and the river looked quiet, deep, cozy. At that moment, my heart also turned tranquil and I can clearly remember myself thinking, "What lies in front of me is also a new world waiting to be encountered. This job might delay my studies, but this new experience with the students here will bring new insight and spiritual nourishment to my life, won't it?" Perhaps it is also a small gift of karma from my life here with my students that I am writing this letter to you today.

If ever you feel you have the time and the courage to reencounter those "high school girls in white summer uniforms" before the Special

> Program for Industrial Workers is closed down entirely, please let me know. But please do not feel pressured, either. You wouldn't carry this letter around for a whole year now, would you?
>
> I wish you good health. In both body and mind.
>
> Yours sincerely,
> Han Gyeong-sin

I read the letter again from the beginning.

Putting it back into the envelope, the way it first arrived, I placed it on my desk and gazed at it for a long time. I wanted to write her back. I pulled out a few sheets from the pile of printer paper, laid them out on the desk and filled my fountain pen with ink. I copied down the greeting from Ms. Han's letter. *Hello.* An hour passed but the only thing written on the sheet of paper was *Hello.* I sat there staring into the dried tip of my pen, then put the cap back on. I inserted the letter between the pages of my photo album from back then, then got up from my chair.

This year, we accepted no new students in the program—The sentence flowed out from the letter and stepped into me as I rose from the desk. The program will probably be closed next year, I imagine. Just a trace, disappearing into the story.

I took out a songbook from the shelf and as I bent down to lie prone on the floor, lifted myself up and called J. I heard her twinkling laughter.

"So you've sent in your manuscript."

"No."

Silence.

"Let me sing you a song."

"Let me hear it."

"Ring-a-ding last summer we met by the sea . . . Ring-a-ding all the things we had to say . . . Ring-a-ding but the night was so short."

Just as the current class has Teacher Han Gyeong-sin, we had Teacher Choe Hong-i. The one who had said to me, Why don't you try writing a novel. He is no longer my homeroom teacher, but in class, while we copy his notes from the blackboard, he paces back and forth between the rows of desks, then leaves a book on my desk. It has a red cover. I stare at it for a long time. Printed at the top is the phrase *Voicing Our History.*

Below is a solid black line, and the title in large black type: *Action and Literature.* Below, I read for the first time, the word "grassroots." *Magazine-style Publication at the Forefront of Grassroots Literary Activism, Inaugural Issue.* Poetry. Fiction. Special Features. Criticism. Vol. 1. 1980. Jeonyewon Publishing. I, eighteen years old, flip through the pages but have no idea what the words mean. I find a work of fiction and start reading. "Mr. Gang from Our Village," by Yi Mun-gu.

Before our factory shuts down, the cram school where Oldest Brother teaches, wearing his wig, is forced to close. A nationwide ban, abrupt and unexpected, on extracurricular private tutoring. Oldest Brother had been excited at the prospect of renting an additional room for us by extending his summer teaching hours, but with the tutoring ban, he is now an unemployed man.

"You guys will have to provide for me now." He takes off his wig and hangs it on the other side of the attic door, putting on a weary smile.

Summer vacation. I, eighteen years old, am sleeping in our country home. Father has closed his shop and is now concentrating on farming. No good with a scythe and no good at weaving straw baskets, Father tunes in to the agricultural report on the radio each morning. He marks the important facts on the Farmers' Co-op calendar on the wall. There is the sound of Mother making breakfast in the kitchen. When I get up, Father calls my name in a low voice. I am about to head to the kitchen but turn around and sit next to Father. He takes down a box from the top of the wardrobe. To my surprise, my letters to Chang spill out of the box. My face flushes red.

"When your mom first said something's going on with you and Chang, I didn't really listen . . ." Father pushes the letters toward his eighteen-year-old daughter. "Now I'm not saying something's really going on between you and Chang, but once you start sending letters and stuff, you'll both get attached to each other and . . . Your mom, she's terribly worried, you see."

Father, who has never played the role of the ill-spirited parent, sounds all muffled.

"Your mom, you see!"

He keeps blaming Mom.

"When it's time for the mailman to arrive, she walks out to the main street to wait, to take your letters to Chang. Now, the mailman brings your letters straight to your mom."

I say nothing.

"To think that you're waiting for his reply, not knowing any of this . . ." In my embarrassment and anger and distress, I break into tears. "There're no parents in this world that wish their child unwell."

I pick up the letters one by one without saying a word and go to the other room. Not knowing any of this, I had been waiting everyday for Chang's reply. I had felt a bitter grudge as I waited. Thinking, "It's because I'm a factory girl, isn't it?" And when my grudge subsided somewhat, I would write another letter. All through spring, all through summer, that was what I had been doing, repeatedly. But this was what Mom had been up to?

Not knowing that Father has told me everything about the letters, all through my vacation Mom keeps asking, "Is anything the matter? What is it?" I do not speak a word. I do not answer when Mom calls. I do not even touch the chicken that Mom has boiled for me. Mom, feeling upset, takes it out on Father.

"This is why children need to grow up in their parents' bosoms, no matter what. Just look at her! Already she thinks nothing of what I have to say. All bitter that she's being put through a difficult life, I bet. Just wait until she's older. She's gonna look away when we run into her on the street. Wonder who she takes after? Prickly as a summer rash she is!"

She might talk like this, but since I'll be heading back to the city the next day on the train, Mom keeps circling me all day, trying to get to eat something. When she serves up a plate of zucchini pancakes, I turn away. Unable to take it anymore, she hollers at me, demanding to know where I picked up such an attitude.

"Just what kind of a person would do that, who? What kind of a daughter glares at her mother like some ruffian?"

I turn around and face her as I shout. "You don't know anything!"

This results in a misunderstanding, pushing things in an unexpected direction.

"You're right, I'm a foolish know-nothing, that's all I am." Mom's eyes fill up with tears.

"Is it so bad what I have done?" Teardrops fall from her dark eyes. "I knew when I took you to Seoul that I'm guilty for this wretched life of mine!"

Little Brother, who had been sitting by my side, pushes me away and goes over to Mom. "Mom, don't cry, don't."

"Sending you, still only a girl, to stay with your fierce-tempered brothers . . . always wondering if the three of you are getting by or arguing or eating at each mealtime . . . if it weren't so far away, I could look in more often but . . . Every time I cook, I think of you and I'm so tormented, I go weak in my knees. You're still young, got so much growing up to do, but I've turned you into a kitchen maid for your brothers, that's what I tell myself, so how could my heart afford a single day of sun?"

I stand outside Chang's front gate. Chang looks like he's returning after a night bath in the brook, carrying a soapbox in his hand. We walk together toward the railroad. We sit down by the embankment. Summer night. Stars glitter. A train speeds through the dark. The long, brightly lit train reminds me of the embankment abloom with flowers. I have inside my pocket the letters that were never delivered. Each time a breeze blows past, the scent of soap floats from Chang to me. He tells me he's taken up painting. That he's planning to go to an art college.

Painting? I had never heard Chang mention anything about painting. Out of the blue, he insists that we should both go to college. College? I am unable to answer as I pick at the letters inside my pocket, the letters that were never delivered to him.

"What kind of paintings are you working on?"

"Traditional ink paintings."

Ink paintings? He says he takes lessons at a studio after school to prepare for college entrance. Says that he will go to college and become a painter. He tells me to go to college, no matter what, and become a writer. "Let's try hard to get into college, we must!" Chang sounds like he's making a pledge.

College? The moment I hear this word, I can no longer smell Chang's soap scent. I head back in the end, without handing him my letters.

I remember that rainy day in the fall. That fall when two months had gone by without receiving our wages. At the factory, where

I no longer had Cousin with me, the locker room is the only place I can find some comfort. I shake in the chill of the autumn rain. This locker room, which I would slip into when I had to stand around all day after failing to get a position assigned in the morning. Those who quit their job leave their uniforms on plastic hangers in the locker. They are required to hand in their uniforms along with their resignation letter, but what with the overdue wages, the severance pay that has yet to be processed, the company is in no position to demand that they follow regulations, nor do the workers care to. There are many faces that never return after getting off work one day, and these are the blue uniforms that they have left behind. On this rainy day, I had been assigned to the engine room but the only thing I could do there was to stare at the machines sawing wood or at the masks on the engine room staff's faces for keeping away the sawdust, which is rising like clouds. The reason I had walked up to the dark locker room and pulled one of the uniforms from its plastic hanger, its shoulders drooping low, and put it on over my own uniform, was because I was feeling cold.

It was for that same reason that I put my hands in the pockets. My hands touch something. I pull it out and it is a white envelope. Only then I check the nametag on the uniform shirt. Yun Sun-im. The shirt belonged not to one of the workers who had quit but to Yun Sun-im, a colleague. Had she gone home early, or was she gone for a short errand? I look into the envelope in the dark. Inside is a crisp new 10,000-won bill. My heart starts beating fast. The quiet, deserted locker room. Yun Sun-im, who had been the object of admiration of the engineering student intern, the one whom Cousin was in love with.

I take off the shirt, hang it in the locker and slip out of the room. I return to the engine room and sit amidst the noise of machines sawing wood. I head to the production department office and submit a request to leave work early. I return to the locker room and undress in a hurry.

I fetch my schoolbag from the top of the locker. I then push my hand into Yun Sun-im's uniform shirt, grab the envelope, and rush out. I walk and walk in the autumn rain, across the industrial complex in broad daylight, and arriving at our lone, remote room in the middle of the day, shut the door behind me, my heart pounding.

Had I fallen asleep? I wake at someone's shaking to find Oldest Brother, who no longer has a job.

"You didn't go to school? . . . Are you feeling okay?"

I keep lying there, unable to sit up, and Oldest Brother puts his hand on my forehead, asking again if I'm feeling okay. He gazes down at me for a moment, then heads out, returning with medicine from the pharmacy.

"You're burning up with fever. You should have gotten out your bedding."

I just lie there. "Probably just a cold. Get some sleep and you should feel better."

When I try to get up, he tells me to stay as I am. He pulls out the mattress from our vinyl wardrobe and slips a pillow under my head.

Bean sprout soup, that's what Oldest Brother cooks for me. He never eats bean sprout soup, so he's put in too much chili powder, turning the soup all red.

Later at night, Cousin comes home from school and, seeing me lying on the floor, asks if I'm okay. As she tells me that she was worried I wasn't at school, she holds a white envelope in her hand.

"I found this letter under our door. Just your name written on it in large print."

"Letter . . . ?"

Oldest Brother, from where he is sitting at the desk, looks down at me, lying on the floor, as if to ask what it's about. When

I just lie there after taking the letter from Cousin, he comes down to the floor and turns on the TV. Cousin goes up to the attic to change, then heads to the kitchen.

"Who's it from?" Cousin asks, craning her neck into the room in the middle of washing her feet on the kitchen floor. She must think it odd that I still haven't opened the letter, asking me "What's wrong?" Oldest Brother also turns his eyes from the TV and looks at me. He presses his palm against the back of his neck, as if he's feeling stiff. The sound of Cousin splashing water over her feet in the kitchen. Oldest Brother sitting back in a languorous pose as he watches TV. I sense fear that the moment I open the letter, the peace in this room will shatter. My eighteen-year-old hand trembles as it pulls out the letter from the envelope.

> I ask you to return the envelope you took from my
> shirt. I desperately need the money . . .
> Yun Sun-im

I pull up the blanket and cover my face. Under the blanket, the letter crumbles inside my hand.

In the morning, I set out with Cousin, but after she heads for the subway, I return to our lone room. I lock the door from the inside, as if someone is chasing me. All day long, I sit frozen in the room. I feel as if someone will snatch me by the neck if I set foot in the world outside the door. I feel like I'll be dragged away and never be able to return. Around lunchtime, someone knocks on the door. "Are you in there?" I recognize that it's Yun Sun-im's voice. My school shoes left outside the door would have told her that I was in the room. I open the door and find Yun Sun-im standing outside. I hurry and pull out the white envelope from my schoolbag.

"Thanks." She smiles as she takes the envelope.

The sound of hammering, drilling . . . There was construction going on since early morning, in the apartment either next to or below mine. Crack and crumble, it sounded like they were drilling through a wall. *Bang, bang,* it sounded like they were knocking the wall down. I had already missed my deadline and could not afford to lose a single morning. I lifted my head and gazed out toward the hills. Red azaleas had blanketed the hills but now half of them were dead. I felt I was lost inside a fog. My eyes were sore. The drilling quieted down. Intense noise followed by intense silence. Was it over now?

As I blinked my sore eyes, the drilling began again, loud enough to knock down not only walls but mountains. They must have been trying to tear down the entire apartment. I went into the room on the other side of the hallway. Was the noise coming from downstairs, not next door? Even when I got out of the room that shared a wall with the apartment next door, the drilling sound followed me persistently, as if my eardrum were being punctured. Just what kind of construction work was this?

I was not very sensitive to noise. I could usually block it out if I tried to. Wherever I was, I was able to maintain my concentration. Even when I was amidst a large group of people, I could focus on my thoughts. I had the number one position on the line, and although we stood with the conveyor between us, the person across from me was in charge of testing the finished product. The quality control staff from the testing department raised and lowered the stereo volume all day to check each product. My ears were exposed all day long to piercing sounds, high notes and low notes, the sound of the air driver fizzing, the rumble of the conveyor belt, the zapping of the soldering iron.

After I left, I had been indifferent to most noise.

. . . Life was always fair. It never gives all or takes away all. It made me open my notebook amidst all that noise and write to Chang, allowing me to feel a tender, warm presence.

. . . But the drilling, and now the hammering. It was as if they were about to drill holes into everything in this world. I stepped inside the bathroom and squeezed out a large amount of toothpaste to brush my teeth, then washed my hands and rubbed my face with soap. *Rumble, crash, bang!* The noises from the past were like a lullaby compared to this.

Shouldn't they have sought consent from the neighbors if things were going to be this bad?

I felt annoyed at the face I could not even see. It was as if my face were being chipped, my calves twisting into a whirl. I should at least find out when it would be done. I slipped on my shoes and rang the bell next door. The woman next door stuck out her head.

"Not us. It's downstairs." It seemed like she was just as irritated, the way she answered even before I could ask. I walked downstairs to find the door open. Peering inside, I could see that the threshold to the balcony was smashed to pieces.

"Excuse me." Unable to hear me, the worker did not even look back. "Excuse me!"

No owner, just the contractors. One of the workers finally looked up, his hands on the drill and his face covered with brick dust.

"Can I speak to the owner?"

"Not here right now!"

"I live upstairs."

I pointed with my finger.

"When will the work be done?"

"It'll take about three days."

Three days? Unbelievable. I returned and washed my hands at the bathroom sink, rubbing hard.

On Saturday, Oldest Brother finally brings it up. "Why aren't you going to work? Have you quit? . . . You don't like working at the factory, either, is that it?"

"..."

"You just need to hold on a little longer, just until I finish military service."

"..."

"Say something!" The more he pushes, the more I clam up. "You got scoops of honey in your mouth or something? Say something!"

But how could I tell him that I did not have the heart to look at Yun Sun-im.

"If you're going to be nothing but trouble, pack up your things and go back to the country." Oldest Brother leaves the room, slamming the door behind him. I put on my uniform and walk out to the alley, carrying not my things but my schoolbag. I don't even have any money for fare. I trudge along, to Jinhui Tailor Shop, by the entrance of Industrial Complex No. 2. I see a man next to Hui-jae *eonni*, cutting a piece of blue fabric, his face marked with a blue spot the size of a palm. To my eighteen-year-old eyes, it all feels sore, the blue spot, the blue fabric.

"What are you doing here?" In the shop's cutting room, Hui-jae opens her eyes wide, her face pale. The cramped hallway. A mess of fabric scraps strewn on the floor. With no chairs to sit on, Hui-jae's tiny body is placed upon a wooden chest that looks like a piece of shipping cargo.

"I need to borrow some money."

"How much?"

"Five thousand won."

She hands me 5,000 won without asking me what I need it for. Instead of going to school, I head to Seoul Station. Each time I think of Oldest Brother, yelling at me to pack up and go back to the country, my heart suddenly feels numb.

Mom.

What will I say to Mom if I go back to the country? I won't go back. I won't go where you can find me. I will go away and never come back. See if you can get by without me. I get a ticket for a night train to Busan. Pledging, I won't ever go back to you, I won't ever go back to that room.

As soon as the train leaves Seoul Station, I want to get off. I see Oldest Brother's heavy shoulders glimmering at the window. His wig hanging on the attic door. His hands washing his socks in the kitchen, as if it were a habit. His movements as he sat up in the dark and headed to the rooftop after his girl left him. The smells his body carried when he came back after a long while, the cold scent of the night wind, the scent of his wounds.

But my neck quickly stiffens as I think of his voice, telling me to pack up and go back to the country. I'm not going back. The train speeds past a trail of lights at the bottom of distant mountains. The train enters a tunnel. *Oppa.* The train is full of a myriad odd smells.

A baby cries and a woman bursts into a scream trying to calm the baby, an old man snores while a group of young women chat and grin, chewing strips of dried squid, and strange men play cards, loud and rowdy. I see my eighteen-year-old self on the window, looking scared amidst the swarm of people. Busan? Where can that be? Each time the door opens, a pungent odor drifts in with the wind. My hearts pounds with a longing to return to Oldest Brother. Getting off at Busan Station at the break of dawn, I buy a ticket back to Seoul then sit there and wait without taking a single step outside the station, to board the train once again. Daylight starts to spread. Outside my window, a flock of baby birds flies from wire to wire. The train's steel wheels go *click-clack-click* as it runs at full speed, back toward our lone room.

From Seoul Station, I take the subway, get off at Garibong Station, walk past the photo studio, past the corner store, and arrive at the front gate. I step inside, pushing the gate open, and Oldest Brother runs down from the third floor.

"Where have you been?" He looks like he hasn't been able to sleep all night. His eyes are bloodshot as he presses me for an answer. His palm lands with a slap on my eighteen-year-old cheek.

"You wretched girl." I am bursting into tears when he pulls me into his arms. "I thought there'd been an accident or something!"

As my quivering tension melts away, tears keep rolling down my face. Oldest Brother tears my face from his chest and makes a thundering sound.

"If you do that one more time, I'm going to kill you, I swear!"

Yun Sun-im. She comes to see me in the middle of the day, as I lay alone in the lone room. I sit up, startled. The sound of radio playing in one of the rooms. Why has she come to me? I sit there fidgeting. Why has she come to me?

"You wanna hear a story?"

Yun Sun-im, with a snaggle tooth that makes her lips roll up each time she smiles, revealing her gums, cheery and red.

"I dropped out of high school . . . You know why?"

". . ."

"I happened to open my desk partner's pencil case, without thinking, really, and found two thousand-won bills. I didn't dream for a second that I'd steal the money. But before I knew it, my hands were picking it up. With this money, I thought, I could buy myself a girdle. I wanted one because I seemed to be developing a paunch. The entire class was turned inside out. We had to have all our belongings checked, even the insides of our pockets. I had the money hidden inside my underwear. The teacher sent a student to the hill behind the school to pick pine needles, enough for the whole class. Then he handed them out, one for each student. He told us to place the pine needle on our palm, then grab it tight while keeping our eyes closed. The pine needles are all the same length, he said. And that after ten minutes, only the needle inside the hand of the one who stole the money will have grown five centimeters. Then we'll all know then who did it, so the person who took the money should just raise her hand now, he said. If you think about it now, it's complete nonsense, isn't it? How can a pine needle grow inside your hand? But at that moment, it really felt as if the needle was growing longer right inside my hand. When I thought about what would follow, my heart began to pound and my head felt as if it were about to burst. I could almost hear the pine needle growing longer inside my hand, rustle, rustle. I got so scared I broke into tears. I even wet myself right where I was sitting. The whole class found out that I had stole the money. I didn't go back to school after that and my life took a strange turn. I would tell my parents I was headed for school, then sit all day by the dam and wander around the marketplace. My parents eventually learned that I stole the money and I got beat up bad. Mom said to me, holding up her rod, 'A thief, is that what you had to turn out to be, of all things?'

"The minute Mom called me a thief, I decided that I should end my life . . . Planning to die as far from home as possible, I stole Mom's money and left home . . . But I ended up here somehow . . . It was five years before I visited home again."

". . ."

"If I didn't need that money desperately, I wouldn't have written you that letter."

". . ."

"Come back to work tomorrow. . . . I don't think of you as a thief. And nobody knows about it. It was just a guess because I'd seen you going home early that day as I was returning from my errand. You could've just played innocent."

". . ."

"They say the company will fold soon. Will be handed over to the bank or something. Just hang in there until then and you'll get your severance pay and the overdue wages also . . . If you stop working now, things'll get a little complicated and they'll most likely cheat you out of that money."

"..."

"You will come to work tomorrow, won't you?"

"..."

"If you don't, I'm going to keep coming back."

I go to work the next day. I get the time stamped on my card. Yun Sun-im puts on a big smile. Foreman, no, Chief of Production now, calls for me.

"You think this factory is where you come when you feel like it?"

I stare down at the cold cement floor. Nothing has changed at work. With no assigned spots at the workstation, workers sit around here and there. On the roof, on the benches, by the water tap. Chae Eun-hui, the young woman who works as the administrative staff at the assembly line, also sits idly in the empty office. It's Chae Eun-hui's job to check production output at the end of each work day, but now there is no output for her to check. The company is emptying out.

I sat amidst the noise, trying to suppress my exasperation by flipping through my book, held up a page of poetry and read it out loud.

> All the little ones of this world
> raise their splendid tails at me
> calling out to me, mama . . .
> How my little one would miss my milk?
> I would cry as squeezed out my milk
> Those innocent eyes
> dared not dream of escape

I cannot abandon you for anything else
for anywhere else
I turn back down from my uphill hike
Ha, in the puddle, rice fish still swim safe.*

I am begging you, please stop this noise. I am on the threshold of a home being crushed and torn apart.

Granny Emily Dickinson
carried me on her shoulders to sea
the distant sandflats where I'd never been
Not a tired beast in sight
just shellfish inside their shells
living in comfort
Granny soaked her green sleeve in the sea
washed my wounded feet
gently
putting them down
like silent tears.**

I beg you, please just come toward me so I can soar above them . . . the drills . . . the hammers . . . they are all coming toward me, stamping and trampling, getting lost between the interior and the exterior of my narrative.

Leaves land on grapes shy and discreet.
Long ago set out a man after the leaf's shadow.***

Like the ocean surf, sleep rushes in. The one stroking my hair, he will soon turn back.

* Ra Hee-duk, "Little One"
** Yi Sang-hee, "Dickinson's Green Sleeves"
*** Yi Si-yong, "Pattern"

> The crashing cascade awakes the mountain.
> The pheasant jumps, a pine cone falls.
> A squirrel raises its tail and the trail secretly lights up.
> Ah! A *pansori* virtuoso giving a full performance
> of his epic song. *

Yes, he will. He will soon turn back.

Tears arise when close / knocking on your room / my ankles shook so . . . Tears arise when close to you . . . I kept my head down but a few steps before me / I saw your fingers locking the door / I saw them now and then.

I find Chang's letter in the mailbox, completely unexpectedly. Oh! My delight released in a single cry. I ran into Ippi. Ippi, my younger sister's nickname. I heard from Ippi about the letters. I thought you weren't answering my letters because of my father. Chang has written my name with affection. So what if we can't exchange letters? I'm going to write in my notebook whenever I want to write to you. I'll show you what I wrote when we meet. You can do the same, too. You'll be home for Chuseok, won't you?

We don't make it home for Chuseok. Cousin has borrowed a camera. We pack a wooden lunchbox and go hiking to Mount Gwanak with Hui-jae. Carrying her borrowed camera, Cousin is all excited. It seems she's mistaken Hui-jae and me for the birds atop the trees. *Click*, under the maple tree, *click*, under the rock, *click*. "Turn around. Sit. No, you stand . . . Hold hands. Try to be more natural . . . Hui-jae, give me a smile now!" After Cousin is

* Chun Yang-hee, "Stepping Into Jikso Falls"

done taking one shot after another, as if we were those birds, we sit down for lunch up on the peaks, when Cousin lets out a scream.

"What in the world is this!"

I jump up at her screams, as if someone has yelled, "Snake!" I jump up, then ask, "What is it?"

"There's no film. It was empty!"

". . . What?"

She puts the film in and we take pictures all over again. Still nothing gets printed. Cousin returns from the photo shop, all glum.

"They said light got inside."

"Light?"

We had disappeared after swallowing light.

A wet autumn day. I recall Gangnam Sacred Heart Hospital in Daerim-dong. For the first time, I visit a hospital funeral parlor. Choe Yang-nim, an employee at Kumho Electronics, smiles from her photo, framed with flowers. Carbon monoxide from briquettes. Her dark-skinned mother from the country sits staring at Choe Yang-nim, barely holding on to her mind. Her little sister is asleep, her head resting on the mother's lap. Mi-seo, our class president, places the condolence money that we have collected in front of Choe Yang-nim's mother.

"Three of them were sleeping in that room. How come only Yang-nim died, I wonder."

Choe Yang-nim's little sister opens her eyes slowly from her dark-skinned mother's lap.

"Can it be real . . . Must be a dream, right?"

The dark-skinned mother is so dumbfounded she has no tears to cry. All she can do is mumble, her blurred gaze on her departed daughter. All she can remember is her daughter's fingernails were cracked and festering when she came home for Chuseok. What pain she must be in, traveling down that long, long path, with such fingernails.

Hui-jae *eonni* gets a perm. Now she never wears her uniform. Instead of her student shoes, she now wears her dark red high heels. Now on her shelf the student shoes sit like a symbol. She's changed. Instead of her white-collared uniform, she wears a blouse, buttoned up to her neck and tucked inside her plaid skirt. Her flared skirt flaps against the wind. I sometimes catch sight of her carrying a slim bag on her shoulder instead of the red schoolbag. Her back to me as she makes a turn at the end of the alley. The tip of her shoes as she descends the steps on the other side of the elevated walkway from me, the movement of her small body as she hastily disappears into the marketplace.

Again, Oldest Brother asks if she works at a bar. I start as if I'd just heard something I shouldn't have, offering a firm denial.

"No, I told you that's not true."

I must sound like I'm on the verge of tears, because he looks at me quizzically even as he kept adding garbled sentences, saying, "Then why does she come home in the morning hours? I saw some man leaving her room early in the morning."

"Man . . . ?"

When I answer back with a question, Oldest Brother says, "Her brother, maybe?" as if it's occurred to him he said something he shouldn't have, and closes his mouth.

I also see the man leaving Hui-jae's room. He goes out the front gate, his head sunk so low his nose could almost touch the ground. On one of his cheeks, I see a blue spot the size of a palm, like the one on Hui-jae's back. That spot? Where did I see it before? Jinhui Tailor Shop. Ah, that's him. The tailor who was working next to Hui-jae when I went to borrow money. The man walks with his hands dipped inside his pockets, deep in thought, almost bumps his nose into a telephone pole and finally exits the long alley.

Cousin makes an announcement. "I'm going to rent a room in Yongsan."

Oldest Brother, a commuting soldier serving military duty, is quiet, refusing to answer. "I can't go on living with your family forever," Cousin says. And her younger sister is finishing middle school so she'll bring her to Seoul and share the room. She says that one of the staff at the district office has promised to find her sister a job there, and that she'll try and send her to a commerce school.

Mambo. A winter's night, our mambo dance. Saturday, we come home from school and the lights are on in Hui-jae's room. Cousin heads straight to her room, still carrying her schoolbag.

"I'm moving out tomorrow."

Hui-jae, in the middle of doing her laundry, opens her eyes wide and looks at me.

She asks if I'm leaving as well. "I'm not moving. It's just her."

"We should have a farewell party."

We agree to meet on the roof in thirty minutes. Cousin and I change clothes, wash up, tell Oldest Brother that we're having a farewell party, then go up to the roof, bubbly with laughter. Hui-jae has already laid out a bamboo mat. There are candles on the low table, and an ample dish of spicy rice cake slices. Hui-jae tells us to wait and goes back down to get her cassette player. When she presses play, "La Cumparsita" comes on.

Pampampampam Pam Pam Pam Pampampam—Pararara Ah—

In the middle eating the rice cake slices, Cousin gets up and sings out "Pam pam pam," her arms straight out, her fists tight, and heads downstairs. Where are you going? Cousin drifts into the distance as she dances. When she comes back, she pulls out from her pocket a bottle of clear *soju*.

"What if *Oppa* finds out?"

"We told him it's a farewell party."

The cheap, potent liquor quickly makes us fragrant with alcohol. Hui-jae hands Cousin a paper shopping bag.

"What's this?"

"A going-away present."

Inside the bag is a pair of jeans.

"Try them on. They'll fit you nicely."

Cousin, who had always somewhat disapproved of Hui-jae, is quiet amidst all the *pampampam*-ing The candlelight flickers then goes out. The rooftop is still bright.

"The moon's out!"

The moon, high and round, above the factory chimneys. Were they working a night shift? The windows in the Design and Packaging Center are lit bright. A train rattles past. Today's last number 118 bus leaves its last stop on the route. Under the moonlight Cousin tries on the jeans, Hui-jae's going-away present. They fit her perfectly.

"I made them myself."

"For me?"

"Well, not exactly . . ."

"For whom, then?"

"My little brother back home is about your size."

"Your brother?"

"Doesn't matter if I made it for a guy or a girl, they're jeans. And they're baggy disco pants."

"Then what about your brother?"

Hui-jae smiles meekly. "I can always make another pair."

Cousin, always cheerful, nodding whenever she hears music, even in the middle of cleaning the floor, starts with the *pam pam pam* again in her new jeans. Swaying, shaking, under the moonlight, on the bamboo mat, like a tree shadow.

"You try it, too."

Hui-jae is reluctantly pulled up and I'm dragged along with her. Like sea crabs that have crawled onto the shore by mistake, we move in side steps, *pam pam pam*—Cousin, with her cute moves, Hui-jae, stiff and awkward, smiling softly. The moon hangs in the sky, on the Design and Packaging Center's steep chimney. The moon on the chimney sucking up the black smoke. The darkening moon. Cousin, who was the first to dance, lets out an exhausted breath and sits down on the mat. I sit next to her. Hui-jae sits next to me. The night wind wipes the sweat off our foreheads, and we quickly get cold. We cuddle closer, arms on shoulders as if in an embrace. We sit like that for a long time. As we sit shoulder to shoulder, the steel wheels of the day's last train rattles by our heads. The dark moon on the chimney of the Design and Packaging Center sticks out its clear white face. On this little island . . . where the frozen shadow of the moon fills up the waves, and a harsh wintry surfs gather. I think of the solemn, beautiful love, inside heart of the lighthouse keeper . . . We are three moons. Warm feelings surge, as if we had shared something in our hearts as we sang.

That winter, after dancing the mambo on the rooftop above our lone room, Cousin leaves the alley. Like a migratory bird. To be Oldest Sister to her little sisters, as Oldest Brother was to me.

I visit Cousin in her rented room in Yongsan. Samgakji Rotary. A long, long alley. Houses clustered close together. Bags of trash frozen in the cold wind. A side door installed between two walls, its lock exposed; from next door, a woman leaps out, her hair dyed blond and wearing red lipstick, black leather skirt, and leather boots. A black man with big, bright eyes steps out after her, his back bent low. The two of them walk down the frozen alley, cuddled close. The wind is cold but the woman's calves are completely exposed.

"Come in!"

"You haven't lit any briquettes?" I blurt out as I step inside Cousin's room.

"When it gets colder I will . . ." Twenty-one-year-old Cousin has suddenly gotten very old. Her expression seems to suggest that there's nothing in the world that will surprise her now. Another lone room, a long, narrow room. My feet are freezing.

⁂

The man who shed blood in Gwangju and pushed the entire country into a state of fear in the name of social purification enjoys going on night inspections. He doesn't like to give advance warning. He will suddenly walk into a police station in Incheon, or appears out of the blue at Seoul City Hall in casual attire. When he shows up, those on duty are shocked out of their wits.

⁂

It is time for bookkeeping class in school. Dark faces slip into the hallway. The back door of our classroom slides open. The president is here. He is no Ha Gye-suk but he steps inside, in the middle of class. Unlike Ha Gye-suk, he is not cautious, nor apologetic. The teacher's face turns pale as he stands in front of the blackboard, writing out his lesson on the double entry system.

The president's broad forehead flashes under the fluorescent lights. His wife stands next to him. Is that man over there an aide? A skinny man in a black suit stands right behind the couple, his eyes flashing. When the president strokes my left-handed desk partner An Hyang-suk's hair, light flashes. A camera. I dunk my head. The camera clicks as his wife picks up my notebook and opens it. My heart sinks with a thump. The cover says "Bookkeeping," but there are no notes on bookkeeping, it is filled only with my letters to Chang, and poems and passages copied from magazines like *Samtoh*. Fortunately, his wife puts the notebook back on my desk and follows after the president, walking down the desk aisle. A black-suited man trailing them farthest behind carries a pair of shoes in his hands. After they leave through the door in the front of the classroom, the bookkeeping teacher walks toward me. He opens my notebook. My heart sinks more heavily than when the First Lady opened it. Since there's nothing in there about bookkeeping, whether it's by single or double entry; the teacher looks dumbfounded as he flips through this and that page, and asks me if this is the notebook that the First Lady looked at. I, eighteen years old, am unable to answer.

"Is this the notebook, I asked."

"Yes."

The teacher tilts his head.

"I wonder why she didn't say anything then. Did she pick it up just for the photo?"

He stands there flipping through the pages for a long time, then puts down the notebook as she had done. A sigh of relief rushes out from me. Following the First Lady and the bookkeeping teacher, this time left-handed An Hyang-suk opens the notebook.

FLOWER SNAKE
The backwaters of □□ □□
Beautiful snake . . .
What immense sadness was it born with, to possess such a vile body.

Just like a flower ribbon.
The . . . tongue that your grandfather used to allure Eve darting in and out of red jaws, deprived of sound
The blue sky . . . Bite, rip, in bitter fury,

Run away. That wretched skull!

An Hyang-suk stares at the notebook, at me.

"You wrote this?"

"No."

"Who then?"

"Seo Jeong-ju."

"Who wrote 'By the Chrysanthemum'?"

"Yes."

An Hyang-suk looks at the notebook again. She asks me what are the four blank squares after "The backwaters of."

"They were in Chinese characters, too difficult to write, so I just left them as blanks."

An Hyang-suk says, "Oh," as if it were nothing important.

"What's 'flower snake'?"

"I don't know."

"Why did you copy it down if you don't know?"

"Because I like it."

"Do you know what the poem is about?"

"I don't know."

"You don't know but you like it?" Left-handed An Hyang-suk stares at me again, as if she's flabbergasted.

Had that been the true for me as well? Just like Mi-seo, who read Hegel, could it have been that, only when I was reading people like Proust or Suh Jung-joo, Kim Yu-jong or Na Do-hyang, Jang Yong-hak or Son Chang-seop or Francis Jammes, only when I was copying their splendid sentences in the corner of my bookkeeping notebook, without even understanding what they meant, I believed that I was different from the faces in that classroom? Could it be that I believed that these books, novels, or poetry would take me out of the alley?

I fell off my bed in the middle of a long nap. As I climbed back on the bed, the spring sunlight from the window hurt my eyes.

On the hills, the parts where the azaleas had withered were now bright green. In the distance, cherry blossoms gleamed white. It was now green where the flowers died, but a black gloom brushed against my feet. How poor we were then. What little money we had. How so very little, and how come? It felt as if a scream were pouring out of the mirror next to my bed. Are you sure you remembered correctly? How could that be? I can't believe it. Don't take it out on me. I can't believe it, either. I called up J for no good reason.

"Finished writing?"

". . . Yeah."

"Wanna make me garlic chive pancakes?"

"No."

"Wanna steam me some blue crabs?"

"No."

"Then let's go out to eat."

"No."

Silence. Embarrassed, J shifts to a bubbly tone.

"Well, let's meet somewhere anyway!"

"No!"

"Then why did you call?"

"To tell you this."

"Tell me what?"

"To tell you no!"

I could hear J turning sullen on the other end of the line.

I turned on the television. Ah—uh—uh—A sound that seems as if it's been around and inside all the rooms of this world. Hair held up in a bun, jade ring, knotted ribbon on her traditional blouse. Kim So-hee, from ten or so years ago, stands in the center, singing "Bonghwa Arirang" with her students. Arirang, arirang, arariyo, I'm headed beyond Arirang Pass, carrying my bundle on my back.

Two days before, a state funeral had been held in her honor at Maronnier Park in Dongsung-dong. Beyond the pass. She would now be walking somewhere down the road to the other world. But at this moment, in this world, she was on television, caught in stop motion, her grief-stricken eyes slightly raised. I'm headed beyond Gaepung Pass, clutching my bitter, sore heart. Arirang, arirang, arariyo, I'm headed beyond Arirang Pass. I had only happened to turn on the TV, but pulled in by the singing, sat down in front of the screen. Ahn Sook Sun, Shin Young-hee, and other students of Kim's were sharing their memories with the host.

Ah, so that's Ahn Sook Sun. Her eyes were teary. The living, I suppose, feed on death. It would be the same for Ahn. She would feed off Kim So-hee's death, thus completing the dead one's life.

The screen cut back to Kim So-hee in her lifetime. She was sitting in a studio. Thin, pale, but elegant. I'm recording, but I'm not happy with my work. If my health improves, I would do it over, but I'm terribly old . . . I feel I should work on it some more but things don't go as I'd like. She is wearing a ramie blouse and has camellia oil on her hair. A singer should have style. Everything should reflect style, even the way your feet move when you step onto a stage. Only then the sound will follow. Singers these days, when they step on the stage, look around to see how many people are in the audience, but one must always think, Just the drummer and myself here, just the two of us.

On this still spring night, I reached out and turned up the TV volume.

*B*irds, birds, birds flying in. All the birds in this world. The phoenix, bird of birds, the good harvest bird at the Gate of Longevity. Myriad birds flying in two by two, responding in song, drunk with spring. The chatty parrot, red-crowned crane the graceful dancer, sing-songy turtledoves . . . Singing's got to come out of your body and your soul, it's not singing if you're just babbling at the tips of your lips, that's not singing. It's got to come from your heart, then echo through your guts and swirl inside your belly, one's got to endure and overcome this to really sing.

That old wagtail looking so frail, it would starve to death even with a dozen scoops of rice in front of her, tottering this-a-way, tail shaking that-a-way, falling rolling shot down, old wagtail crying flying left to right, pigeon flying into the garden, boy, come and throw some beans. Singing's got to come out of your body and your soul, it's not singing if you're just babbling at the tips of your lips, that's no singing . . . Her words seemed to grow distant, then came closer, grew distant, then close again. As she walked out of the screen and slipped quietly into my heart, her hair shiny with camellia oil and carrying an earthenware jar on her head, an ibis lets out a cry . . . Startling one's soul, startling one's spirit.

FOUR

I have spoken with the voice you gave me and written with the words You taught my parents, who taught me. I pass down the road like a donkey, head lowered, loaded with bundles, who makes the children laugh.

—Francis Jammes

Over the weekend, the school takes just the seniors on a field trip. It's an overnight trip, so a good many students working extra shifts on Sunday cannot join. My first and last trip with them. I remember, from our trip to Gyeongju, the color of Ha Gye-suk's face, the same Ha Gye-suk, who called me up asking, "How come you don't write about us?" I remember the color on the faces of left-handed An Hyang-suk and the Hegel-reader Mi-seo and Min-suk from the fur company. Their faces yellow against the green mounds of ancient tombs. I remember Hyang-gyu and Myeong-hae and Min-sun and Hyeok-gyu. As our train passes through a tunnel, we scream along. Woo! . . . We hide our teacher's shoes and jacket while he sleeps, then act innocent. We strut down the night streets of Gyeongju, clad in jeans and plaid shirts, tight and scampish. Wearing red hats, we swagger and sway.

But we are soon overcome with awkwardness. The sunlight is to blame. It is the awkwardness of encountering, under the bright sun, faces that we have seen only at night under fluorescent lights. Having never met during the day, we are at a loss how we should act toward one another, as we direct our awkward gazes toward the Tomb of the Heavenly Horse. Toward the Cheomseongdae Observatory. We climb up Mount Namsan. My cousin—her gaze is fixed on her camera. My cousin, who wanted to be a photographer, pushes her camera lens in any direction she feels like. She makes me and the Hegel reader Mi-seo put our faces close together and smile. Feeling awkward in the light, we try to smile and end up scowling. Cousin makes An Hyang-suk position her face atop a statue of the headless Buddha and looks into her viewfinder.

"Smile."

An Hyang-suk, who had to wrap 20,000 candies in plastic in a day, also feels awkward about being on this trip and tries to smile but ends up scowling.

"Idiots."

Cousin, eager to take pictures, grows tired of her unwilling, pale-faced models.

"I'm going to photograph birds . . . I'm going off to photograph birds instead of idiots."

At any given place, on any given night, there is someone suffering from the agonies of love. Yi Ae-sun, in love with the union leader of the textile mill where she works, lets out a long sigh on this night in Gyeongju. The word "user" pops out of Yi Ae-sun's mouth. We turn quiet all of a sudden. Our users who use us.

"Wish we didn't have to go back."

Ring-a-ding last summer, we were singing, but abruptly come to a stop.

"Things are unbelievably scary at work. He was investigated at the Martial Law Enforcement Headquarters then court-martialed. Isn't it terrifying? Court-martialed, for asking for a wage increase."

"Then what happened?"

"He was released, but they labeled him as a subject of purification, demanding him to resign, but he's resisting."

"What do you mean, subject of purification?"

"Beats me, some sort of social purification campaign going on."

Our night away fills up with anxious whispers.

"They don't assign work to union members. It's a plot to make them resign. They send all the work to outside contractors, then hand out brooms to the unionists, telling them to clean the factory instead."

"It's the same where I work. The police seem to be stationed there permanently."

"Maybe we would've been better off without the Seoul Spring or whatever they called it—things might not have gotten so frightening . . . Everyone protested for wage increase back then, refusing to work extra hours, they've all been taken in to this Joint Investigation Headquarters for questioning."

"It's same where I work also. Sheer terror, that's what it's like. Last winter, they didn't even turn on the heat where the unionists were stationed. More than two hundred workers quit before spring arrived and there're less than ninety left. A sly scheme, making people quit so that the management can temporarily close down the factory. Anyway, I'm going to need a new job if they really close, so see if there's an opening somewhere, will you?"

The night I return from the trip, Oldest Brother calls my name as we get ready to sleep. The room feels deserted with Third Brother and Cousin gone. Oldest Brother says nothing after calling me, which makes me anxious. Does he have an ache in his chest like last time?

"What is it? . . . What is it? Do you feel pain in your chest again?" Recalling the way he looked, clutching his chest in pain, I push away the covers and sit up. I am already scared out of my wits, without Cousin here.

"So you want it that bad? To go to college?" My startled eyes open in the dark with a sparkle. It feels for a moment as if moonlight, or starlight, is pouring over me. I climb back under the covers. "Are you still trying to be a writer?"

I turn reticent. I have never mentioned to Oldest Brother that I wished to attend university. Not to him, not to anyone.

"To be a writer, one needs to read a great number of books, acquire a great amount of knowledge."

Ah. He has read my notebook while I was away on my school trip.

"College admission is tough enough even for students who didn't have to do anything else but study for three years straight." His voice carries the weight of worry and woe. I push off the covers and poke out my face toward Oldest Brother, lying over there with his tired back to me.

"Don't worry, *Oppa*. I'm not going to college."

As I step out to the kitchen at dawn to cook breakfast, I open my schoolbag and search for the notebook. What had I written in there, that made Oldest Brother say what he said last night? The notebook isn't in the bag. I look here and there, where I might have left it, unconsciously, but to no avail. I carefully climb down the attic and go to Oldest Brother's desk. There it is. Under my copy of *The Dwarf Launches His Tiny Ball*, wrapped in a book cover. I must have left the notebook on Oldest Brother's desk after scrawling down this and that the night before leaving for the trip. It would have looked as if I had left it there for him to read. I head up to the roof, taking the notebook with me. Dawn is breaking. The stars in the sky are fading out one by one. Under the fading starlight, someone is perched on the guardrail, looking like she's about to fly away any minute. It's Hui-jae. Like a bird she sits on the roof guardrail, watching daylight breaking, not between peach and apple trees but between tall, imposing factory chimneys. The light of dawn appears blue, even amidst the greasy smells. In the light of dawn, everything in this world exudes the scent of soft, splendid shoots budding anew. Even the factory chimneys.

"Hey." I approach Hui-jae, slapping her on the shoulder. She is startled.

"What're you doing?"

"Hanging laundry." How long has she been up, to be done with the washing already? On the clothesline hang a tablecloth, a pair of men's cargo pants, and socks. When I stare at the men's pants, she puts on an awkward smile.

"What are *you* doing up here so early?" I hide my notebook behind my back.

"What is that?"

"Nothing."

"Then why are you hiding it if it's nothing?" Noticing that Hui-jae's feelings are hurt, I push my notebook toward her. "So it's a notebook."

She flips through the pages. "Do you want to go to college?"

She asks in a faint voice, her gaze on one of the pages. I want to go to college—the words have been written over and over on top of each other and stand out from everything else on the page. This was what Oldest Brother read as well. On any given page, the sentence has been slipped in, like a prayer—I want to go to college, I want to go to college. It all began when Chang told me last summer, "Let's try hard to get into college, we must." I end up feeling guilty and embarrassed toward Hui-jae, perched on the guardrail up on the roof, toward Oldest Brother, deep in his weary sleep.

"I'm not going to college." I say this as if I'm choosing not to go when I can. As I take my notebook and head down, Hui-jae calls to me from behind.

"You see, I've . . ." She stares into my face when I turn back to look at her. She looks pale.

"What is it?"

"It's that . . ." She stammers.

"Tell me, what is it?"

"Well, it's just that . . ."

I, nineteen years old, stare back at Hui-jae, unable to bring herself to say what she's trying to tell me, repeating her fragments over and over.

"I decided to let him move in with me . . ."

Him? The man at the Jinhui Tailor Shop, the one with the spot on his cheek?

"I just felt that I should tell you . . . When I save up two million won, I'll give the money to my younger brother and we'll be able to get married then."

Get married. Yes, of course, they'll get married.

I gaze blankly at the pair of men's cargo pants hanging on the clothesline.

As I returned home after handing over the galleys for my essay collection to my publisher, I pushed the key into the keyhole of the empty apartment, and felt a tingling quiver at the tip of my fingers. I released my hand and stood outside my door for a while. The yellow sticker advertising a lock repair service filled my field of vision. All I wanted to do as I got out of the taxi was to hurry inside and lie down, but now I felt as if I had stumbled upon something.

I opened the door and headed to the bathroom sink after I stepped inside. I put down my shoulder bag on the basin rim. When I turned on the tap, drops of water splattered on the bag. I moved the bag to the tub. What was it, what was the sentence that my heart had stumbled upon?

I opened my palms and put them against the mirror. What had I done with these hands? I saw myself and my hands clash with my eyes in the mirror. I quickly pulled back my hands, placing them under the running water.

Running water.

It appeared as if my fingers were swelling and swelling under the water. My hands, so insecure when they are not touching, grabbing, or writing something. The loneliness contained inside each of my ten fingers. What were they trying to do, cuddled together here in this state that they were in, squirming and squiggling?

The water flowed over. I pressed the plug to let the water drain. The gathered water escaped down through the pipes, making a sound that was desolate beyond words. I turned off the water and gazed for a moment into the mirror. My heart was desolate as well. I did not want to budge an inch. I slid down and sat with my legs stretched out, my back against the tub where my bag lay. The crammed bathroom seemed as vast as a prairie. When I pushed the open door with the tip of my toes, the door closed and everything turned dark.

What was it, what was the hidden sentence that had thrust a blade into my heart when I opened the door?

. . . A strange silence.

The sound of running water within that silence . . . The sound of slapping footsteps mixed within the desolate sound of water traveling back up the pipes and through the darkness. Slip-slop . . . Someone walking barefoot? Slip-slop . . . Traveling back through the moonlight, through the deep seas, through nets and mudflats . . . Slip-slop . . . A pair of discreet calves that I seem to remember from somewhere . . . Slip-slop . . . The flared skirt with tiny flower patterns . . . Slip-slop.

"Why did you call me here?"

"I have something that needs to be finished."

"What do you mean?"

This is final. I am no longer nineteen but thirty-two. When I first started writing this book, I hoped that by the time it was done, I'd be able to say that I have told the story of my past, and that I feel better for having done it. But that's not the case.

. . .

It's in your hands now.

. . .

Tell me about that morning.

. . .

Why did you ask me to lock your door?

. . .

Why me of all people?

. . .

Even after I left that place, whenever I spotted someone who looked like you, or a room similar to that one, my heart would race, leaving me breathless. I'd go blank or become restless. I would lose focus and wake up in the middle of the night, unable to go back to sleep. Sometimes I suddenly lost my judgment, as if I were a child, and get caught up in the urge to lose myself in someone . . . Depression would come over me in the middle of reading a book . . . and when crossing bridges, I would feel the impulse to jump off the guardrail . . . Sometimes it felt as if drapes or clotheslines were about to attack me. Did you know that? You were my handicap. A handicap in building relationships, making me push him away even when I was happy to be with him . . . You know better than me the fatigue that comes from a state of being overly alert . . . I never went back to that place. Not even within the vicinity. But in my mind, words and names like *factories, workers, train station, Garibong Market, Doksan-dong,* and *Guro-dong* at the entrance of the industrial complex have turned into a flood of images, locked inside a dike . . . It's in your hands now . . .

Why was it me of all people?

. . .

Why me?

. . .

I was only nineteen.

Sitting in the dark, I lifted my back from the bathtub. That was it. My encounter with death. I walked out of the bathroom and called my publisher. The sentences that had thrust a blade into my heart when I opened the door upon returning to my empty apartment was part of "My Encounter with Death," a section newly included in my essay collection. I had revised them over and over, but the blade was still there. The blade with its edge pointed toward me.

I got a cab and headed back to the publishing house. They had already finished putting in the page numbers. An awkward silence . . . Between my insistence—I need to erase some lines—and the publisher's questioning—What is this about? The galleys were handed over to me one more time. I positioned the pen between my fingers.

I moved my fingers and changed "My aunt's son died" to "an older cousin." I scrapped "Aunt" and replaced it with "a relative." My aunt did not read fiction, but this was a book of essays, and how much pain would it bring her, a loss that took place more than ten years ago, if her daughter came across the essay and read it to her? I changed "Aunt's family" to "her family." I changed "his crushed, chopped, blood-covered body . . ." to "his body, no longer recognizable . . ." "In the face of my cousin's death" to "In the face of death, of a man hit by a train." This, however, was not the reason this sharp-edged blade had appeared in my heart.

I marked the manuscript to delete an entire section on what had gone on that morning with her. Sentences being erased right before they went to press.

She is standing there inside the erased sentences.

I tell Hui-jae that it seems as if the man cannot speak, asking how come he never says anything. She does not understand what I'm trying to say.

"What do you mean he never says anything? He's also a good singer, you know." Hui-jae answers back with a question instead.

"But I've never heard him say anything." Or sing, on top of that! I thought to myself.

"No, he's good with words. And he's a good singer, too."

Perhaps between the two of them, words were none other than Jin-hui Tailor Shop itself. Inside the shop where he cut the patterns according to size, where she sewed the patterns that he has prepared. Perhaps their conversation was flowing between the cut-out patterns and the sewn-up dresses. Between his cigarettes, which she would light for him during break; between his fingers, lifting a strand of loose thread from her hair while she is immersed in her sewing.

Between the two of them, they had words that were nameless and unknown to the world.

Not having had the chance to take a good look at his face, it is difficult for me to speak about him. He remains, for me, that pair of cargo pants, a pair of unfamiliar shoes on Hui-jae's kitchen shelf. She defends this man even though he looks the other way when we run into each other, saying it's because he was not cared for as a child.

"No one looked after him. He said that ever since he was little, he knew that there was no one in this world to care for him. So to build up courage, he went into the mountain with his friends and asked them to tie him up to a tree. Asking them to come back and untie him after three days."

"Why did he do that?"

"To build up courage, like I said . . ."

"Courage?"

"You got to have courage to not live in fear."

"So he was really alone in the mountain for three days?"

"That's what he said."

"For real?"

"You think he's lying?"

"No, it's not . . . it's just hard to believe . . ."

"Well, he says that after spending three days in the mountain, he became even more scared. Even at the smallest rustling noise, and when dusk falls and night approaches, he got goose bumps on his arms. Still does, even now."

"Even now?"

"That's right, that's why he leaves the light on when he sleeps." Hui-jae grins as she turns to look at me. "Without my care, my brother will end up with the same expression as him . . . He'll be okay now. I take care of him."

Since they began living together, his shoes now take up the spot on the shelf next to Hui-jae's school shoes, which she used to wear when she was a student like me. I only remember him as a pair of shoes, a pair of cargo pants, and that spot on his face. He would remember me as the girl carrying fish in a plastic bag, or the girl walking up to the roof on Sundays with laundry in a washbasin. Perhaps he thinks he has never heard me speak, just as I believe I've never heard him speak. If what he and Hui-jae shared was a nameless language unknown to the world, between him and I flowed a nameless solitude unknown to the world.

Thinking back now, we might have lived close at each other's side but we didn't like the same food, nor did we spend much time together. I have no memory of us arguing. We had nothing to fight about. She had no desire inside her heart. Except for matters regarding her brother and the man whom she had to take care of, I don't remember her ever mentioning anything that she planned to achieve or anything she hoped to become . . . or anything that she liked. My cousin always said, I'm going to become a photographer. Just as I always said that I was going to become a writer. Cousin's vivacity or my melancholy had perhaps sprung from the constant recognition that we were different from the people in that place despite the fact that we also lived there.

Cousin and I had no intention to remain there for long. Cousin had now already left and I would soon as well. Cousin and I knew we had to leave, which was why we had things we wanted to do, were sure about what we wanted to become, wanted to see many things, even if we could not own them. This was why Cousin and I had so much to argue about. This was not the case with Hui-jae. She was the alley itself. She was the power pole, the vomit, the inn. She was the factory chimney, the dark marketplace, the sewing machine. The thirty-seven lone rooms were her, the venues of her life.

The two of them seemed to love each other dearly. I never heard them say the word "love" so I can only write, "they seemed to."

I could not find the right word to address him so one day I referred to him as "Uncle." Hui-Jae is washing plums in her kitchen and bursts into a laugh.

"Uncle? He'll think that's hilarious!" Getting a basket to drain the plums, still glossy with water, she breaks into a broad grin as she playfully splatters water toward me with her wet hand. I am sprinkled with that water, fragrant with the scent of plums.

"Well, 'Fist' is what he calls me."

I am the one who laughs this time. "But you have such tiny hands!"

Her hands are much too tiny for her to be called Fist. Tiny hands. Hands that constantly push the marked fabric under the needle of the sewing machine. Such delicate hands, covered with scars from the needle.

"He says that my hands are in tight fists when I sleep, like someone marching to battle."

Such lonely hands.

Singing. There was a night when we sat singing, on the roof of the buildings that housed our lone rooms. Hui-jae, me, and the man I called Uncle. Cold rain falling in the woods erasing the footsteps of love. Like Hui-jae said, Uncle is a good singer. It is as if he has always sung instead of speaking. It is your round face I see as a gentle wind blows in the morning. His singing is smooth, even on the difficult high notes. There is no hesitation, as if the song is flowing out of the red spot on his face. Burning like a camellia on a dark cliff, enduring cold dew, a flower, is that what I shall become. When he is done with one song, his voice finds another. He has been singing for over an hour, yet he still keeps finding more songs. If I become a flower will mountain birds fly to me, will the soul of my beloved become a flower as well . . .

From a distant darkness, Oldest Brother calls to me. The singing stops and an awkward silence circles us. A silence heavier than the factory building.

"What're you doing over there?"

"Get going." Hui-jae pushes me along. Back in our room, Oldest Brother turns his back to me, stiff and stubborn.

"Didn't you hear what I said . . . I told you to stay away from her." Oldest Brother's voice is thunderous. I wish he'd speak more quietly . . . if Hui-jae heard his cold voice, she would cry.

It was around six o'clock. I must have dozed off while reading. Younger Brother, attending university in Incheon, was on the phone, rousing me from my sleep. He blurted out, "You're okay," when I picked up. I asked what he was talking about, and he said he's in a restaurant near school and the TV reported that a department store had collapsed so he thought he'd call. Just in case.

"A department store? For real?" I turned on the TV, one hand still on the receiver. The screen only shows the building before the collapse. The newscaster was reporting the disaster in a flustered tone, but it did not feel real since the scene of the incident was not shown. It was Sampoong Department Store in Seocho-dong in the Gangnam part of Seoul, south of the Han River. As the names of the dead and the injured began to appear on the screen, I got anxious and hung up to call Oldest Brother, who lived in Gangnam. Just in case, I also thought. Live scenes came on air and I went blank. How could this be? It was like a battlefield. I thought a collapse meant a corner of the building had crumbled, but no, the five-story building, with three underground levels, had collapsed completely, as if it had been a carefully planned demolition. It seemed like the building had never existed on this site. The streets were heaped with debris from the collapse and people were being carried out, covered in blood. Sounds of screams. Complete mayhem. My mind went blank. Witnesses who made it out of the building reported that they heard an explosion before the collapse. Explosion? Terrorist attack? Because it was a department store always crowded with people, a luxury store located amidst luxury apartment and office buildings in Gangnam, it never occurred to me that poor construction or safety issues could be the cause. The scene turned even grislier as time passed. People were buried under the debris of a five-story building. Five stories above ground and three stories below. Smoke from toxic gas was soaring up. The news reported that while survivors were trapped inside, there existed the dangers of a toxic gas explosion or the collapse of what remained of the building, which kept even the news cameras at bay.

The collapse had occurred at around six in the evening. The basement floor was mostly the food section. Trapped in the basement, the most difficult to reach for rescuers, would be mostly housewives who had been getting groceries for dinner. The news reports continued.

. . . Many children were found dead in the children's clothing section on the basement floor.

. . . There are about fifty people currently trapped in the basement restaurant.

. . . A woman's amputated left leg has been transported to the hospital. If they can find the injured person right away, they will be able to save the leg.

It is Oldest Brother's birthday one Saturday. Mom arrives from Jeongeup. I am walking to the bus stop after class when Cousin calls out to me, all out of breath. Since she moved to Yongsan, Cousin and I no longer ride the same bus. After class, most students take the night bus back to the industrial complex from Singil-dong in Yeongdeungpo District, but Cousin walks in the opposite direction to catch the bus that gets her all the way out of Yeongdeungpo.

"Hey! Are you training for a track meet or something? Look how fast you're walking! Didn't you hear me call?"

"Call, me?"

"What? You ask if I was calling? A deaf man could've heard me."

"Uh . . . sorry. Mom's probably arrived, you see."

"Auntie?"

"Yes."

"Come on, let's get going."

"You're coming, too?"

"Of course, it's *Oppa*'s birthday, isn't it?"

"You didn't forget, did you?!"

"What do you mean, 'forget' . . . Would've been better if it was tomorrow . . . Did you make him sea laver soup for breakfast?"

"He doesn't like laver soup, remember?"

"Oh yeah, that's right. So how come he won't eat it? He doesn't eat bean sprouts, either."

"He went on a school field trip in sixth grade and at this restaurant he saw one of the cooking ladies step into a giant bowl in boots to toss the bean sprouts with a shovel."

"A shovel?"

"Uh-huh."

"What enormous amount of bean sprouts would they have been preparing to need a shovel?"

"I know."

"Still, that was ages ago. He still won't eat it because of that?"

"You still don't know him after all this time? Would he ever eat it, after seeing someone stand inside the bowl in boots with a shovel?"

"What about laver soup, why doesn't he eat that?"

"That I don't know. Maybe someone stepped inside the pot in boots to serve the soup?"

Cousin and I burst into laughter. Oldest Brother, who would not eat laver soup, or bean sprouts, or bean curd. We, who did not buy dried laver or bean sprouts or bean curd because of him. We, who, left without much to choose from, used to linger in front of vendors that sold spinach or mackerel.

I step inside the alley with Cousin, the first time in a while. After we pass the sign for the inn, the alley turns dark. It used to be that when we stepped inside the alley the light from the corner store kept the alley lit past midnight.

"The store still closes so early?"

"The granny is sick."

As we walk past the power pole, then past the store, Cousin glances at the chair outside the store.

"Still no news from *Ajeossi*?"

"No."

The storekeeper who used to make Virgin Mary statues from plaster does not return. The granny, who has heard nothing after losing her son to men who had barged in in the middle of the night, grabs at anyone at the subway station and asks after her son.

"Look here now, please tell me where my son is, that's all I need to know. I'm dying here, like my guts are on fire."

Passersby stand looking lost, one of their arms caught by granny's grasp. One day I see her holding on to Oldest Brother.

"You look like a learned man, so you ought to know. He's done some wrong in the past, but he was all set, to settle down good. Already done his time, his body paid up for all the wrong he's done. Why drag him away in the middle of the night, why not send him back home?"

Speaking in a thick northern dialect, the granny pulls out her heirloom double ring and hands it to Oldest Brother.

"It's gold, weighs twenty *don* at least . . . I'm going to give you this, all I need you to do is let me know now, if he's dead or alive, and if living, where he is, that's all, you hear now?"

Older Brother says nothing.

"Whatever wrong he's done, all in the past now. His body paid up for all the wrong done . . . That's why he's got no wife, no kids at his age. What hope can I have at my age. Worthless in the world he may be, he's the only child I got. Back in the north, my life was a decent one. Had a husband, five children. All of them dead in the war, except for this one . . . Makes no sense, that he survived even back then, but now after all this time I don't know if he's dead or living, makes no sense."

"I wouldn't know, either, ma'am. All we can do is wait."

"Wait, you say, after so much time's gone by . . . If he's still alive, he would've sent word, wouldn't he? You used to work for the government, I heard, so how come you don't know? My ring's not good enough, is that it?"

"Granny, please!"

The granny throws to the ground her double ring that she was trying to hand over to Oldest Brother.

"What good's all this . . . Someone just tell me what's happened to my son!"

The granny's store no longer stocks laundry soap. No Sando crackers or toilet paper, either. The granny just sits in a chair outside the store, gazing at the alley. When young factory workers ask for cigarettes, she says, "Take them." Does not check if they pay the right amount. Just sits there, in the spot where her vanished son used to open up the store at the crack of dawn, where he would set out a crate of fresh bean curd, or carry in a bucket of bean sprouts.

Look what Mom's done. She's locked up inside the kitchen of the lone room a rooster, its comb red and erect, with feathers scarlet and sleek. The bird, its feet tied up with straw rope then bundled up inside a blue wrapping cloth, jolts with a startle as Cousin and I fling open the kitchen door, calling out, "Mom, Auntie. We're unable to step inside," our schoolbags still in hand, just standing there staring at the chicken, ignoring Mom and her broad smile.

"What's this chicken doing here?"

The rooster is in quite a fury. The way he's glaring and squawking, he seems ready to nip my calf the minute the rope comes undone.

"Mom, you brought a live chicken?"

"Is the rooster all you see, not your mother?"

Mom herds Cousin and me into the room and sets the table for a late dinner. The factory no longer provides dinner for student workers. Having returned home hungry with an empty stomach, we gobble up the food.

When Oldest Brother returns and sees the chicken from outside the door, he is also aghast. "What's this?"

Mom looks out to where he's standing. "What's the matter with all of you. All you see is the rooster, not me!"

Only then Oldest Brother's face fills up with an affectionate smile for Mom. We have a hard time sleeping with Mom's chicken squawking in the kitchen. "That darned rooster," says Oldest Brother, tossing in his sleep each time it crows. It seems the city is a strange place for the chicken as well. Mom is affected by none of this. She even snores quietly, as if the rooster's restlessness is music to her ears. After Oldest Brother has turned over several times, Cousin taps my back.

"What is it?"

"Come, follow me."

"I'm too sleepy."

"Come on—" Cousin takes the rooster and its flapping wings in her arms and walks out of the kitchen.

"Where're you going?"

Cousin takes discreet steps, as if she were a chicken thief. I follow behind, trying to be discreet like her. Where Cousin arrives at, carrying the rooster, bundled in wrapping cloth with its feet tied, is the rooftop. Once we get there, Cousin drops the chicken to the floor. *Squawk!* The rooster crows in the dark.

"Let's head back down."

"What about the chicken?"

"This'll be better for him than the crammed kitchen and we should get some sleep." When I glance at the chicken, hesitating, Cousin undoes the bundle to release him. "That should help him breath."

After tying the chicken to a laundry pole with the rope on his feet, we climb back downstairs.

The next morning, Mom tells Oldest Brother, "Butcher the rooster, will you."

"Mom, but I've never done it."

"Well, I haven't, either."

"So why did you bring a live chicken in the first place?"

"I wanted to feed you fresh meat."

"Well, I can't do it."

"Am I asking you to slaughter a cow or a pig? You're a man and you tell me you can't even butcher that little chicken? You've seen Father do it a hundred times, isn't that right?"

"That doesn't mean I can do it. I can't."

"A lame job I've done raising you!"

Disappointed with Oldest Brother, Mom glances at Cousin.

"Auntie! I can't do it!" Cousin jumps, waving her hands. I'm amused, seeing that Mom is at a loss about a live chicken. Turns out there're things that Mom can't do.

It was always Father who butchered the chickens. Mom set out the big pot on the brazier in the backyard, and Younger Sister and I would start chopping garlic. Little Brother . . . you can rest your head on my lap and take a little nap. If I lay your head down on the floor, find your way back to my lap and sleep some more. Father would call out my name from the yard.

"Bring me the water when it starts to boil."

Then Mom would pour the hot water into the pail. "Careful now."

Three chickens lie dead next to Father, their necks twisted. Father soaks the chickens in the hot water and plucks the feathers. Little Brother has followed me out into the yard and joins Father at his side. When he is done plucking, Father pulls out matches from his pocket and burns the feathers. The flesh stench spreads through the yard.

Mom can make many different dishes with chicken. She makes spicy chicken stew with potato chunks thrown in; she chops the meat into pieces and drains them for frying; she shreds boiled meat to serve cold with vegetables . . . Ever since I moved to the city, Mom piles up my plate or bowl with heaps of whatever dish she has cooked. The chicken porridge, made with garlic and rice, fills up the bowl in front of me. When she finds a drumstick in her ladle while serving the porridge, Mom slips it into my bowl.

"Eat up before it gets cold."

Little Brother picks out a drumstick from his bowl and dips it into mine, imitating Mom's words. "Eat up before it gets cold."

Younger Sister plants her knuckles on his head, saying, "You little rascal."

Food. Mom's way of encouraging the family is to cook food in the old kitchen of the house. Whenever the family encounters unbearable grief, Mom steps into her old-fashioned kitchen. The men of the house. Father, whom she loved but was sometimes difficult to understand, and her sons, who were growing into adults—whenever they disappointed her, she would go into the kitchen, her steps feeble. As she did when she was in shock, at the daughter lashing back at her, "You have no idea!" By the fuel hole of the furnace, or the shelf lined with upside-down bowls, inside the old-fashioned kitchen of that house, that was the only place where Mom could endure the grief that has invaded her heart. And there she would regain her courage, as if the kitchen spirit had breathed a new energy into her. When she was delighted, when her heart ached, when someone left, or came back, Mom made food, set the table, made the family sit down, and pushed the bowl, piled with food, in front of the one who was leaving or had returned. Offering, endlessly, "Have some more. Try some of this. Eat before it gets cold. Have that, too."

Mom and Cousin and I bundle up the rooster on the roof and carry him across the elevated walkway, to the chicken vendor at the market. To ask him to butcher the chicken for us. It seems the market isn't open. The chicken vendor is closed. So is the fish vendor, the vegetable vendor, the snack stall where Cousin and I often go. We manage to buy two salted mackerels from a street vendor and also a steamer made of nickel silver, to make rice cake. Mom is disappointed since she wanted to cook up something special for Oldest Brother. Back on the roof, as she ties up the rooster again, Mom tells us, "I have to go back on the night train, so as soon as you can find the time, I want you take the chicken to the vendor at the market and ask him to butcher it, and boil it slow and long for you and your brother to eat.

"I brought lots of garlic, all peeled and cleaned, so when you get that chicken butchered, fill up its stomach with garlic and simmer, then rinse a bowl of rice, add it inside and simmer some more."

"All right."

"It's homegrown domestic-breed chicken, different from the kind you buy at the market. I fed him real well. Do as I say now, all right?"

"All right."

Left with no other choice, Mom relents and prepares Oldest Brother's birthday dinner with the other ingredients that she's brought. She hulls peas to steam with rice. She cubes radish and braises the mackerel. She steams red beans to make sticky cake with the rice flour that she has ground. She makes kimchi and prepares wraps with the young radish and cabbage she brought from home. She dices the zucchini she's picked from our vegetable patch to cook bean paste soup, and serves in a basket a heap of green peppers, baby cucumbers, perilla leaves, radish greens, and yellow cabbage leaves to make wraps with rice. Also green peas steamed inside their pods. When the rice cake is done, she sets the steamer on the table and a large bowl of water next to it. She plants candles in the rice cake and lights them. This is what she does back home, cooks rice cake, makes an offering of pure, clear water, and lights candles, even when the family member celebrating his or her birthday is far away.

Cousin has a present for Oldest Brother, a white button-down shirt. "You're getting out of the military. Then you can wear this."

The dinner table that Mom has prepared carries the smells of home. The smells from the rabbit hutch, the pigsty, the wooden floor of the veranda in midday, streaked with chicken poop, from the roses by the brook. The chili paste dip mixed with chopped garlic and green peppers contains Mom's vegetable patch. And Mom's own corner of the garden behind the sauce jar terrace. The faint shadows of our family mixed inside the smells of home. Little Brother's snot-stained sleeve, Father grilling marinated meat on the sizzling gridiron, my older brothers making extensions for my tiny pencil ends with pen stems. The flutter of Younger Sister's bob cut as she calls to me, *Eonni*. I remember, at the house, there's a shed for hanging farming tools. There hang sickles, shovels, hoes, pitchforks, giving off the smells of soil. The pitchfork. There's a sudden sensation of pain and I stop in the middle of taking a spoonful of the bean paste soup, and touch the sole of my foot.

I remember, at the house, there's a well. And there is a sixteen-year-old girl, who pulled down the pitchfork from the shed that had pierced her foot and headed to the well, dragging her foot wrapped in cow dung, to throw the pitchfork down deep inside.

In the afternoon Cousin is the first to leave, taking some rice cake for her sister. Around dinnertime Mom packs up her wrapping cloths and emptied bags and sets out to head back home. Oldest Brother goes to see her off at Yeongdeungpo Station. As she walks out of the alley to catch her subway to the station, she urges that I take the chicken to the vendor at the market and ask him to butcher it and eat it with Oldest Brother.

"You hear?"

"Yes."

With Mom gone, the kitchen of the lone room, which had given off the smell of home, feels desolate. My eyes well up as I sit alone on the threshold. I take some rice cake to Hui-jae's room but the door is locked. I clean the kitchen cupboard, and rinse with clear water the bowls and spoons and cutting board and knives and pots. When I am done putting everything away, the only thing left is the nickel silver steamer that we used to make the rice cake, blank and quiet. The shiny steamer looks out of place in this kitchen. I rinse the steamer, dry it with a kitchen cloth, and put it away on the shelf.

I head up to the roof with a small bowl of water. The rooster is lying down, utterly exhausted. I place the bowl by his beak. It must have been thirsty and I feel sorry for the bird as it rushes to drink from the bowl, floundering. I come back down to get a fistful of rice and scatter the grains in front of him.

I leave the rooster on the roof instead of taking him to the chicken vendor. Hui-jae watches as I turn over the large rubber basin that had been left upside down on the roof, to see if he can stay released.

"How can you raise a chicken inside a rubber basin? Are you going to keep a lid on it?"

"What should I do?"

"We have a huge wooden plank at the shop that we don't need. Should I ask him to bring it and put it up over there?" She points to a corner by the railing.

"Wooden plank?"

"He'll get rained on if you leave him out here like this."

I go up there the next day to find a wooden plank set up over the railing and the rooster moved under it. The straw rope tied around its feet has also been replaced with a long string woven with yellow and pink thread, extending over the plank through a hole. Thanks to the string, the chicken can now walk around freely under the plank.

At work and at school, from time to time I think of the rooster under the plank on the roof. It makes me happy to bring him water and food. When I step up on the last set of stairs to the roof, he starts to squawk, as if in recognition.

Ever since I've been keeping the rooster on the rooftop terrace, I often run into Hui-jae's man up there. It looks like the chicken recognizes his footsteps as well. The man even plays his harmonica to the rooster. Sometimes Hui-jae is next to him when he plays, her face on his lap.

One day I find next to the makeshift chicken coop a planter made out of styrofoam. Inside, little trees are squeezed in together, abloom with scarlet flowers. Then one day I find next to the planter a large apple crate filled with soil. When I ask what it is, Hui-jae says that the man has lettuce seeds planted in there. A few days later there really are green lettuce leaves lifting themselves out of the soil, toward the chicken. It seems that the two have decided to build a home on the roof. Sometimes they lay out a bamboo mat and take a nap, next to the chicken coop, the flower bed, the vegetable patch.

Once I walk up to the roof with chicken feed and find the man already there. He is mumbling something to the rooster while feeding it. I know how awkward it can be when someone catches me talking to myself. Sometimes I say out loud what I mean to say to Chang, who is far away, but sense that someone had heard me and quickly extend my syllables to turn them into a song. Ah-ah-ah—where can he be? I see him conversing with the rooster, his back to me, and turn around and head back down.

The rooster is theirs now, that's what's happened. Without knowing it, Mom has given them a huge present.

I receive a letter from Chang, who is now a university student, and it contains the term "library card." He checked out *An Introduction to Aesthetics* with his library card. He was writing the letter with the book under his letter pad. The term "library card" has left me feeling awkward and I stand for a long time leaning again the gate of the house with the thirty-seven rooms. "Freshman, College of Art Education." I gaze for a long time at Chang's new address on the envelope.

We all leave the places of our birth in order to grow up. It seems that Chang has also left the village where we grew up in order to attend university. When I get to thinking that Chang is no longer there, suddenly the lights in the village go out all at once.

A woman I met today told me that the place of her birth was Ningan County in Heilongjiang Province, China. Her name is Kim Yeong-ok. Her book was published in Korea under the title, *Madwoman.* Her author bio read as follows:

> Born in 1971 in Ningan County in Heilongjiang Province, China, Kim Yeong-ok won first prize in the National Ethnic Korean Children's Writing Contest at the age of eleven in fourth grade in elementary school, acquiring a reputation as a literary prodigy, a genius writer. When she was fifteen, in third year of middle school, she was selected as one of China's Twelve Young Geniuses by the influential *Hainan Daily*, and at seventeen, included in the fifty-six Young Stars of China selected by the government, to the amazement of the nation's 1.2 billion citizens. She was the only ethnic Korean in the list, a source of great pride to Koreans. Upon graduating from middle school, she went straight on to the College of Korean Language and Korean Studies at Yanbian University, and after earning her bachelor's degree, worked as staff reporter covering arts and literature at the Yanbian Daily. In April 1994, she began her master's studies in the graduate school at the Academy of Korean Studies in Korea. Her nickname is Dallyeo—a woman always on the run.

I was signing books at Kyobo Bookstore after giving a talk a few days ago when I saw her, this woman who was nicknamed "Dallyeo," standing in front of me with a journalist that I remember meeting. She had a bob cut and wore a sky-blue cardigan over a tight skirt. She said to me as she handed me her copy of my book, "I'd like to get together some time."

We met four days later. We went to have jumbo dumplings at Sogong-dong. After having tea at the coffee shop in the Seoul Press Center, the journalist left. I suggested that we head to Kyobo to get a copy of her book. She was shy, and I said, "You've read my work but I don't know you at all and that makes me uncomfortable." We got the book and walked to Insa-dong. We sat down in a corner of a tearoom named Volga and I asked her to autograph her book.

She said she'd been in Korea for a year and a half now. I asked if there's anything awkward or inconvenient about living here and she said she didn't feel that way at all. That she never felt like she was in another country. That perhaps it's because there was nothing unfamiliar, whether it was food or customs. That she had the choice of studying either in Japan or Korea and she was really glad that she ended up coming to Korea. Our conversation naturally turned to the collapse of Sampoong Department Store. She was shocked, she said. Of course, I thought, but she explained that it was not the collapse that shocked her but the fact that the entire scene of the catastrophe was shown to the public and the fact that people showed their anger.

I went blank for a minute.

"If something like that had happened in China, they wouldn't have broadcast it."

". . ."

"Watching the Korean people expressing their anger, I felt there was hope. The Chinese do not care even if they see something happening right next to them. Even if in broad daylight, a pregnant woman is being harassed in the middle of the street, people simply stand around and watch. It could go on for three hours and no one would stop the men. Unthinkable, in this country."

". . ."

"Once a woman fell in the river, in Heilongjiang Province where I'm from. There wasn't a single person who jumped in the water to try to save her before her family arrived. Everyone stood there, their arms crossed, watching the woman flounder as she drowned. When the family arrived and offered money, they started negotiating how much they were going to pay, and the woman died while this went on."

". . ."

"That's how things are in China nowadays. Nobody cares if someone dies in front of them. But everyone's more and more interested in money. The collapse should never have happened, but watching the people showing interest and expressing anger I feel a kind of hope in the people here."

She adamantly defended the ethnic Koreans living in China. She said that the Korean people can never erase their national color no matter where they live. Whether they're in America, in Japan, in Australia, or in Sakhalin, ethnic Koreans formed Koreatowns. And she said that no matter how much time passed, Koreans were Koreans, they could never be Chinese.

"Do you know how fortunate you are? Your writing carries the untainted sentiment and spirit of the Korean people. Something I could never have. I was born as an ethnic Korean in China. From the beginning, my motherland was far away. Reading your work, I can sense a strong scent of one who grew up on this land. Whether it's about death or love or separation. It's not something you can set out to acquire. You don't have ancestors who had no choice but to leave this land, do you? You don't have family in the North, do you?"

My ancestors?

I looked up at her face from my *omjia* berry tea as she asked about my ancestors. She was right. No ancestor of mine had to leave this land. Mine was a clan that once had thrived and had much to protect. Their lofty gate collapsed as colonial rule and epidemics and war swept past, but there were still elderly members who updated the family tree. For years and years my ancestors had maintained the family gravesite here in the South, and the clan's rice paddies nearby. We had not experienced the pain of being separated from family in the North. My ancestors had never left our corner of the South. I had encountered cities like Sinuiju or Hamheung only in books, as I did numerous other place names. Most of my family and cousins and second cousins still lived in the area. Moved only as far as the nearby towns or cities like Jeonju. None of my family had left for America or China. This city was the furthest that any of my family had traveled, and we were the ones who had done it.

She then told me, "You and I are different, as different as the fact that your family is here on this land in the South, and that my family is far away on Chinese soil, always possessing a nomadic soul. In China, I am an ethnic Korean, and here, I am someone from Heilongjiang Province. But you are wholly a Korean, whether you are in Heilongjiang Province or here. This is why you will be able to fit in wherever you go."

As we parted she put on my wrist a filigree enamel bracelet that she said she brought from China. The green bracelet, inlaid with leaf and flower patterns, shimmered in the sunlight. She seemed sad somehow and I suggested we meet again when August arrived. I suggested we go to Mount Gaya and visit Haein Temple there.

•

One day Yun Sun-im asks me to come along to check on a colleague who is unwell.

"Who is it?"

"Miss Lee."

"Is she sick?"

"Ssh." Yun Sun-im brings a finger to her lips. When I give her a curious look, she whispers into my ear. "You mustn't tell anyone that we're going to see Miss Lee."

"Why not?"

She looks around then places her finger on her lips again. I feel a sweep of chilly wind watching her cautious behavior. Spring is here but the lilacs in the flower beds of the factory lot show no signs of blooming. We stop by administration and get a pass. I thought we were going to a hospital but we head to Miss Lee's rented room. As we pass through the entrance of the industrial complex, I glance toward the Job Training Center where I stayed when I first arrived in here, as if someone were pulling me that way. There was the teacher who wrote on the blackboard for us who had been learning soldering skills. How beautiful, to behold from behind, one who goes knowing clearly when it is he should go. There was Mom, who escorted me to this city then turned back again. There was Oldest Brother, visiting every Sunday and buying pastries for us to eat. Three years have passed since then. I worked hard, but nothing has changed in those three years. Nothing except that I started high school and am now in going on to my third year. Nothing except that the white scar left on my thumb by a hot clump of solder paste had splattered while I learning soldering skills at the Job Training Center had now turned faint.

Snow has yet to melt on the slopes of this Doksan-song neighborhood. I have on flat shoes but Yun Sun-im is wearing heels. She looks just as cautious climbing the hilly road as she did when she placed her finger on her mouth.

"Should we get some clementines?"

We buy some clementine oranges, displayed discreetly in a corner of a tiny store on the slope, and start heading up again. We turn downhill and continue for as long as we've climbed up the slope, then come across an alley lined with stovepipes.

"It's that one."

Yun Sun-im points to one of the houses, perhaps the fourth one in the alley. It is a single-story building. We push the gate, which is open, and step inside to find two doors, numbered 101 and 102, respectively. There are some ten rooms down the corridor and there are small cooking stoves lined outside in the corridor. And next to the stoves are pots, strainers, and baskets with bowls placed inside upside down to dry . . . a dizzying array of cookware without a kitchen for them to be placed in. We open one of the doors and enter. Miss Lee is lying down. She tries to sit up but Yun Sun-im stops her.

"Stay as you are, it's okay."

It seems she can't get herself up even if she wants to. She lies back down, her face crumpling.

"How are you doing?"

Without answering Yun Sun-im, Miss Lee straightens her frown and gives me a smile, saying, "It's you."

Yun Sun-im says to me, "Sit down," and to Miss Lee, "You said you missed her, so I brought her." She missed me? I lower my head, feeling shy. I've always been on the other side of what Miss Lee's been doing. When the union walked out on overtime shifts, I kept my place in front of the conveyor belt; when the union handed out ribbons that read, "Let's Claim Our Rights," I kept them inside my pocket. But still she says she missed me? Miss Lee asks Yun Sun-im, "Still no news from Chief?" Yun Sun-im shakes her head.

"He mustn't get caught. If he does, he'll be sent to purification training. I received a D grade and managed to be released, but there's no chance Chief will get a D grade."

A look of concern appears on Yun Sun-im's face. "Don't worry too much. You'll hear from him, I'm sure."

At Miss Lee's words, Yun Sun-im probes my face. Ah, Yun Sun-im and the union chief? The two of them?

"Those inhuman thugs. Saying this nation's in disarray because of people like myself." When Miss Lee says this, discouraged,

Yun Sun-im lifts her blanket. Underneath, Miss Lee's legs are encased in plaster. The legs that used to scurry about, always busy.

"How's your shoulder?"

"Better now."

"What in the world did they do to you?"

". . . I was kicked on the stairs that led to the basement and rolled all the way down. The interrogation room was in the basement, you see. My hands and feet were tied, so the injury was bad."

"Were they trying to kill you, pushing you down the stairs with your hands and feet tied?"

"But I'm alive, aren't I?"

"Listen to you!"

"I got out, that's what counts. Chief will never make it out if he gets caught. So if you hear from him you have to tell him this. They mean serious trouble, these people. I heard that if they shave your head, it means they're going to kill you. Some got beat up so bad, their intestines got ruptured."

Yun Sun-im closes her eyes tight then opens them. "You should have lunch."

Yun Sun-im goes out to the hallway and lights the stove to cook two packs of *ramyeon* noodles. The soup is warm and tasty, more so because the room is so cold. Miss Lee puts down her chopsticks after a short while and Yun Sun-im peels a clementine to offer her.

"How are you managing to prepare food?"

"I have Seo-seon next door . . . She's got a strong spirit."

Miss Lee stops in the middle of speaking about Seo-seon and looks at me.

"You should, too. Be strong-spirited . . . No reason to be discouraged. Are you continuing to write? . . . Whenever I saw you write, your notebook on the conveyor belt, it made me feel good somehow."

"It wasn't my writing. I was just copying someone else's."

"When you become a writer someday, you should write about us, too." Miss Lee smiles, patting my head.

Now more people show up at the factory to pick up their severance pay or overdue wages than to work. The company no longer seems intent on production. Our employers no longer seem intent on employing us. Our employers want us to forget about the time that we were employed and evaporate into nowhere. We miss the times when we rejected overtime shifts to demand shorter work hours, welfare and hygiene, higher overtime pay. Our hands feel anxious now that they have stopped producing goods. Our employers no longer carry out mass dismissal. Dismissals call for severance pay. The security office, which used keep a strict eye on promptness, is now silent. It's hard to believe that it was once a venue for so much conflict, cutting an hour's pay for being one minute late to work.

One morning, Oldest Brother brings up a question at breakfast. "Are you allowed to keep attending school after quitting work? You need to study if you want to go to college."

Oldest Brother thinks for a while then asks, "Since Cousin is not experiencing trouble continuing with school after quitting work, things should be okay for you as well, right? Whatever the regulations are, you're in third year now, so they won't throw you out or anything, will they?"

". . ."

"You should quit."

Quit? That would be what the company wants. They want us to leave of our own accord. Three months of pay was overdue. So even if we get paid, we are getting paid for work that was done three months ago. But how can I quit, when Oldest Brother is unemployed as well, after the tutoring center closed down.

"I'm being discharged from military soon. I'm going to quit civil service and get a job at a corporation."

"Corporation?"

"A big corporation. Have you seen the tall building across the street from Seoul Station?"

I have seen it. The building that appeared like a gargantuan beast when I first got off the night train in this city with Mom. She had told me that it was nothing to be afraid of, nothing but steel frames.

"That's where I'm going."

"Into those steel frames?"

"Just hold on for a while. When I quit my civil servant post, I'll get some severance pay. Then we'll move."

"Move?"

"Yes, we're going to move." Oldest Brother smiles again, making an effort.

Oldest Brother brings it up again in the evening.

"Did you hand in you resignation?"

"No."

"I told you to!"

The next day he asks again. When I say I haven't, he looks at me incredulously.

"You have a slim chance getting into college even if you do nothing but study from now on."

I stare back at him incredulously. Even if he's going to start working for a corporation, if I quit my job now, how will we pay rent and . . . ? Oldest Brother seems not to care what I think, and points to the desk. There are three shopping bags filled with books.

"I got you books you need to start studying for the entrance exam. Don't even think about math or English, just focus on subjects you can study by rote."

He pulls out money from his pocket.

"Study home economics as your elective. I didn't know which study guide I should get for that. Go to a bookstore near school and ask for one that most of the daytime students use."

I put down my spoon, startled, and stare at Oldest Brother. I swallow hard the food in my mouth without chewing.

"It's a late start, but if you work hard you'll be able to get into a junior college at least." His voice is like a stream of water. It seems as if somewhere, where it is I don't know, my favorite flowers are blossoming all of a sudden, all at once.

"Let's eat."

Oldest Brother's chopsticks head for the steamed spinach on the table. He gazes at me, sitting there still and blank. "What is it?"

I put down my spoon and pull up closer to him. "*Oppa*!" Oldest Brother stops eating and looks at me. "Do you really mean it?"

"Mean what?"

"Do you mean it, that I can start studying?"

"I do."

"For real?"

"Yes."

He puts down his spoon and once again smiles, making an effort.

·•·

The girl's name was Yu Ji-hwan. She was miraculously rescued thirteen days after the collapse of the department store. She moved her toes. The girl was being carried out on a gurney, rescued from the pitch-black darkness and the violent rubble of steel rods and cement. She gently lifted the yellow handkerchief placed on her eyes to prevent blindness from the attack of sudden sunlight. Then she gazed out at the world with fearful eyes. My eyes were fixed on the TV screen. A face I seemed to have seen before. A face I once loved. My heart sank with a thud.

. . . I want some iced coffee.

. . . I think I slept for about five days.

. . . I thought of what Mom used to tell me, that I should never lose hope no matter what.

That face, the face I once loved. It was she. The face that had come back to life from pitch-black darkness.

I was unable to tear myself away from the TV. The girl was pretty and lovely. I cut out her pictures from several different papers. How pretty. Ever since the building collapsed, I had felt desolate, as if all thought had been abruptly cut off at once. This was not a war we were experiencing yet so many human lives could be lost in an instant. I had a deep sense of defeat about life, bringing down with it the meaning of it all, of the struggle to live.

What was it that we should try to uphold in life? The unexpected shock had stripped me of will, making me respond cynically, causing a blackout in my concentrated and continuous contemplations about man.

But then this girl?

The girl had fallen asleep while receiving IV fluids and as soon as she opened her eyes, her older brother asked her this question.

"Isn't there anything you want to eat?"

The girl answered, beaming a smile at him.

"I want a bowl of clear beef soup, but I can't have it right now, so you should go with your friends and have some for me."

I was engrossed in my thoughts about the girl, as if I was determined not to overlook a single word, a single movement of hers. The deeper I thought about her, the more my shaken mind turned calm, and I felt a genuine intimacy, as if I had know her for a long, long time. Ji-hwan, thank you, thank you, for living.

Summer was here. Yet another summer, like summer of that year.

I don't seem to remember. Whether I received my overdue wages or my severance pay, or not. How I wish I could write, I don't seem to remember that summer, either, I don't seem to remember.

I visit Mr. Choe Hong-i, the teacher who is no longer at the school with us. Upon hearing that I plan to study for college, he ponders the situation. He seems concerned, saying, "Starting this year, you have to submit your high school records as well. But your bookkeeping and abacus grades are a mess, aren't they?

"Fortunately, only grades starting from your second year are reflected, so start focusing on school work now. Improve your grades. High school records are divided into fourteen levels—you want to be at least in the middle."

Only then I open the bookkeeping textbook. Debit, credit, balance sheets. All I get is a splitting headache. I sit with a scowl and Cousin comes and asks, "What is the matter?"

"I don't understand any of this."

"I don't, either."

"But I have to now."

"Make some time during the day and go to a bookkeeping class then."

"I thought they closed down all the private academies."

"Not the ones offering adult classes. I heard that a lot of students attend those now."

Cousin hands me some money and I turn sullen.

"You'll be able to catch up in a month. You just need to learn the basic principles—it's only that you've never tried. Someone told me that these academies can teach you in one month what takes you three years to learn in school . . . They probably offer an accelerated class. Sign up for that. Once you take that, school tests will seem like nothing."

Still, I stay sullen and Cousin grabs my hand, holding on to the money.

"Take this and sign up for the class." My dear cousin picks up her schoolbag and speeds off before I can say anything. My dear cousin, who said she would never end up a nobody; my dear cousin, who brought her younger sister after she finished middle school in the country and enrolled her in a commerce school—So what it it's not a regular school, I cannot bring myself to send my own sister to a factory . . . You should never end up a nobody, either.

. . . I remember. Summer of that year. My memories of that summer are not all those that would not detoxify. There were moments that I loved. It was also that summer, the night that Chang and I walked and walked . . .

Little Brother hands me a note. I'm about to ask what it is, but he lifts his finger to his lips, stealing a glance toward the kitchen where Mom is working. The note is from Chang. He wrote asking me to meet him by the railroad. After dinner I wash my face. Also wash my hair. I take Mom's toner and pat it onto my face. I pretend I'm getting some air out in the garden, then slip out the gate. Chang is standing at the railroad, whistling a tune. He stops as I approach. Stars twinkle in the sky. On the ground the day's heat still remains. Chang and I walk side by side along the tracks of the southbound railroad. Since starting university Chang has turned reticent. Melancholy. Taciturn. His face now reminds me of Third Brother, who, at the urging of Oldest Brother, had to pack up his law books and leave for the farm. We walk on and on, circling the village.

"Have you heard about Gwangju Incident?" Chang is attending university in the city of Gwangju. "It was no incident but a revolution."

Silence.

"I was shown numerous photos at the club I joined . . . Things we cannot even imagine happened in Gwangju. Is it thinkable that a soldier stabs a civilian with a bayonet? Not any civilian but a pregnant woman?"

Silence. I suddenly feel burdened by my silence. I feel I have to say something. How come everyone's face changes like that when they go to university?

"I don't work at the factory anymore." I'm not sure how I got to saying this out of nowhere. We walk on and on and now we've arrived at the causeway on the far outskirts of the village.

"Let's stop here for a while." Chang lies on his back in the middle of the causeway. The fresh air of the summer night seeps into our bodies. Moonlight, leaves of grass, light from the distant village, the sound of water.

"There was a day, when I joined the protest on campus and I was chased by the riot police, all the day down a dead-end street where I hid behind the sauce jar terrace of a small inn. They came chasing and beat me up."

". . ."

"That night, I slept with a woman I'd never met before."

". . ."

"When I woke up I reached out my hand thinking I might as well feel her breasts, but ran off, got myself out of there."

". . ."

"Her breasts were shriveled, all dried up. I noticed only then that she was my mother's age . . . When I returned to campus, I threw up terribly."

". . ."

"I'm sorry I'm telling you this." Chang lets out a quiet chuckle as he fumbles inside his pocket and takes out something as if he's just remembered. "Here, take this."

Something small, the size of a thumb, glimmers on Chang's open palm, like a star. It's a tiny, tiny teddy bear charm. A fluorescent bear. Amidst the soft bristle of the night wind, Chang seems to be lifting himself to sit up. But it turns out he's kneeling. Don't do this.

A sadness surges up into my heart. I, nineteen years old, grasp onto the fluorescent bear. Nevertheless, the sadness does not stop. This realization that Chang and I will someday grow apart. It seems like a dream that we're together like this. We could wake up any moment from this dream and I, nineteen years old, feel immense pity for Chang. So much so that a tear escapes from my eye. I search for Chang's hand as he sits on his knees, his eyes gazing out somewhere.

"Do you want to feel them, just once?" I take Chang's hand and place it on my breasts. When we've grown apart, when this dream inside my heart has been broken, where will I be? And where will you be? Where will we be, looking back at this moment?

No matter what other roundabout path I took, my writing remembered that summer. No matter how I pushed it deep inside of me, that year's summer would surge up again and again. It would seep in, even into the moments that I shared with him, smiling together. Even in the most unexpected moments, like the night wind, the rising tide, the fog.

One day, upon returning late, Oldest Brother asks me, "Do you think you can manage living alone?" He's been coming home even later since he was discharged from the military.

"Where will you be?"

"Looks like I'm going to be sent to a post in Chungmu."

Chungmu?

"I tried everything to get a post in Seoul but it seems I'm going to have to go. It won't be long. I'll be able to come back in two months or so. Will you be okay on your own?"

My heart sinks. I'm going to be left alone here in this alley, in this lone room.

"There's no other way."

I know this. If there was any other way, Oldest Brother would not go off to Chungmu by himself, leaving me here alone. He cherished me like a precious stone.

"I'll be okay. I can manage on my own."

"Stay away from the woman downstairs." Ever since the man moved in with Hui-jae, Oldest Brother is uncomfortable about her. He used to refer to her by name but now it's the woman downstairs. It's not that he's said anything to her face, but Hui-jae also knows that he feels uncomfortable. When she stops by with a bowl of noodles she's cooked and Oldest Brother is home, she places it on the counter and heads down the stairs, as if she's being chased.

"Is there a library at school?"

"There is one."

"Then do your studying there."

I look at him quizzically.

"You need a good environment . . . but here all you see and hear is . . . Pack your breakfast and go to school to study in the morning."

Oldest Brother has no idea that I've been attending Hallym Academy located behind Yeongdeungpo Station with the money from Cousin. Nor that my month-long course is not done yet but I am now the best student in my bookkeeping class. Nor that Hui-jae gets our groceries for us every night ever since I started studying for college. Oldest Brother says it is a cowardly person who gives up before trying. No doubt he does not approve of Hui-jae, who has dropped out of school. A man of upright character, he has reservations about a woman who comes home in the morning and lives with a man without marrying him. He is concerned that his younger sister is bonding with such a woman.

Oldest Brother brings home a wheeled suitcase and I put yellow melons in water to chill. He packs the suitcase with dress shirts, underwear, socks, handkerchiefs, and comfort wear. He also packs toothpaste and toothbrush and soap case and razor. On the last night before he leaves, I slice the yellow melons for dessert. When I scrape out the seeds with my knife, he says that's the sweeter part of the fruit.

"You don't know the right way to eat a melon."

"But I don't want to get an upset stomach."

"That's nonsense! That's the sweetest part." Even as we're getting ready to sleep, Oldest Brother once again asks me to stay away from the woman downstairs.

"She's not a bad person."

"I don't want to hear it!"

"I mean it, she's not!"

"Don't want to hear it, I said!"

In the middleof listening to Rostropovich playing the *Bach Suite for Unaccompanied Cello*, I unplugged my telephone.

I cannot put it off any longer. I must finish writing this. Everything is set. I have made arrangements so that I have no one to meet, no other writing I need to work on except this. My desk is neat and I've finished cleaning the bathroom sink. I have no laundry to do; I have filled my fridge with groceries; and I have nothing to work out with anyone. Yet I cannot bring myself to sit at the desk, doing nothing but listening to Rostropovich's cello all day long. In the liner sheets of the record, the elderly cellist states that for a long time Bach had been a sacred name for him. He says that ever since encountering Bach when he was sixteen he had worshipped the composer, which kept him from recording the complete unaccompanied cello suites, and all I can do is gaze blankly into his face on the liner sheet.

> I have made two recordings of the Bach suites. Forty years in Moscow, I recorded the *Suite No. 2*, and in 1960 in New York, the *No. 5.* I cannot forgive myself when I think about these two recordings. But anyone who looks back at the past would be self-critical and there would be things that he wishes he would not have done. What can you do about something that's already been done, life will continue to flow on, proud and imperious. So now I must work up the courage to record the complete cycle of Bach's unaccompanied cello suites, a body of work deeply connected to my life. There is nothing I treasure more than these suites. I discover something new each time I listen to them. Each hour, each second you spend thinking about these compositions, you will reach a deeper understanding about them. You might one day think that you know everything about

> these suites, but then discover something new the next day.

He continued on with the same expression. That Bach was never vulgar, temperamental, or caught up in rage, that even when close acquaintances grew distant, he never spoke ill of them.

Was I in awe of Rostropovich's cello playing, or was I enchanted by Rostropovich's interpretation of Bach, this man who himself was enchanted by Bach? I'm not sure what it is I feel. When he discusses Bach, Rostropovich's face wears the majesty of the sound of cello. At times it even takes on an air of solemnity.

He says, "Now I must work up the courage to record the complete cycle of Bach's unaccompanied cello suites."

Rostropovich seems like someone who recognizes life's passion, grief, and intensity. He searched and searched for the right place to perform the suites, and found a cathedral that was built nine hundred years ago.

The cycle includes an amazing sarabande . . . It possesses a special kind of honesty and seriousness, and also a musical vulnerability. This piece cannot be played for the audience by for oneself only. The audience simply gets to glimpse at an artist deeply focused in his music, at an intense solitude that is cold and at the same time hot. Many times, I have played this sarabande for those lost in grief.

I adjusted the CD player to *Suite No. 2*.

For those lost in grief? Immediately I examined Rostropovich's face again. He's been playing for those lost in grief?

Hui-jae sits in front of the dead rooster. She wears a cold expression. It was Hui-jae and the man who loved the chicken most dearly, but the man cannot be seen. When I say it looks like someone fed the chicken poison, Hui-jae's profile turns even chillier.

Even during the rainy season, construction continues in the lot. An excavator digs up the cabbage growing in a nearby patch. Steel beams are raised and bricks are carried in. Now we can no longer see the subway station outside the window. What we see are workers walking up and down the ramps of the construction site, and men wearing scarlet plastic hardhats the shape of gourds. I remember one Sunday, by this time we could no longer see passengers pour out of the subway station like the rising tide, and one day the pile of briquettes collapsed in the cellar, in the house with the thirty-seven rooms. If it hadn't been for the collapse, I would never have known that the house had a basement.

Hui-jae is in the basement scooping up the crumbled black briquettes, her face streaked with charcoal.

"Where can everyone be, the water is rising."

"Where's Uncle?" Hui-jae streaked face turns even darker. She descends into the basement again. Then she emerges with a pail brimming with black water.

"You can't take care of this by yourself. Get out of there."

"Half of the briquettes in the basement are ours."

"Where's Uncle?"

"He's gone." Hui-jae enters the basement again. Gone? Where? At a loss, I follow her downstairs. The water in the basement reaches my ankles. The broken briquettes have turned the water black.

"Where did he go?"

Hui-jae stops to brush her hair away from her face behind her ears. The charcoal stains her face. "Don't bring him up again."

"How come?"

"He's not coming back, ever."

I clamp my mouth shut. Hui-jae keeps quiet as she bails the black water from the basement. I cannot leave her side. She tells me to stop and go study but I can't. At one point Hui-jae squats down in the basement and starts to vomit.

"*Eonni*, you need to take a break, go back upstairs." She doesn't seem to have heard me, as she's continuing to scoop out the wet pile of briquettes. It's already afternoon when we're finally done. She bends down in her kitchen and vomits terribly. I get scared that she's about to die and I boil water on the kerosene stove and wash her. I wipe and wipe but her body still smells of rotting food. Then I think I must have fallen asleep. I feel someone clipping my fingernails. I open my eyes to find Hui-jae clipping my nails, sitting crouched with my hand on her knee.

"Your nails are black with charcoal." Feeling warm and peaceful, I sit still for her to finish.

"How's your tummy?"

"Better." She's almost done with both of my hands when her face turns cold again as she brings up the dead rooster.

"Remember the chicken?"

I can understand how disheartened she is and respond, "Who could have done something do terrible?"

"It was me." My mind goes blank. I must have heard wrong. "I gave him poison."

My body jerks with startlement, and the nail clipper in her hand tears a tip of my finger. She stays calm. At that moment she is not the same person I know. She is firm and cold.

"Why did you do something like that?"

"Because that was what he loved most dearly!"

He? I retrieve my hand from her knee. What he loved most dearly? The wet stench from the basement has seeped into every corner of her body and mine.

The sun comes out in the afternoon. There's me, nineteen years old, washing my clothes and after hanging them on the roof, opening her door to check inside. She is asleep with her face down. There's me closing the door gently, taking care not to wake her. There's me opening her door again, thinking, She'd be awake now. There's me opening her door three, four more times. She sleeps without even stirring. The sun goes down. I bring in the laundry from the roof. I make dinner and take some food to her on a tray but she still hasn't moved. I leave the tray there and am about to close the door behind me when I suddenly get scared. There's me flinging the door back open and turning on the fluorescent light. The fear that I sense in her body on the floor, appearing and disappearing in the flicker of the light. It occurs to me that the flesh under her birdlike shoulders might have turned cold. There's me sinking to the floor, lifting her blanket. She is curled up in a ball, her fists clenched tight. Her black hair hides her profile, her skin pale and yellow.

I shake her awake. "*Eonni, Eonni*?"

There's me shaking her, gently at first, then harder. She turns over, whimpering. I'm still not relieved and before I realize it I am slapping her cheeks, screaming.

"Wake up!" She opens her eyes. Pupils blurred. She sits up.

"What is it . . . ?" She gazes into my frightened eyes. She doesn't look like she's been sleeping all this time.

". . . What is it? Tell me."

"No, it's just . . ."

I, nineteen years old, cannot bring myself to say, You looked like you were dead.

"Come on, you're being silly."

She opens her door and says, surprised, "Goodness, it's night already." She seems unaware that she's slept all afternoon, her fists clenched, that I shook her, all frightened, that I slapped her cheeks . . . all she does is bring her palms to her waist, as if the only thing she's surprised and embarrassed about is that it's night already. She is back to her blurred self.

It seems that Hui-jae no longer goes to work at the tailor shop.

She no longer keeps two jobs. While school's out for the summer, when I return at dusk after sitting through the day at the school library, Hui-jae is already home from work, asleep in her room.

From this point on, she is always asleep whenever I see her. Her fists clenched tight.

•◆•

Chang is in Seoul for a visit. I am hanging laundry on the roof, shaking water off, when I see someone waving at me from below. It's Chang. He's not alone. A cute girl stands by his side, her black hair bouncing on her shoulders. I shout at Chang to wait down there. I do not want to show him our lone, remote room. I hurry and change, then run out to Chang. I'm not wearing my uniform and Chang is a college student, so we head for the Green Meadow Tearoom near Garibong Market.

"I'm entering military service."

I spill the coffee on my skirt.

"What's there to be so surprised about?"

"Who's surprised?"

Chang asks me for a tour of Seoul. Tour? The only part of Seoul I'm familiar with is Yeongdeungpo. Outside of Yeongdeungpo, the only places I've been to are the Myeongdong Cathedral and Korea Theater, where Oldest Brother took us at Christmas; Jongno Bookstore, which is just outside the Jonggak Subway Station; and the alley where Cousin lives in Yongsan. But I want Chang to have a good time. Sit here for a bit, I tell him and call Cousin to ask where I should take Chang, who's visiting, to give him a tour of Seoul. Cousin tells me to take him to Mount Namsan. I get the bus route from Cousin. At Mount Namsan, we rent rackets and play badminton. The girl that Chang brought has never played badminton. Chang and I have played since elementary school so the two of us end up playing. The girl sits at a distance. Chang says from time to time, "You must be bored," and she waves her hand, saying, "No." She seems nice. As dusk falls, Chang asks if I should be getting to school, and I tell him that I'm not going. After dinner we go to another tearoom. One on the foot of Mount Namsan this time. Chang takes out from his bag a notebook and photographs. It's the notebook that I sent him, where I copied down *The Dwarf Launches*

His Tiny Ball. He hands the notebook to me, and the photos to the girl. I open the notebook and the margins of the pages inscribed with my handwriting he has filled with his drawings.

"I made these drawings whenever I thought of you." The stifling feeling that has persisted in my heart dissolves at his words. It is late now and Chang asks me to make a phone call.

"To whom?"

The girl looks down without saying anything. Chang pushes a note toward me and says it's the girl's older sister's number. He asks me to tell her that the girl will spend the night at my place.

"My place?" I look up at Chang, startled. The girl does not look up and Chang smiles shyly. He writes down the girl's name on the note. So her name is Hae-seon. Chang calls her Seon-i, so I thought her name was Seon or Seon-hui. I get up and dial the number. A woman with a high-pitched voice answers the phone.

"Hello, this is Hae-seon's senior from school. It's getting late so I invited Hae-seon to sleep over at my place."

"Where do you live?"

"In . . . in Garibong-dong."

"Can Hae-seon come to the phone?"

"Yes."

"I'd like to speak with her."

I hand over the receiver to the girl who is standing next to Chang. While she is speaking to her sister, I ask Chang when he's heading back to the country.

"Tomorrow . . . Hae-seon was coming to visit her sister so I came to see her off."

"Did you get your train ticket?"

"I'm going to take the express bus."

"When do you enter service?"

"Day after tomorrow."

I return to my lone room after parting with Chang and the girl, and stay wrapped under my blanket for a long time without turning on the light. Then I get up, turn on the light and open the notebook that I got from Chang. I fiddle with the fluorescent teddy bear in my pocket. What is he doing, at this hour? I sit gazing into Chang's little drawings, then walk down to Hui-jae, carrying my pillow.

"I'm going to sleep here, *Eonni*."

Hui-jae says okay. "Is anything wrong?"

"No."

"Talk to me. Talking makes it feel better."

I don't talk. Hui-jae looks at me, with my mouth shut tight, then gets up, goes into the kitchen and puts a pot of water on the kerosene stove.

"What are you doing?"

"I'll make you some noodles. You'll feel better with a full stomach."

In the morning, I, nineteen years old, take the subway to Seoul Station and from there take the bus to the express bus terminal. My face is puffy and swollen after having Hui-jae's noodles at a late hour. I wait for Chang at the booth for the tickets to Jeongeup. Past noon, and still Chang does not show. It's past three in the afternoon when Chang finally appears in the distance, walking with his shoulders drooped. His eyes widen when he sees me.

"Since when have you been here?"

"A short while now."

"But you didn't know when I'd come."

"I felt I'd see you if I came."

We just sit there, on the waiting room bench.

"Your studies going well?"

"Uh-huh."

Neither Chang or I mention the girl. I want to tell him something nice but instead blurt out something completely different. "I'm not going to write you!"

"I know."

"How do you know that?"

"It's been a long time since you've written."

The harder I try to speak cheerfully, the stifling ache in my heart worsens. It makes me so uncomfortable to put on an expression that is opposite of how I feel inside. I get to thinking that from now on I will start living in a manner opposite to my feelings. Laugh when I feel like crying, say I'm not angry when I am, answer that I've been here a short while when it's really been a long time. His departure time arrives and Chang gets to his feet. At the ticket gate he looks back at nineteen-year-old me and says, "I'll be back soon." As if he's going on an errand for his mother, not entering military service.

⁂

A thunderous summer night. It looks like the typhoon is about to blow our roof off. Startled by the lightning rays assaulting the lone room, I head down to Hui-jae's room, carrying my pillow. She is sitting with her door open, staring into nowhere.

I close the door behind me as I step inside but she remains still. *Eonni.* I cover her eyes with my palms. My palms feel wet. She's crying.

"Why is life so hard?"

I sit there clasping my pillow.

"Is it just me? Or is it hard for other people as well?"

⁂

Oldest Brother sends money from Chungmu. My oldest brother. In his letter, he writes as if he was born into this world to take care of me. Pay rent on time, don't be too frugal, the weather's hot so buy some melons to eat.

⁂

Since I began writing this, fall, winter, and spring have come and gone, and now it is summer. I should finish before summer was over. Ever since I began I hoped it would be done soon, but now my heart felt stifled, as if I'd never contemplated an ending for this. The phone had been unplugged for more than ten days. But only now I made myself sit at the desk, just barely. During those days, with my phone unplugged, I just lingered by the desk day and night, laying myself down, then lifting myself up again. To keep myself from getting anxious amidst continuing rain, I closely followed the news in print and on TV. The typhoon passed and an oil tanker hit into a rock off the southern coast. The TV screen showed black oil slicks formed on the southern seas. Oysters and fish in aqua farms were afloat on the water after dying en masse. As I watched choppers spray dispersant over the sea, my eyes attached to the screen, I wondered if I was memorizing everything I was reading and seeing. No living creature will be able to live in those mudflats now.

Why did they fire at civilians waving white flags? The prosecutors' office decided not to indict any of the fifty-eight men accused of charges related to the May 18 Gwangju Uprising. They said they will not take the case to court for a criminal trial. The prosecutors' approach to solving the May 18 Uprising case is to conclude that they do not have power of prosecution. That a successful coup cannot be penalized. This man, who had pushed for a civilian government every chance he had, who had solemnly declared, as he abandoned his path as an opposition leader and joined the ruling party, that in order to catch the tiger one had to enter the tiger's cave, the same man was now saying that we should leave the May 18 Uprising case to history.

Why aren't they going after the tiger? He responds to my question with a smile, as if to say it's nothing new. How come there are people who died but no one who killed them? His expression remains sullen.

"The top leaders of this country view the citizens as mere subordinates. Why should they be afraid of their lackeys? When a subordinate disobeys his superior, their impulse is to court-martial them. There's this radio drama titled *The Fifth Republic* and . . ."

The mention of the term *Fifth Republic* pulled me in.

"In the early days of the Fifth Republic, the harvest was bad and in 1982 they had to import rice. The show featured a scene where the chief executive of the Fifth Republic reminisced about those times . . ." He stopped mid-sentence and straightened his neck. Then he spoke in a voice that imitated that of the chief executive. "I engaged in psychological warfare at that point. The people of this country were anxious with worry about food because of the bad harvest. I sent down orders for the trucks to drive six, seven times through downtown before unloading the rice subsidies at Gwangju Station. The same thing for the trucks headed for Daegu. I was waging a psychological war."

He seems to be putting on a comedy routine and I let out a chuckle, but his face hardened.

The government imports rice after a bad harvest—how does that call for psychological warfare? He took power after a sweeping victory at the battle in Gwangju in May 1980, so even after he became President, he is engaged in a war against the people. It might be understandable if we were at war and the military was running out of rice provisions and the soldiers' morale was at stake, but this president was waging a psychological war against civilians in a time of peace . . . There was no other way of looking at it, that he saw the nation as military barracks, and the people as subordinates under his command.

I feel as if my face and my heart were swelling up, puffy and plump.

I have sat myself down at the desk now, so my writing will be done before long. I will now finish it. Soon I will no longer have more to say.

At night, when I sat at the chair with all the lights turned off, I saw the forest outside my window. When the wind blew, the pine trees shook and swished. When it rained, magpies sat at the tips of white pines, making a fuss. Have you ever gazed out at the forest stirring and shifting under attack by rain and wind? Have you ever heard pines trees, laceshrubs, and crape myrtles, stirring and prattling? It seemed that at night trees turned into spiritual beings. They seemed to bring back those who were forgotten. Bringing back to mind what we still remember—the person's finger, neck, even the spot under one eye. Have you ever felt that this person was walking toward you down the narrow path between the trees, this person you can no longer be with, this person who has lost his words? If you have never felt a chill in your heart at the forest stirring and prattling on a windy, rainy night, it means you have no sin to repent. I, for one, get scared. Nevertheless, each night I turned out all the lights and sat in my chair, gazing out at the forest. Whenever I was overcome with fear, I straightened by body and placed my arms on the window frame.

Yes, say what happened that morning. Get it done and over with.

That morning I ran into her in the alley. Thinking back now, we did not run into each other. She would have been waiting for me. We walked out of the alley together and as we were about to part, she tells me something, as if she just remembered. She's going on vacation. She's heading to the country in the afternoon but she forgot to lock the door. She'll be in the country a few days, so would I lock her door when I come back in the evening, she asked. Adding that the lock was hanging on the door latch. It was no big favor and I answered that I would. No. I think I might have asked, what about during the day, wouldn't it be safer if you went back now and locked it? There's nothing to take even if I don't lock it, she said. Which was true. We did not own anything that others would want to steal. In the evening I returned from school and before heading up to our room on the third floor, I fastened the lock on her door on the first floor. The lock was hanging on the door latch, unfastened. I think I might have peeked into the kitchen for a second as I hooked the lock onto the latch. Her washbowl and soapbox were arranged neatly, like any other day. I could sense the traces of her hands in the dishcloth that had been washed and wrung, and her pot, wiped and scrubbed with a metal pad, sat upside down on the kerosene stove, quiet and twinkling. I think I might have also caught a glimpse of her student shoes, which she had worn for a short while. But that was all. All I did was to take the lock that was hanging on the door and fasten it to the latch, as she had asked.

I will not leave the desk, I tell myself . . . If I leave now I will not be able to come back.

Many days pass. Her door stays closed, the lock fastened. Each morning I, nineteen years old, make new rice to pack my lunch and walk past the subway station, leaving behind the locked door on the first floor. At Industrial Complex No. 3, I take the number 109 bus to school. At the library I memorize the home economics test sheets, my skirt hiked up to my knees, until I head back home. As Oldest Brother instructed, I don't even think about studying English or math. On some days I change into our PE uniform and practice the hundred-meter dash alone in the empty athletic field. Practice hanging on the chin-up bar.

Exiting through the school gates around dusk, sitting inside the bus to return to the lone, remote room, I think about her. Wishing she'd come back now. Cousin has gone to Yongsan, Third Brother to the farm, Oldest Brother to Chungmu, so I wait for her, desperately. Since everyone has left, I am all alone.

Getting off the bus at Industrial Complex No. 3, walking past the subway station, past the vacant lot, and stepping inside the gate in the alley, I glance at her door, as if it were a habit. Locked. Still locked. Nothing else of note. How can she take such a long vacation, I'm wondering, when the man approaches. I greet him with a bow, and he asks after her awkwardly.

"She went on vacation."

"Vacation? Where?"

"To the country, she said. Back home."

"Home? But she has no home in the country."

Only then I sense there's something wrong. I realize that all this time she has never mentioned visiting her home in the country. Even during the holidays, she remained alone in her room. But now she's gone to the country on vacation? The man sits outside the locked door for a while then leaves.

In the middle of the night, my doorbell rang, long and loud. The person, whoever it was, kept her finger on the bell. The bell ringing long, nonstop. "Who is it?" My irritated voice from inside the door was met by, "It's me," the voice of Younger Sister outside the door.

What's she doing here so late at night? I opened the door, and Younger Sister, baby in her arms, throws a fit.

"Why aren't you answering your phone if you're sitting at home?"

Phone? But the phone never rang? Ah. When I told her that I unplugged the phone, she seemed even angrier, plugging it in as soon as she stepped in and tapping a number, then pushing the receiver into my face.

"Who is it?"

"You'll find out when you take it!"

She was furious. The voice on the other end of the line was Mom's.

"Why aren't you answering for days on end? I got scared something must have happened and told her to go and see!"

I glanced at Younger Sister as I spoke with Mom and she was washing the stack of coffee mugs and bowls in the sink.

"Have you been eating anything decent at all?"

She was opening the rice cooker and the large soup pot on the gas range. Disappointed that they're all empty. Her baby turned the sugar bowl upside down. Her husband slapped the baby's bottom and the baby bursts into a sob, clear and transparent. I see off Younger Sister's family and unplug the phone again.

Six years ago, I had written about the events that followed those next few days.

•

I recalled, out of the blue, like a legend, the events that followed. That I happened to be passing the subway station for some business and a pain . . . a pain, sharp and deft, sped past, faster than the subway train. That she never came back, and that the man tore down the door. Unable to bear the smell, unable to wait any longer.

And that . . . no one was able to step inside the room.

•

I, nineteen years old, run to Cousin, trembling. Inside my pocket, the fluorescent teddy bear from Chang rolls and bounces. Would it still glow inside the pocket? I stand outside the door, frozen pale, and Cousin brings me some water.

"What happened?"

No words would come out of me, only tears. At first Cousin tries to comfort me, but then my dear cousin, my other guardian, says my name, and I see her eyes about to break into tears. When I hear Cousin's warm, teary voice, I bury my face on her lap and start to sob. Cousin caresses my back, on and on, unaware what has happened.

That day I ran out of our lone room, out of the alley, and I never went back. When I refused to ever go back again, Cousin brought my belongings and school supplies to her room. She told me, it's okay, that it's nothing. But she was trembling herself.

Oldest Brother returned from Chungmu before the construction in the vacant lot was completed and we moved to Daerim-dong, leaving behind his wig on the attic door of that room.

How was the anonymous death handled? And the fact that the door was locked from the outside, inexplicable even if they had found a suicide note in her room.

This I had written.

For a long time I dreamed that the attic ceiling was collapsing . . . and remembered . . . then forgot, the man's despair, mingled with fear and grief. I'd told her to get an abortion. I wasn't breaking up with her, the timing was just too . . . too . . . But that I did not think that it was his words that turned her into food for maggots. Her faint smile . . . her tiny waist, the size of a fist . . . the bank account she left behind, with a million won in savings . . . The man had said, Get an abortion . . .

And I had fastened the lock, leaving her inside as she wore a faint smile, or perhaps cried faint tears, leaving inside on the shelf her school shoes, which she had worn for less than six months.

The place we move into after leaving the lone room is a unit in Wujin Apartments, in Daerim-dong. An old building with electric heating. It seems Oldest Brother used his severance pay and got a loan from his new job to pay for the place. The apartment has two rooms. We even get a telephone installed. Oldest Brother comes to get me at Cousin's after moving all our belongings from the lone room. Third Brother also returns from the farm and goes back to school. Since moving into this old apartment, I get scared of leaving home except for going to school in the evening. I don't want people getting close to me, either. I don't want to see anyone. I stay home alone all day long and when the sun sets, I make dinner for my brothers, cover the table with a cloth, then take the bus to school. Cousin is the only other person who knows that I am studying for college.

I am alone in the apartment all day long, sitting at the desk or lying down on the floor. The rain falls then lets up. A transparent autumn sun pours in through the window. It's too bright in the room and I draw the curtains. Dazed, I doze off then awake with a start. I see her in my short dream. Her body, heavy and slack, swarming with maggots. I am covered in cold sweat. I feel like a snail inside a levee. I drag myself up, lift the curtains, and open the window. The sunlight, speckles after the rain, fills up the space between the ground and the sixth floor. I am gazing out at this transparent air when I feel a tight clamp in my bottom jaw. A chilling thought passes through me and before I know it, I see myself on the ground, fallen, sprawled out. Terrified, I rush to close the window.

I, nineteen years old, rapidly lose my words. There are days when I do not utter a single word. Left-handed An Hyang-suk and Mi-seo the Hegel reader try to make me talk but end up losing their tempers instead.

My cousin does not try to make me talk. She keeps quiet as well. She'd be curious but Cousin does not ask me anything about her. Neither does Oldest Brother. Since I was especially close to her, perhaps they believed that just the mention of her name would be painful for me.

Once we were at a family wedding where we were served noodles, and Cousin wanted to give me her boiled egg (back in our days in the lone room boiled egg halves served in noodle soups or spicy noodles or cold noodle soups were my favorites) but it fell to the floor. At that moment, Cousin sighed, "Ah," and gently called out my name, twice. Now a housewife married to an airline pilot, Cousin glanced at me with an expression that seemed to be remembering something, but quickly erased it and said we should hurry and eat. I gazed blankly into my bowl of noodles. The past had already washed up next to me. That time when the three of us sat waiting for our spicy noodles at the snack stall in the Garibong-dong market. When we were served our three bowls of noodles, she and Cousin picked up their egg halves with the wooden chopsticks to move them into my bowl. It wasn't because they disliked eggs but because I liked eggs. While trying to move the egg halves into my bowl, as if it were a habit, their arms bumped into each other and an egg half fell to the floor.

In the old apartment where we lived until Oldest Brother got married, whenever I woke in the middle of the night I snuck into the room where my brothers were sleeping, carrying my pillow. And I would try to go back to sleep as I listened to their breathing. While I listened to the sound of their breathing, I was able to forget the anxiety and loneliness, growing more distant every day. Only when my chest filled up with the breathing of my family, my blood relations who would never abandon me, only then I was able to go back to sleep.

I take the physical fitness test with the daytime students. The autumn day is so clear and bright. I, nineteen years old, am wearing my PE uniform, the sky-blue V-neck shirt. The breeze feels cool and soft on my face. It seems there is sweetness in the scent of leaves in the wind. My turn to do sit-ups. Six students form a line and lie down on the white mat. Go! Hands clasped behind the head, elbows jerk forward to touch the bent knees.

After finishing six, I can't bring myself to lift my torso.

From amidst clear white clouds her face emerges. It approaches, then pulls back, each time I sit up then fall back down. I give up doing sit-ups and lie on the mat, gazing up at the clouds. Before I realize it, a tear rolls down my cheek. The proctor in charge of counting calls out, "Twelve!" probably thinking I was crying about my poor performance.

Thanks to this, perhaps, I get eighteen points, an unexpectedly high score, on the fitness test.

I sit among strangers, not a single face I know, and take the scholastic achievement test. There are far more questions I can't answer than ones I can. The last test is math. I fill out the answer sheet without even reading the test. When I leave the classroom, the first one in the room, parents are waiting outside the gates. I do not bother looking around since I don't expect anyone to be there, then hear a familiar voice call my name. It's Third Brother.

"*Oppa*!"

I rush toward him. Who knows where he got it, but he's carrying a thermos bottle, filled with hot coffee.

That's what my brothers used to do, appear in an unexpected place or situation, calling my name. Then reach out to caress my hands and my face, quickly growing old since leaving that lone room.

While writing this, from time to time I would be filled with a feeling that someone was watching me. When this happened, I would look back, nervous and tense. For a while it seemed that the gaze visited me regularly, at a specific time. This would make many things impossible for me. I could not sleep, could not lock the doors for the night, got sick and tired of having to be honest, could not bring myself to be gentle to him.

Looking back now as I am about to come to an ending, I realize that the person watching me was none other than myself. That I was trying, awkwardly, to have a conversation with myself.

It is now August. I have nothing more to say. I should send off the manuscript to my publisher, but the other me within me keeps whispering to me, tenaciously, Start over from the beginning . . . Start over from the beginning.

Start over from the beginning . . . from the beginning . . . from the beginning . . . once again . . . from the beginning . . . once again . . . start over from the beginning . . .

When putting certain events down in writing, there is much that does not go as planned. Important parts get reduced to short passages and parts that had seemed vague become long and extensive. I am the one writing it but I cannot do as I intend. These moments that keep surging and vanishing. But I start thinking that now, whichever story I choose to tell, the story should not be aimed solely at myself.

•◆•

Since that day when I ran out of that place, my hands empty save for the fluorescent teddy bear that Chang had given me, I never went back, not even once. I tried so hard never to think about the room that sometimes it really seemed as if that time in that space has vanished within me. But then I would once again see her in my dream and everything would be vivid again. My heart would beat rapidly, making me feel as if I were suffocating, then I would turn blank, in a state of excessive alertness. But now the dark and damp shed inside of my heart is calling to me. Whispering, "All you need to do is take the subway bound for Suwon at Seoul Station or Jonggak, and get off at Garibong Station. Walk down the steps that lead to the Design and Packaging Center, not to Industrial Complex No. 3, and you will arrive at the vacant lot. No. You will arrive at the building that was under construction in what used to be the vacant lot." Will the photo studio, where Cousin used to rent a camera, still be there? Will the barbecue place, where Oldest Brother used to treat us to pork belly, still be there? Will the storekeeper granny still be alive? Does the number 118 bus still make its last stop by the vacant lot? What was the high-rise building they were constructing on the lot? Will the house with the thirty-seven rooms still be there?

Will the rubber basin still be there, placed upside down? What about the clothesline?

Trying to avoid this growing urge to visit the lone, remote room, which was amassing like a snowball, I called him on the phone. Asking if he would give me a ride to the bus terminal because I was visiting the country. He willingly drove me to the terminal, my luggage loaded in the trunk. It was 10:20 when we arrived and 10:40 tickets were available at the booth. I got a seat on the 10:40, but exchanged it for an eleven o'clock ticket. I didn't want to part right away. We had coffee at a tearoom inside the terminal where the tables were arranged haphazardly. As I got on the bus he waved at my back, saying, "Have a good trip." We had gone a short while after the rest stop. It was still a long way until Jeongeup Interchange, but the bus came to a stop. The door opened and people climbed on, covered in sweat. The bus before us must have been in an accident. I didn't give it much thought at first, but seeing the shards of glass scattered on the pavement, I wondered, The bus ahead of us? They said it was the 10:40. The seat that I gave up because I didn't want us to part right away. If I hadn't felt that way, I would have gotten on the bus in the crash. The bus was parked in the middle of the highway at midday, crushed and contorted. They said people had been injured and taken away by ambulance. His face passed before my eyes.

When people say, "Back when we lived in that house," or, "Back when we raised chickens," they seem happy. I start wishing that this book would contain such happiness.

There are dishes I crave when I visit this house in the summer. Sweet potato sprouts, peeled and pickled like kimchi, and bean paste mixed with freshwater snails.

They were dishes that Mom often cooked in the summers before I left this house. Mom seemed to just throw these dishes together like they were nothing special, but when I tried to make them in the city, I couldn't get them to taste that way. How mouthwatering, to take a spoonful of rice, mixed with thick bean paste, cooked with snails from the bogs, and some chopped young radish. But I would be afraid of green chili peppers. When my brothers picked up the long, plump peppers and dipped them in bean paste sauce before taking big, juicy bites, I would stare, saying, "You're going to scream soon that they're too hot." But instead of screaming, they would reach with the other hand to grab another pepper.

Mom is stubborn, as stubborn now as she's always been. What I really want is sweet potato sprouts, peeled and pickled like kimchi, and bean paste mixed with freshwater snails, but she insists that Father head out to the butcher in town. He takes his motorcycle and brings back a large bundle of meat for marinated beef and leg bone soup. Mom gets a large white pot of water boiling on the gas stove in the backyard for the soup. She said she had a pumpkin this big (she stretched out both arms to make a circle) growing old and fat in the patch behind the house but, sadly, someone had taken it.

"Our vines had crept next to the ones in the neighboring patch, so I gather they must've taken it, thinking it was their vine."

"Why don't you go ask, then. Asking, those vines are ours, and I thought you took our pumpkin thinking it's from your vines, maybe?"

I stick out my chin enacting the conversation, and Mom quickly forgets about her disappeared pumpkin and laughs, her large eyes narrowing into slits.

"Just that it was my first pumpkin of the year. Every day I looked into it, thinking when it fattens up, I'm going to simmer it for my daughter to eat, but just like that, it was gone, that's why."

Concerned that my face and my feet are prone to swelling, each year after the harvest was done, Mom would make pumpkin juice and bring it to the city in a kettle for me.

After dinner Mom and Father discussed the house at length over slices of red watermelon. Father wanted to rebuild the house. He'd been renovating an old structure over and over, so things stuck out here and there, giving the house an unstable air, as if it were just a temporary accommodation. There was no room for guests, either. Mom was against the idea. Ours was one of the best functioning houses in the village and if we wrecked it and built a new one, the villagers will not look at it kindly, she said. But that the veranda was too narrow, letting too much sun into the rooms, so we need an extension, and that was all.

At first I sided with Mom, then with Father, going back and forth. Mom said they didn't have that much longer to live, not long enough to wreck the house and build a new one. That they should use the money to get Little One an apartment when he graduates and finds himself a wife. Father said that he could never live in any other place, and that if he didn't build a new house, no one would visit this place after he's dead. I was leaning more and more toward Father. He seemed to be having a discussion with Mom, but I could tell that he'd already made up his mind. Father was not a man of many words. This was the first time I'd seen him engaged in such a long conversation with Mom. He was not discussing the issue with Mom; he was persuading her.

"Is it just for us that I want to build it now? Doesn't matter what kind of house we live in. Our children, they visit because we live here now, but do you think they'll come visit when we're dead? We gotta leave behind a new house so that they'll visit long after we're gone, that's what."

"Aigu, who's gonna come live here when we're gone?"

"So what if no one lives here? We'll make a key for each of them. First, Second, Third, Fourth, Fifth, Sixth . . ."

Father counted all our siblings, as if he were counting the stars.

"Six in all, so if they each take turns, it's six visits a year, at least. And if there's a house here, they'll want to come. They'll meet here, even if they can't see each other often in Seoul."

Again, I was leaning more and more toward Father.

It was not Mom that Father had won over but my thinking that he had transformed.

Sitting here in the night breeze listening to Father's thoughts about our house, I began to get curious about what I played with when I was a baby, who was the first person I smiled at, which corner of this house I had held on to when I first started walking, which color shoes I had on the day I first set foot outside these gates.

I awoke deep in the night. I had to go to the bathroom. Perhaps it was all the watermelons. Only after I opened the bedroom door, then opened the door to the veranda, stepped into the yard and walked all the way to the outhouse, I remembered it had been closed up. A bathroom had since been built next to the sauce jar terrace, with a toilet installed. The renovation was done a long time ago, but I kept forgetting the new changes in this house, searching for old traces. I couldn't wait so I squatted under the persimmon tree, and noticed the summer stars twinkling in the night sky. Who was it that said that things left unsaid inside one's heart ascend to the sky and become stars? When tiny things are gathered in large numbers, there is a sadness to them. Pebbles, sand, rice grains, seashells. The same with the stars in the sky. The difference, though, from pebbles, sand, rice grains, and seashells is that there are myriad stars, yet each one of them gives off its own glimmering light.

I couldn't bring myself to go back inside and was sitting on the veranda when I saw the well in the distance. No bucket next to the well. Now there was a motor that pulls up water from the well and sends it gushing out from the kitchen faucet. The well kept getting bigger until it filled up my field of vision. I walked quietly across the yard to the well. I lifted off the roofing slate covering the roof and slowly gazed inside. Nothing but darkness. The well had been covered up for a long time and the damp smell of moss stung my nose. When we used the bucket to fetch water, we never thought of putting a lid over the well. Back then, I could feel chilly air around the well even before I got near it. I sat and let my arms rest on the rim.

When I was little, the well seemed very deep. Whenever I cried, Mom would try and spook me and distract me with the story of a ghost inside the well, who'd come chase after me, wanting to be my friend. This didn't scare me at all. I liked the well, so if there really was a ghost in there, I thought I could be friends with her. If she lived inside the well, hiding the sky deep inside it, she'd probably resemble the well. Memories came back to me, of fetching water, when I'd put away the bucket, dripping with water drops, to look for the sky hiding inside the well, when I'd sit like this and quietly gaze in. When I used to live in this house, my favorites places were the well and the shed, you see. I could hide or hide things in them. I would hide inside the well things I could not hide in my body. My brother's harmonicas, Mom's brooches, the golden carp that Father caught in the swamp or the azalea petals that he picked in the spring mountains.

I rested my face on my arms on the well rim and gazed inside for a long time.

Later, while strolling along the river, pebbles turned up everywhere, rolling and bouncing. As I gazed inside the well, thoughts turned up, here and there, just like those pebbles.

Yun Sun-im gives me perplexed look as I tell her that I am handing in my resignation. She tells me to wait until I get my wages and severance pay.

"I don't have the time."

"Time for what?"

"I have a chance to study."

"Are you going to college?"

"If I get in."

Yun Sun-im no longer dissuades me. I take down my purple winter uniform hanging in my locker and wash it. I have to hand it in along with my resignation and my blue summer uniform, too.

As I folded the uniform after washing it and drying it in the sun, I slipped my hand into one of the pockets. Who could it be, who first invented them? These pockets that have comforted me through my four years at Dongnam Electronics, whether I was punching in my work hours in blue or overtime hours in red. After handing in my union withdrawal statement, when I could not join the other working in refusing overtime, whenever I got a scolding from the foreman, whenever I headed to the cafeteria on the roof for lunch, I had slipped my hands inside these pockets.

I hand in my resignation and return my uniforms, and as I walk out the gates of Dongnam Electronics, I notice Yun Sun-im following me.

"How about doing your studying here? . . . It's not like you have to study at home."

". . ."

"You'll lose your wages and severance pay and that's a shame. Your cousin didn't get paid, either."

"I hope you can help us get paid."

"You know how things are here. Why do you think people who've already quit keep coming to work every day? They're worried that if they don't show up, the company will never pay up. The company's in such a bad state, the bank or the government won't be able to look the other way. If they take over, they'll process everyone's severance pay. So why don't you come and study here, just until then?"

". . ."

"Hold on for just a while . . ."

She insists once again that it's not like I have to study at home. I tell her I'll do as she says.

The next day, out of habit, I try to punch in my card. I am embarrassed by my hand, reaching out to the slot and finding that my card is no longer there. The TV section is the only place that's still in production. Even there, two lines have been stopped and only one is in operation. I, nineteen years old, sit where it's quiet, on the roof or on the bench or the cafeterias, reading my language arts test book, then head back home. When I see resigned workers gathering or making noise, I pop in to see what is going on.

One evening, Oldest Brother asks why I keep going to work after resigning. When I tell him I'm trying to get my severance pay, he says with a sigh that I should stop going. That it's more important that I focus on my studies without wasting time. When I still keep going to work, he throws a fit, asking if it's worth it, my severance pay, which will only be a puny sum.

I go to work for one last day, without telling Oldest Brother, to let Yun Sun-im know that I can't show up anymore.

"Your brother's wrong. Getting our severance pay is very important to us, even if it's a puny amount."

I feel guilty and hang my head low without saying anything. "We'll be able to see each other again." Yun Sun-im smiles as she sees me off and I say good-bye. "Back in the days, we'd have thrown you a farewell party." Her voice remains in my ears.

Yun Sun-im . . . I never saw her again.

She wouldn't have stayed locked inside this genre painting of industrial labor that I have in my mind. She would have built herself a home somewhere in this world. Even when she sat in front of the conveyor belt, she carried the scent of home. Even when she gazed for hours into the circuit of wires, tangled like a labyrinth, tying, fixing, soldering, planting new wires, I could picture her peeling garlic or cleaning water parsley. Somewhere, she would have made her home into a cozy cave. She would be picking up, rinsing, hanging, folding endless loads of laundry. She would have kept her first baby's swaddling clothes wrapped in white muslin and taken them out for her second child. In the summer she'd head down to the basement, stacked with household appliances, to bring up the fan, squat down to finish her ironing, her neck covered in sweat. In the evening she'd finish setting the dinner table and step outside to get her child, wiping her hands that still carried the smells of sauce and seasoning. Sometimes she'd listen to the sounds of nature in circulation, her narrow eyes closed, and on some days she'd speed down the road on her bike, and she'd have used the serenity and fierceness kept inside of her to build a beautiful home for herself. She'd still be somewhere in this world trying to understand the people around her, battling the emptiness of fleeting relationships. The movements of women inside their homes . . . that was it. Even when she sat in front of the conveyor, contained inside her movements were a sense of peace and a nostalgia for a traditional home life.

It was my teacher Mr. Choe Hong-i who told me about the Seoul Arts College on Mount Namsan. He said the school has a creative writing department. My scholastic achievement scores were terribly low, and I don't bother applying to first and second tier universities. My application number is 155. The entrance exam is a writing assignment. We are given the topic "Dream." We can write prose or verse, whichever we choose. I, nineteen years old, write about my fourth-grade teacher whom I had admired. I write that she was a beautiful person, her science classes filled up with endless sad stories about the constellations, and that my dream is to become a deliverer of beautiful stories, just like her.

Later, during my interview, the professor who later would become my mentor looked up at me and commented, "Your scholastic achievement test scores are low." As I walk out of the room, his words circle inside my head, round and round. It's all over now; a tear escapes from my eye as I walk down Mount Namsan. To head back home, I had to get on the bus at Lotte Department Store. I am unable to find the crossing from Toegye Boulevard to Lotte, circling the Namdaemun Market area again and again like a hiker losing his sense of direction on a ring route. Each time I exit the underground walkway I end up in the same place, so I go back down, then end up at the same exit, over and over. When I finally get home, I get under the covers and weep. Third Brother asks how the interview went and I scream out, "Don't talk to me," which shocks him.

Third Brother goes to see the admission results. I'd get lost again in the unfamiliar part of the city, unable to return easily. Third Brother called and said, "You got in. Congratulations."

I've just started college and Oldest Brother tells me he's going on a business trip. But the next day, after telling me he'll be away on business, he calls me from Jeongeup, Mom by his side. I think it was a Saturday. Oldest Brother says he's getting engaged the next day, and tells me to come down to Jeongeup. Engaged? I couldn't believe it but it didn't seem like he was lying, so I take the night train home. I don't even have time to tell Cousin. The next day, at a restaurant in Jeongeup, I meet my brother's fiancée-to-be for the first time. It was their engagement ceremony, so we met for the first time as family. She has large eyes, light complexion, and is short in height. It seems that Oldest Brother doesn't know much more about her, either. Except that she went to university in Seoul; went back home to the country to stay with her father; and that she was a delicate and understanding woman who, despite her father's difficult nature, never once made him upset. What more could he know, having been introduced to her on Friday and getting engaged on Sunday. Right away I take a liking to Oldest Brother's fiancée. But even during the cake cutting, I just stand there blankly, unable to believe that he is getting married. Then when he put the engagement ring on her finger, I begin to sniffle. I can't understand my tears, so I don't know how to stop.

People turn and stare at me. Mom comes over to me and tells me to stop. But I can't. Mom gets teary as well while trying to comfort me. That was their engagement and a month later they get married. At the wedding, Cousin starts to sniffle, just as I did at the engagement. She sniffles and sniffles, and this time I comfort her.

Oldest Brother's wife was diligent, her eyes clear and kind.

All of a sudden I am addressed as Sister-in-Law. Everything—the cutting board, the kitchen knife—is hers now. Only then I realize how much I enjoy sharpening a dull knife on the little stone that Father gave us, rinsing the rice to steam in a pot, chopping and seasoning radish to make a spicy salad. I realize that as I focused on moving my hands to sort out unhulled grains in the rice, I was comforting the undulating solitude deep inside my heart. Is it because my room is the one closest to the kitchen? No longer allowed to work in the kitchen, I start to hear the smallest sounds that she makes. The sounds of her wiping her hands on her apron, the sounds of her skirt brushing against the refrigerator. Early one morning, after days of sitting in my room trying to guess whether it's a ladle or strainer or rice paddle that she's taking down from the rack on the cabinet, I paste on my window a black cardboard of the same size. The sunlight at daybreak is blocked by the cardboard, turning my room into a cave. While I am out, she takes down the cardboard. I come home and put it back up. She takes it down again. I put it back up. She would disapprove, of course. How inappropriate, a dark, cavelike room in her home for the newlywed couple, where pink sheets and white drapes should be more fitting. One day she throws out the cardboard. I go see her next to the washing machine, where she's doing the laundry and ask her, in a barely audible voice, not to come into my room. She bends down toward me.

"I can't hear you, *Agassi*, what did you say?"

"Don't come into my room!"

This time I scream, out of the blue. She is surrounded by the scent of fabric softener as her eyes well up with tears. Oldest Brother comes out of their room and takes her inside. A while later he comes over to my room. He looks into my eyes and says he wants to get me a present to celebrate my new start in college, asking me if there's anything I want.

I tell him I want books.

"What kind of books?"

"Novels."

The next day the complete set of Samsung Publishers' *Contemporary Korean Literature Collection* is delivered to me. I count the books, with their ivory and scarlet covers, as I arrange them on my bookcase one by one, one hundred volumes in all.

My conflict with Oldest Brother's wife was quickly over, thanks to the books. I no longer put up black cardboard since I had to read the books, and while reading them I forgot about the kitchen.

As my eyes grew accustomed to the darkness inside the well, I could make out the black surface of the water. As my eyes grew accustomed to the black surface, I could make out the myriad stars glimmering on the water. The stars were floating on the water, like some sentence. For a moment, the stars in the well tossed and rolled, as if a wind was sweeping across the sky.

These were the sentences that I went after my publisher to take out of my essay collection right before going to print.

•◆•

The wound left behind by Hui-jae's death, which I had inadvertently gotten involved in, turned me into an infinite blank. Her traces still exercise their influence over me. Ever since then, I have possessed a great fear in establishing relationships with others. She was a ruined part of my heart, keeping me from building more intimate ties. Whenever I got close to someone, I felt compelled to tell the person that it was me who had locked that door. And I feared that this new relationship might again impose on me, without giving me a choice, a role that I cannot comprehend. I contemplated that my secret might be revealed after my death. I could accept the revelation but I feared distortion. To prevent my secret from getting distorted, it would have to be either that my life was thicker than the life of the discloser, or that I never tell anyone. I chose the latter. Never tell anyone, which meant never establish relationships, with anyone. I kept my lips sealed for ten years, suffering from blame, grudge, and longing. And after ten years, I tried writing, not to a person but within my work, that I had fastened the lock on that door. More years accumulated. Having spent so long keeping it inside of me, not letting it out, now it seems like a dream. Perhaps it was a dream . . . I try thinking. Yes . . . perhaps it was a dream . . . My heart insists and my hand sneers. The hand remembers. What it felt like when I fastened the lock, the clicking sound it made. I gaze down at my hand.

The body remembers in a way that is more placid, frigid, precise, and persistent than the way the mind does. The body is more honest.

Twenty some years ago in this house I learned to ride the bike. Before I was able to pedal all the way down the hill, I crushed my nose and skinned my knee myriad times. On the day I rode my bike to school for the first time, I got so flustered on a downhill road on my way back home that I forgot to grab the brakes. The bike sped downhill and threw me, in my white uniform, into a rice paddy, my hands trembling as I held on to the handles. The textbooks in my schoolbag got soaked in the water at the bottom of the paddy, and I had to study with these yellowed books all year long. But after this incident I was able to grab my brakes at the right moment and through three years of middle school rode my bike to school, my schoolbag in the back. Later I would even let both hands go as I pedaled, feeling the wind on my face. I haven't had the chance to ride a bike since arriving in the city.

Have not even seen one. It seemed that my mind had forgotten about biking. But it was my body, wounded and hurt while I learned to ride, that never forgot it. I would not ride one for a year, sometimes two, then when I happen to come across one I'd start pedaling and the bike would push forward with a swoosh.

I have been thinking again and again all this time. If I had opened the door, just once, before fastening the lock, would things have turned out differently. Would they?

Inside the well the night wind blew and the sky settled. A fresh fragrance flowed into me. Forgetting that I'd been gazing into the well, I look around, trying to find the origin of this fragrance that was flowing into me. Somehow I felt that if I didn't try to identify this smell right now, I would regret it for a long time. It was the scent of water, the scent of moss. Ah, I looked into the well again. It must be that the damp smell of the water and the moss, covered up for a long time under the roofing slate, has sucked up the new air and new stars after the lid was lifted. The wind inside the well died down. The stars died down. Her face floated up inside the well like a sentence. That bashful expression she used to wear when she said something from her heart.

". . . No need to feel sorry for me. I've lived in your heart for a long time. Open your heart and think of the living. The key to the story of the past is in your hands, not mine. Spread the grief and the joy of those you've encountered to the living. Their truth will transform you."

A wind seemed to blow, making ripples inside the well. She is inside the fresh-scented water, searching.

"What are you looking for?"

"The pitchfork you threw inside."

"What for?"

"I'm going to pull it out . . . then your foot won't hurt anymore."

She lifts the pitchfork, from the bottom of the most remote gorge inside the well. What myriad water routes within a water route. The pitchfork drags inside her grip, scraping the ground. A spray of water. All that had sunken to the bottom of the well stirs up in a whirl. Where is she headed now as she departs from my heart? I do not know where, but I imagine it will not be somewhere inside a whirlpool, under the sediments or within dead silence. For inside my heart new stories are springing, of hopes and wishes.

I ran into Hui-jae's man exactly once. It was on the busy streets on Myeongdong and I was on a bus. As I stood, my body rocking, my hand gripping the handle, I saw someone standing under a tree, off the sidewalk. Since the crowd at the bus stop was crammed in one direction to get on the bus, he stood out, standing on the road under the tree. The sight caught my eye and only then did I realize it was him. He just stood there. He didn't try to get on the bus or walk on, just stood there on the road, his back against the tree. Grimacing each time a cab passed, as if the lights hurt his eyes.

A cold wind swished by. I felt a chill on my face in the middle of this summer night. I even started to shiver. I walked away from the well, leaving it uncovered. I crossed the yard and stepped onto the veranda, and when I looked back as I opened the door, I saw the starlight flow into the well, filling it up. The water and the moss, nourished with starlight, will take on an even fresher scent. I stepped inside the room and buried my face on the pillow. Mom and Father were lying asleep close to each other, the room filled with the sound of their breathing. Mom went out to the vegetable patch in the afternoon and picked a basketful of sweet potato sprouts.

•◆•

I was returning to the city on the 6:40 train. Mom peeled the sweet potato sprouts, one by one. Insisting they wouldn't taste as good if she seasoned them in advance, she made kimchi with the sprouts right before I set out, stuffing them into a container for me to carry in my bag. Father pulled out his motorcycle, started the engine and gave me a ride to the station. On the country road that led us out of the village, he picked up speed. I tightened my grip around his waist to keep from rocking. Father would soon build a new house. If he discreetly seeks our opinion, I will offer support. I will persuade other family members who are hesitant. The new house in Father's vision for the future contains six keys. The keys will tie us together, keep us from separating. Father got a ticket for me and carried by bag to the platform. "Call home when you arrive." When the train arrived, Father loaded the bag on the overhead rack above my seat. In the seat next to mine, a boy sat sound asleep. His hands grasped the armrest to keep from rocking. He had dirty fingernails. They looked like they were stained with oil, or were unwashed, filled with scum. His profile gave off a cold impression, his forehead covered by his locks. The boy slept and slept until the train pulled into Suwon. When they announced that next stop was Yeongdeungpo Station, I stirred him awake.

"Have we passed Yeongdeungpo?" Only then the boy opened his eyes, startled. His body was frail but his eyes were big and bright. I told the flustered boy that we'd made a stop at Suwon Station a while back and would be arriving soon at Yeongdeungpo, and the boy folded himself into his seat again, saying, "Oh," sounding relieved.

•◆•

If I get off at Yeongdeungpo Station, I can go there by subway.

Once again I ignored the surging inside my heart. Go there, carrying that heavy bag? My large bag, with the container of sweet potato sprout kimchi. I got up to pull down my heavy bag, gazing down at me from the rack; the boy offered to get it. He effortlessly fetched the bag and placed it on the floor. His body giving off the scent of a skilled steel worker.

"Thanks."

The boy smiled shyly. Revealing a row of teeth, white like pomegranate seeds. He didn't sit back down but headed straight to the door. He carried nothing, not a single bag, and I noticed from behind that he had a sturdy build. While I oscillated between hesitation, anticipation, and resignation, the train arrived at Yeongdeungpo Station. I shifted seats to where the boy had been sitting. How nimble. He had already made it to the far end of the platform. When he was asleep, crumpled up in his seat, he had seemed pitiful, but now, striding down the platform, he was full of vigor. It occurred to me that perhaps he was no longer a boy. With his mop of hair lifted off his forehead, his long profile, which had seemed cold somehow, reminded me of a giraffe. The train started and he began to run, as if he were racing the train.

Ah! My eyes opened wide. Was this a mirage? They were a beautiful pair of legs. Faster than the steel wheels on the train. They were perfectly toned and tempered, ready to run at the speed of seventy miles an hour. The boy's beautiful legs left the platform before the train got out of Yeongdeungpo Station. A sigh of relief escaped from my mouth. I placed my hand down on the window of the speeding train car, its wheels clanking, *clickety clack*. My gesture, small and natural, brought back, albeit faintly, a promise from the past, a promise about to fade into oblivion.

On its way to its final destination, Seoul Station, the train would pass through Garibong Subway Station.

During my solitary days lived inside the industrial labor genre painting, the image I often made an effort to bring to mind was that of the birds in the photography book that Cousin showed me that night we arrived in the city—the birds sleeping under the vast night sky, facing the stars, sitting high and beautiful. I endured those days inside the genre painting by promising myself that there would come a day when I would go see these birds with my own eyes. In the years that followed, even when I got lonely in the midst of life's fatigues and the absence of human ties, I never abandoned my wish that I would go see them one day, those egrets in the book in Cousin's arms, the flock of egrets in the forest where night had fallen, leaning close to one another, tight and round, blanketing the trees with their beautiful sleep, as if they had forgiven all the goings-on in this world. One day, I shall set out, beyond the ridge that blocked my view, my arms rocking as they rested on the window of the train car. I told myself this on the days of grief or solitude, and never let anyone else know. Seventeen years had passed since I made that promise and I had yet to travel to see the birds.

Was I here?

Where Oldest Brother had waited, wearing his wig, for the subway train to Anyang; where Cousin set out for Jonggak, instead of coming to school, in hope of becoming a telephone operator; where Third Brother stood and waited before he headed to the farm, carrying on his back his luggage filled with nothing but books. Does left-handed An Hyang-suk still write with her left hand?

I looked out the window, my eyes glowering.

In the distance factory chimneys stood tall and impetuous. How I wished the train would slow down. Shine some light on that place. I looked at my arm resting on the windowsill. It rocked this way and that, to the tremors of the train. The moment it occurred to me, that I was here, in that place, an egret flapped its wings inside my heart.

Fly away now, no need to hesitate, fly to the forest. Soar beyond the ridge blocking your vision. Go on, sleep, under the vast night sky, facing the stars, sitting high and beautiful.

For I shall never forget you, year after year, come on back some day, come back as a new sentence. Come back to deliver the truth that arose then vanished in places where my breath cannot reach. Let us say good-bye now. We didn't get to do so back then. I lifted my arm from the windowsill and got up. I headed for the door, as if I were following the boy. It was as if he were racing across the plain. I stood where they boy's toned and tempered legs had lingered before dashing down the platform, and pushed open the door with all my might. I stuck out my hand, grabbed a fistful of air, then released it.

Good-bye . . . I will hold dearly in my heart how you cherished and cared for me.

In any situation, in any relationship, I was never able to speak or behave as I intended. By the time I lifted my head, determined to say something, he would already be far away. What was left unsaid and undone to him has become a novel. Which is to say, he has never heard me speak. I am now utterly baffled, though. I long to go back to the time when all that was left unsaid and undone had yet to become a novel and remained as a future. Back to a time when revision and addition and the questions to myself had all remained intact . . . August 8, 1995.

I am on Jeju Island. I have returned to the place where I first began writing this. August 26, 1995.

I remember writing a year ago, at this same place, Here I am on an island, Jeju-do . . . It is my first time writing away from home. Yes, it's already been a year. This past year has gone by while I wrote this book. This past year I was unable to work on any other fiction except for this. I had an impulse, from time to time, to start a short story, but never went ahead with it. During the writing of this book, I've suppressed so many of my heart's desires, again and again, that now I'm starting to worry whether I can go back to the way I used to be. I am hoping that while I am here, spending my days going over and polishing the book, the submerged layers of my heart will recover. It has also occurred to me that my habit, of stopping myself midway, wherever it is I am going, and trying to return to the beginning, might be a vanity that lies outside the realm of life. It is August 26, 1995.

I went swimming at Hyeopjae Beach at night. It was my first time swimming in the sea. I suffer from an unbearable headache from time to time. It's less frequent now, but there was a time when I battled the pain every single day. When it attacked, I lost all will, and my knees would buckle, wherever I happened to be. When it got to a point where I felt so shaken inside my head I had difficulty getting out of bed and out the door, the doctor recommended that I take up swimming. I followed his orders. That was how it was for me.

There was nothing I wouldn't do if only my head would stop aching. So I went to the pool and learned to swim. Freestyle, backstroke, breaststroke. When I was in the water, I was able to forget everything. The water caressed my headaches with its warmth. Doing the backstroke relaxed me so much I'd get sleepy. Ever since, I've considered swimming a cure-all, heading to the pool for back pain, for a sore in my shoulder. But I never expected that I'd be swimming for fun in the middle of the night, in the sea. Neither did I expect that my first swim in the sea would take place at night. I floated on my back and head out as far as my arms would take me. The sensation of the water on my back warmed my heart. Floating on top of the water, I felt that the city I left only ten hours ago was now a distant place. My empty apartment, my busy life in the city, all seemed unreal. My desk cleaned up, the gas range quiet. The phone would ring and the answering machine would pick it up instead of me. The stars in the night sky poured into my eyes. The moment I took notice of the twinkling of the stars, I lost my balance, floundering. I got salty seawater in my mouth, in my eyes. Who was it that said the seawater was the closest fluid to amniotic fluid. August 26, 1995.

All morning long I sat facing the sea. August 28, 1995.

I took the bus to the town in Hallym. I bought a sewing kit from a street vendor, made up of spools of thread in different colors and needles of different sizes. I had been looking all over for one but all I had found in the city were disposable kits, and here, they were just selling them on the street. When I was young I used to play with my mother's sewing kit.

There were all sorts of things in there. Colored threads, broken buttons, thumbtacks, scraps of cloth, thimble, scissors, pins, big needle, small needle . . . When I am asked this question about my writing method, whether I have the novel's complete structure worked out before writing or not, I think of Mom's sewing kit. I don't have to work out the novel's structure. I don't take notes, either. If I had notes to work from, my thoughts would lose fluidity and refuse to move ahead. Often, it was whatever popped up in my subconscious or unconscious that formed into sentences. They were sometimes explosive, emerging, without my knowing, as I followed the preceding sentence. This is why at times I don't know how my writing will turn out until I am done with it. All I do is simply open the sewing kit and gaze into the colored threads, scissors, needles, and broken buttons. As I follow the preceding sentence, making my way through the sewing kit, sometimes there are certain threads or buttons that hide deeper in the layers of my mind. Like a terrapin pulling its neck deep into its shell, I was not able to pull out by force what kept itself hidden until the end. But that was what I was attached to. I believe that the truth in what hides away, refusing to be pulled out, would come back to me someday as a certain aesthetic sensibility that would allow me to view life from a different perspective. That wherever you are, whatever life you live, not even literature will overlook the nobility of his truth.

I went deeper into the market and bought a large towel. I also got a camping stove, a fuel canister for the stove, a kettle, and a box of Maxwell House instant coffee. At another store, I got two bowls of instant noodles and a box of biscuits, and turned back on my way out after paying for them and bought two cans of Hite beer. August 29, 1995.

In the middle of the night I went out with all the coins I had and called up people in the city. P said I had it too easy, and J asked, "Did you have dinner?" H said she was going to visit her father's grave, since it had been three years. Younger Sister asked if I was here alone. When I said I was, she asked, in a melancholy voice, "Do you want me to come, *Eonni*?" I too felt a rush of melancholy and asked, "You want to come?" Beyond the phone booth, the night sea was swelling and slopping. August 30, 1995.

I was having breakfast in the lobby, flipping through the morning paper, when I felt a grain of rice catch in my throat. My photo in the paper. When will I stop getting startled at encountering my photo in unexpected places? The large print next to the photo read, "Sixteen-year-old Country Bumpkin Factory Girl Dreamed of Becoming a Writer." I felt my cheeks flush. Worried that the front desk staff would recognize me, I pulled out the page with my photo and took it upstairs to my room. August 31, 1995.

I was out on a walk and I followed the sign to Hallym Park. Once inside, I was stunned. It was not a mere park. There were thousands of rare subtropical trees, breathing and sighing. The arboretum had been built on a desert wasteland by transporting 2,000 truckloads of soil and spending twenty years cultivating after planting the seeds of these subtropical trees. And that was not all. There was enormous scale of the surrounding caves and the trees bore splendid flowers, their colors so vivid no paint could have produced them. My hand would reach out before I realized it, wondering, "Can they be real?" Some plants had leaves hard and sharp enough to prick your hand, a necessity, presumably, for surviving in the desert. I got my arm pricked while walking past a Mexican agave, which left a bleeding wound and I had to apply ointment when I got back. These plants made me realize how tame and prudish our indigenous plants are. At the pond where tens of carp were swimming, a tortoise was resting on a rock, craning its neck toward the sky. Or was it a turtle, not a terrapin? I always have a hard time telling them apart. I followed a guide to look around the two caves, Hyeopjae and Ssangyong. As we approached, I could sense a release of chilly air. One step inside and I felt a shiver. The guide flashed the light on a section of the cave and pointed out that there were stalagmites growing here that cannot form in lava tunnels. Stalagmites? How do they grow? The guide explained that stalagmites are precipitates formed on the ground of a cavern by rainwater that contain dissolved compounds from the thick layer of shell sand on the earth's surface, and that they grow a centimeter every hundred years, fed by limewater dripping from the ceiling. A centimeter every hundred years? I was frightened, not amazed, by the myriad dripstones of varying sizes, revealed by the guide's flashlight.

The guide pointed at one of them and said, "That one is twenty centimeters tall, which means it has been growing for two thousand years. The floor of the Ssangyong Cave was not just sand but shell sand. A long, long time ago, it was probably part of the sea. What processes does a seashell go through to turn into this fine sand?" The guide pointed the flashlight to the ceiling, toward what he explained was a trace that a pair of dragons left behind as they escaped the erupting lava. The flashlight exposed the elongated silhouette of two dragons. One had its head, and the other its tail, reaching out toward the light outside the cave. The movement was swift. Light seeped in only through the part of the ceiling through which the dragons had escaped. I felt a chill on my forehead, to think dragons had once lived here. With the hot bubbling lava pouring in, how had the dragons made their escape toward the light, making what kind of sounds, bearing what kind of emotions? I was frightened by the force of nature engulfing the cave. The twisted rocks that had formed from boiling lava that quickly hardened appeared either elaborate or misshapen, and there were myriad holes on the cave's floor, made by endless drops of limewater dripping onto the exact same spot. I was also hit by cold drops of limewater. It was the naturally formed rocks that soothed my fear somewhat. How could such shapes and silhouettes have surfaced naturally? There was one that seemed like an exact replica of the Pietà. The mother stood, full of sorrow, carrying her son. I took an instant photo in front of a rock that resembled a bent over bear, and one that was like a turtle carrying a rabbit on its back. In the image that appeared, then and there, I am wide-eyed with surprise. September 1, 1995.

Younger Sister and her husband arrived for a visit with their child. He has been in this world less than two years. He maintains about a meter's distance from me. I want to hold him but he only wants his mom. He relents into my arms only when I am clapping or barking with a funny look or performing a funny routine singing, "Heading out to sea, going fishing." And even then, only when his mom was next to me. I found it moving, how his instincts immediately sense her whereabouts. The baby seemed to have entrusted everything to this being called mother. Even while he's sleeping, he calls out, "*Eomma*." When she answers, "Yes," from wherever she is, he goes back to sleep. But if he does not hear her respond, he immediately opens his eyes and looks around, calling, "*Eomma* . . ." And when she does not come into view, he will be wide awake, waddling toward the door and banging, crying, "*Eomma*." A boy sobbing, his face covered with his two hands. It's no use no matter how I try to comfort him, but when his mom comes and holds him, his sadness is over. He evens smiles with a sigh, winking his teary black eyes. There would have been a time when I was like him. When Mom's scent was all I believed in, when all I had to do was follow where she went, when all I needed was Mom. September 2, 1995.

I was gazing into the water and there were conches rolling around. Not one but many, so I picked one up and looked inside to find a hermit crab. I picked up another and again a crab. Hermit crabs crawling inside the shell, eating up the conch and making a home. September 3, 1995.

Younger Sister and her husband left early in the morning with their child. When he arrived, the only things he could say were choo-choo, twinkle twinkle, *Eomma* and the second syllable of *Appa*—ppa. During the three days he spent here, I whispered in his ear every chance I got as I pointed to the sea, *bada*. And finally, yesterday, he said, bba-da, stressing the first syllable. I have no way of knowing whether he was actually referring to the sea or to the tip of my finger, but as we said good-bye, he pointed to me and shouted, "*bba-da*."

Returning alone after seeing them off at the airport, the crystalline voice that he left behind lingered in my ear—bba-da. The child's every movement brings out enormous sympathy and affection. His soft bottom, twinkling eyes, his fingers, tiny and cute. This vulnerability seems to be the child's method of survival. Instinctive movements that compel those who possess power to protect him. At the sculpture park, while we were captured by the impressive works of art, he ran off to the yellow butterfly on the lawn. At the museum of miniature trees, while we were lost amidst the rows of trees trimmed to perfection with scissors, he got down on the floor on his tummy to watch black ants crawling. At the beach, while we were gazing out at the distant sea, he waddled after the minnows scattering by his feet. He showed interest only in the unadorned, in what moved.

I came back to the hotel and slept all day. The stain on my sheet, of a spill that the baby made. The child's smell left on my pillow.

Each time the sunlight stirred me awake, he appeared, over in the light, glimmering. September 5, 1995.

How fortunate that Jeju-do is part of this country. September 6, 1995.

Tomorrow is Chuseok. I was also here for the harvest holidays last year, trying to start this book. For two years in a row I am spending Chuseok on this island. September 8, 1995.

Is this a sign of growing old? Remembering that it was Chuseok, I suddenly felt lonesome to be here by myself. Around noon I went down to the lobby and ordered lunch, but the soup tasted sour, like yesterday's leftover. I put down my spoon and came back upstairs. On television, the women who worked at the traditional rice cake house in Nakwon-dong were engaged in a Chuseok cake making contest. In their hands, the half-moon cakes took shape swiftly, taking on a glossy sheen. All day long I waited. For what? A phone call? A visit? Outside on the beach villagers were playing volleyball on the camping ground. I followed with my eyes a young man with a strong serve, rooting for him. The phone did not ring. In the late afternoon, I put on a jacket and headed out to the beach. The sea, at low tide, had revealed a thousand-meter stretch of mudflat. In the last surf of the ebbing tide, children were catching moon crabs, and a pair of foreign tourists, a man and a woman, sat on folding chairs, their backs exposed. A man stood with his feet in the water after casting his fishing rod. One of the children catching crabs, a girl, recognized me. A few days ago she was gathering clams out here with her brother and I had joined her, digging into the sand. "Look." The girl opened the plastic bag for me to see and inside there were about ten moon crabs wiggling around. Their sand-colored shells were radiant. I'd never seen sand-colored crabs. I poked my finger inside for fun and one of them snapped its claw. I dug into the sand trying to catch one for her and I couldn't get a single one. Over where the mudflat ended two young women were taking pictures. I gave up catching crabs and was walking down the beach along the tide when the two women asked me to take a picture for them. I see the distant sea through the viewfinder. For a moment I forgot to press the button, enchanted by the sea inside the viewfinder, standing there with my feet in the ebbing tide. The women took back the camera from me and walked toward the other side of the mudflat. They looked at each other and laughed, like they were sharing a joke, holding hands, slapping each other on the back. Ahead of them two dogs played, covered in sand. The man standing with his feet in the water, his fishing rod cast, threw me a glance. I walked on then looked back without giving it too much thought, then realized he was glancing at me again. I walked faster, getting myself farther away from him. I'd been thinking, each time I was out on the beach, that all beings, people or animals, are more natural in the company of others. Even clams and moon crabs. Even a rock in the sea catches attention when it's off on its own. Much more so for me, a human. As I leave the mudflat, I notice that the sun is setting but the volleyball game on the camping ground is still going on. September 9, 1995.

Autumn seems to have arrived. In the mornings and evenings, I get goose bumps on my arms. The sea wind is colder as well. I have no autumn clothes in my suitcase. Must be time to head back. September 10, 1995.

Only now I call them my friends, they who had to continue moving their fingers, all ten of them, and keep producing things, without end, their names forgotten, their efforts completely dissociated from material riches. I shall not forget the social will that they have spread in me. That they, my anonymous friends, have given birth to a piece of my inner world, just as my mother gave birth to my essential self. . . . And that I, on my part, must give birth, through my words, to their own place of dignity in this world. September 10, 1995.

Early morning, after washing a white shirt and hanging it on a clothes hanger out on the balcony to dry, I walked out to the beach. The tide, which had ebbed overnight, was coming in, filling up from afar. I could hear the swooshing sound of the blue tide seeping in on the white mudflat. Water and sand. What other pair shares a relationship as perfect as that of seeping and scattering, between water and sand? Seeping in, then gone, in a flash.

The white sand on this beach was so fine it formed a hard, dense mass. I stood watching the tide and took off my shoes. I thought the water would be cold but it felt warm. The sand felt nice on the soles of my feet so I kept walking. My feet left imprints on the smooth sandbank. I ran toward the tide then turned around to check, and my footprints had run after me, then cut off right where I was. I sank down on the mudflat. I felt someone sitting down next to me, which for a moment distracted my vision. It would be a long time until the rising tide reached me. As I waited, I kept glancing at my side. Why did I keep feeling someone was next to me when there was nothing but sand around? The water rose. It felt soft where it touched my feet. I released my raised knees and stretched. As the tide flooded in, tickling the top of my feet, my calves, my buttocks, my waist, I wanted to call out his name. I seemed to know his name, but perhaps I didn't. I wanted to call out his name tenderly but I also seemed to have forgotten his name. It seemed he was very close to me, and at the same time very far. This was agonizing. He was always at the other end of the line. After my consciousness was swept up by sensual desire, it would be left with solitude, so close to death, like the white mudflat behind me. Nevertheless, by feeling his existence, I was able to taste the euphoria of taking a step deeper inside of me. The tide moved on past me. He moved on past me as well. Even when I had come to a halt, unable to flow with time, just as I sat on the mudflat now, he had moved on past me, like this rising tide. Behind me, he and the tide intertwined. I looked back to find my footprints being washed away by the tide.

I walked out to the beach again at dusk. The tide was ebbing. The beach, which had been underwater all day, revealed its white bottom as the tide went out, the way it looked in the morning.

The ebb and flow were opposite phenomena, but at one point, the ebbing and the rising tides appeared the same, like identical twins. Once that moment was over, they take on clearly opposite traits, but at one moment before they head in opposite directions, they reveal the same scenery, brilliant and fleeting.

He and she, ebb and flow, hope and despair . . . life and death. Aren't they pairs of words that are one and the same?

On the white mudflat at dusk, two children were digging clams with their mother. If you followed the ebbing tide until the end, how far could you go? I looked back and my feet had left imprints, as they had in the morning. I ran around wild on the mudflat. My footprints also ran wild, following me right behind. I ran and ran until I caught up with the ebbing tide, then stomped into the water before flopping down. The water reached my chest. The boy who was digging clams lifted himself and looked my way, probably thinking I was acting strangely. The tide went out, slowly. The water left my breasts, my waist, my buttocks, then the tops of my feet. The water left me behind all alone on the white mudflat, growing more and more distant. When the tide was far, far out, I looked back and the only thing vivid on the mudflat was my footprints. It seemed that, unlike in the morning, the tide had ebbed in order to keep my footprints intact. Yes. I had turned a deaf ear to my girlhood with my silence. It was a time when I was unable to love myself, so I had to go from fifteen straight to twenty. Whether I started walking out of my past or walked into it from the present, my footprints always came to a stop in the same place. I would go from being fifteen to twenty, or go from being twenty to fifteen. If I set out from the past, I had to ignore sixteen, seventeen, eighteen, nineteen, and skip straight to twenty. If I set out from the present, I had to ignore nineteen, eighteen, seventeen, sixteen, and skip straight to fifteen. Those years always remained vacant, like naked sunlight, like the well with its bottom completely covered. For a long time, inside my mind, my girlhood had left behind no other human ties except for family. I made an effort not to remember anyone from that time, not to remember Hui-jae *eonni*. But my consciousness would suddenly, vividly, reveal these past relations and I would behave like someone afflicted with amnesia.

The traces of my footprints continue endlessly on the mudflat. What kind of lives are they living now and where? For a long time, whenever I thought about them I would be overcome with a sense of inexpressible solitude that kept me from thinking that life was beautiful. I wasn't aware but they have always been in the present for me. They gave me the courage to embrace the squalor of life that I encountered since I was twenty, and helped me examine myself and resume my life, coming from a place of preposterous desires. I got up from the mudflat and walked off the beach, placing my foot upon my foot. The footprints made on the beach today seem to be connected to the lone room. To that place I ran out of and was never able to return to. Today, my most evident present, I feel that if I follow the footprints I made here today I will be able to step straight into nineteen. And perhaps I shall be able to walk back out the other side, from fifteen to sixteen. This was the path that would allow me to walk out of that lone room once and for all. This path kept appearing before me. I walked off the mudflat, step by step, pressing my feet firmly into the sand. For a long time, Hui-jae was what all of my moments of fate looked like to me. To me she was the ebb and flow. She was hope and despair. She was life and death to me. And all of it was love. September 11, 1995.

I stepped off the beach and onto the paved street and walked on until I no longer could, like someone who had learned to walk for the first time. On one of the coastal roads sea birds sat in a row. When I approached, the birds flew up into the air, all at once, then landed a little farther out. I would approach again and they rose again. I looked out at the beach and there were thousands of birds by the sea, their wings tucked. I gazed out at the edge of the sea while following the trace of the birds, at the childlike sky above it. I felt the past, once locked up, now mingled with the scattering clouds. Felt the birth of new beings entering the world at the edge of memory, giving off a new smell. On my way back I saw a child crying on one of the beaches. It looked like she wanted to play on the rocks for a while longer but her mother was taking her home. Inside a car, parked off in the distance, the child's father was honking the horn, *beep-beep.* The child was carried away from the beach in her mother's arms, growing farther away as she continued to cry. Will she remember that she had cried on this beach? That she had even existed on this beach?

My body was utterly exhausted but my head was getting clearer and clearer. September 13, 1995.

This book, I believe, has turned out to be not quite fact and not quite fiction, but something in between. I wonder if it can be called literature. I ponder the act of writing. What does writing mean to me?